LIFE & SPICE

LIFE & SPICE

Vita e Spezie

A NOVEL BY

Myers & Reed

LIFE & SPICE

This book is dedicated
to those who face some form
of heartache or loss every day.
And to those who persevere
despite the hardship.

ACKNOWLEDGMENTS

We could not have completed this book without the expertise and skills of the following: Kelly Newsome, CPNP-PC for her generous guidance regarding arterial stenosis; Mr. and Mrs. Rick Silvestro and *Trattoria al Giardino* (GiardinoItalian.com) for the authentic dining experience; our intrepid editor Vivian Freeman (Yellow Rose Typesetting); our graphics artist for our brilliant and beautiful cover, Stephen Marshall, (StephenMarshallPhotography.com); Liz Etheridge for her photography and video help when two writers were beyond busy and exhausted; Lisa Lowry for "the voice"; and, always, Leslie King for tirelessly and creatively keeping our web presence updated and online.

HRM: During the writing of this book, both of my parents passed away within eleven months of each other. It concludes the journey of taking care of the senior members of my family that began in the early 1990s with an aunt and uncle. The last two years were by far the most challenging, but also the most educational and humbling. My parents had a mercurial relationship and, inevitably, or consequently, so was ours. If it were not for some special and dear friends and neighbors, I would not have survived, and so I gratefully thank, Gail Reed, Dolores and James Dugger, Norma Wilkinson, Linda Broday, Laura Taylor, Paula and James Rogers, Donna Robertson, and Billie Kear. To borrow a phrase from the late Pat Conroy, "Great love."

MGR: I am so thankful God blessed me with such incredible friends and family who have stood beside me through the best and worst times. Helen Myers; Lyndon and Rita Reed; Waymon, Diane, Trey and Jennifer Newsome; Harold and Betty Lightfoot; Lisa Lowry; Kay Harper; and Terry McGonagill—you all own pieces of my heart.

From the very dawn of my existence, my sister, Joy Silvestro, has been a part of me. To my brother-in-law, Rick Silvestro, who came to the United States at thirteen and could only speak Italian, yet overcame insurmountable difficulties to become a successful American businessman, you have my complete admiration. Thank you both for your stories and inspiration for this book.

Robin, Steve, Blakeley, Brooks, Sara Grace, Laura, Clint, Evagail, Morris, Reed, Keely, Bryan, Thomas, Brylan, Keegan, Michael, Meredith, Emmersyn, and Easton—you are the source of my light, my love, and my laughter.

I love all of you, la mia famiglia!

AUTHORS' NOTES

While we took great pains to research all factual events, locations, Italian and Cajun phrases and expressions, as well as foods, we take full responsibility for any errors. (Special thanks to blogger Sugar Bee: Cajun French Language Dictionary.) For the sake of story, however, *Vita e Spezie* (the restaurant) is fiction, and while Post Office Road does exist in The Strand, the popular dining and shopping district, our post office was inspired by a photograph from another time and location.

We would also like to point out that there is no cemetery adjoined to St. Mary's Catholic Basilica, nor—to the best of our knowledge—is there a bocce court in Galveston. However, Fisherman's Wharf continues as a successful seafood location, and the items chosen by the characters in the story are directly from their menu.

LIFE & SPICE

*Life is an end in itself, and the only question
as to whether it is worth living is whether
you have had enough of it.*

—Oliver Wendell Holmes

To maintain a joyful family requires much from both the parents and the children. Each member of the family has to become, in a special way the servants of the other.

—Pope John Paul II

PROLOGUE

September 8, 1900
Galveston, Texas

DEAR GOD...

Those two words had Nathan Burroughs dropping his pencil from rain-soaked, shaking hands. They overwhelmed him as did the raging storm beyond the four walls of his temporary sanctuary, and for good reason. He'd meant to write, *Dear Mia*, his pet name for his beloved wife, Amelia. Instead, he seemed to have begun a prayer. Incongruous, since he was neither a church-goer, nor devout, which made him one of the last people who might offer words of worship, let alone write a letter to the Almighty. Yet, proof lay before him on someone's abandoned desk.

His penmanship confirmed his state of mind—pathetic, shaky and desperate. Nevertheless, with a slow nod, he uttered a fatalistic sigh. His subconscious had recognized what his conscious mind still rejected: he was fast running out of luck, and should have no expectations of surviving the night. What's more, it would be foolish to write to Mia when—by the time this ungodly storm was through with them—there would likely be no letter left, let alone a place to send it.

"So be it then," he murmured, his saltwater-cracked lips barely moving.

With what time he had left, he would make peace with this world and the Lord he respected, but too often put in second place to earning a living. He would write to God and hope his beloved would somehow come to know that in his final hours, he had humbled himself. After struggling and failing to make a better life for his family, only to succeed in putting them in new danger, he, a shrimper, would atone to the Father. The Father whose son was the fisher of men.

A storm unlike any he'd experienced in his one score and five years was taking direct aim at the largest city in Texas. The last time people in these parts were subjected to nature's wrath was back in 1875. He'd been little more than the frown of concern between his pregnant mother's eyes in those days, when his parents left Oklahoma and headed for the Texas coast. As so many already had done, his father had given up on farming, surrendering to the relentless punishment of draughts and tornadoes. Willing to try his luck at sea, the senior Burroughs had heard how the Port of Galveston was booming. He'd sold their homestead, packed up his family, along with their meager possessions, and headed south.

Shortly upon crossing the Red River into Texas, they'd heard the news, then increasingly harrowing reports about a storm. To avoid the worst of the assault, they'd detoured and paused in Austin for a few days as their destination, Indianola at Matagorda Bay took a direct hit. The second largest city in the state had been brutalized. Having come from a place that proved lightning would strike twice if conditions presented themselves—as did tornadoes—Nathan's mother had been full of doubt about their new home, especially once they saw the depth and breadth of the devastation. Nevertheless, Nathan's father kept a single-minded focus on opportunity.

As was so often the case, "opportunity" meant living in their covered wagon for months until improved, yet still temporary, housing could be acquired. It was pure hell for a pregnant woman, but such were the times.

Only days after they had a solid roof over their heads, Nathan was born. As relieved and hopeful as the family was, their struggles and heartache continued.

Fulfilling Nathan's mother's fears, another storm struck in 1886 killing his father, and many more. By then, many residents decided they'd endured their fill of coastal living, and chose not to remain to rebuild a third time. Some moved inland; however, his mother's priority had to be attaining a livelihood for herself, and her children. She took him and his younger brother up the coast to the state's largest city, Galveston. There she quickly found work as a cook and, within months, married the proprietor of the restaurant, who also owned the hotel next door. For the first time, the new family knew what it was like to live in comfort. Yet, neither he, nor his brother stopped watching the Gulf of Mexico, or the horizon, without trepidation.

"Stupid," Nathan muttered, thinking back upon his life. History proved repeatedly how a man, who didn't learn from his mistakes, was apt to repeat them. Even so, Nathan saw fortunes could be made in shipping and, like his biological father, became a man of the sea. But his plans were to only be a sailor for as long as it took him to have his own fleet. He had worked his way up to first mate on a shrimper, and had enough saved to purchase the boat from his captain, who had been preparing to retire. That would never happen now.

Yesterday, in the late afternoon of September 7, the craft had capsized in the storm. Everyone onboard, save him, had been consumed by the riotous waves and angry sea. Nathan shuddered at the memory of the cries of his crewmates, soon drowned out by the storm's fury.

The crew had experienced their share of squalls before, but nothing like this, and all had already cursed Captain Hardin for demanding they risk everything when most everyone else had refused to go out. In fact, a group of captains had relied on instincts and experience to move their crafts from port and head along the coast down to Mexico to avoid having their property decimated. "Hardhead" was the crew's name for their captain, and they decided Hardin had earned it for eternity when he ignored every warning, including the ones coming straight from Washington, D.C., and President McKinley.

"The sea will be alive with shrimp churning to the surface and begging to be scooped up," Hardin had declared to his anxious men. "We'll make it back to shore before conditions grow serious. Either follow my orders or find yourselves jobs elsewhere, you sniveling cowards."

Hardhead couldn't have been more wrong. The seas had been too rough to manage the nets, let alone control the vessel and, thanks to the captain's blinding greed, the *Miss Melissa* would sail no more.

A sudden jolt and boom knocked Nathan out of his tortured reflections, and shook every wall of the post office. When he'd reached the place, he'd been surprised to find it abandoned, since it was constructed of concrete, and one of the sturdiest buildings in the area. It was also two stories high. Now, he had to accept his initial sense of good fortune would be short-lived, just as it was when he'd been flung onto land by a brutal wave and believed he had outlasted nature's wrath. Although they were blocks from the beach, he was beginning to believe the entire sea was about to slam onshore, determined to reclaim him and whatever other unlucky souls remained in the area.

As the post office took another blow, Nathan heard both human and animal screams. "Heavenly Father," he croaked. He guessed some hapless individuals were seeking a belated escape in a horse and carriage. Undoubtedly, the momentum of wind and water had carried the entire party into the side of the building.

A spontaneous impulse to help had him pushing himself to his feet. He reasoned it might be possible to grab someone from the doorway, and drag them into safety—temporary as it might be. However, brutal logic soon overrode the thought. Galveston was less than ten feet above sea level. He'd ventured to the roof to glimpse conditions from his current vantage point. What he'd seen was waves starting to destroy the wharves and buildings closest to the water. Conditions had to be far worse now. If he opened the front door, would he have the strength to shut it again?

A last, brief shriek of human or animal terror had him covering his face, then his ears. As he shuddered with shock and shame, the storm mocked him and beat at the building repeatedly promising utter annihilation.

Doors and window panes began to creak and groan louder, a reminder of how everything had its limits, especially those manmade. Convinced his own death was near, Nathan's gaze shifted to the papers across the room. Determined to leave something behind, he grabbed for the pencil and began writing with fervid determination.

Dear God.
Forgive me, for I have sinned. I remember that much of
my Catholic upbringing from my good mother. She tried
to prepare me for Confession, Mass, and Communion.
But it's been close to twenty years now, and You know I
wasn't an inspired student from the beginning. Things
changed inside me once Papa died in the Indianola
storm, and we were forced to move here. Pray, remember
my heart is with You now. You saw reason to spare me
a grave in the sea, but I suspect You think I'm not fit to
rejoin my beloved family again.
    I ask for this one thing—spare Mia, sweet Lizzie, and
baby Paul. Lead them to safety. Let them know a husband
and father's last thoughts were of them.
                         Amen.
                    Nathan Burroughs

With his breath rattling in his chest, Nathan went from desk to cupboard until he found a stack of envelopes. He put his letter in one, licked it, and pressed it closed. After addressing it simply: To God, he hurried across to the brass mail slot just inside the entryway of the post office and slid it in. Where it would land, he didn't know. The door to the area was locked. In all likelihood, it would end up sucked into the ocean like everything else, and remain forever unread. Oddly enough, the prospect didn't trouble him. If their Lord was all knowing and seeing, then Nathan trusted his words had already been received.

The building took another blow, and a front window on the far side burst into jagged shards of glass and splintered wood. As water and debris poured in, Nathan pressed himself against the wall. The noise was deafening, while the calamity it created triggered his flight instincts. If he didn't get to higher ground fast, he would be crushed amid the chaos intensifying in the bowels of this structure.

By the time he reached the base of the stairs, he was soaked to his chest. Just as he grabbed the bannister, the same momentum that was turning the world into a giant washbasin slammed something sharp into his leg. He screamed in agony and collapsed under water.

Salty sea and filth rushed into his open mouth and beyond. He gagged and choked, wildly flailing to regain a handhold. He had to get back on his feet, yet his attempts were a folly. Everything he grasped at were items with little substance and only sent him deeper. Then, just as his lungs threatened to burst, his grappling fingers found the bannister again.

Frantic, he held fast and fought to regain his footing. As his injured left leg failed him, he discovered he knew nothing yet about excruciating pain. All but blinded by it, in sheer desperation he dragged himself up and out of the water until he could discern what had happened. It was then he discovered only Satan stood with him on this night, and his mood was murderous.

Nathan's pants were ripped wide and exposed a compound fracture of his thigh bone. Understanding what that meant, an animal-like cry broke from his lips.

He was done for.

1

The Present

"ASSASINO!" LEO ANGELONI CRIED, AS HIS BUM LEG SLID OUT
from beneath him. Dreading what was coming—brutal contact with
the restaurant's tiled kitchen floor—he made a wild grab for anything
to break his fall, only to cause himself greater injury. The first came as
he clipped a stainless-steel work station with his funny bone, followed by
banging his head on the metal stool behind him. Blinded by stars giving
birth to stars, he hit the floor, and lay dazed like a fish flung onto the deck
of a boat in the brightest and hottest part of the day.

"Leo!"

Several voices called out at once, but being closest, Alfredo "Tiny"
Busto reached him first. Awarded the unfortunate reputation by
co-workers as being the most expendable member at *Vita e Spezie*,
he lived up to the criticism by simply resting his hands on his knees
to stare at his boss. What Tiny lacked in height, he made up for in
girth, and the few steps to Leo left him panting as though he'd been
sidetracked in the middle of a marathon. Nevertheless, he was the
cousin most devoted to the baker, and not just because Leo was the
only relation willing to work with him. Both men tended to be social
wallflowers and misfits, although for entirely different reasons, and
were most comfortable in each other's company.

Hearing the guttural sounds emanating from Leo's slack mouth,

Tiny extended a hand. "You sound like you're choking, are you okay? Let me help you up."

Leo lifted heavy-lidded eyes to deliver a scathing look at the younger man. "Do I look okay? Damned people and their stupid letters."

Groaning, he eased to a sitting position then scanned the area, his dark brown eyes narrowing as he finally spotted the white envelope, now blemished with the footprint from his non-skid shoe. With an angry growl, Leo kicked at it with his good leg, a motion that had Tiny performing a clumsy jig to avoid being struck in the process.

"Hey!"

"You big baby, I missed you by a mile." Leo motioned for the corpulent man to offer his pudgy hand again. "Come on! Get me to my feet before somebody puts a cell phone over the counter to take a picture. If I become the latest joke on social media, it's on your head." Standing again, he derided the rest of the staff. "Thank you for all the assistance."

At his initial cry, everyone had turned into a cluster of gapeseeds, but as soon as he'd started grumbling, they'd returned to their work. Sure, the restaurant was packed; it was, after all, Friday night; also, not the first time Leo had experienced an encounter with a letter pushed through the ornate brass mail slot located in the entryway. Yet that was the point! Was it too much to ask for a little concern and compassion given how many indignities he'd suffered thanks to that antiquated tourist attraction?

Over a century ago, the building had been a post office—one with a wildly romantic history. Even after the Angeloni family purchased the building and turned it into a *ristorante*, people had come to also see what some journalist whimsically described as a "conduit to Heaven," after a couple of people left their own letters. From then on, the postings to God increased. Consequently, no one knew when another missile of hope—and danger to *him*—would appear.

"You still got the moves, *paisan*," Vincent Sirocco called, grinning over his shoulder from his place at the stove. The head chef and father of six took Leo's rebuke with his usual good humor, since Leo characteristically exhibited a singular repertoire of moods—all gloomy. "And look on the bright side—that knock to the noggin might have cracked loose your rock-hard jowls. Let's see if you really have forgotten how to smile."

As he began to share his opinion of Vinny's ancestors—carefully phrased in Italian to protect the most tender ears of their diners—Leo was thwarted by his older sibling. The restaurant's owner came bursting through the swinging doors connecting the kitchen to the main dining room. Waiters and waitresses immediately stopped giggling, grabbed plates from under the heat lamps, and exited in haste.

"Can you get any louder, Leo?" Seething, Salvatore Angeloni strode through the kitchen to stand toe-to-toe with his brother. "You had half the customers turning to look this way. In case you haven't noticed, 'assassin' sounds the same in several languages, and that's not a word people react well to, especially these days."

Pausing in the middle of rechecking his injuries, Leo went full out melodramatic, and pressed a hand to his chest. "Oh, excuse me. My brains have to be spilling from the back of my head before I can get any sympathy from you."

"Sympathy I have," Sal replied, staring him down. Two years older than Leo's fifty-seven, he looked a good five years younger, his features bold, dark and romantic, without any of Leo's cragginess. "And I'd have more if you would take the doctor's advice and have that hip replacement surgery he said you need. Maybe then you could maintain better control of your body."

"Bah! Who has the time for doctors? Besides, you have no one to replace me with if I did do it."

The arrogant challenge in his reply had Sal lowering his voice to a whisper. "Try me."

Looking increasingly anxious and eager to put an end to the brotherly dispute, Tiny grunted as he struggled to pick up the soiled envelope. "It wasn't Leo's bad hip to blame for the fall, Sal. It was this."

Leo tried to beat his brother from grabbing the envelope. In the last second, a faster, feminine hand intervened.

"Give me that."

Soft-spoken Valentina Angeloni-Pastore had also entered the kitchen. Graceful and quiet, she was an elegant vision in severe black, her equally dark hair brushed into a neat bun at her nape. Folding the letter, she slipped it into the pocket of her maxi dress.

"You know I handle these."

"Valentina." Leo's gravelly voice took on a wheedling tone. "Enough already. We have to put a stop to this. Once and for all, somebody screw a metal plate over that mail slot before one of us is killed."

Five years his junior, fifty-three-year-old Valentina rose on tiptoe to place a gentle kiss on her brother's temple, still bruised from another incident where he'd judged distance poorly and banged into one of the lower cabinets. His ruddy complexion might hide some of the bruising, but there was no missing the pain in his brooding eyes; a misery she knew went much farther back than his last mishap.

"Leo, you know you're supposed to pay more attention to what you're doing. And you also know many people are drawn here because of the 1900 storm. That lure will always be bigger than all of us. The best we can do is make peace with it. Thankfully, Sal is the one with business sense among us, and his marketing idea has worked. Summer has barely begun and we're already fully booked for next Valentine's Day, thanks to the fascination triggered by the Burroughs letter."

"Booked with people who want the free red-velvet cupcake, instead of ordering from the dessert list," Leo all but spat. His expression changed to one of suspicion. "And what's going on with those letters? You used to tell us about them. Now you say nothing. I know why," he continued without giving her time to reply. "Because even you have come to realize it's all a joke. I bet most of the time you get some kid writing obscene stuff or asking for a waitress' phone number."

Her expression disappointed, Valentina shook her head slowly. "You've just answered your own question. I don't tell you because all you do is ridicule them, and me, for showing interest."

"At least we know an ambulance is unnecessary," Sal told her. "His mouth is working just fine, and he's still standing on his own two feet." Sal's eyes radiated the passion that exuded from every inch of his well-toned body. His hair showed only a fine dusting of gray, much like Valentina's; however, his hairline had begun to recede, so he kept it short, sometimes not much longer than his relentless five o'clock shadow. "One thing I'll give you credit for," he added to Leo. "Your thick skull."

Turning to the rest of the kitchen staff, Sal clapped his hands to encourage their team. "Come on people. There are too many tickets piling up, and the Campisi wedding rehearsal dinner is about to start. Seventy extra guests to make happy. Put a fire under it."

Valentina touched her oldest brother's shoulder. "I'll go light the candles back in the banquet room and make sure the flowers and everything look their best."

"Good," he told her. "I'll do another walk-through of the dining room before paying my respects back there." Usually he would check out how things were going in the bar and lounge, too, but there wouldn't be time until much later tonight.

Vita e Spezie had been at this location for over twenty-five years. Prior to that, the Angeloni family had owned a smaller restaurant in another part of the city. Because of the former post office's fame, along with their multi-generational business, they had worked their way up to being on the chamber of commerce maps as one of Galveston's "must see" destinations, as well as for being an historical landmark. The achievement was no small feat, considering the failure rate for their kind of enterprise, and he was proud of it. Lately, however, a great deal had been weighing on him as to what the future held. Leo's momentum for injuring himself only added to his concerns.

As the current head of the Angeloni family, his siblings, along with some members of their extended family looked to this place for a paycheck, and him for advice and guidance. While he continued to see that as an honor, he was growing increasingly troubled as to how there were no Angelonis on the horizon to carry on with the business, once he grew too old to keep things going; someone with the touch to achieve the fine balance between harmonious kitchen and happy dining room.

His brother should have been an easy choice. A bachelor didn't have to deal with the influences and distractions a wife and children naturally created. Sal had learned that lesson the hard way. Unfortunately, Leo also had other troubles besides needing surgery, some of it dealing with issues from the past, some with the argument voiced by many middle-offspring: the I-don't-get-no-respect syndrome. In Leo's case, it was mostly self-inflicted. He was prone to walking away from discussions as soon as he heard things he didn't like. To Sal, those character traits weren't conducive to being a good manager. Even in the kitchen where he'd known everyone for years, Leo preferred to work alone.

As for their sad, but beloved kid sister, Valentina, she was a treasure as a hostess and his right hand. Unfortunately, she didn't have the strength to take on the full responsibility of running the business.

They were coming to the end of the line of skilled Angelonis. With every day, the promise of *Vita e Spezie* staying in the family was growing dimmer. It all proved that no matter how hard you worked or what financial comfort you had achieved, there were always thunderclouds on the horizon threatening to ruin everything.

He had to act, and act soon. A potential heir needed to already be apprenticing for his position. No matter what, though, he would settle for nothing less than an individual who had a fire in the belly for this kind of life.

Pausing to straighten the jacket of his black suit, Sal sought comfort by stepping into the dimly lit dining room full of animated patrons, brisk, yet amiable waiters and waitresses in their crisp white shirts and black slacks. This was his arena and he felt as confident as Caruso or Pavarotti on an opera-house stage. He was in his element when he strolled around to shake hands with the regulars and compliment the ladies.

Noticing a pair of new faces, he paused to offer a particularly warm smile. "Welcome to *Vita e Spezie*. I see you ordered *Linguine Tutto Mare*," he said, nodding to the middle-aged gentleman's plate of sautéed mussels, shrimp, scallops, calamari, and baby clams in wine sauce. "It's one of my favorites. Not to put you on the spot, but what do you think?"

With a groan of pleasure, the equally well-dressed man sat back in his seat and rubbed his belly. "Fantastic. It's such a generous serving, I'd love to take this back to the hotel room with me, but I'm worried about the shellfish, you know," he added with an apologetic shrug.

Sal dismissed his concern with a wave. "Everything in that recipe was caught fresh today, and we're very liberal with the wine, which is extra insurance." He added a wink to assure the diner.

The woman sitting across the table leaned forward exposing a discreet amount of cleavage for her age. Her décolletage was tastefully enhanced with gold jewelry a cut above what one found at the chain jewelry stores. Sal had an eye for such things. Always circumspect, he warmed his smile by subtle degrees. "Dare I say that you look like another happy guest, *Signora*?"

"Oh, indeed. And I just love the name of your restaurant, even if I really don't know what it means."

Beaming into shy blue eyes enhanced by the electric candlelight provided by the wall sconces, and the smoky quartz fixtures overhead, Sal spread his arms wide, inviting everyone around them to participate in the moment. "Life and Spice. What else can anyone ask for?"

"Oh, that's lovely," she replied, with a girlish scrunch of her shoulders that accentuated her delight. "I knew it had to be something sensuous and artistic, just like the atmosphere in here. I can't wait to tell my friends back in Georgia."

"You've made my week, *Signora*," he said with a hint of a bow. "Now be sure to leave room for dessert so you can share that experience, as well."

"I saw tiramisu on the menu. Do you recommend it?"

"I can do better than that." Sal signaled to their waiter. "Tony," he said to the young man, who appeared instantly at his side. Placing a paternal hand on the shoulder of cousin Anthony Riva's eldest son, he continued, "We'll have two tiramisus for this couple when they're ready. My compliments."

Leaving the charmed diners, he continued his way around the room. Out of the corner of his eye, he saw the wedding rehearsal party beginning to arrive, and knew it was time to return to the kitchen to supervise their dinner preparations. On the way, his attention was drawn to the one undesired table in the restaurant—always the last to be used. The cramped seating for two was compromised due to its position by the second series of swinging doors. While those doors provided access to the kitchen, they were mainly used to reach the office, more storage rooms, and staff restroom facilities. It struck Sal as criminal that tonight it was inhabited by a young woman dining alone. Such mother-of-pearl skin should be enjoyed by the entire patronage, even if her short, blond hair looked like she'd just stepped off stage from some local performance of *Peter Pan*. However, no one with such dewy eyes and bowed lips could ever be mistaken for a boy no matter how youthful.

Pausing before her, Sal offered a remorseful smile. "Another new face. I apologize for the poor seating. We're extra busy tonight."

"Oh, I completely understand," the young woman with the big

blues and equally intriguing smoky voice replied. "But I'm compelled to ask—is there an alley in back where you can discretely pull in an ambulance for your chef?"

Before he could stop himself, Sal cast a quick glance over his shoulder into the kitchen. Leo was nowhere to be seen. Had something else happened, or had he misjudged how badly his brother was hurt?

"I admit I'm being nosy," she continued, "but this seat does give me the best view of his part of the kitchen. When the hostess offered it as my only option, I grabbed it for exactly that reason."

Expecting anything but this admission, Sal was momentarily taken aback. Who was she—a food critic from a national magazine? He should be so lucky. More likely, the competition was spying on them. He was always anticipating one of the resort hotels to put in a restaurant with Mediterranean fare. Either way, he was immediately on guard.

"Leo is my brother," he admitted with a grimace. "And he's been accident prone for years. But we also know never to underestimate his durability."

"I was just wondering if there's anything I can do?"

"Are you a chiropractor or in pharmaceutical sales?" Sal asked drolly. It wasn't smart to prolong the conversation, but he couldn't help himself; he had always enjoyed the company of a pretty woman, and he found this one particularly appealing. "I'm ready to consider almost any tweak if it means improving his overall disposition. Nobody can believe such a sourpuss likes to work with sweets."

With a brief laugh as smooth as suede, the young woman replied, "I'm neither." She extended her hand. "I'm Olivia Dumont—Livie to my friends. I happen to be a pastry chef, too. One who's looking for employment."

"Salvatore Angeloni."

Another few members of the Campisi group entered and continued the procession toward the banquet room triggering a new impetus for Sal to return to the kitchen, but curiosity and an indisputable sense of destiny had him taking the bait she offered with her engaging smile and sparkling azure-blue eyes.

"Well, I can see you as a model from one of those cordon bleu school commercials, but you don't look old enough to be a short-order cook, never mind a pastry chef."

"Do you have your cardio specialist's number close? I graduated with a culinary arts degree from the University of New Orleans, and then spent three years in Paris honing my skills as a pastry chef before returning to Louisiana."

"*Complimenti*," Sal replied, his eyebrows raised. "So, you're not a BOI?"

Olivia looked momentarily startled. "Pardon?"

"Not boy. B-O-I. Born-on-the-island. I knew I would have seen you around somewhere if you were a native. What made you leave New Orleans?"

Livie offered a one-shoulder shrug. "A need to continue broadening my horizons. I'd like to show you what I can do before anyone else hears you might be seeking backup."

As tempting as the idea was to Sal—what he could do with the talents of a bona fide pastry chef—he knew there were too many complications to prevent him from taking her up on the offer. "As I said, Leo's my brother."

"A brother who doesn't look like he'll find it easy to get out of bed tomorrow."

Her eyes weren't merely gemstone riveting, they held wisdom. Despite his initial doubts, Sal glanced back at the kitchen in time to see Leo return to his station, grab a washcloth, and wipe the sweat from his forehead. Mentally willing him to have the presence of mind to toss the thing into the laundry basket, he returned his gaze to Olivia Dumont. She was a sharp cookie and he liked the vibes he was getting from her. Dare he trust that Providence was sending him a sign—and a gift?

"Okay, Miss N'awlins, I tell you what. Be here tomorrow morning by seven-thirty, and you can show me what you've got besides guts and sass."

He'd already started for the kitchen when he heard, "You've got it!" from behind him. Raising a hand in acknowledgement, he pushed through the stainless-steel doors and in the process forced thoughts of her to the back of his mind—especially once he saw the latest commotion before him.

Entrees for two tables were waiting to be delivered; waitress Kat was flirting with Benny, taking the sous chef's mind off his work; and preppers Joey and Stu were arguing again over whose responsibility was what. Oblivious to it all, Vinny's head was bent over the stove as he scrubbed violently at something.

"What the hell?" Sal snapped. "Kat—are those plates going to deliver themselves? Benny if that calamari comes out of the fryer anything beyond golden brown, I'm going to bread and cook the parts of you you'll miss most. And why aren't you controlling your people? Joey, Stu, less hot air and more work."

Returning to Vinny, he continued in a moderated tone. "What's happened? I see a dozen orders not getting filled." He nodded back to the slips of paper fastened with magnetized clips to the stainless table behind them.

"Ech. I accidentally knocked the spoon out of the Alfredo sauce, and it gummed up the burner."

Sal squeezed his chef's shoulder to signal his appreciation for managing the ill-timed error. "At least you caught it before it started to smell up the place. Let me know if you want me to dive in and give you a hand."

He turned back to his prep crew. "Half the wedding rehearsal party is here and I don't see seventy salads ready to go."

Joey Farina hooked his thumb toward the cooler behind him. "It's under control, boss. We'll bring them out when you give the word. I was just about to ask Benny if he was ready for us to bring him the asparagus to go with the veal parmigiana."

"Bull, he was hounding me about the salad dressing," Stu Ciccarone countered. "He claims that I put too much garlic in it last time, like I don't have the recipe memorized. I could make the stuff in my sleep."

Sal picked up a clean spoon, dipped it into the bowl of dressing, and tasted their house specialty. Smacking his lips, he dropped the utensil in the plastic bin with the other dirty dishes by the sink, where Ruben, the Hispanic dishwasher, was hard at work.

Passing Joey, Sal snapped, "You two don't just look like bookends, you act it. Mind your own business and get the asparagus."

Two more waiters came in to check on their orders, and Sal weaved between them to confront Leo. His long-faced brother was muttering over the cake for the Campisi wedding rehearsal party.

"Now what's wrong?"

Leo grunted his distain. "You can't see? The bride-to-be asked for a spiced rum cake with almond and cocoa frosting, and to use the darkest variety of liquor. Now I have an ugly and uglier brown cake. How appetizing is that?"

Sal studied the two-layer concoction. "It's too late for a do-over, but at least it smells damned good. What can she say when it's what she asked for?"

"Women have a Geiger counter monitoring everyone's reactions to their big events, and that can trigger instant amnesia as to what they claimed they wanted," Leo informed him.

"So...add some white chocolate shavings?" Sal suggested, not wanting to remind Leo, this was something he should be figuring out for himself. "Hell, use whole truffles if you have them, and get a bride and groom figurine from the stockroom."

"It's a rehearsal cake, not a wedding cake." Leo massaged his back. "I guess I could make a nosegay from the white roses left in the cooler. But I swear, Sal, I'm hurting so bad, it'll be a miracle if I can do anything else tonight."

The admission should have sent Sal into a panic considering how it would leave him short-handed. Instead, the news was like 7s across a slot machine screen. "Are you telling me you want to go home now?" he asked, careful to keep emotion out of his voice. "Say the word and I'll have Tiny drive you." He would sacrifice an employee to chauffeur them both home if it meant an end to tonight's drama. "Valentina can serve the cake, and I can help her." Logistically, it would make better sense for one of the waitresses to do it, but that couldn't happen while Leo was around. Last time Sal suggested one of them assist, his brother went rabid, insisting how their glitter-and-decal-adorned nails were borderline board-of-health violations.

Sal pulled over a stool. "Sit down, and let Tiny get the flowers and whatever else you need."

"Okay. Thanks," Leo muttered, as Fredo Busto wasted no time to hurry to the cooler. "And I should warn you now—I don't know about tomorrow."

"Not a problem," Sal assured him. "As luck would have it, I may already have a solution for that."

"What are you talking about?"

As soon as he heard the suspicion in his brother's voice, Sal regretted opening his mouth. "It's nothing. Someone saw your fall and introduced herself, that's all. She's coming to show me what she can do in the morning."

"Apologies. If I'd killed myself, you could have spared her the trouble of an audition."

Sal glanced around feeling trapped. There was no time for this, and yet he couldn't walk away. "Leo...consider the possibility that she could take some pressure off you. She seems to have good credentials."

Drama was a given in families, and the Angeloni clan was no different. Growing up, Sal remembered how their dinner table was a stage for operatic intercourse. Leo didn't disappoint as he dropped his chin to his chest, only to rock his head back and forth in abject dejection.

"So, this is what it's come to."

"Not now," Sal warned under his breath. It felt as though he had two hundred lasers burning into his back coming straight from the dining room.

"Excuse me for needing to have my say. It's always about *your* precious time. Me, I have no voice."

Praying that the comely blonde had left by now and wasn't watching all of this, Sal drew a sustaining breath. "I'll save you samples of whatever she makes. You can opinionate then."

"She...she...who is this *she*?"

"A chef from New Orleans with a culinary arts degree. She also trained in France."

"You know this for sure? She showed you papers?"

"Yeah, she pulled her diploma from the pocket of her size two jeans."

"You're hiring an anorexic pastry chef!" Leo snorted. "I knew it. She's a looker. Your Achilles heel is showing again, Salvatore."

Nothing got under Sal's skin faster than that accusation. For years he'd heard the innuendos and rumors floating around. He even understood the reasons behind them. It was a crime to be alive, for all intent and purposes single, and denying some poor unmarried Italian girl the full cycle of her life. But he resented the branding that followed, even if it was simultaneously impressive and ridiculous given he worked seventeen and more hours a day, six days a week. When did he have time for a social life, let alone to act like a playboy?

Taking his brother's silence as a sign he was gaining leverage, Leo gestured to encompass the kitchen. "Besides, how many women do you see working in here? Eh? None."

"Maybe it's time that changed."

"It can't. They don't fit in."

"That's what our parents said when I hired our first waitress."

"I remember. And you just had to warn the worst of them to quit flirting. Again."

"Why can't you just accept that I'm trying to get you some help?"

"Stop it, you two," Valentina ordered as she swept into the room. "The Campisi group is seated and starting toasts. Unless you want to have to refill the breadstick baskets two or three more times, and offer complimentary drinks from the bar, I suggest we get the salads out there."

The tension between the brothers had to be put aside. Sal called to Joey, "You heard her. Move it."

Belatedly, Valentina noticed the cake and leaned toward Leo, her expression pained. "That's it? It looks pitiful. Delicious, no doubt, but so plain."

Leo sucked in a deep breath. "Over my dead body," he muttered, and went to work on the roses and ribbon Tiny had collected for him. He drew out three of the long-stemmed beauties and cut them down to size. Then he tied the shortened ends with ivory-lace ribbon. Creating a dainty bow, he gently laid the mini-bouquet on the top of the cake.

"How sweet," Valentina said with an approving nod. "Tiny, help me move it to the cart and I'll wheel it to the banquet room." To Leo, she said, "You did good, dearest."

"You're the only one who thinks so."

Kat's arrival stopped Valentina from replying, as she plopped a dessert plate before him. "My customer is complaining that we cheated him and left the cream out of his cannoli."

"*Cannolo*," Leo intoned. "One cannolo, a tray of cannoli. How many times do I have to tell you?" Inspecting each empty end of the confection, Leo offered, "Amazing. Your diner is a lizard or did he suck it empty with a straw?" Without waiting for a reply, he dumped the remnants into the trash, reached for a new plate, and took another pastry from the display case.

Accepting the replacement, Kat puckered up and gave him an airy kiss. "Take it as a compliment. He obviously likes them."

"Sure, sure," Leo groused, as she went off to make the delivery. "I'm such a success, I'm being pushed out of my own kitchen."

THE KINETIC ENERGY continued for the rest of the evening, testament to the increase in tourism and special-event bookings. By closing time, everyone looked spent, but satisfied. Once the dining and banquet rooms emptied, cleanup went into full speed. Valentina had stayed with the Campisi party for most of the evening. As a result, her twenty-one-year-old niece and assistant hostess, Janine Tucci, struggled a bit managing the busy dining room, even though this was her second year in the position. However, the recent college graduate was all smiles, since she was finally *legal* and could join the others in the kitchen for one of their ritual weekend celebrations.

Sal opened a couple of bottles of sparkling wine to toast everyone's dedicated efforts. Leo held back, which compelled Tiny to do the same. The two of them continued to scrub their side of the kitchen with the fervor of workers expecting the Pope to arrive the next morning to bless the place. It finally got to be too much for the modern-day Sancho Panza, and he gazed mournfully at his Don Quixote.

"Aren't you even a little thirsty? I could use a sip. My throat is so dry."

"I've already got a headache from the fall," Leo replied. "That sweet wine will only make it worse." Yet he glanced at the tray where two glasses remained. He tilted his head in acquiescence. "Go ahead. Drink. I can't blame you."

Tiny still hesitated. His expression went from enthused to doubtful and then distressed. "If your head feels that bad, maybe it's time for a little Green Fairy?"

Ever since the accident that initiated Leo's physical woes, relief from chronic pain was impossible, no matter what prescription doctors offered him. It was by sheer coincidence they came upon a solution.

One day a customer who had just suffered an injury asked their bartender Rocco if by chance they had a forgotten bottle of absinthe in their inventory. They did, and Rocco later told the story of how the customer left the bar almost walking like a new man.

Leo remembered how the history of the green spirit went back centuries, and at one point was outlawed in various countries, including the United States, due to its hallucinogenic reputation. Hemingway made it famous again by creating the cocktail, *Death in the Afternoon*, which involved absinthe poured over ice-cold champagne. Recently, the spirit had enjoyed a revival among the younger crowd, who were always game to try what was new or unique. For Leo, it was the miracle he'd lost hope in ever finding. To this day, he swore the elixir was the one thing to provide any reprieve from his most debilitating pain. He did, however, restrict himself to only indulging at home when the menacing spasms were at their worst.

Now he glanced guiltily around the room before waving away Tiny's suggestion. His siblings would make a fuss and increase their nagging.

"At the house," he told Tiny. He kept a case of the stuff as insurance, and the way he was feeling, Leo knew he would empty what was left in one bottle tonight. "Listen," he warned his assistant. "If I'm not able to make it in tomorrow, I need you to be here on my behalf. Somebody is coming."

"I heard. What do you want me to do?"

"Everything you usually do for me—sift flour, cream butter...but most of all watch *her.*"

"Is having some backup such a bad thing?"

If that was all it was, Leo might have accepted Sal's news with some appreciation; after all, he wasn't getting any younger and could use an easier schedule. Unfortunately, he suspected his brother's concern over his welfare was lip service to conceal his real interest.

"There are no accidents," he replied, keeping his voice so low Tiny had to lean close to hear him. "Think about it...five minutes after I fall, some pastry genius walks through the front door?" He laid a careful finger against his bruised temple. "I may not be as sharp as some of Vinny's knives, but I still have enough up here to recognize when something doesn't smell right, *capire?*"

Tiny's wide eyes and small mouth shaped in an O made him look like a chubby perch gulping in shock at being yanked out of a pond. He quickly nodded his reassurance. "I understand. I'll be here, Leo. And I'll take notes to make sure I remember to tell you everything I saw and heard."

"I know you will."

"Did I ever tell you that I've always loved watching the Batman and Robin TV series reruns? I even dressed up as Robin for Halloween once."

"Don't ruin the moment," Leo told him.

AFTER THE LITTLE celebration, Sal and his head bartender, Rocco Mancini, did a liquor count. Rocco was a good-looking guy in his early thirties with muscular arms and a quick smile. He also had a head of hair that would have made Samson envious. Even when he wore it in a ponytail during work hours, women remarked that he should be a billboard model, then got giddy as they teased about how many traffic accidents he would cause. Oddly enough, men saw him as a man's man. He could talk sports, guns, politics, or brainstorm a problem under the hood of a car or truck. After five years at *Vita e Spezie*, Sal was dreading the day when one of the big hotels or even Vegas succeeded in stealing him away.

As soon as they had the numbers, Sal gave the younger man a high five. "Well done. That's a new record for a Friday night."

"If it wasn't for the fire code, we could have squeezed in a few more bodies and done even better," Rocco said. "The sidewalks were as packed as I ever saw them in Atlantic City during the good days there. I'll go back to the store room and restock what we're low on, but if it's okay with you, can I come in earlier tomorrow to draft a purchase list?"

The restocking was heavy work and would take him another half hour. Sal valued quality employees, especially someone like Rocco, who had taken a bad turn earlier in his life and had worked hard to get himself straightened out. "Tell you what, I'll handle that. You've earned the chance to get off your feet. See you at the regular time tomorrow."

"You're sure, boss? You know I owe you a year of Sundays."

With an understanding smile, Sal said, "I've got this. Go enjoy yourself for a change."

Once he locked up, Sal returned to the front to make sure everything was secure. That was followed by the final check of the bathrooms, the coat room, and all the places that needed to be inspected in a business like theirs. Finally, after he secured the night's cash and credit card receipts in the office safe, he found his siblings and Tiny waiting on him at the back door. Regardless of how tired or sore they felt, there was a standing rule that Valentina would be seen safely to her apartment upstairs before they left.

"Thank goodness," Valentina said, groaning in relief. "You took so long I thought you were figuring out the deposit. My feet are killing me, and if it wasn't for the wall holding him up, Leo wouldn't be standing."

"Sorry, sorry. Just making sure everything is locked tight and the security cameras are on." Avoiding Leo's hard stare, Sal turned off the interior lights and opened the back door. "After you."

Instead of exiting, into the brightly lit rear parking area, Valentina gasped at the silhouetted figure standing before them.

"Luca!"

"Hi, Aunt Val."

Sal stared at the man leaning forward to kiss Valentina's cheek. Seconds ago, his heart beat dropping, he'd begun to reach for his sister, intent on drawing her to safety behind him. But, then he heard that name and the same organ threatened to quit functioning altogether. *Holy Mother... what had she just called him?*

"Luca?" Leo croaked. "You're a man."

"Well, it has been twenty-five years." As Luca endured his aunt's smothering kisses, he reached out to cup his uncle's cheek. "You weren't exactly easy to recognize, either. What happened to my merry uncle? And your forehead—in this lighting, I didn't see the bruise until now."

"You should see the egg on the back of his head," Tiny offered.

"He had a terrible fall tonight," Valentina explained.

Luca grimaced. "Sorry to hear that. Do you remember you gave me my first soccer lesson? You were so fast on your feet."

For the first time in a long time, Leo smiled. "You can't remember that. You were only a baby."

Luca began to answer, but his gaze shifted over his uncle's shoulder. "Hi, Dad," he began tentatively.

"Does your mother know you're here?"

2

HIS EXPRESSION BEMUSED, LUCA'S TONE TOOK ON A GENTLY cajoling note. "Dad, I'm thirty—a little old to be asking anyone's permission for anything."

Sal raised a hand, signaling the need for a moment to collect his wits. Theirs had been a full day, one compounded by Leo's latest accident. Add the shock of seeing a man instead of the sweet boy—an image memorized from the cherished photograph he kept by his bedside—and he had every good reason to be saying nonsensical things.

He also used those precious seconds to take stock of the handsome man Luca had become. Sal wasn't one to be falsely modest about his own physical appeal, and he could see himself in his son's Italian features. The boy—*man*—had the same perpetual five o'clock shadow that women would forever complain about when exposed to hungry kisses. Yet, Sal could see there was something of his mother's sensual mouth, too, and her Neapolitan eyes.

"You're right, of course," he finally replied. "I'm just shocked." Which was why he didn't know whether to offer his hand, try to hug him, or what? Luca sounded friendly enough; however, there remained the question of what Rosa had filled his head with in all this time? If his son had been raised to think the worst, Sal could do without being humiliated in front of his siblings.

"Who wouldn't be surprised?" Valentina declared, taking hold of Luca's arm. "Come in. We should all have a drink to celebrate. Leo, do you think you're up to staying a few more minutes? A little glass of something might do you good."

"The way I feel, two would be better."

Tiny circled the group and backed away from them into the night. "I'll go move the car closer, Leo, so you don't have to walk so far."

Glancing over his shoulder at the retreating man, Luca said with more concern, "That must have been some fall."

Leo's first response was to make the age-old gesture of dismissal. "It's that damned mail slot in the entryway. You were still in diapers when we opened this location, so you probably don't know the story."

Luca glanced toward Valentina before replying. "This used to be a post office. I get it. I did a report on it for English class when I was in junior high, after Mom gave me a head's up about the building's historical credentials. So, it's still capturing people's imagination? They really continue to leave letters, like the guy did who rode out the 1900 hurricane in here?"

Leo pointed to the kitchen. "*Stupido!* Go to church if you want to talk to God. I beg your father and aunt almost every day to close the thing so we can have some peace. But no. Your father claims it will hurt business, and your aunt—" his shrug reflected resignation "— if she's not lighting candles for everybody and their aging pet, she's bringing leftovers from here to the homeless she's befriended. She listens to angels, not me."

"Mom calls you a saint, Aunt Val," Luca said.

"She might as well have joined a convent," Leo muttered.

"All right, enough with the griping," Sal said, as they reached the bar. While the others slid onto stools, Sal went behind the black-marble counter and turned on the low-hanging lights. Their smoky-amber, glass shades cast an intimate glow around them, but still provided plenty of light for Sal to reach for glasses. "You know the Texas Historical Commission would give us hell if we tamper with anything other than what we did to make the restaurant work. We had enough trouble getting them to agree to let us close the street slot so we could extend the kitchen."

Valentina leaned closer to Luca. "Your father had to prove how mischief makers were shoving trash and water bugs into the opening at night, jeopardizing our Board of Health certification."

"And you were the one who wanted the pastry area in the front to have easy access to the display counters for customers who are only buying dessert to go, or ordering for a special function," Sal reminded his brother. However, he gentled his rebuke by pouring Leo a generous portion of *VSOP Courvoisier* into a snifter.

Leo eyed the amber cognac with surprise then offered a nod of appreciation. *"Grazie."*

"Thank you, brother," Valentina said softly.

Sal knew she had taken a glass of the champagne this evening, but had only wet her lips with it and nothing more. This time he poured a mere splash of her favorite Cabernet in a delicate liqueur glass to let her know he was observant about that and what had been transpiring since he opened the back door.

With a tender look for Luca, he asked, "And so...what are you drinking these days?"

"I experiment. It comes with the job." Luca eyed the well-stocked glass shelves. "You know it's been years since I've had a Tuscan wine. I bet if anyone has a quality Chianti, you do."

"You bet." Sal reached for a bottle set in the famous woven basket. "This has a plum base, we have a lighter one for people ordering antipasto, but the lasagna lovers and late-night drop-ins really go for this." As he poured, he asked, "Where've you been, that you had to deny yourself some of your heritage?"

After casting a discreet, almost impish glance at his aunt, Luca said, "Most recently? The White House."

Sal didn't miss the exchange and took his time filling the glass above serving standards. As he slid it toward his son, he asked, "What the hell? Are you telling us you're Secret Service?" Although dressed only slightly above beach casual in jeans and a black polo shirt, Sal had already gauged him to be in too good physical shape for someone whose job kept him behind a desk.

With a chuckle, Luca replied, "The other department that's expected to take a bullet for the top guy, especially if we mess up a state dinner. I was a chef."

Could the day hold any more surprises? Still adjusting to the idea of having such a grown son, Sal was forced to look at Luca through new eyes. The kid could have said he'd been at the *Le Cordon Bleu* in

Paris, or was Wolfgang Puck's right-hand man, but a bona fide chef at the White House? Not in his wildest dreams would Sal have imagined his own flesh and blood getting to walk through the kitchen at 1600 Pennsylvania Avenue, let alone working there. It was one surprise too many and he reached for his standard stomach stabilizer, a little shot of *Campari* with soda. He knew it was a dead giveaway if his son had the education he'd just insinuated he did. For his part, Luca probably chugged the American over-the-counter version—milk of magnesia— straight from the bottle, given what the stress level must be there.

"The White House," Sal murmured. "Well, you know how to create a moment."

Looking more serene than surprised, Valentina reached over and hugged Luca. "We're so proud of you."

Leo uttered a gruff, "Wow. What's that like? Anyone ever come down in the middle of the night to raid the fridge?"

Luca laughed. "Some more than others."

Valentina pressed her clasped hands to her heart. "Salvatore, did you ever imagine?"

Having recovered from the first wave of shock, Sal found himself dealing with emotions dammed up far too long. "No. But I'm the guy who never imagined his wife would desert him and steal away his only child, so what do you expect?"

His bitterness had Valentina wincing. "Can't we just enjoy each other?"

"This family has lost the ability to enjoy anything." Leo punctuated his pronouncement by downing most of his fine cognac in one gulp, as though expecting Sal to reconsider his generosity and snatch it away.

"Please." Luca leaned forward and looked at each of them in suc- cession. "I didn't come to cause trouble. I apologize for not calling first to give you time to adjust to the idea."

Suddenly brothers and sister did a complete turn-around and pro- tested simultaneously. "No!"

"This is wonderful," Valentina added.

"You did right," Leo assured him.

"Ignore the sarcasm," Sal said. "We have to monitor ourselves so much in front of others, we get carried away when we're alone. Why don't you tell us what brings you back to Galveston? I didn't think they gave you guys much of a vacation."

"It is demanding. In fact, that's part of the reason I recently re-signed." Luca paused to let his elders take in the news. His father simply raised his eyebrows, his uncle reared back his head, as though dodging a blow, and his aunt's look of compassion was accompanied by a soft throaty mew. "Hey, it's all good. You see, someone on our staff lost a family member a few months ago. Watching him struggle with split loy-alties reminded me of my own circumstances. It struck me that I have been needing to come back here and reconnect."

"Isn't that wonderful?" Valentina gushed to her brothers.

Despite his previously voiced bitterness, Sal blurted out, "It is if it's the truth. Seriously, Luca, you're not waiting to break the news that there's something wrong with your mother?" He couldn't help himself. Since the day she'd left, he'd sworn her name would never cross his lips again. Heaven knew, he'd tried not to think about her; yet tonight was like no other and, apparently, he had about as much control over his tongue as he did his imagination.

"No, no, she's great," Luca assured him. "Just getting a little older."

Valentina scoffed, "Your mother never ages."

Whether it was due to the confidence in her voice, or how quickly she'd reacted, Sal felt a cold something congeal in his gut and he put down his glass. "How would you know?" he demanded.

Momentarily flustered, Valentina waved her hands like a trapped bird unable to take flight. "You've forgotten how young the entire Na-varro family always looked. They all have such good genes."

He hadn't laid eyes on any of his estranged wife's family in years, and Valentina knew as much. But as the heavy silence began to feel awkward, Sal said to Luca, "We appreciate you wanting to come. How long can you stay?"

Looking hopeful, Luca replied, "It's up to you. I could hang out here and lend a hand if you need it."

"That would be great—as long as it doesn't take away what time you have planned with your mother."

"She understands," Luca assured him. "In fact, she encouraged me to do this."

"Great," Leo said before Sal could recover from yet another shock. "You can help me. Your father is about to replace me with a Twinkie from New Orleans."

Luca laughed. "Come again?"

Sal made a face at his brother. "We both know it'll take a miracle for you to get out of bed tomorrow. What's more, the pace of things has been wearing you down for some time."

Ever the diplomat and intermediary, Valentina told Luca, "Someone promising happened to come in tonight. Your father says she's qualified."

"You really do look like you could use the rest," Luca told his uncle.

With a growl of disgust, Leo eased himself off the stool. "I can see talking is useless. I'm going home."

As he limped to the back door, Valentina rose, too. "Leo, wait. You're in such pain. I'll signal Tiny to help you get to the car."

Watching the little commotion play out, Sal shook his head and downed the rest of his drink. He needed something more substantial if he was to deal with his son by himself. As his gaze fell on Valentina's barely touched wine, he reached for it.

"Do you think my being around would really be okay with Uncle Leo? He sure sounds uptight," Luca said.

"Your uncle thinks he's the only one having to deal with the clock ticking away. You give him sympathy, and he wants independence. You give him that and he accuses you of not caring." At the sound of the door shutting, Sal took advantage of their privacy. "So, are you married or involved?"

Luca smiled wryly. "Neither. Got serious twice. Considered proposing once. You know how it is. We chose a profession that's almost a calling, which is demanding on our personal lives. Things just didn't work out."

Sal had thought about that a good deal over the years and still held fast to his original theory. "I've always believed it can be done—with the right partner."

"Well, in my case, she wanted to return to her comfort zone—San Francisco—which wasn't my scene. We'd both been offered jobs in New York, too, but she was adamant." Shrugging, Luca asked, "What about you?"

Sal wasn't prepared for the question, although he should have been. He hadn't felt so vulnerable since the time he was eighteen and had dragged into the house at daybreak. His father had met him at the door with a pointed look at his zipper and one comment. "At least assure me that you double-wrapped it?"

"You said it yourself," Sal told his son. "Who has time for a personal life in a business like this?" He risked a covert glance. "I suppose your mother is with somebody by now?"

"Do you really want to know, or is your curiosity based on old Latin possessiveness?"

A few words shouldn't have the power to scrape the scab off an old wound so easily, but coming from his only child, they did. "Possessiveness? I call it marriage vows."

Luca smirked. "Are you going to tell me there's been no other woman since mom? I mean you took the same vows."

Before Sal could reply the back door opened and Valentina reappeared. "Oh, Sal, he's more thick-headed than you. Leo was so agitated, he tried to bully Tiny into letting him drive."

Grateful for the interruption, Sal replied, "Wait until tomorrow morning. He'll have to be on oxygen in ER to miss being here."

"Because you dangled that girl under his nose."

Sal gave his sister a level look. "Any dangling is in Leo's head. I invited her to audition, nothing more."

"She must be something," Luca said, drawing the attention from Valentina.

Slapping the counter with the flat of his hand, Sal snapped, "Your uncle almost suffered another crippling injury tonight, but we'll never know because he won't get to a doctor to see about his hip, let alone his head." Then he pointed toward the front door. "By chance, someone walks through the door that seems to be the answer to an unspoken prayer. I would be an idiot to reject such a gift."

"But you are going to check her out?" Luca urged, continuing to look doubtful.

His father gave him a sarcastic look. "She's not applying for a position at the White House. If she can make decent cannoli, she'll do for now."

Looking anxious at the rising tension in the room, Valentina took Luca's hand and stroked it soothingly. "Have you already made arrangements for where to stay tonight?"

"Not yet. I only just drove in."

"Good. My couch converts into a bed. You'll stay with me."

"Are you sure?"

"She lives upstairs." Sal was oddly relieved not to have to offer his own house—formerly *their* home—knowing it would mean too much opportunity to dig up old pain. "The birds roosting on the roof complain she recites her rosaries all night. You'll do good to get any rest."

"Shame on you for exaggerating," Valentina said, though her smile was all amusement. "It's a good thing for you, Salvatore Angeloni, that God knows your heart."

Luca had only tenderness for his aunt. "After all these years, I'd hoped you would have found happiness again."

She demurred, all but tucking into herself like a soft-shell crab shying from attention. "I had my family. I had my time. I'm okay."

"Yeah, I can see you're still good at telling fairytales, too," Luca countered. With a subtle move, he changed their positions to where he was stroking her hand. His ministrations were gentle, as sensitive as a sculptor's as he tested the different effects time and the elements had made on a beloved piece. "Mama sends her love."

"Thank you." Tears welling in her eyes, Valentina leaned over to kiss the young, strong hands cradling hers. "What a fine young man you've grown up to be."

With a deep groan, Sal gestured to his son. "Luca, take her upstairs before she has us all crying like babies." The image was too much for him tonight. "We all need some shut-eye if we're going to get through tomorrow. *Buonanotte.*"

"HOW WAS your night?"

It wasn't yet 7:00, Saturday morning and Valentina stood next to Sal in front of the expresso machine. She was dressed in her usual black—today a matching tunic-and-slacks set—and her pale olive skin looked as delicate as rice paper. Sal was in a uniform of sorts, as well; his a crisp, white, tailored shirt, and black dress slacks. They both craved strong coffee in the morning, and Sal's guttural tone acknowledged as much.

"About as good as yours."

"I'm fine," Valentina said. "It's good to have Luca here, isn't it? He's so considerate. He insisted on me having my shower first this morning. He'll be down in a minute. Imagine...someone from the White House thinks I'm more important than he is."

Sal ignored her whimsical chatter. He had other things on the forefront of his mind. "I noticed you didn't ask him how his mother was. Is that because you already knew?"

"Sal—"

He held up his hand to silence her. "The instant you opened the door last night, you knew who he was."

"Well, he looks just like you did at his age. It was the first thing I thought of."

Sal shook his head. "You never were a good liar, Valentina. What other secrets have you been keeping from me?"

The espresso machine gave a last harsh spurt; it had Valentina reacting as though there'd been an unexpected shot outside. She looked nervously from the machine back to her brother, one hand at her throat.

"Brother, maybe this isn't a good time. You have so much going on today."

With a bitter laugh, he picked up one of the two cups on the machine's tray and handed it to her. The skin on his face felt so tight, every inch seemed ready to burst. "You've already told me all I need to know."

The china shook in Valentina's hands, and she turned away to place the cup and saucer on the table where they usually sat. But before she could say anything they heard sounds like the front door opening. Sal had expressly unlocked it for their morning appointment. In all the commotion last night, he hadn't thought to direct "N'awlins"—as he'd begun to think of her—to the rear entrance.

When Olivia Dumont stepped into view, Valentina leaned toward Sal. "Please. Keep whatever you're feeling toward me in the family. Don't make a scene."

Ignoring her, Sal lifted his espresso cup to Olivia. "Welcome Girl Wonder."

Olivia paused, her smile faltering as she looked through the partition into the kitchen to consider the two people waiting there. The tension that stirred between them gave her pause. "Was I right to come?"

"Absolutely." Sal beckoned her with a tilt of his head. "And you're early, which is good, too. We're having our first dose of caffeine." As the pretty blonde came through the swinging doors, he continued, "Olivia Dumont, my sister, Valentina Pastore."

Her expression brightening, Olivia quickly set her shopping bags and chef's knife tote on the main prep table before extending her hand. "It's a pleasure. I really admired you last night. You were so busy handling the banquet room and main dining rooms, yet you looked totally calm and collected. And now I'll stop prattling. I'm sure I already sound like a first-timer sucking up to authority."

"Not at all. Even though I've been doing this for years, there was extra pressure last night, so I'm grateful you think I looked confident. You mustn't be nervous, either," Valentina added, ever reassuring. "If my brother asked you to come this morning, I know you're qualified to work here."

With a nod of appreciation, Olivia gestured to the bags on the table and said to Sal, "I did a little shopping. I know you have the basics, but I thought after reproducing one of your regular desserts, I would show you what else I can do."

"Nice," he replied. "We'll leave you to it—unless you'd like to join us for a coffee?"

"Thanks, but I'm good."

"You don't mind having an audience, do you? We usually camp out here, until the rest of the crew comes in to prep for lunch."

"I don't mind, at all." She pointed at the view of the dining room. "Besides, it's clear you invite diners to watch, too. That's been the case at several places where I've worked. I actually prefer it. It can be a long day when you're stuck within the same four walls with the same few people, who aren't always compatible."

Her expression pinched, and her sigh genteel, Valentina said, "I'm so sorry. I was afraid you'd witnessed us as you arrived."

"Oh, I was referring to my own experiences," Olivia assured her. "But...how is your brother?"

"I haven't talked to him yet. Hopefully, he's still in bed counting his blessings."

As Olivia went to work, Sal returned to the espresso machine for another hit of caffeine. Valentina came up behind him.

"If my presence upsets you, I could retire to the office and do some bookkeeping."

"Don't you dare," he muttered. "You're my witness that this is about a job and nothing else. I don't need to feed Leo's innuendos. The office work can wait. Besides, you should have something to eat. You're extra pale this morning."

"I'm not really hungry, but I wouldn't mind trading this espresso for a cappuccino. The strong coffee is a bit harsh on my stomach."

As she reached for her cup and saucer the back door opened and Luca entered. That had Valentina whispering another entreaty. "Please try to believe that he's here because of you. He wants and needs your approval."

"He said something to you?"

"Not in so many words, but he was beyond delighted you invited him to stay."

Sal had his own wishes and fantasies, but only time would tell if what his sister claimed was true. However, if needs had any weight, the scales should tip his way. His son could be a tremendous help, and not just on a temporary basis. His son...despite Sal's tight hold on his emotions, he felt a lump in his throat, Fortunately, Valentina spoke first.

"Here, Luca—take this seat and the espresso."

"Isn't that yours?"

"No, I want to be able to dunk some biscotti. *Prego.*"

"*Grazie, Zia.*"

Luca didn't wait for a second invitation. He'd slept in spurts, only partly due to his excitement at being back in Galveston. His *zia* had endured a difficult night, and from everything he could see and sense, it had taken its toll on her this morning. The dark circles under her eyes were a giveaway; however, the new lines of tension or strain around her gentle mouth were new. He'd often seen her looking peaked when she would come for a visit to Houston, but never this frail.

Recognizing questions had to wait, he kissed her cheek before taking the seat on the left side of his father. That was when he noticed the little blonde, as she stepped from behind the refrigerator in the dessert portion of the kitchen. Embarrassing as it was, his concern for his aunt momentarily fell off his radar, and he dropped onto the stool as though someone had knocked his feet out from under him.

With his next breath, he cursed himself for dressing so casually— only a clean white T-shirt and the jeans he'd worn yesterday. In contrast, she looked crisp and professional in her starched white chef's jacket, and spotless black slacks. She couldn't be more than five-foot-four, or over twenty-five-years-old, but every movement she made spoke of experience and confidence. No wonder his father had been so quick to offer her an audition. This was someone worth watching.

"Pick your tongue off the floor before she notices." Sal's words were barely audible from behind his demitasse cup, and his tone matched his expression—pure amusement. "Nice to know there's nothing wrong with your eyesight."

"Good morning to you, too." Fighting an odd sense of annoyance, Luca finally admitted, "She could replace the craving for caffeine."

"Well, if this works out, don't consider testing the theory. I'll be investing a lot of stock in her." At Luca's double-take, Sal said, "At the very least to earn us another star in future reviews."

Luca nodded in understanding, but as he savored his first sip or two of espresso, he thought of his uncle. "Which means Uncle Leo wasn't being completely paranoid."

"Give me a break. Your uncle's tendency to jump to conclusions drives me nuts. He's family and he'll always have a place here, only business is business. If you tell me that you're a wiz at desserts, speak up. I'll thank Olivia and show her the door. Just let me add that your abilities could be put to better use elsewhere."

Luca's gaze kept returning to Olivia. At the same time, he tried to gauge his father's sincerity. There was no denying his old man remained a good-looking guy, and Luca had come from a city where young women commonly hooked up with men old enough to be their grandfathers if the payoff was big enough. Add that Leo had practically insinuated Olivia had put a spell on his father, it was difficult to determine which of the brothers was being clear-minded, and which had an overactive imagination.

In the end, Luca had to admit his weakness. "I'm competent in desserts, not inspired. And look at her—she's far more adept at eye measuring ingredients than most people I've met."

"She was either raised in a kitchen and taught the basics before she was knee-high to a sack of flour, or it's a genuine gift." Glancing over his shoulder, Sal added, "Did you and your aunt stay up talking all night? She looks as limp as the table linens we used to soak in the washing machine before we started using a service. For that matter, your eyes look as though you dipped them in cayenne pepper."

Leaning over so their shoulders touched, Luca said, "I'm glad you asked. "Are you aware she's a tortured sleeper? She either talks or walks, all through the night. Moans, cries...all in more Italian than I understand."

Sal uttered a low sound of acceptance and regret. "She never wants to admit to having a bad day, yet she has plenty. What can I say? We all know the Marios still prey on her mind."

"Mom would never talk to me about that. Once when I was in college, I pressed her. All she would share is that she'd tried without luck to get Aunt Val to see a therapist. Aunt Val is old school and says she has the only therapist she needs. God."

"As you'll learn, she goes to church every day and then some."

"You don't approve?"

"You ask that after telling me she's tortured?" About to inquire what words or phrasing Luca might have grasped, Sal saw Olivia signal him.

"May I have a word, Mr. Angeloni?"

"Of course. What's up?"

"While I told you I would start with one of your stock desserts, I wondered if I might add my own twist to the cannoli?"

Sal beamed with satisfaction. "Very respectful of you to ask. By all means, do what inspires you."

As Valentina finally sat down on Sal's right, Luca said to Olivia, "This must look as daunting as the judges table at one of those food network reality shows."

"Not quite," she said with a one-shouldered shrug. "No hot TV lights to make me worry about my delicacies melting."

She sounded totally serious, but there was a mischievous twinkle in her blue eyes that drew an appreciative laugh from Luca. He glanced over at Valentina and Sal, but they were preoccupied with each other and hadn't caught the double entendre.

"I'm the son," he told Olivia. "I guess you'd already left by the time I arrived last night."

Sal reacted as though poked with a cattle prod. "Excuse my lack of manners. Olivia Dumont, my one and only, Luca. He's a chef, as well."

"Nice to meet you," she said. "You don't have any hint of an Italian accent the way your father and aunt do, and yet I don't hear a Texas one, either."

"There's no hint of French in your voice for someone named Dumont, and yet I'm catching a lyrical something here and there," he countered.

"N'awlins is Cajun by birth, French by training," Sal told him. To Olivia, he offered, "My son just finished several years at the White House. The rest of us have spent as much time speaking Italian as English, but we were all born here."

With a slight arch of her elegant eyebrows, Olivia focused on Luca. "Now that's an achievement. If you don't mind my asking, why did you leave? I mean, you're still quite young. I imagine the pressures of maintaining job security would wear me out, yet I would guess anyone who gets a job there strives to stay put until retirement."

"He just missed his family," Valentina piped in. "He surprised us all."

"All?"

Sal's sardonic, but quiet query had Valentina adding brightly, "We're so proud of him!"

The awkward vibrations had Olivia's gaze shifting from one Angeloni to the other. "As you should be. Thanks for sharing. I feel so much more challenged than when I first arrived. All I need is for your other brother to walk in and share that Martha Stewart once asked if she could borrow one of his recipes." Instead of them chuckling, the three of them exchanged concerned glances. "Did I say something wrong?"

"No-no," Sal said. "Only I expected him to be here by now."

"But you told him to stay home," Luca said with a frown.

"Which I never believed would happen. Valentina, go call. I would have bet twenty bucks he would have arrived a second after you did."

"So true." Looking every bit as worried as Sal, she headed for the office.

Sal turned to Luca. "Speaking of not worrying family, did you let your mother know you made it here safely?"

"I called her before I turned in last night. She had only made it home herself."

The news soured Sal's mood. "Is that so? She really has a rich nightlife, huh?"

Luca cast an embarrassed glance toward Olivia. "Don't make it sound like that, Dad. Work like hers requires a real calling, and take it from me—she works hard."

With a dismissive toss of his head, Sal replied, "What else could a father expect a devoted son to say?"

"Dad...*Ci sono altre orecchie ascolto.*"

There indeed were other ears listening; nevertheless, Sal's conflicted state of mind was such that he only felt shame when he saw his son's disappointment in him. He tried to make amends with a compliment.

"You criticized your Italian earlier, but I can see your mother taught you well enough. Credit where credit's due."

"Sal. Leo's not answering."

Valentina's rushed return had Luca rising from his stool. "Where does he live? I'll go check on him."

Before his aunt could reply, they heard the back door opened again. Leo limped in with the aid of Tiny. Dressed in a white shirt so loose, and pants equally ill-sized, it was immediately clear clothing was a discomfort, and he'd reached way back in his closet for something he'd worn when he was younger and more robust.

"Merciful Father!" Valentina rushed to him and cupped his bruised face with her hands. "You can barely walk. We should have taken you to the hospital last night. My poor Leo. Come sit down. I'll get you some coffee."

"I did try to get him to stay home, Miss Val," Tiny said. "Check the knot on the back of his head. He may be hatching a goose soon!"

Leo sent him a quelling glance, then squirmed away from his sister as she tried to inspect the wound for herself. "Let me be. I only need to sit."

As he shuffled over to the table, Olivia set down a stainless-steel bowl. "Maybe we should put this off for another day?" she asked Sal.

Leo offered a ceremonial, though stiff, bow. "No need. But thank you for the consideration. The...professional courtesy is appreciated. Only a delay would defeat the purpose of you being here, wouldn't it?"

As soon as he saw everyone's reaction to his formal and eloquent comment, he bristled. "What are you all staring at? Valentina, I'll take a regular coffee, thanks."

"Immediately, dearest. Sweet and creamy, the way you like it. I'll get you something to eat, too."

"Hold on." Leo looked over to Olivia. "I take it we'll be sampling soon enough. I can wait."

His near-elder statesman comment had Sal relaxing. "You may feel like hell, but I can see that brain of yours is working. Maybe better than it usually does."

"Mi lasci in pace."

"I'll leave you alone, but only because I need to settle some things with Luca." He turned to his son. "Back to business—are you still planning to stay a bit? If you are, I'm going to try to convince this one to take off the rest of the weekend. If I succeed, I'll definitely be able to use your help."

Leo looked taken aback. "What are you talking about? I have a say in this. I'm a partner."

Technically, a silent one, not that he'd ever paid attention to the understanding initiated by their parents. "You'd drop dead before you admit you should be home in bed," Sal replied. "It hasn't crossed your mind that with one more bruise, you might scare off customers?"

"Dad has a point, Uncle Leo," Luca said, his expression sympathetic. "I mean about putting the customers first."

Initially, Leo looked ready to take on both of them. He clenched and unclenched his fists, and the veins at his temples bulged. However, he deflated just as quickly, and the way he leaned on the table seemed to imply he was struggling to keep his pain in check. "Maybe I didn't give things enough thought. My head. It feels too heavy for my body."

"That does it." Valentina delivered his coffee, but lingered beside him. "As soon as you finish this, Tiny is taking you back home."

"But Leo wants me here to—" Tiny sent Leo a look of panic "—uh, help?"

"It's more important for you to see he isn't alone," she replied. "Leo, dear, did you take anything?"

He made a dismissive gesture. "Extra strength something, but I couldn't keep it down."

With a sound of distress, Valentina took hold of each side of his face and forced him to look her in the eye to check his pupils. "I knew it. I'm sure you have a concussion. Sal, I'm not taking no for an answer. He's going to the hospital."

As Leo began to protest, Sal raised his hand to silence him. "You've upset your sister. Shut up. If I'd insisted last night, we would have the situation taken care of already. Now you want to throw us even further behind, and worry Valentina sick? Be my guest."

"Salvatore!" Valentina cried. "It's not helpful to heap guilt on him."

"Why not? Common sense hasn't worked."

For the next few minutes, the family went back and forth over what would be the best thing to do. At the other end of the room, Olivia was either a pro at concentration, or she'd secretly put in ear plugs and had succeeded in blocking out everyone.

When she finally set a platter of beautiful cannoli before them, the squabbling ended abruptly. Valentina and Tiny uttered whispers of appreciation. The plate looked perfect for a photo shoot, the pastries adorned with a fine dusting of confectioners sugar, pistachios, and framed with sprigs of mint cuddling fresh raspberries.

"My mouth is watering, and my stomach is pulling with hunger," Sal said as he admired the rolled sweet with the creamy, mocha-ricotta filling.

It was obvious to anyone with eyes that this young woman was the real thing. She had addressed more attention to presentation than Leo could ever dream of achieving, and the aromas spreading through the kitchen had them all salivating.

"Olivia that smells heavenly, and looks so elegant," Valentina said. "This is as beautiful as anything a five-star hotel's restaurant would present."

"What matters is flavor." Leo snatched one pastry and stuffed most of it into his mouth, as though it was imperative for him to get the first taste, as much as the last word.

As soon as they realized what he had done, everyone else reached for the tasty pastries. For a while the only sounds were of munching and moaning.

Once Leo wiped his mouth with one of the napkins Valentina had passed around, his initial comments were for Sal. "If you would have told me you wanted the ends dipped in chocolate, I would have given you fancier cannoli."

"When was the last time you let me suggest anything in your part of the kitchen?" Sal asked.

"You don't listen to my suggestions about that stupid letter slot, so why should I?"

Looking beyond frustrated—and embarrassed—Sal muttered, "How about cutting the crap and admitting this is good?"

As Leo's face turned an angry red, Valentina gushed, "It's so light, Olivia. I feel as though the filling is melting in my mouth."

Only after he'd licked his fingers did Luca offer his opinion. "She's right. And it would have been easy to overdo the pistachios. You definitely have a French touch."

"Thank you, Mrs. Pastore, Chef." Olivia kept her expression blank, her chin up, and her hands clasped behind her back.

"Call me Valentina, please. Only our youngest wait staff is required to be more formal."

Olivia warmed to the invitation. "Then please call me Liv or Livie."

"I couldn't." At Olivia's startled look, Valentina explained. "I love your name. It reminds me of Shakespeare's *Twelfth Night*—the very brave Viola. Are you familiar with the character?" When Olivia shook her head to communicate she didn't, Valentina explained. "She was the sole survivor of a shipwreck—or so she believed—and dressed as a boy to gain honor for her beloved brother believed to be drowned."

"From the sister who was also named for a romantic," Sal drawled, gesturing to his sibling.

"And who loves both of her brothers," Valentina added tenderly.

With a reluctant nod, Sal indicated what remained on the plate. "Given the added ingredients, we'll have to raise the price on these, but I'll be surprised if anyone complains. You mentioned you wanted to show us other options. What did you have in mind?"

"I'd like to make a Doberge cake, along with a sweet potato cheesecake to be served with praline sauce and whipped cream. Then I thought it would be fun to offer children a cream puff swan, which you could serve with a dollop of ice cream."

As Leo grew more grim-faced Valentina clasped her hands. "Something for all ages. Wouldn't the children love that, Leo?"

"It sounds like too much work for something that will be desecrated in seconds. 'Oh, look, Mom,'" he mimicked, "'a headless swan.'"

Luca almost choked on a mouthful of espresso. "Now, Uncle Leo, you know food is meant to be eaten, no matter how you go about it, and what better reward for us who present it than to witness utter enjoyment?"

"Who knew? I have a food philosopher for a son," Sal said, saluting him with his demitasse cup. He turned to Olivia. "It does sound ambitious, but I remain intrigued. Keep track of your cost per item so we can get the pricing figured out. Also make sure you prepare enough for at least one hundred fifty people. Maybe a little extra. Tonight would be a good time to comp some desserts to see how people react to the new offerings." He leaned over to view Leo's granite-hard profile. "Agreed?"

"Bah!" Leo growled, and rose from his stool. "What do you care what I think?"

"Damn it, Leo, enough is enough." Sal rose, as well, his stool screeching harshly against the floor. "Nobody is usurping your place. But could you face facts? We're not getting any younger, and we need to look to the future. I'm supposed to wait until the day Tiny comes in here with you on his back, or not at all?"

"I don't mean to complain," Olivia began softly. "But I almost dropped an egg just now. Any more bitterness and I'll worry about you curdling my next dessert."

"She's right," Luca said. "To be fair, I think we should move this discussion elsewhere."

"No need. We're leaving," Valentina looped her arm around Leo's and drew him toward the door. "Come, dearest. I'm taking you to a doctor. You know it's the wisest thing to do."

"Give me a ring when you know something," Sal called after them. "I'm heading to the farmer's market for the fresh produce, and then to the docks. Is there anything I can bring you, Olivia?"

She scanned the area, then peeked into the cooler. "One Doberge will serve forty-five to fifty, so I'll plan on two of those. Maybe another few pints of berries for decoration?" After that she pointed to the ice cream machine. "I see you make your own—or is that gelato? Do you have enough ingredients to make extra? If we serve the swans with either, you may require more dairy for tonight. As for the sweet potato cheesecake, I'll make four and they can last a few days in the cooler."

Tiny held back looking torn. "Leo, what do I do? She's going to bake."

"You follow us in whatever vehicle you came in," Valentina told him. "Because I'll have to come back here, and I told you, I don't want my brother alone—if they let him go home."

As the door closed behind them, Sal uttered a sigh of relief. "Thank God that's resolved—for the moment. Now to get back on schedule. Luca, how about you come to the market with me? Get to know the area and meet a few people?" He turned to Olivia. "I'll lock the front door. The prep people will start knocking within the hour to start on lunch. We won't be long. Just introduce yourself. They'll love you."

"Yes, sir. Thank you very much. I'll make you proud."

Sal hesitated. When he smiled, only one side of his mouth turned up. "You'd better. What you just witnessed is only a small fraction of the grief Leo can put me through. Make sure you're worth it."

3

THE RESTAURANT BUSINESS WAS MANY THINGS, INCLUDING back-breaking, foot-aching, hard work; however, although it tended to be a high-risk endeavor, it didn't quite have the 90 percent failure rate often reported. Closures in the first year were closer to 27 percent, and after three years, 50 percent. In the end, though, it was true it wasn't a business for everyone. Fewer than 70 percent of restaurants were still around for their tenth anniversary.

It was a testament to the Angelonis' dedication and determination that *Vita e Spezie* was well into its third generation of operations. Olivia had noticed the proud notation on the menu last night. It helped her to not take Sal's attitude too personally. He would have said as much to anyone applying for the position—and justifiably so. However, this family had a lot going on and it affected the atmosphere like static electricity ready to explode like a blue fireball prior to a super-cell thunderstorm. It wasn't what she was hoping for when she'd walked into the dark, elegant, but welcoming *ristorante* last night. Nevertheless, she needed a job and this place represented the best opportunity she'd come across so far to use her skills.

Squaring her shoulders, she met Sal's serious stare with a firm nod. "Absolutely, Mr. Angeloni. And I'll pass on your message to the others. Excuse me—what's your head chef's name?"

"Vincent Sirocco. We call him Vinny. Vinny the Nose. You'll soon find out why."

Only after Sal gave her a quick summary of the outlay to the back of the restaurant, and retreated down the hallway leading to his office and the employee restrooms did Olivia allow herself to breathe. She hoped he would soon be leaving for those errands he'd mentioned. Along with the Italian machismo he exuded, Salvatore Angeloni was an intense and brooding man, who all but stole the oxygen from a room. The charming restauranteur she'd met last night was a seasoned actor. She would do well to remember his complexity.

Her heart was racing as she unpacked the rest of her supplies. She could feel the air conditioning cool the flush that heated her face, another symptom warning her to relax.

Not now. Not now.

Olivia had been instructed by her specialist that if this momentum persisted, the smart thing would be to sit down for a few minutes and breathe evenly to allow the feelings to pass. Easy enough, if you had a desk job, but that option wasn't possible here where she was exposed on so many levels. Then the room spun before her eyes, and she had no choice but to grip the table to stay on her feet.

"Are you all right?"

She had shut her eyes to stop the nausea. The sudden sensation of warm breath on her cheek, and gentle words caressing her ear gave her a start—but she knew better than to meet the prodigal son's too close gaze. The magnetism he exuded was every bit as compelling as his father's; she had no desire to experience it at this proximity. And yet, she had no choice, unless she wanted to explain everything and find herself back on the street hunting yet another job.

"Yes. Thank you," she murmured. Summoning all her resolve to meet his troubled inspection, she added, "Are you?"

Luca took an abrupt step back, and several seconds later purged a short breath. "Frankly? No." Stuffing his hands into the back pockets of his jeans, he asked, "How often do people ask if you're wearing contact lenses? I've never seen that shade of blue before except in photos of the coast by my family's ancestral homeland."

"It happens. I'd invite you to lean closer to see for yourself, but I've already breathed in enough of your carbon dioxide."

The corners of his sensual mouth twitched. "Cute. But you were already swaying on your feet before I was near you. Want to try again?"

Wise or not, Olivia strived to match him stare for stare. "No. But you could explain why you're trying to intimidate me."

Luca lowered his gaze to her hands gripping the table. "You need to know my father's reputation for being a bear disguised as a Romeo goes way back, so if you are more vulnerable than first impressions suggested, you might want to rethink taking this position."

Releasing the table, Olivia squared her shoulders. "Is that what you want me to do?"

His voice almost a caress, he replied, "Want...want...we'd better not get into my gut reactions to that question. In a few minutes, I'll be riding with the boss, and it wouldn't be smart to have to explain why your handprint is still on my face."

Olivia's laugh lifted into the air like a sweet flautist's reply to a songbird's herald of spring. "*Pomeé*," she said, breathing shallowly from the exertion.

"What's that?"

"Cajun. It means what you're doing to me—making me laugh too hard to breathe. Be careful how you describe him—you strike me as a chip off a hardy old block."

"Ouch."

"Trust me, there's enough of a compliment in that to keep your ego intact." Clearing her throat, Olivia began the explanation she used the few times someone had caught her in a weakened moment. "What you thought you saw? I contracted a bad bug a while back, and I'm still regaining my strength."

She returned to her work, her movements economic and steady, but Luca remained where he was, studying her. "That sounds logical enough—only I'm not sure I totally buy it."

"I can't help what you've already indicated is a vivid imagination. What I can do is assure you I have the required health certification." She stepped around him to reach into her tote and drew out an envelope. "In fact, you might give this to your father. He'll need a copy for his files."

Luca eyed the thing, but kept his hands in his pockets. "Do you trust me with that?"

"I don't know you well enough for trust. However, given your last position, I suspect you were checked out adequately to where I probably don't have to worry you're a stalker or identity thief."

"Despite my bruised ego, I thank you," he replied, finally taking the envelope. "Then I'll leave you to it. I look forward to working with you—and tasting more of your...delicacies."

AS SOON AS Sal and Luca were in the restaurant's white van, Sal spoke his mind. He was through with waiting for things to build into a new crisis. From now on, he intended to address matters as soon as they became apparent, so everyone would know where he stood on any given matter.

"I meant what I said earlier," he began, as they buckled their seatbelts. "Easy on the flirting with N'awlins. I have enough drama going on without a budding romance bursting into full bloom under my nose, thanks to all that comes with it."

Fortunately, Luca didn't pretend confusion. When he'd turned away from Olivia, he'd seen Sal watching them from the back door.

"I had a serious reason for going over to talk to her. Didn't you notice she was having a weak spell? For a moment, she looked ready to collapse."

"Say what?" That was unsettling news, and Sal considered the reasons she hadn't mentioned any problems. None of them were good.

"She was white-knuckled and glassy-eyed. I made small talk as an excuse to stay close and make sure she didn't end up in the same shape as Uncle Leo."

"Huh. Did she say what was wrong?"

"She claims to have caught some bug, but supposedly she's over it."

"She seemed fine while she was working. Last night, too."

Luca shrugged. "I'm just saying."

After several introspective moments, Sal nodded to the envelope Luca had placed on the console. "Open that and check the dates. Surely, she's not contagious?"

There were several sheets of paper inside, including Olivia's resume. "Everything looks in order. Her health certificate is only a couple of weeks old. She got it in Houston."

"Houston? That's a bustling place. Why didn't she get a job there? They have ten times the opportunities we have down here."

"Could be just what she said—she's rebuilding her strength and doesn't want to dive into anything too ambitious yet."

"Smart. Except, I don't need to train a new person only to lose her in a month or two if she suddenly decides she's up for bigger challenges. It's bad enough when that happens with wait staff. When you start to change the quality of the food, we're talking real money at risk." Sal slid his son a wry look. "Not that I expect you to know anything about such things considering where you've come from. Given the chance, people would stampede over each other to get to work inside the White House, even if they were only cooking chicken nuggets. How long does the kitchen staff tend to stay? Do they switch with every new president?"

"Every new administration can trigger employee changes, but adjustments are often more about menus than personnel," Luca began. "The long-term people are seriously dedicated and patriotic. They really care about being part of history and serving the country. I've met some who've stayed through two or three administrations. But to correct your misconception about me, I have restaurant experience. I didn't start at the White House straight out of culinary school."

"When did you realize you were interested in food?"

"I was a junior in high school, and my first job was at the neighborhood deli."

"Oh, yeah?" Sal asked too casually. "Where was that?" Luca didn't answer and Sal waved away the question. "Fine. It's none of my business."

"I just want you to know if you have a question about Mom, ask it openly. I'll answer if I can."

"I'll hold my breath."

With a sigh, Luca returned to the subject that started all of this. "About Olivia—I take it you aren't interested in pressing her for a better explanation about what happened?"

"What for? I don't want to get hit with some discrimination accusation. I'm not even allowed to ask her age or whether she has kids. I'll take a closer look at her paperwork later, but unless we start dropping like flies from something she has, I have no right to give her the third degree. She's a professional and deserves the benefit of the doubt, until she shows me otherwise."

"Okay. Sorry for intruding."

Hearing a decisive withdrawal in his son's voice, Sal mentally kicked himself. He should have remembered the tough times he'd experienced working for family when he'd joined the business. He'd been told up front he was just part of the hired help, and often thought the alley cats were treated better by *Nonno* Angeloni than he was. If he hadn't loved the work, he doubted he would have stuck with it. He'd also promised himself if he ever ran his own place, he would never treat anyone the way he'd been treated.

"You didn't intrude, and you have to ignore my blunt way of talking," he told his son. "That's more about worries than being a hard ass."

Luca accepted the verbal olive leaf with a single nod. "Good to know. It can't be easy to be the head of the family *and* keep a successful restaurant going."

"It's all worth it, especially when I get to do this every day."

Grateful to have avoided deeper conflict, Sal lowered his window. The temperature was still relatively mild, and the salty air had the briny aroma that preserved his soul the way saline did food. There were none of the refinery fumes you got up the channel and he enjoyed the seagulls and pelicans gliding between the cruise ships, freighters, and fishing boats, as they scouted for their next meal.

"I can't imagine having to live inland, or in a big city where I couldn't breathe in the ocean air every day. I guess you were too far away from Chesapeake Bay to acquire a craving for that, or the soothing sounds of waves rolling onto shore or lapping against docks?"

"On the contrary—I went over there as often as I could," Luca replied. "And for the record, as soon as I came to the island bridge last night, I rolled down my windows."

The admission won a soft chuckle from Sal. "Son of a gun."

"Do you know there's a word for people who prefer to live by the sea? Paralian. It goes back to the Greeks on the coast near Athens in the sixth century."

"What, did you minor in history in school?"

Luca grinned. "No, just like to do crossword puzzles to relax, and look up words I don't know."

"All I thought when you said it was peril and piranha."

Luca grinned. "I guess it depends whether you have a glass half full or half empty mindset. At any rate, you might enjoy knowing I often frequented Main Street Fish Market in Washington, D.C. It's within walking distance of the Jefferson Memorial."

"You don't say?"

"I thought about you most then," Luca continued, a wistful note entering his voice. "I was trying to hold on to memories of you taking me with you shopping for the restaurant. It got to where I wondered how much of what I recalled was real, and how much was a little kid's wishful thinking."

Touched by the confession, Sal had to clear his throat. "It was real. Come rain or shine, you were up at dawn, dragging your clothes to our bedroom, worried I would leave without you. I was fool-grinning proud, while your mother complained about having twice the amount of laundry to do because you always came home smelling like fish, and she would have to change you."

"I can imagine. If anything, she's even more of a stickler for cleanliness now."

"Do you remember everyone cheering you on as you climbed over mounds of fish to pick out your idea of a good one?"

"Yeah...and getting my finger caught in a crab claw."

"More than once. Your mother went through lemons by the pound to get the smell off your hands, so you wouldn't be made fun of at church and friends' houses."

"Now I remember *that* because I cut myself on a fin or scales all the time. Man-oh-man, to this day, I cringe at the thought of acidic juice in a wound. But thanks for filling in the gaps," Luca said.

Although he'd enjoyed the reminiscing, past pain bound Sal to his bitterness. "It was a long time ago," he replied with a shrug. "I'm surprised you remembered what you did."

The Farmers' Market was located farther down Post Office Street, and even though it was officially only open on Sundays, some vendors trickled in throughout the week and sold their goods out of the bed of their trucks. Today's supply was such that Sal filled much of his list within minutes.

"Those eggplant prices? Insane." Luca couldn't get over the cost as they carried their bounty to the van. "We pay twice that in D.C."

"Yeah, well, the growers aren't far away. But why are you complaining? Up your way, you can charge virtually anything for eggplant parmesan and get away with it."

"I know. It's still an adjustment. So, what's next?"

"Seafood." Sal continued to have his own connections among the fleet of boats docked along the wharfs. Through the years, he had learned the hour fishermen would usually return, as well as who was trawling for what. He quickly got his shrimp then argued with two newer suppliers over the quality of their sea bass. In the end, he opted for some beautiful red snapper instead.

Throughout, Luca stood back to watch his father do his thing. He was learning despite the friction that occurred between him and Uncle Leo, his dad tended to say little and speak fathoms with a look or a gesture.

"You're a force to be reckoned with," he said, once they loaded their last purchases and started back to the restaurant. "You had those guys with the sea bass all but swallowing their tongues."

"I'm no better than my suppliers, so I count on them not to screw around with me, especially about freshness. They'll learn."

Luca's failure to respond triggered doubts in Sal. Had he come on too strong? What if his kid was wondering if the tough talk he'd witnessed meant his old man was affiliated—as in part of the "organization?" Considering what was in the movies and on TV these days, he doubted any kid living in a comfortable Italian home didn't wonder at times.

Sal decided to bite the bullet. "Are you sure your mother is okay with you spending time with me? I swear to you, I am my own man. I don't want to be accused of being a bad influence."

"Dad, Mom never said anything negative about you, which is an accomplishment, considering how many questions I asked growing up. I especially pushed her buttons as a teenager because there were things my friends asked I didn't have answers for. Mom pretty much kept you a mystery. Credit her job for finally making her relent however slightly. She recognized for better or worse, I couldn't be a whole person without knowing both of my parents."

While Sal was curious as to what his son's buddies asked about, his predominant interest went in another direction. "What the hell does she do that suddenly she's become so fair and open-minded?"

Luca looked taken aback. "Honestly? You don't know? Dad, she's a hospice nurse."

With perfect, though ironic timing, a traffic light changed to red. Already dealing with one shock, the other caused Sal to overreact and slam too hard on the brakes. Behind them, boxes and ice-filled tubs slid. Vegetables tumbled out of their containers and rolled through water that sloshed from the pails holding fresh flowers.

"Son of a—" Sal caught himself just in time, and once he came to a complete halt, Luca released his seatbelt and displayed youthful agility by climbing in back. He quickly set things in order as much as the situation allowed. "Sorry about that," Sal said, once his son settled back in front.

"Glad to be able to help. Except for the water, nothing seems damaged, not even those good-looking tomatoes."

The light turned green, and Sal knew he had to correct his son's impression, even if it made him look worse than he already might. "I mean about your mother's work. Of all the things you could have said, it sure wasn't that."

"She's an extremely intelligent and compassionate woman."

Sal had long concluded Rosa had been something, all right—a clever, vengeful cookie, who had kidnapped their son. He wanted to believe Luca's praise was nothing short of long-term brainwashing.

"If you say so," he finally replied.

"You never saw that side of her? You married her."

Sal could have laughed, but it would have been from embarrassment. They had been a normal, hot-blooded couple who fell instantly into passion. Barely over the legal age to get serious with a guy nine-years her senior, the relationship had a strong consideration working in its favor—their Italian immigrant families. In their culture, the age difference was considered an asset, especially since Sal had his culinary arts degree—with a minor in business—and was on the path to taking over the family restaurant. Rosa's intellect hadn't kept Sal up nights. Getting his hands inside her blouse and under her skirt did. He would *not* share such truths with his son.

"Don't be ridiculous," he grumbled. "The night I met your mother, the music was loud, the place was packed with people yelling at each other to be heard, and the drinks were free. All I remember her saying is that she wanted to become Miss Texas."

"And yet you asked to see her again."

"Smartass." Sal swallowed his annoyance and dealt with another morsel of his own curiosity. "You're telling me she went to college?"

"Became an RN, all while working full-time. Then, after she got me through school, she shifted to hospice care. That had been her intention all along. It wasn't easy, Dad."

Sal snorted. "She had only herself to blame. I would have helped her if I'd known she was so hell bent on the work."

"I guess it became a point of pride with her."

"Pig headed, that's what. She had to show me she didn't need me or any man."

He saw Luca look out his window and dealt with a spasm of contrition, but what did his son expect him to say? His Rosa was content to be in his arms and be adored. Her friends and family saw her as the princess who'd won her prince. Things only changed after she got bored with the daily grind of being a wife and mother. Was it his fault he couldn't drop everything every time she wanted a change? He had more responsibilities than her and Luca; it was up to him to keep building the business, so they could afford to get the loan to move into their current location, pension his grandfather, and look toward doing the same with his father. *You want to talk about not having it easy?* Sal thought. But one glance at his son and Sal felt his anger cool to disgruntlement.

"Okay, it's good she made something of herself," he said. "But I don't know the woman you're talking about."

"It wasn't my intent to upset you," Luca said.

"We're unfinished business, that's all. She's like a big red boil on my back."

Luca winced at the analogy as much as his father's pantomiming. "I see … which my presence can only compound."

"No, listen—"

"I should have considered the possibility your feelings didn't match mine before showing up on your doorstep."

"I'm glad you're here!" Sal declared. "But I have to know—what do you want from me?"

"Whoa!" Luca raised his hands in the sign of surrender. "I don't want anything except some of your time, a chance to get to know you. Financially, I'm plenty comfortable. More so since I sold my townhouse the same day I listed it."

"Good for you," Sal said, impressed. "Only … you need to understand, in the world where I operate, everything either has a price or a string attached."

Luca slumped in his seat. "Wow. You would fit right in with some of the characters where I worked. That's the mindset there. Nothing is simple cooperation or a gesture of goodwill. Everything is suspect as having an ulterior motive."

"It's called life."

"It's not the version I'm interested in living. I'm just looking for fresh air and a place to really call home."

If true, his son was a dreamer and in danger of having his heart broken and his spirit trampled. Sal hated the very thought of his flesh and blood experiencing such disappointment, and at that moment another phenomenon occurred. His heart swelled at the thought of the fine human being he'd helped bring into the world.

Pulling into the restaurant's parking lot, Sal backed to the rear exit and shut off the van's engine, only to stare at the young man about whom he had so much to learn.

"I owe you another apology," he said simply.

With a boyish smile, Luca replied, "Not as long as we can keep trying to get things right."

"Sounds like a plan."

AWKWARDNESS DIDN'T ONLY occur between father and son. While Olivia was well-pleased with the layout and equipment in her corner of the kitchen, it soon became apparent that Sal Angeloni may have expected too much of the rest of his team. Despite their polite greetings as the small group wandered in, they were subdued as they set to work and whispered among themselves. However, it didn't take Olivia long to figure out they thought she was part of a conspiracy.

She caught only a phrase here and there, but what she could put together was that at some point—and at the behest of Leo—Tiny had phoned Vincent Sirocco with the warning to "watch your back." By the time Sal returned with Luca, Vinny had worked himself into an agitated state and was ready for "the big deal from Washington D.C." to try to push him out at *Vita e Spezie*.

Sal only added to a simmering situation. Visibly preoccupied, he stumbled over introductions. It left the staff looking at each other with new speculation and concern.

"You've met Olivia and now this is my son Luca," Sal announced. "He's here to reconnect with the family." Thrown by the wary looks he got in return, Sal put his arm around Luca's shoulders. "I—uh—gotta say his timing couldn't be better, considering Leo and everything."

"Did you hear that?" someone in the background muttered. "'And everything.'"

Emboldened by that, Vinny jutted his chin. "I thought Olivia is taking over for Leo? Who's he replacing?"

"Nobody," Sal replied.

"Yeah, sure."

While slow to catch on, once he did, Sal gave an adamant shake of his head and responded with authority. "Nobody is replacing anybody. In case you haven't noticed, we've been so busy, the only time off anybody gets is Sunday. It's a killer schedule and can't continue."

"I noticed," Vinny grumbled. "Why do you think I haven't bothered asking for vacation?"

"If there's anything I can do to alter the situation for any of you," Luca said to the room at large, "I'll be glad to fill in."

While the others exchanged hopeful glances, Vinny promptly dismissed the offer. "We'll see what happens. I got kids to feed. And one is turning eighteen, I gotta think about school. It'd be smarter to take my vacation time in pay and put it in the bank. Maybe even for a rainy day," he added with a speaking glance toward Sal.

Clearing his throat, Luca discreetly excused himself. "I'm going to continue unloading the van."

"Joey, Stu," Sal said. "Go help him."

As they hurried off, and Olivia returned to her area, Sal faced Vinny squarely. "What's going on with you?"

"Nothing." The surprisingly tall, long-limbed man corrected himself. "Nothing that's my business."

"Spit it out," Sal demanded. Vinny had been promoted to head chef when Sal's father retired, while Sal had assumed the responsibility of the overall management and operations of the business. To his way of thinking such trust and support deserved nothing less than complete honesty.

Vinnie crossed his arms over his chest. "You said it yourself. Despite what happened to Leo, we broke records yesterday. Yet this morning, there are two new employees. Only not just anyone. I got the word about their credentials, and you know I can't compete with them. What am I to think?"

Frowning, Sal demanded. "What word? Who's been filling your head with these crazy ideas?" He didn't have to wait for an answer; it came to him immediately. "Leo. My brother could be a one-man intel bureau—and ruin the country overnight."

Stepping closer, he laid a reassuring hand on Vinny's shoulder. "Listen to me. What you have is experience. You were mentored before you came here, then you were trained by my old man, who was taught by the best chefs his father could send him to. That puts you on equal footing with anyone as far as I'm concerned.

"And you were here when I told Leo why I was bringing in Olivia," Sal continued. "None of what she's doing has anything to do with your work. Now, can you be relieved we won't be left in a lurch with Leo being out, and happy for me that I get to see my son for the first time in twenty-five years?"

Vinny took his time mulling things over. Only when Sal saw a twinkle of humor in his eyes did he utter a playful growl and hugged the man.

"Complimenti, Salvatore."

"Grazie, amico mio."

RELIEVED TO HAVE the tense situation resolved, Olivia resumed her baking. Sal retired to his office taking Luca with him, while Vinny and his people addressed their part of preparations with renewed verve.

"We put pecan pie on the menu around Thanksgiving and year-round the traditional cheesecake with fresh strawberries, but I've been wondering about the variety you're making from the moment you asked to cook sweet potatoes beside me. I must say the aroma is unexpected for this time of year, yet festive and comforting."

Focused on her work, it took her a moment to realize Vinny was speaking to her. "Oh—you have an impressive sense of smell, Chef Sirocco."

"Why do you think they call me The Nose? Thank goodness my daughters all look like their mother."

There was no missing the proportions of that facial feature, even if his head hadn't been narrow. With his expressive, large round eyes, he made her think of a parrot.

Olivia found his self-deprecating humor sweet and picked up her knife to point at the first cake she'd finished. "What would we do without sugar and butter to tantalize our olfactory senses and taste buds? I would appreciate your feedback." She brought him a sliver glistening with a touch of the praline sauce. "Only your honest opinion, please. I'm not as used to an Italian menu, as I am some others, and I'm having second thoughts about it being too rich or heavy to follow your sumptuous entrees, especially in the heat of summer."

As serious as Solomon about to voice a decree, Vinny drew the almost terra cotta-colored cake into his mouth. He closed his eyes to savor the moment. "Ah, the flavors blossom and seduce. It's nowhere near the density I expected, and the creaminess...it caresses my heart."

"Chef, you're a poet. I'm honored."

Swelling with pride, he said, "Grazie, *piccola*. Usually only my wife notices. If you have any of that left tonight, I must bring a sample to her and my children."

"I would be delighted. You mentioned them before, how many are there?"

"Six. All girls. Our home is ridiculous. I'm blessed."

Warming to the chef by the minute, Olivia assured him. "I'm making plenty. It would be my pleasure to box some for you as we close for the evening."

WHEN LUCA RETURNED to the kitchen, they had an hour remaining before opening their doors for lunch. He was grateful to see a jovial, harmonious atmosphere had replaced the earlier tension. Stopping at Vinny's side, he watched the seasoned chef making the spinach ravioli.

"Do you mind me observing, Chef?"

"Not at all. Now. We serve this with a crabmeat topping. The recipe for the Angeloni version is in the book over there."

Luca followed his nod and saw the half dozen black loose-leaf binders on a shelf above where the take-out boxes and bags were stored. "I'll study them after the lunch service. Who makes the pasta?"

"I used to, but Sal told me to start giving the job to Benny. You love it, don't you, Ben?"

The curly-haired, sou chef with the wire-rimmed glasses that kept sliding down his nose grunted his opinion of Vinny's humor, as well as the task. "My mind is willing, but it's like I got bear paws." He held up his short-fingered hands as evidence. "The dough won't cooperate."

Vinny mischievously added, "I told him to think of it as his girl-friend. Persuade instead of impose."

The younger chef, who appeared to be around Olivia's age, didn't exude anything close to a dominant nature. Luca watched him accept the executive chef's teasing, even though it earned him snickers from the preppers. Presently working on one of the side dishes—braised eggplant and tomatoes—his technique looked capable enough, but he needed more confidence if he was going to survive in the business, let alone rise to head chef anywhere.

Luca glanced over his shoulder at Olivia. The way she was studiously removing another cheese cake from its pan told him she'd heard, but was pretending otherwise.

"Have you ever tasted *filindue*, Chef?"

With a look of respect, Vinny replied, "I haven't heard anyone speak of it in years. Don't tell me you championed that?"

Filindue pasta was only made in the town of Nuoro, Sardinia, because there were but two or three women who had the training. The recipe was simple enough—merely semolina, water, and salt. The challenge came in working the dough properly. It took hours, and required a keen sense of knowing when to add salted water to stretch the product, or plain water for moisture.

"Like a bunch of other arrogant guys, who thought they had the patience and schooling," Luca replied, "I couldn't get past 119 of the 256 even strips required to be stretched along those wires on the circular frame, and it took me ten hours to get that far. The woman who instructed me did the whole thing in under seven, which she pointed out was an off day for her."

"That's pretty good," Vinny said. "I never saw it done myself, but I heard each strip is half the width of the angel hair variety."

"You feel like you're working with a spider's web."

Vinny paused and studied Luca. "I think you should join Benny making the pasta." Catching Benny's expression of dismay, he took on a fatherly tone with the younger man. "Take it from me, I'm giving you a gift."

"Yes, Chef," Benny sighed.

Luca wished the subject had been handled more privately. "I don't want to intrude on my father's directives."

"Let me handle that. Sal was trying to make things easier on me. But something needs to be done before a reviewer who knows his business comes in on a day our ravioli resembles gnocchi. So far, I've been able to cover things with extra crabmeat sauce." Vinny added too casually, "Sal is a gifted pasta maker, too."

Luca knew he was swallowing the bait like a starving fish, but he was hungry for any-and-all information about his father. "He is?"

"His father and grandfather recognized that quickly and relinquished the role to him," Vinny said. "He would have to come in hours before the rest of us. By the time we arrived, the place looked like a Chinese laundry with the pasta hanging everywhere."

Was that part of what destroyed his parents' relationship? "My mother once said my father preferred to work instead of sleep."

Vinny agreed wholeheartedly. "Sure! You can sleep when you're dead."

"And I guess his father and grandfather saw how well-made pasta would further establish the restaurant's reputation." Luca contemplated everything he was learning. "In a way, Dad created his own *filindue*."

"Now you understand." Vinny pointed a flour-covered index finger at him. "Tell him the story you've just told me. Ha! Angeloni pasta is back!"

Caught up in Vinny's enthusiasm, Luca considered going to talk to his father right away, but a brunette server chose that moment to introduce herself. The waiters and waitresses had been scurrying around the dining room and in-and-out of the kitchen for several minutes, as they prepared the tables for first service. Introducing himself was another thing on his list, but it appeared one of them couldn't wait, so he smiled politely as she blocked his way.

"Hello," she began in a tone that had the effervescence and tang of *Limoncello*. "I sure didn't know Sal had a son. You're as good looking as he is. Lucky us. I'm Delilah. Not the one in the Bible. My mother was a huge Tom Jones fan."

"Giving new credence to the possibility of reincarnation," Vinny opined as he passed to put a tray of ravioli in the cooler.

Although Delilah playfully slapped at the head chef's arm, it didn't appear she took any offense. "I, for one, prefer not to waste time on beating around the bush. Are you married? Attached?"

"Neither."

Delilah gasped at his hesitant reply. "Shy! I adore shy men."

"She adores testosterone," Vinny whispered, returning from his task. "Delilah, I seem to recall Valentina asking you to tend to the flower arrangement up front in the reception area if she's running late. She *is* running late. Because of Leo. I see Tony on duty, so I know he's passed on the word. Remember any of that?"

"Okay, okay, I'm on my way." With a flirty wink for Luca, Delilah made her exit.

Vinny watched her retreat, only to put his palms together like a clergyman in prayer. "Believe it or not, she's a good employee. Works double shifts if we need her, and except for Tony, she's the best at training the new kids. Just be careful. She switches men more often than a Vegas show girl changes costumes."

With an amused shake of his head, Luca said, "For what it's worth, I'm not here for anything but helping out and catching up with my family. *Vivi e lascia vivere*, I think is the way you put it."

"*Saluto*," Vinny said. "'Live and let live' is the only way to be."

BY NOON, THE only conversation going on in the kitchen was Vinny's precise announcements as he read orders, and Benny notifying some- one that a plate was ready to be delivered. The steady stream of diners soon filled the restaurant to capacity, which had the wait staff constantly checking on their orders. Not surprisingly, the females used the oppor- tunity to have a closer look at the new man on the premises. Olivia would have found the latter scenario hilarious, except for the disap- pointing realization that she had yet to receive one dessert order—until Luca encouraged a waiter to recommend something to a particularly cheerful group in no hurry to finish their lavish lunch experience. Soon after, Luca himself ventured into the dining room the way Sal and Valen- tina did in the evenings and, suddenly, she was as busy as everyone else.

At the end of the lunch rush, Luca came over to inspect how little was left of the first cheesecake. Several other dessert menu items were depleted, as well. A satisfied smile played around his mouth, but he restrained himself from commenting.

"If you're waiting for me to admit I noticed what you did," she grumbled, "I noticed. Happy?"

"There's no need to be piqued. I may have helped things along at first, but primarily your success is your own," Luca told her. "Unless there's a banquet or some other celebration, the trend is for desserts not to move well in the middle of the day. Take these results as a testament to your fine baking."

"Realized only after your skilled nudging."

"Dad does expect me to do my part."

His smooth reply and courtly bow grated as much as his deft control of every situation in which he inserted himself. Yes, he was doing his job superbly, Olivia thought as he retreated, but did he also have to enjoy toying with her in the process?

The kitchen was empty save for the two of them, the dishwasher, and the last two waiters closing out their shift. Vinny and his team had left for their lunch break, or to run errands. Aware she had too much work to take a break, Olivia stayed put and moved on to focus on the evening service.

Well into preparing the light batter for the swan-shaped cream puffs, Luca returned from the back. *Now what?* she wondered, tensing.

Not wanting to waste energy on his idea of cat-and-mouse games, Olivia looked hopefully beyond him. "Where's your father? I haven't seen him in hours."

"He's gone to make the deposits, and to check on Leo and Valentina. My aunt called and said they're doing some tests on my uncle."

"He must feel miserable."

"And he's being uncooperative." Luca leaned against the work station. "Some of us are going to take a break outside in the wine garden. Why don't you join us? You've been on your feet longer than anyone. That can't be good for someone who's recovering from a nasty bug."

Knowing better than to look at him considering his nearness, Olivia kept working and merely shook her head. "The hot afternoon sun and ocean breeze would put me to sleep. Besides I have to dive right into evening inventory or you won't be thanking me for not being able to provide what you're selling."

"Can I help? Without even Tiny to assist you, you're going to wear yourself out."

"Tiny strikes me as a devoted employee, but even your polite reference to his role here seems generous. Adding his allegiance is to Leo, I'm counting my blessings for not having him underfoot."

Luca murmured his agreement. "You do understand? It's all about *la famiglia* around here."

Before they got busy, Vinny had given her a brief recap of who was related to whom. "I'm not criticizing. Cajuns are big on family, too."

"Speaking of... you know I'm an only child. How about you?"

Olivia hesitated, not wanting to go down that path; only the way Luca effortlessly controlled conversation, he didn't leave her much choice without sounding uptight. "Three brothers. All of them older."

"The baby girl," Luca drawled.

"If you go for the cliché and suggest I was spoiled, I'm going to be deeply disappointed in you."

"Okay, but I'll bet you had hell trying to date as a teenager with those watchdogs standing guard over you."

"Wrong again. I didn't date." From the corner of her eye, Olivia saw Luca smile. The unexpected mixture of surprise and satisfaction was hardly what she expected.

"Overly protective parents?"

"They didn't need to be. They understood I had priorities and plans."

"You really are one bombshell after another. I want to hear all about it."

Instead, she pointed at him. "If your chattering ends up making me forget an ingredient or measuring incorrectly, you're the one who'll explain the wasted product to your father."

"You're a hard woman, Olivia Dumont. To be continued then."

Steeling herself against the slight tremor his promise triggered inside her, Olivia watched him follow the others outside. "Not if I can help it, Golden Boy," she whispered under her breath.

4

MUCH LIKE FAILING COMPUTER SOFTWARE, OLIVIA'S INTERNAL
mantra to resist Luca Angeloni needed rebooting repeatedly throughout
the day. In comparison, by the time customers were being seated for
dinner, the rest of the staff appeared to be unanimously onboard with
the idea of Sal's son as heir apparent to *Vita e Spezie*. His presence lent
a new atmosphere to the environment—an impressive feat considering
how Sal Angeloni's influence and abilities deserved their own respect.
Nevertheless, Luca soon had the staff working with renewed enthusiasm.
To Olivia it was as though Fate was playing yet another cruel joke on her.

Her strange mood wasn't due to finding any fault in her co-workers' judgment. Obtuse, she wasn't. Thanks to her own training and
experience, she saw as fast as Vinny did how genetics and instruction
would make Luca Angeloni elevate the restaurant to a new level. She
couldn't have been more pleased for Sal. Delighted. At the same time,
however, she felt hamstrung by a unique melancholia—that of witnessing an enviable future being laid out before her. A future in which
she had no place.

"You know what your trouble is," she said under her breath. "You
think too much."

Keeping busy was her panacea. Never one to stand idle, she polished her area to perfection, then offered her services around the
kitchen; however, that still left her with too much awareness of Luca.
He had a deft touch in handling Benny's battered ego, to where in a

short span of hours, the sou chef was hanging on his every word like a kid idolizing his older brother. With patient counseling, he had Joey and Stu down to arguing and competing half as much as they had been—at least not until Delilah or Kat lingered in the kitchen.

"There's one challenge you won't resolve overnight," Olivia drawled to Luca as he waited for her to box a take-out order of desserts. She nodded across the room. Kat had been whispering in Joey's ear to the point where Stu forgot what he was doing and cut himself. Worse yet, when she saw what she'd caused, Kat found it flattering and giggled.

"Baby steps," Luca said, looking more disappointed than annoyed.

"Mm, but the problem with that baby," Olivia told him, "is that she has eight legs like a black widow. Go ahead and take care of them," she added. "I'll get this to your customer."

It was well after six o'clock before Olivia received her first order for dessert, but it was a considerable one. One of each of tonight's selections for a table of eight ladies on vacation from the Texas Panhandle. The request had her scurrying and, before she realized it, she was skidding on something. Fortunately, Valentina had been coming to speak with her and was close enough to offer a steadying hand.

"My dear, do be careful in this area. Remember? This is exactly why Leo fell."

"Thank you for the quick reaction," Olivia replied. "Goodness! I thought I had been watching, but I guess I'm over-excited to have such a great order. Where did you say that slot was?"

Valentina pointed out the offending location, now all but hidden by a stainless-steel table. "We keep a basket under it to catch the letters, but sometimes visitors are either too enthusiastic, in a hurry, or shy about being seen posting something. In any case, the envelopes occasionally miss their target and float onto the floor."

Retrieving it, Olivia handed it to Valentina. "I read a little about the backstory in a flyer I picked up at the tourist center. So, people still write like the man in that awful storm?"

"Oh, yes. Did you take time to read any of the newspaper stories we have framed in the entryway?"

"I saw them, but the area was packed last night."

"Nathan Burroughs thought he was going to die. His letter and story has been published all over the world. I believe our success is tied to his experience. We've made it possible for people to continue the tradition he started when they're experiencing…special circumstances." Valentina gazed down at the letter and ran her long fingers over the single word written in a delicate cursive on the front. *God.* "I never tire of seeing this duplicated. It speaks to a person's faith, even in times of distress. As you witnessed, Leo thinks it's all nonsense, but at least Sal acknowledges the story has been good for business."

"Well, considering the shape Leo's in, I can understand his reluctance to find merit in the tradition."

"I wish you could have known him before all of his troubles," Valentina said, wistfully. "He was a different man than he is now."

"Will you fill me in when time permits? The brothers seem to be at odds with each other. When he returns, I'd like to convince Leo that I'm no threat to him, rather we could help each other."

"Of course."

"What happened to the man?" Olivia added. "The one who wrote that letter?"

"Nathan?" Valentina went to the cooler and took out two bottles of cold water. "He survived and made it back to his family, who had reached safety, too."

"Yes, but who was he? What was his story?"

"I don't know."

"You weren't curious?"

"My dear, those were hectic times. We were working with an even smaller staff than now to try to pay off the building as soon as possible. I just prayed, as I pray now—that our Lord will help those in need."

"Livie! My desserts for table nine?" Tony called softly to her from where he picked up entrée plates for other diners.

"Right away." Olivia got back to work, while Valentina carried the water bottles up to the reservations table and her niece. Questions continued to nag at Olivia.

"What happened to the letters? Have there been many?"

"More than I can tell you," Valentina said, answering the belatedly voiced question during her next trip to the kitchen. "Dozens—hundreds over the years."

"So, what do you do with them?" As Valentina appeared to deflate at the question, Olivia apologized. "Sorry. It's none of my business."

"No, it's good of you to take an interest." But Valentina's smile was sad. "More should be as caring as you. I do read everything. Then I go to Mass, where I pray for the people involved and their various plights. Afterward, I light candles, especially for those who are ill, or those who have lost loved ones."

"But what if someone writes something that makes it clear they need immediate help—maybe rescuing?"

"There hasn't been any of the latter, but if there were . . . there are no addresses, Olivia. Never a full name let alone an address to go by. You can't investigate something intentionally cryptic. Besides, these are letters to God. I have no right to invade people's privacy."

"Yet you read them."

"Yes, because I can't bear the thought of my brothers throwing them in the trash without some advocate keeping the authors' hopes alive. To me, Nathan made this building a place of trust. We're not a church. We're not sanctified, although we had the place blessed upon moving in, as we've always done our homes. Nevertheless, I believe something is going on here and it continues for a reason."

"But—"

Valentina squeezed her hand. "I assume that no one has told you about my past. No, of course, they didn't," she said, studying Olivia's confused expression. "Suffice it to say that I ache for what some of these people are enduring because I understand too well. But that's the best I can do for them."

Pain radiated from her eyes and her skin grew almost translucent compelling Olivia to assure her, "No one told me anything. Thank you for sharing what you did. I do love culture and history—partly because it inspires us to make the food we create as geniune and rich in flavor as possible. And maybe, sometimes, it reminds us how we're all connected, however fragile the link."

Valentina's expression gentled. "What a lovely thought. I have a feeling you're going to be every bit as good for us, as Luca will be." As though the clasped fingers proved inadequate, she quickly added a hug. "We'll talk again, but I must return. My late husband's niece is quite capable, until it gets pressure-cooker busy. Janine can grow flustered if she doesn't remember a regular's name, or where someone else likes to sit."

Another hour passed quickly, and this time it was Luca who stopped by for a bottle of cold water. "How are you holding up?" he asked, after taking a long drink. "Are you sure your feet aren't killing you by now?"

Olivia hadn't experienced another sinking spell, which was a relief in more ways than one. It also meant she didn't have to fabricate another story. "I got to sit down a while early in the service," she reminded him. "Don't worry. As I assured your father, I won't let you down."

Her slightly defensive tone had Luca frowning. "You're still assuming too much when it comes to my authority. I'm simply asking from a point of friendly concern."

"Uh-huh, except you didn't have to audition. Face it, you're the latest beneficiary of nepotism."

With a husky laugh, Luca drawled, "That tells me what you don't know. For the record, I half expected to be bounced out of here on my butt the second Dad realized who I was." When he saw her surprise, followed by skepticism, he mused, "You haven't been told."

"I'm hearing that phrase a lot tonight. Told what?"

"Until yesterday, I hadn't seen my father in almost twenty-five years. I was just five when my mother left him and took me with her."

"Holy smokes!" After the near yelp, Olivia offered a sheepish look. "I would have never guessed," she continued in something closer to a whisper. "You people do appearances better than British royalty. Well, except for your uncle."

"He does rather look hatched from a separate pod," Luca mused. "He must take after a different branch of the family tree."

"At least it appears as though distance has made the heart grow fonder. Anyone can see your family is beyond thrilled to have you back."

"I hope so, considering I wasn't a party to whatever happened. But I do see there are wounds besides mine in need of healing. If only they weren't all so content to live with the status quo."

Since he sounded as though he was thinking out loud as much as speaking to her, Olivia hoped she would respond wisely. "And yet if they hadn't put their all into this place, it wouldn't be what it is today."

"Also true. But a kid wants to matter more than a job or business."

Somehow Olivia knew Luca had yet to share this perspective with Sal. It reminded her of a quote she'd read a short time back about all parents damaging their children and why it can't be helped.

"You're one of those," she said.

"I don't follow."

"People who give a thousand percent every day, yet at the end of each one still wonder, 'Is that all there is?' In other words, despite your accomplishments, and your outward confidence, you have a big emotional hole left unfilled by the family you were denied."

Eyeing her with new respect, Luca asked, "Is this where you tell me that aside from culinary school, you also did a stint with the Dalai Lama? You barely look old enough to get into a casino without ID, but you talk like someone working on her second Masters."

"I'm twenty-eight and no wunderkind. However, I do admit to being an avid student of human nature."

He returned to his playing mode. "And yet you've made one incorrect assumption after another about me."

Despite her lectures to herself, Olivia used the same tone back at him. "I only met you for the first time this morning. Unlike the male members of your family, I'm willing to correct my faulty perceptions."

"Then I can't wait until tomorrow."

The tingling sensation evoked by Luca's parting glance and caressing tone was still fluttering through Olivia when Sal came in from the dining room to inspect the momentum in the kitchen. Caught in his own moment, he moved from station to station, until he finally joined Olivia. She finished adding berries to two plates of swans and ice cream, and handed them over the counter to silver-haired Pat before acknowledging his presence.

"The ladies seem to enjoy those as much as the kids," Sal said.

"Romance is as powerful as fantasy."

"I'll take your word for it. I know nothing about the latter, and I've forgotten more about the former than I ever knew." He nodded to her depleted inventory. "But I recognize success when I see it."

"Thank you. Several people have ordered desserts to go. Someone took an entire cheesecake for a party tomorrow. I couldn't be more pleased."

"You're surpassing my hopes, as well as my expectations. Except it means you'll have to come in extra early Monday to restock."

"A rather flattering variation of cause and effect."

"And you're up to it?"

"Pardon?"

"Luca told me you'd been ill before joining us."

The last of the fairy dust lingering from her conversation with Sal's son went up in smoke. "Oh. It's old news."

"Glad to hear it. Between you and Luca, I feel as though we're launching an entirely new enterprise. How do you think it's going for him?"

"You should ask Luca."

"I'm asking everyone."

Having some experience with that tactic, she offered, "He has a disarming personality, although I sensed at first the others were more cautious about him than they were with me, but he's either winning them over decisively or putting narcotics in the water."

Laughing, Sal said, "Of course, the girls are thrilled with the new eye candy."

"Something would be wrong if they weren't."

"Yet he gravitates to you."

Glad that she'd read him correctly, Olivia belatedly sensed a little possessiveness in his attitude, as well. Having just been reunited with his son, Sal wasn't ready to share him much. "I'm just here to work, Mr. Angeloni."

"Sal. But you're the only one playing hard to get."

"I'm not playing, Sal."

After another long look, he said, "Maybe that's what worries me. You're an interesting woman, N'awlins. Keep up the good work."

A HALF HOUR before closing, Luca returned to the kitchen carrying a loaded bin of dirty dishes to the wash area. Intended or not, it signaled that he didn't see any job too demeaning, nor was he above lending a hand wherever it was needed.

Olivia couldn't resist taunting him a little when he grabbed another bottle of water and ventured her way. "The new broom is putting us all to shame, he's sweeping so clean."

"Ha, you're one to talk," he replied, eyeing her spic and span area. It looked as though no one had worked in the section all day. "Did you see the bus boy? He must have been fired as a jockey for eating the last s'more between races."

"He's our dishwasher's son, R.J., short for Ruben Junior, and too young to have a driver's permit, never mind climb on the back of a million-dollar racehorse."

"I know. I was just feeling sorry for the kid." Luca took a thirsty gulp of water before settling on the same stool he'd claimed earlier. It was close enough to easily lean over and inspect her shopping list. "Wow…you were busier than I guessed. Can you get everything re-placed by lunch on Monday?"

"I can give it a good start and move on from there. If someone could be here to let me in by six o'clock that would help a great deal."

"I'll talk to Dad. I'm sure it can be arranged." He took another swallow of water. "So why did you leave New Orleans?"

"My, that's a subject leap."

"Not really. You don't need me or anyone else to tell you New Orleans' loss is Galveston's gain. Besides, I'd wager most people—es-pecially chefs and musicians—think if you're lucky enough to be born or live in the Big Easy, it remains your home port."

"Well, since you brought up music, I guess I was born under a wan-dering star. Then there's a small technicality of fitting into the family business."

"Now we're getting somewhere."

"No, you have not found my Achilles' heel. The problem is my old-er brother runs the family smokehouses, my middle brother runs the restaurant, and my youngest brother handles commercial distribution."

"Good grief, even the bayous have become a conglomeration."

"Exactly. The family is as busy wholesaling as they are retailing. As a result, the menu doesn't often deviate from their stock successes, mean-ing—as proud as the family is of my achievements—there's not a great deal of call for my culinary arts, except when there's a wedding or polit-ical function to cater. They understood I needed more than that."

"But I bet they miss you like hell," Luca said softly. Before she could reply, he changed the subject again. "Where are you staying?"

"After a bad night in a respectable, but bug-infested motel, I found this secret garden-like place that rents out rooms. My landlady grows her own herbs and vegetables and said she would allow me to use her kitchen."

"Lucky you. I'm going to need to make more logical arrangements."

Olivia knew he'd spent the night upstairs at his aunt's, who also tended an impressive herb garden on her patio. "I'm sure your father would be more than happy to put you up at his place."

"After spending sixteen hours or more a day together? Not a good idea."

"Couples that are also business partners do it all the time."

"You're talking from experience?"

"No, but I've met people for whom it works."

Luca's expression turned skeptical. "I can only imagine."

"Oh, now *you're* the expert?" When he held up a hand in appeasement, she continued, "You learn to set boundaries. If all else fails, I hear making up is totally worth it."

"Now you have my attention. Ideas are blossoming in my mind like Fourth of July fireworks."

"An easy man, how novel."

Instead of laughing or voicing a smart comeback, Luca said thoughtfully, "Despite the Latin blood pumping through my veins, I've chosen a discerning path ... and having met you, I'm glad."

"I wish you wouldn't say that."

"Say what?" Sal asked joining them.

Before Olivia could think of a reply, Luca said, "Livie's being overly modest. She once reduced the mayor of New Orleans to tears for the cake she made for the reception following his mother's funeral. I read about it online—only I didn't realize it was her until minutes ago."

At Sal's curious look, Olivia had to think quickly. "The inspiration was really provided by his wife, who showed me a photo of the dear woman's birthplace. And, in fact, Luca misunderstood. It was the governor of Louisiana's mother."

Luca coughed.

Sal patted his son on the back. "Take a drink of water. Everyone makes mistakes. The good thing is that this is a boon for us. We can use it in our next interview or review."

"Uh—Dad."

Olivia was about to confess her teasing when something caught her eye. An envelope teetering on the edge of the basket beneath the table slid to the ground and she hurried to grab it.

Her conscience told her to pass it on immediately to Valentina, but the pink-glitter heart that had popped loose from the back had her scanning the dining room. Unbelievably, despite the late hour, a young family sat looking miserable in a far booth. Unable to resist, Olivia took out the slim piece of paper and almost gasped at the emotions poured onto the page.

> *Dear God,*
> *Did you here? We are moving. Mommy and Daddy*
> *loosed it, and say stuff I don't get. They say they can't*
> *live together anymore, so I have to leave my school and*
> *friends. They tell me they still love each other. Then why is*
> *Daddy giving Mommy back to Grandma and Grandpa,*
> *and us, too? Can you please help? Love, Sophie.*

Glancing again at the sad group, she quickly plated four desserts. "Excuse me," she said to Sal and Luca, and carried the tray to the dining room.

She placed the saucers with the swan puffs in front of the children. "I know there are days when serious food is just too much to swallow." She turned to the parents and set a slice of cheesecake in front of each of them. "I'm the new pastry chef and my grandmother always told me that desserts made a bad day better. Would you like coffee, espresso, or cappuccino? And for the children? It's my treat."

When she reached the coffee machines, Valentina came up behind her. "Let me help. That was so good of you, Olivia. I noticed that family has been struggling. And to be out so late with young children."

"That's what caught my attention, too." Olivia discreetly showed her the note. "Look at this. I think the little girl wrote it."

Valentia stiffened. "I told you that I take care of these."

"I didn't open it. The sticker didn't hold. I couldn't resist Valentina. As soon as I read what was happening to them and saw that scene out there, my heart ached."

Once Valentina read the brief note, she pressed her hand to her chest. "Oh, will it never end?" she crooned softly. Slipping the letter into her pocket, she said, "Of course, you did the right thing. They might have left before I saw this. It's such a pleasure to be able to finally talk to someone about these things. Do you need help serving them?"

"No, I'm good. Besides, you look like you could pass through these walls without the help of a Ouija board."

"It has been an exhausting day. I'll ask Luca to escort me to my apartment as soon as I send my niece home. Thank you, Olivia. Forgive me for overreacting."

Olivia got the children chocolate milk and carried the drinks to the family's table. They were still being very quiet, but the children were enjoying their desserts. The parents had yet to touch theirs.

"It isn't often we get children at this hour. It's a treat for me," she said.

"We're traveling and had to make a great distance today," the mother said. "But this was very nice. And we appreciate your kindness."

"You're most welcome. Are you at the end of your trip?"

The man sent his wife an uncomfortable look. "Yes. This is my wife's hometown. She and the children will—visit with her parents for a while."

Moving in permanently, from what the letter suggested. "What a treat for you!" she told the children. "I'm from New Orleans, and if I can't get to the beach every day and walk in the surf with the seagulls asking me for groceries, I would get homesick."

"I like fishing better than everything," the little boy said, with blossoming enthusiasm.

"Grandpa will take you," his mother assured him.

"Well, I hope you'll come back and see me sometime while you're here," Olivia told them, giving the little girl her warmest smile. "You know you remind me of someone I went to school with when I was your age. It was the middle of the year and she was new and so shy. We became best friends. Her name was Sophie. What's yours?"

The child gasped. "That's *my* name!"

Olivia returned that with an open-mouth stare. "You're not just saying that?"

"My name is Sophie Michelle Jenkins. Tell her Mommy."

"Sophie was her paternal grandmother's name. Michelle her maternal grandmother's."

"Both are beautiful. Well, Sophie, thank you for bringing back sweet memories. My name is Livie, short for Olivia and you made my day. I hope to see you again."

"Oh, you will," the mother said. "This is one of my parents' favorite restaurants and they share the story about the building and the hurricane with the children every visit."

Upon returning to the kitchen, Olivia paused to tell the waitress serving the family that the extras were on her tab. Then she went to explain things to Sal and Luca, only they had discretely followed the scene and had a general idea of why she'd abruptly taken off. Olivia filled them in on the rest of the story.

"I'll reimburse their waitress as soon as they leave," she assured her boss.

"No need. I would have done the same thing. You did right."

Thanking him, Olivia turned to Luca. "Your aunt isn't feeling well. She thought you might help her get up to her apartment as soon as she sees her niece on her way home."

"Absolutely." Luca exchanged glances with his father. "Unless you would prefer to escort her?"

"She asked for you because she knows I have questions she doesn't want to answer. But it's been a wild couple of days. One more won't change anything. Go ahead—but you'll be back?"

"Absolutely. I intend to help finish cleaning up."

Sal took in the condition of the kitchen. "That's pretty much taken care of. My intent was for you to get to know Rocco a bit better, and Chanel is working tonight. You haven't met her yet."

"She's the Eifel Tower-tall redhead who has to constantly wipe off the bar for all of the drooling guys hanging out in her area?"

Sal's laugh lifted over the other chatter, as well as the music being piped throughout the building. "And a chance to drool is all they can hope for because they know she's not only a personal trainer, her husband is a cop. All six-foot-six of him."

Olivia had begun to move away, only to feel Sal touch her arm to delay her. "On Fridays and Saturdays, we have a tradition—a little celebration after we close. The whole crew has a drink, but there's no pressure."

"Lovely. I haven't met anyone in the bar yet."

"Do you have a way home?" Luca asked. "I missed seeing you arrive this morning, so…"

"I have my car, but thanks. I mean, the place where I'm staying is close enough to walk, only with all I was carrying, and the long day, it wouldn't have been practical."

"Just checking."

"Appreciated."

IT WAS ALMOST an hour before the front door, and the side door leading to the wine garden off the lounge were locked. Rocco was already setting out glasses and bottles of bubbling wine for the crew's weekend libation reward.

Sal started things off. "Another great night, kids," he declared. "Thank you!"

Cheers and hoots filled the room. Olivia clapped along with the others, until she noticed Luca standing beside his father. When he winked at her, she looked away.

"Most of you have met my son Luca," Sal continued, "but for those who haven't, take a minute to introduce yourselves to him, and to Olivia Dumont hailing from New Orleans, who is filling in for Leo."

"How's he doing, and where's Valentina?" waitress Rosemary asked. Not only was the bookish graduate student the only blonde in the place other than Olivia, she was one of the few employees not related or otherwise friends of the Angelonis or Pastores.

"She sends her regrets," Sal replied. "It was a full day for her, and Tiny is trying to keep Leo from sneaking out of the hospital. They kept Leo overnight for observation, due to the concussion he experienced, and while he's there, the doctors are doing some tests on his older injuries. Thanks for asking. Now, enjoy, everyone!"

Another round of cheers and applause filled the room, and most of the group reached for filled glasses. Olivia went in the opposite direction seeking out Chanel, who stood behind the bar, separate from the noisy group.

"Hi," Olivia began. "I actually first saw you last night."

"You were considering eating at the bar." Chanel extended her hand.

"As swamped as you were, you noticed that?"

"Constant lecturing from my sweetie. Never stop being aware of your surroundings. He's a police officer."

"Wise advice. Well, I'm glad I took up Janine's offer of the little table or I might not have gotten Sal's attention," Olivia said.

"I hear you may be the one to finally appease my husband's discriminating sweet tooth. I got Tony to box a slice of the cheesecake everyone is talking about, as well as the Doberge. Mitch is going to have to do twice as many pushups in the morning, but I'm convinced he won't be complaining. Which," Chanel continued, "brings me to the question—how do you stay so thin while creating all that confectionary decadence?"

"A different kind of training than yours," Olivia admitted. "You have to learn to be satisfied with tasting, not indulging."

"Willpower. I can see it in your eyes."

"Where?" Rocco asked, joining them. He stooped from his own impressive stature to mimic an ophthalmologist's inspection. "Nah, from what I hear, she's the first test robot aimed at replacing bakers. A visually delightful combination of Barbie and Peter Pan programmed to memorize the entire Library of Congress collection of cookbooks to produce any dessert on demand."

Playing along, Olivia raised her hand in acceptance. "Guilty. But they're recalling me for reprogramming. Something about my software not taking into consideration elevation and barometric changes and their effect on a recipe, not to mention its individual ingredients."

Rocco leaned closer to Chanel's ear. "I think she's ridiculing my theory."

She nudged the ponytailed hunk away with her elbow. "I think you're so out of your depth, you don't know when to quit. And I'm right about her willpower, too. I glimpsed it a minute ago, when Luca winked at her. Mitch would still be a free-wheeling bachelor if I'd let on that he had me at, 'Do handcuffs scare you?'"

Rocco immediately shifted to cover Olivia's ears. "Not in front of the innocents, you insatiable Amazon."

Olivia enjoyed their playful nonsense. "Now I understand why the later it gets, the more likely there's such raucous laughter coming from here."

With a grimace, Chanel nodded toward Rocco. "Blame him. I keep telling him to try stand-up comedy at some open mic event."

"Why take a pay cut when I'm cleaning up in tips here?" Rocco replied, only to give Olivia a seductive smile. "Although I occasionally have been known to do a one-night-only performance."

"She doesn't date. And she has a plan," Luca said, appearing at Olivia's side.

Olivia didn't react well to Luca's unexpected arrival, or his using her own words during a private conversation to discourage Rocco's attention. Couldn't he see the *Vita e Spezie* bartender was still on an adrenaline high from his long shift? And what business did Luca have acting possessive? The long-stemmed glass he put in her hands began to tremble from her embarrassment and agitation.

Rocco apologized immediately, his gaze shifting back and forth between them. "Are you two—?"

"We are not," Olivia said flatly.

Looking unconvinced, Rocco told Luca, "In any case, we were just having a light moment."

"Luca was, as well." Olivia placed the glass on the bar before she ended up spilling the contents on everyone. "It's just that after so much time in a formal atmosphere, he hasn't yet washed all of the starch out of his clothes."

Snickering at the subtle put down, Chanel held out her hand. "I like you. If you find yourself needing a break from the killer restaurant world, I'm a night owl, since Mitch works the graveyard shift. I wouldn't mind hanging out with a girl pal to get my mind off where his job takes him."

"Thanks, as long as you don't check my lack of muscles and try to get me on an exercise program," Olivia replied.

"You have a firm handshake," Chanel said. "That'll do."

Excusing herself only moments after, Olivia wasn't surprised when Luca did the same. Insisting on seeing her to her car, she didn't protest, deciding the sooner she made a few things clear, the better.

"Liv—I didn't mean to upset you." He caught up with her just as she triggered the remote and unlocked the white Prius.

"I shared something private with you, and you used it to insinuate we had a relationship. Luca, we haven't even known each other twenty-four hours."

"It was a signal to let you know I've been listening to you."

"Then listen to this signal—go away. I got almost no sleep because

I was so excited to get this job and, as you said yourself, I've been on my feet more than anyone. I need some rest."

"I know. I *know*. But...okay, I'll put it out there. You didn't even taste the wine. And you were shaking so badly, if you hadn't put down the glass, I would have done it for you."

"Good night, Luca."

He raked a hand through his hair. "Please. Talk to me. If you have a problem, I'm not going to judge. It's been said that eighty percent of people have alcoholism in their family tree. Frankly, I suspect if you add prescription drug abuse, the addiction rate is even higher."

"I agree. Only that has nothing to do with me."

She got into her car and started the engine. She would have put the vehicle into reverse and backed away, but Luca was in her window entreating her.

"*Livie.*"

Lowering the window, Olivia said, "Make sure you check on Valentina before you turn off the lights. If you want someone to worry about, she's the most deserving."

"Who do you allow to worry about you?"

"No one," she answered. "I leave my future in Higher Hands."

5

"SO, IT LOOKS AS THOUGH I HAVE A JOB—AT LEAST THROUGH tourist season."

Sunday mornings tended to be lazy, even in a popular resort city. No loud music pulsated from cramped row houses, their lively colors looking as cheerful as the keyboard on a child's xylophone. Aside from the natural seaside sounds, the only conflict came from the rhythmic cycling of an air conditioner, and the aggressive squawk of a seagull venturing inland, warning garden birds they claimed first dibs on any appealing morsels.

Olivia had been stunned when she first opened her eyes and rolled over to see her alarm clock displayed a hairsbreadth from eight o'clock. The next jarring moment came as the tang of chicory-laced coffee permeated her senses. The aroma was so much like the blend her mother made it caused Olivia to make a quick scan of the bedroom. Noting the buttery yellow walls and turquoise furnishings, she relaxed somewhat.

You've made it to another day. It's Tempest Fleuraugust's house.

She'd quickly pulled on one of her brother's LSU T-shirts over the tank top and jogging shorts that served as pajamas, and followed the scent of exotic caffeine to the kitchen.

When she'd first inquired about the room-for-rent sign in the window of the turquoise, two-story Victorian home, she'd admitted she was in search of work and didn't know how long she would be staying. It was a relief to be able to offer some reassurance to the woman who had been so welcoming.

"See, baby?" Tempest declared. "I told you not to worry. I can tell these things."

Sister Tempest thought she knew, and could do a great deal. There were signs attesting to that all over her colorful yard. In the flowerbeds full of pink and purple gladiolas, and swaths of zinnias in a rainbow of other shades was a stake bearing the announcement FLOWER SEEDS! By a birdbath one announcing HERBS. On the porch were pots of geraniums in almost neon fuchsia, and deep salmon with more notices—HEALING BALMS, LOTIONS, SOAPS. By the door a barrel of white impatiens bore an equally pretty, hand-painted sign adorned with a butterfly and bee hyping *SELECT* SOUVENIRS. Olivia hadn't yet had the opportunity to see what select meant.

It was the advertisement for personal palm and Tarot readings that had given her pause. Such services were common back in New Orleans, where the French Quarter was rife with individuals of all nationalities setting up tables around Jackson Square. She'd even sat for a few readings through the years; however, no one had offered anything to surpass her own instincts and intuition, and she remained dubious of anyone making an honest living that way. Until yesterday, when Tempest sent her off with the startling observation, "Be prepared for the little people today. You'll be needed."

Still fighting yawns, Olivia indulged in a rare mug of strong brew from the pot on the coffeemaker. But she doctored it with a heaping teaspoon of sugar, and generous dollop of milk.

"I'm ready to hear all about it," Tempest said.

Not yet prepared, Olivia hedged. "It was like all first days—busy, overwhelming, exciting, and exhausting. I think I did okay."

"And I think you're being too modest."

"Oh, they're happy with my abilities, and my products are selling even faster than I anticipated."

"So, what's the problem?"

"There's no denying I'm just one link in a very complicated chain."

"The other staff," Tempest guessed with a huff. "You cannot tell me they are anything less than delighted with you. I am an excellent judge of character. Do you think I let just anyone rent one of my rooms?"

Wanting to avoid the subject of Luca, Olivia turned the conversation to what she'd really come down to talk about. "I'm flattered and grateful. But about what you said when I left here yesterday morning? About little people? You were referring to children, right?"

"What else would I mean?"

"I don't know. My mind was so full at the time with my shopping list and recipes. I began to think you'd made a joke about leprechauns or something."

Tempest paused in her work. "What do I know of such things? Do I look Irish to you?"

She was methodically grinding stalks of lavender from a dried bouquet in a mottled gray-and-white stone pestle, about the width of a dessert dish. Each movement was accompanied by a tinkling sound from the selections of bracelets on her wrists.

Even with the high ceiling and the open window beside them, the scent was heady, and seduced Olivia into feeling more comfortable sharing her thoughts about the strange experience. "Please stop confusing me. A family came—almost too late to be served, and this letter came through the slot—and it struck me...you meant children."

"I don't know what I meant. I only had 'children with needs' come to mind. So, I told you."

Olivia looked at her with new respect and a bit of fear. "This is very unsettling."

"Don't let it trouble you," Tempest crooned. "I just use more of my senses than other people. Sometimes you do, yourself. Tell me what happened?"

"You don't know?"

All but rolling her eyes, Tempest gestured behind her. "I left my crystal ball in the other room."

Amused, Olivia chuckled, then shared the story about the little girl and her penned cry for help. "I still can't believe it," she said when she finished. "It's as incredible as your premonition. I got to experience a part of history. The letter sailed right by my feet."

"You had a beautiful day."

The observation triggered a cloud over Olivia's pleasure, and she shifted in her chair, uncomfortable with Tempest's description of her day, since nothing had changed for the family. "I should have done more. Asked for an address or phone number."

"To what end? You're not with Child Protective Services. You said nothing to suggest there was evidence of child abuse."

Startled, Olivia almost choked on a sip of coffee. "Of course not! It was simply a sad situation."

"And for a few moments, you provided comfort and pleasure to the little ones. Who knows, your act of kindness may have affected the parents, as well, and stopped them from quarreling in front of their babies."

With her *café au lait* skin shimmering from the humid air, as much as physical exertion, her eyes artfully made up to resemble an Egyptian temple goddess, and her strong body swathed in a vibrant caftan every bit as colorful and flamboyant as her garden, Tempest evoked mystery and drama. But as intrigued as she was, Olivia missed the bare-faced, livelier, playful Tempest dressed in her knee-length housecoat who had given her a tour of the house on Thursday.

"I'm listening," Tempest said.

Heat burned in Olivia's cheeks as she realized her expression must be exposing her every thought. "I was just wondering if you were open for business today?"

The jingling bracelets went quiet, and Tempest gazed at Olivia from beneath the sweep of her heavy false eyelashes. "Girl, you should see me when I put on my headscarf. I look like a phoenix is rising from my head."

As the middle-aged woman spread her arms wide like a bird about to take flight, and a husky laugh rose from deep in her chest, Olivia shook her head. Getting to know Sister Tempest Fleuraugust could turn into a full-time job.

"There's a fundraiser for the maintenance of one of the cemeteries this afternoon," Tempest explained, as though nothing had happened. "I'm donating my services."

"That's . . . very generous."

"You can say that again. Last year, I matched the total of what all the other booths combined brought in."

"I think I get that."

Tempest reached over and patted her hand. "About last night, it was a moment in time. Let it go. The work that needs to be done belongs to those parents, not you."

"I don't know how Valentina lets go," Olivia said. "As I told you, she handles all of the letters."

"What does she do with them?"

Olivia shrugged. "Once she reads them? I'm not sure. She only told me that she lights candles and prays."

"A tender-hearted soul."

"Oh, she is, but there's something so sad about her. It's like the weight of the world is on her shoulders."

"The lady in black," Tempest said, glancing out the window. "I've seen her. She's a widow in mourning and more."

"What do you mean?"

"Lost a husband and her child. Both at the same time."

Olivia gasped. "You know the story?"

"There was an accident."

"No wonder she has this other world look about her. How awful."

"Don't you get caught up in her sorrow, darlin'. You live your life, and stay ready to receive the gifts prepared for you."

Olivia held the still-warm mug against her heart, appreciating the soothing feeling, as much as Tempest's advice. "Getting this job was plenty."

"How's Golden Boy?"

Feeling more comfortable now—and awake—Olivia gave her a rueful look. During the phone call to announce getting the job and her later hours, she'd mentioned Luca and her concerns how he, not Leo, might prove an obstruction that could shorten the length of her employment. Tempest had dubbed him "The Golden Boy."

"I got upset with him last night," Olivia admitted.

"So now he's a tarnished golden boy."

How did she explain without venturing into territory she couldn't share with anyone? "Not at all. Everyone is thrilled he's there."

"You aren't?"

"My feelings are immaterial."

"Maybe not as far as he's concerned."

"Well, he should mind his own business," Olivia blurted out. "I can't let my guard down for a second. If I do, I have this combination white knight and guard dog at my shoulder."

Tempest chuckled as she poured the remaining contents of the bowl into the half-filled glass jar beside her. "Child, asking a man not to respond to a beautiful woman is like telling a bee to ignore the rarest flower in a garden."

"Oh, please. I told you where he worked before. Comparing us is like using chateaubriand and bayou oysters in the same sentence."

Tempest brushed the remnants of the lavender from her hands into the jar. "Don't get yourself upset again." At Olivia's doubletake, she acknowledged, "I only made it home from a private reading minutes before you arrived last night. I heard you getting in and out of bed. Old houses, you know."

"I'm so sorry!"

"Don't be. I'm at an age when sleep becomes a friend that visits too rarely." Her alto voice flowed like an old library cat purring as she sprawled across the checkout counter, observing all the two-legged souls as though they were her kittens to be monitored. "What will you do today? I don't remember if you said the restaurant is open or not?"

"It isn't. I thought I'd have a walk on the beach before I do my laundry."

"Want some company? I feel closest to God when my toes are in the sand."

Nodding, Olivia replied, "This bayou girl doesn't feel quite right without water within view."

AN HOUR LATER they made it to the beach, discovering they had the area mostly to themselves, except for a lone surf fisherman and a teenager jogging in the frothy edge of the water with his black lab. Seagulls swooped over the newcomers hoping there might be a bite of something to snack on. Olivia didn't disappoint and dug into the plastic shopping bag she'd filled with leftover dinner rolls from the restaurant. She held up the scraps of bread, laughing as the aerial scavengers squawked and dove, racing to be the first to reach her offerings.

Keeping her distance, Tempest picked up an iridescent pink shell that she examined closely before slipping it into the pocket of the caftan floating around her ankles in the mild breeze. It was rare to find a shell intact due to the seawall built after the big storm. "You'll learn to stop doing that once you have to wash your hair three times over to get it clean again."

Olivia gently chided, "What happened to 'We're all one in the universe?'"

"We are. We're also the life form that finds it acceptable to be a bit hypocritical where things like bird shit are concerned."

Accepting the wisdom of her words, Olivia threw pieces of bread into the air, which were deftly caught by diving birds. "How did you get so wise? And your accent...I know it's Caribbean but from where specifically?"

"Haiti. I was one of the 'boat people,' as they called us."

Tempest looked out into the Gulf and beyond. The morning sun caressed the majestic geography of her face. The sea mist bestowed upon her a dewy look any woman would envy. At the moment, Olivia couldn't tell whether she was seventy or closer to forty.

"I was a teenager and ran away from home, sold on the lavish dreams my man, Javel Caprice, spun like endless lengths of silk in my mind. Only reality was so different. Our journey was the most horrible thing—worse than life in destitute Haiti ever was. Javel died trying to save me from the men who owned the boat. I was beaten, raped, and almost drowned, too."

The terrifying scene was too visual for Olivia not to react. She began to reach out to Tempest, only to catch herself; however, compassion for the poor woman who had been such a brave and trusting girl compelled her to ask, "How on earth did you survive?"

The older woman's silence spoke of a past not far enough behind her to escape all the pain. She sighed, and her breath merged with the salty breeze. "I pray that neither you, nor anyone you love experiences what I did. I wanted to die, but God told me I was not allowed to quit. I did not like Him so much in those days."

"And yet you endured. You made it from there to who you are now."

"They say a person is really three people—'who he thinks he is, what others say he is, and who he really is.' But I was done with anyone defining me."

"You had to have landed in Florida," Olivia mused. "What brought you to Galveston?"

"Life. Men. Business. Weather. Did I ask what brings you here?"

"No, you didn't, and I thank you for that, but I'm beginning to think you already know. Why else do you have a sign offering readings?"

"To keep myself from losing my mind."

Before Olivia could react to the stark admission, the woman took hold of her hand. Peeling back fingers Olivia instinctively curled into a fist, Tempest gazed at the open palm and the fine lines mapped on it.

"Okay, wait a minute," Olivia pleaded. "You're making me very uncomfortable."

"What are you worried about, girl? It's not like I'm asking personal questions like the man who makes you walk the floor when you should be sleeping."

"And there she goes," Olivia said to the massif of clouds coming into view on the horizon. Trouble. Out there and most definitely here on land. "I mean it, Tempest. I don't want to know if you see something. Not now, at any rate."

Tempest dropped her hand as quickly as she'd grabbed it. "It's just as well. Didn't see no Golden Boy anyway."

LUCA HURRIED DOWN the stairs of Valentina's apartment, intent on following his aunt. Something about the way she'd left this morning told him this wasn't an ordinary trip to church. She carried a tote. Granted, a check of the weather on his Smartphone last night left him aware of a tropical disturbance forming in the Gulf; but so far, computers were forecasting the system would be forced west into Mexico.

Who needed a tote just to carry an umbrella?

As soon as she quietly shut the door behind her, he'd jumped up, splashed water on his face, while hastily brushing his teeth with a mouthful of mouthwash. He pulled on cargo shorts over his boxers, dragged a clean T-shirt over his head, and slipped his feet into flip flops.

By the time he made it to the road, Valentina was a half block ahead of him. His sad and lonely aunt was the only other person on the sidewalk this morning, and there were few vehicles on the streets. She looked like someone from another time with her black gauzy dress flowing around her ankles with every step. The black lace shawl over her shoulders wafted in the soft breeze like raven wings. Luca slowed his long-legged stride in order not to give himself away.

To his surprise, Valentina passed the entrance to St. Mary's Catholic Basilica, continuing a few dozen yards beyond to the cemetery next door. Pausing at the last traffic light, Luca tried to decide if this was a routine for her on Sundays, or was today an anniversary he didn't remember or know of?

When the signal changed, he continued after her, then paused by a sizeable, white oleander. Using it for cover, he peered into the fenced enclave.

Valentina had stopped at the far side of the cemetery, next to side-by-side plots on the last row. Drawing a small mat out of the tote, she set it on the grass and kneeled. Then she proceeded to remove a few gardening tools, gloves, and bottled water. Slipping on the gloves, she went to work tending the pairs of potted geraniums set in the ground on either end of each headstone.

"So that's it," Luca whispered.

As much as he could remember, this was the first time he'd been here. He'd been so traumatized at the death of his cousin, his parents refused to let him attend the funeral. His maternal grandmother had stayed with him, while the rest of the family attended the joint service and burials. Now, seeing the smaller version of Mario Senior's granite marker left him weak-kneed. The buzz of bumble bees in the oleander blossoms merged with what seemed like gears grinding in his head. Time didn't stand still; it was forced backwards.

He and "Little Mario," as everyone had addressed his cousin, had both been five years old at the time of the accident. The loss had thrown Luca into psychological shock where, to this day, his memory of the event and the first few days afterward were lost to him. Even years later, thinking about the tragic event was like trying to drive at night in dense fog. He'd learned to avoid the subject entirely, especially after he and his mother moved away. The aching loss of being separated from his father was difficult enough.

Tears too long denied burned Luca's eyes as he saw the physical proof of how small his cousin had been. How small he would remain forever.

The last time they saw each other was a morning when Luca had misbehaved badly. They had been at the Pastores' grocery store, tempted by the five-gallon tubs of gelato in the freezer showcase. Luca had dared the youngest Pastore to have a quick taste without getting caught. Of course, one tantalizing lick wasn't enough, and they were spotted just as they sunk gooey fingers in the barrel of their choice. Hoping to save himself from a spanking, Little Mario blamed him, and Luca got sent home by Mario Senior with a scolding that he would not be allowed to join them on the afternoon deliveries.

Luca bit back a moan as pain—like sutures being ripped from a deep wound—split open his memory. The boy he'd been, sitting on the foot of his bed, his stomach pulling with hunger. He'd been sent to his room without lunch. Then the telephone rang, followed by screaming—such screaming, wailing, and wrenching sobs, he'd covered his ears.

Valentina worked quietly. She snapped off the dead blossoms at their joints, and loosened the soil around them. Then she poured a bottle of water on each plant. Luca felt the urge to go sit beside her, only to check the impulse. His sadness was nothing compared to hers.

When she collected her things and rose, he retreated behind another oleander at the far end of the cemetery. There he waited for her to exit, and watched until she tucked her tote out of sight behind a column of the church, lifted the shawl over her head, and entered the sanctuary.

Understanding she would be gone for a while, Luca retraced his steps and for the first time visited his cousin's grave. Dropping to his knees, he whispered, "Oh, my friend..." Tears locked painfully in his throat, his heart did the communicating as he pressed his palm to the grass where Little Mario's heart might be. "I've missed you so."

Reaching into his pocket, he stroked a Liberty silver dollar between his fingers. Both he and Mario had received one for their fifth birthdays from their Grandfather Pastore. Luca had fingered the coin so much through the years, it was rubbed almost bare of any details. He could almost hear his grandfather—a small, thin man, who always wore suspenders—as he'd pressed a coin in each of their hands.

"Always remember, money is important. *Importante, capire?* But *la famiglia* is priceless."

On impulse, Luca dug a hole with his fingers beside Mario Junior's pot, and buried his coin in the soil. "I don't know if angels need luck, but I've had my share. Here's to you, cousin."

When his aunt emerged from the church, Luca stood waiting for her, the tote in his hand. She hesitated for a second, then lifted the lace from her head and came to him.

"Oh, Luca. You are your mother's son."

"What does that mean?"

"Born snoops, but so dear." She linked her arm through his and they started walking back to the apartment. "I should have expected it. I'm so used to being alone, I don't look over my shoulder anymore."

"That's not good."

"There was a time I would have agreed with you, but it's less important these days."

"Why?"

"That doesn't matter, either. What did you do while I was inside? You should have come in. The first Mass doesn't start for some time yet."

Luca slid her a wry look. "Aunt Val, I may not be a regular church-goer, but I do have respect. I'm not dressed for church."

She squeezed his arm. "You just made God smile."

"As for your other question," he continued, "I finally visited their graves."

Her gaze fixed on the ground only a few steps ahead of them, Valentina said softly, "I'm so glad."

"You might not say that if you knew how dizzy I still feel from the experience."

"He was your first best friend."

"He's been my only best friend."

"Oh, my poor dear. We who live in grief often forget what others are enduring."

"I just made myself not think about it." He uttered a brief, wrenching sound. "I feel so many emotions. Guilt, Aunt Val. I realize I've been running from the suffocating blanket of guilt."

Valentina stopped and wrapped her arms around him. "Darling, you were a little boy. You two got into mischief as all children do."

"But it was my idea."

"And he needed so much coaxing," Valentina said with a sad smile. "Let it go, Luca. Don't spend another day being like your Uncle Leo."

"Excuse me? What do you mean?"

Valentina searched his face with growing concern. "You really don't remember?"

"Obviously not."

She crossed herself and looked as though she was going to try to change the subject. Moments later, she relented and said wearily, "The day you didn't get to go on the deliveries, the day of the accident, Leo offered to help Mario because he was done at the restaurant, and Mario was extra busy. Those two got along so well. Mario admired your father tremendously and always looked up to him, but he and Leo were pals."

Luca started shaking his head, already rejecting the words she had yet to say. "Don't say it. Uncle Leo was with them that day?"

"Sweetheart, Leo was driving. How else do you think his leg was so messed up?" As they approached a bus stop bench, Valentina forced him to sit down. "Breathe, Luca. If I knew you never put it all together, I wouldn't have told you out here in the street."

It didn't matter to Luca. Shock made him oblivious to their surroundings. Leo had been driving the Pastore delivery truck. In a way, he had taken his place because there wouldn't have been room otherwise.

"Who was at fault?" he forced himself to ask.

Valentina tried to wave away the question. "It doesn't matter. It's ancient history. It can't change anything."

"But apparently it mattered a great deal to Uncle Leo. He's nothing like the man I remember."

As he rose and started walking again, Valentina caught up with him and, as before, linked her arm through his, gripping it even tighter. "Luca, listen to me. It was an accident. There was plenty of fault all around, even the police said so. Leo and Mario were talking and laughing too much and when a signal light turned green, he accelerated too quickly. His vision was blocked by Mario, and he didn't see the truck on the other street that had tried to beat the yellow light."

"Oh, God."

Luca's tortured words had Valentina leaning her head against his shoulder. "Now you will better understand why I was so grateful for the times I went to Houston to visit with you and your mother. I needed to get away from here. The two of you saved my sanity."

"I don't know how."

"It was bittersweet, of course. Yet, Luca, don't you see how you belong to many people, including me?"

"Oh, man." When he exhaled, the sound was as shaky as he felt. "One of the reasons I couldn't wait to get off to culinary school was due to the feeling of being pulled in several directions. I didn't want to be a part of that. I still don't."

"What if this is one of those moments when it can't matter what you want?"

Luca couldn't believe his ears. "Who are you? That's the most assertive thing I've ever heard you say—and oddly enough, it almost makes me angry with you."

"Well, you'll have to get in line. There's your father to deal with first."

"What on earth did you say to him?"

"Salvatore caught my blunder when I instantly said your name the other night at the back door of the restaurant."

"I did notice something was going on. Only, I was too pumped to be back to let myself dwell on it. Sorry, Aunt Val, but there's another lesson why not to keep secrets."

His aunt held doggedly to her opinion. "Please don't judge yet. There are things you don't know."

"I hear you. That said, you're all on notice. I'm fed up with this family secrecy stuff."

SAL LIKED SUNDAYS in the restaurant. While the rest of the staff couldn't wait for a break, he enjoyed the chance to look around and think, without having to juggle everything that needed to be done on a normal business day. He saw it as the equivalent to several hours on a therapist's couch. The ambiance brought on by the lingering scents of last night's cooking, the images of racks of wine, and the lushness of leather seating made him swell with pride and power. At times like this, he could think, *To hell with anyone who doesn't get it.*

As though commenting on the thought, a knock came from the back door. Peering through the security hole, Sal unlocked the deadbolt. If anyone could make him change his mind about solitude, it was his son.

Luca hesitated on the other side of the threshold. "Hey. Do you feel like some company?"

"Sure." Sal stepped aside for him to enter. "Is everything okay? You look...upset."

"I am. Dad...Uncle Leo was driving the truck that killed Uncle Mario and my cousin?"

The distress evidently disturbing Luca now spread to Sal. This was the moment he'd feared would come. He clenched his fists at his sides, and dealt with another wave of anger at Rosa. She had stolen all the joy of watching their son grow, and left the pain and mess for him to deal with. How was he supposed to make explanations easier for a son he barely knew?

"So, your mother never told you?"

"She did not. But you can bet we're going to have a conversation as to why pretty soon." Checking himself, he said with more sympathy, "Aunt Val had another bad night, so when she left this morning, I followed to make sure she was okay. Low and behold, she didn't go directly into the church. She went to the cemetery."

Sal gestured toward the bar. "How about I make you an espresso over there? With it being tourist season, and business on an upswing, I was adding to Rocco's liquor order."

"Please. I left the apartment still groggy. Add everything I'm learning and I feel as though I ran head first into a mountain."

"Have a seat." As he started the machine, Sal looked over his shoulder to see his son with his elbows on the counter rubbing his face. It was a characteristic trait he'd done himself countless times through the years when he got bogged down with thoughts of his wife, boy, and the tragedy that had destroyed Valentina's young family. "I hate this for you," he told Luca.

"How were you to know what Mom would decide to keep from me?"

A door had opened. Sal had to decide whether to reach for the opportunity it offered. "I should have hired a private detective to find you," he said abruptly. "What to tell you, when to tell you, wasn't for her to decide on her own. But after several calls to her parents and being told to respect her wishes for time and space, I talked myself out of trying to bring you both home. I was concerned about what our fighting would do to you."

Slow to respond, Luca finally admitted, "Maybe you were right. On the other hand, believing you're not wanted by your father is no cake walk."

His son's words made it more difficult to bite back his bitterness towards Rosa. How dare she let his son grow up with that idea in his head. Every day in the news were stories, crimes committed by young men who had grown up in fatherless families. No doubt Rosa had made sure Luca had access to her father and brothers—there was no denying the boy had become a fine man, so she'd done something right—but he'd been denied that reassurance, as well.

Wanting badly to hear what else Luca had to say, Sal hesitated. Their relationship still felt fragile. Was it too early to probe old wounds? "Damn it," he muttered.

The sound of the gurgling brew claimed Sal's attention. He poured the espresso and set the cup and saucer in front of Luca. "About your aunt...I did the same thing for a while."

"What do you mean?"

"Follow her." Sal was loathed to go back to those early months, since, in a way, it was the beginning of the end of his life, as he'd known it. "Valentina couldn't bear being in her house," he continued slowly. "There were too many memories. As for the store—well, she wasn't well enough to deal with it. Mario's family bought her out."

"Yeah? Is it still there?"

"Nah. The memories were just as hard for them. They sold out a couple years later." Sal pointed toward the ceiling. "Anyway, I moved her upstairs. It was a bad time. I had to be here, but I also had to be able to watch her. That's when I started sleeping in the office...to hear her when she got up and left. If you can believe it, she went to church a lot more back then, but I was concerned she might walk into the ocean or the bay."

"Did she ever try?"

Sal stared down at his order sheet, but saw his sunken-eyed, listless sister as she'd been in those days. "She probably wanted to. Thank God for her faith. Even so, I figured it was touch-and-go there at times." And it was hell on his marriage. Of course, Rosa wanted to be supportive of her sister-in-law and best friend, but seeing little Luca was impossible for Valentina and she fell apart so easily back then. As a result, Rosa was isolated. She had no husband coming home at night, she couldn't come here…until the one time she did. Then the rest of his world crumbled around him.

After a fatalistic sigh, Sal continued, "We coped as best we could. As best we knew how, but there were more casualties. You for one."

Luca took that in. The details were helpful at closing confusing gaps in his youth, Sal could see that. But when he tried to speak, he abruptly pulled back and sipped his coffee instead.

"You can tell me anything," Sal said quietly. Of course, inside he was quaking with dread, while his mind mocked him with the old saying, *"Be careful what you wish for."*

Finally, Luca offered, "Dad, I've lived with shame and guilt, and couldn't even put it into words."

It was the last thing Sal expected. "For what?"

"I didn't take ownership of the fact that Mario wasn't here anymore."

Sal bit back an expletive. "You were a child. You did nothing."

"I got into trouble and it changed everything. You know Little Mario and I were supposed to go with Uncle Mario to help with the deliveries. If he'd been driving, he would have been paying attention to the traffic. At least his line of vision wouldn't have been compromised like Uncle Leo's."

"Are you kidding me?" Sal clasped his head. The notion of his son in that truck threatened to rupture his brain. "If you had been there, we probably would have lost you, too." He beat his chest with his fist. "I'm the guilty one. I should have insisted Leo stay home. He'd already had a busy morning and a hectic lunch. He should have had a break before the dinner service. Even before the accident, your uncle wasn't all that great dealing with pressure. But your Uncle Mario was busy, too, and just as short of help as we were. So, when Leo insisted he was fine and wanted to go, I ignored my better judgment and let him. It's family. You do what you have to do." He slid his hand to his belly. "But, Luca, it will be a miracle if I don't die of stomach cancer from all the misery and remorse I carry."

Luca winced, got up, and circled the bar to embrace his father. "I'm sorry. I don't know what else to say."

Sal's eyes burned from restrained emotions, but he hugged his son fiercely. "There's no need to say anything. I'm just so grateful you're here."

Regaining his composure, Luca gripped Sal by the shoulders and said insistently, "Well, I know one thing for sure. There have been too many secrets. I say we clear the air, and get back to being a family again. I told Aunt Val the same thing."

"Fine. Add your mother to that list and see how far it gets you."

"Here we go again." Luca returned to his seat, massaging the back of his neck. "Don't you think I tried? Mom doesn't want to talk any more than Aunt Val. Aunt Val gave me this line about the time wasn't yet right to reveal everything. When will it be okay?"

"Don't ask me," Sal muttered. "One thing I do know is there's been some collusion going on between those two that I didn't know about."

Luca nodded, his expression apologetic. "Not to be a rat, but after what you've told me, you have a right to know. On occasion, Aunt Val did come see us in Houston. But more than that, I couldn't tell you because they were always careful to wait until I was asleep or gone to do their talking."

"It had to be on Sundays," Sal began, "because she knew I was busy with other things."

"Yeah, I think you're right. During high school, I was deeply involved with extracurricular activities and didn't pay as much attention anymore. By eighteen, I was off to school and working. Staying busy kept me from thinking too much about the family."

With a soulful look, Sal said, "Thank you. You've told me more in the last minute than either of them ever shared with me."

"I realize as much now. But I was conflicted about coming," Luca told him. "I was afraid that after the divorce you simply didn't give a damn about me, either."

Sal went slack-jawed and felt the blood draining from his face. "What divorce? There was never a divorce."

6

IN THE ERRATIC TRAJECTORY OF RELATIONSHIPS, SOME OF man's greatest missteps come as a result of passion, stubbornness, and bottom-line awful communication. As truth struck another home run, the two men of different generations stared at each other for several seconds before the elder turned away to collect himself, while the younger sought to hide the idiocy of the situation...and failed.

Luca buried his face in his hands again, only this time to burst into laughter. "Oh, jeez, Dad. You can't be serious. Are you two for real?"

"Okay, Mr. Bachelor, what do you know about relationships, let alone love?"

"I already told you I've been burned—and at a considerable price, although, thankfully, not so much to my heart. That's because I don't believe you should take vows until you're convinced enough to know there's give and take, and you can talk things through and communicate when there's trouble. But you and Mom have defied everything you supposedly know and believe in. Good grief, you're not only still married, you've literally been holding each other hostage all these years."

Energy radiated from Sal like Vesuvius before raining sheer hellfire over Pompeii. It was one thing to carry the pain, disappointment, and anger, but he'd always felt there was some honor in protecting the privacy of his marriage. Now to have this young lion openly mock their lives was an unacceptable offense and he exploded.

"I'm the joke because I left the door open for her to come back? She heard no threats from me."

"Yet, she cried a lot. I don't remember hearing particulars—"

"Because there weren't any. Crocodile tears. She's some actress, your mother."

"I think you're leaving out a critical detail," Luca replied. "What did she get wrong that would cause her to leave?"

"An aberration," Sal insisted. "I was working seventy to eighty hours a week getting this place going." He tapped the counter with his index finger. "We had just settled in this building. It's twice the size of where your grandparents started out, okay? Double the responsibilities and opportunities for failure. Then we lost the Marios. Your mother was pretty young to have to deal with so much at one time. Life overwhelmed her. She needed more attention than I could give her, and her imagination got the best of her."

Luca slid him a suspicious glance. "Are you saying that Mom believed you messed around on her?"

"I told you, it was an aberration. There was an incident in my office. Remember, I was sleeping there for a few weeks to keep an eye on your aunt. At the same time, I was training new staff. Bigger place, more help. As you should know yourself, it's tricky trying to recreate the same intimate relationship you had in a small *ristorante* and carry it here. Anyway, someone took my open-door policy the wrong way. That's when your mother walked in."

Luca held up a hand to stop him. "Okay, I get it. You can quit now. Well, maybe except for one more clarification—are we talking about a blue-dress incident?"

"Knock it off! I'm still your father."

"And when I talk to Mom—and I will—I'd like to be able to support if not entirely defend you."

"It was a kiss, damn it, and not even a good one because the girl caught me off guard."

"How much off guard?"

"I was changing my shirt," Sal ground out. "As soon as it started, it was over, believe me because I ended it. But your mother, she was already heading out the door."

"You didn't go after her?"

"How could I? The safe was open. There was cash on the desk. But as soon as I got rid of the girl, and finished putting the deposit together, I detoured to the house. Only it was too late. She was already gone, and she took you with her. *La vendetta di una donna.*"

"The revenge of a woman," Luca said slowly. A heavy silence hung in the room as he processed the information. "And now?"

He'd asked the question the night he'd arrived, but Sal had lucked out and Valentina had saved him from having to answer. There was no such good fortune this morning. "Now, nothing."

"After all this time, you're telling me there was never anyone else?"

Sal looked everywhere but at his son. "I'm a man and your mother left *me.*"

"That's not what I—I'm talking relationships, Dad. Love."

Sal couldn't stand seeing his flesh-and-blood preparing to be disappointed in him. It was the only reason he was willing to confess what he'd shared with no one else. "If you must know, I've only been in love once—and that woman was your mother."

Luca purged a long breath. "I can't tell you how grateful I am to know that. I'd begun to doubt my own ability to have a meaningful relationship."

"I'm sorry you question yourself," Sal said. "Was it Miss San Francisco who busted your *coglioni?*"

"Me and my big mouth," Luca said, under his breath. "In a manner of speaking. Zarina Silver."

"Now why does that name sound familiar?"

"Because she's the daughter of Alexander Silver of Silver Enterprises," Luca replied.

"The guy whose name is on almost as many buildings as Trump." Sal whistled softly. "And you made it sound like the split was a simple matter of geographic incompatibility."

"I'm not a name dropper. Besides, it was a lose-lose proposition. Zarina's father really wanted me in New York for his newest hotel's premiere restaurant, but to keep his little girl happy, he would have arranged for me to settle nicely in San Francisco. Either way, though, I couldn't hack the idea of a wife leading me by a ring in my nose, and my father-in-law controlling what I could and couldn't serve."

Sal slid him a look of new respect. "You've been dealing with some high rollers. I feel like a johnboat fisherman anchored next to a yacht."

"Don't say that." Luca's sweeping gesture encompassed the entire building. "What you've created here is special. I know our family has had its problems, and there may be things we don't or won't agree on, but even after only a day here, I can see integrity. And there's no missing the respect and affection your clientele has for you."

Initially smiling with pleasure, Sal was soon pinching the bridge of his nose. "You'd better quit with the flattery. I haven't cried since we buried the Marios." That wasn't entirely the truth. In the privacy of his empty house and empty bed, he'd wept several times through the years with anger, fear, and finally pain for his lost marriage and parenthood.

"I'm grateful my opinion matters to you."

Nudged out of his dark thoughts, Sal shrugged. "Why wouldn't it? You're an accomplished man in your own right. Besides, you've heard the old saying, 'You're never a hero to your own family.' Compliments don't flow like wine around here, especially from your uncle."

Luca chuckled softly before growing serious again. "Dad . . . please try to consider something? Mom suffered, too."

"She made her bed," Sal snapped. "She damn well should writhe in it."

Swallowing the last of his drink, Luca noted, "You know, a shrink would probably say you have to feel something for someone to stay angry for so long."

"I do. I'd like to wring her neck."

Luca slid off his stool and carried the small cup and saucer to the machine, where he made himself a refill. "Then I guess it means nothing to you to know, I've been the only guy in Mom's life?"

"How would you know? You said yourself, you've been away from home since you were a teenager."

"I asked her, and have no reason to question what she told me."

"And I believe Valentina is going to stop going to church two and three times a day." Nevertheless, his conscience got the best of Sal and with bowed head he began to shuffle his feet. "You're not blowing smoke, are you? Your mother was a stunning woman, and I can't imagine her looking anything less than beautiful today."

"You're right, and she gets plenty of male attention. The fact remains, she's devoted to her work."

"Huh. You said she's a hospice nurse?"

Smiling proudly, Luca nodded. "I don't know how she does it. There's seldom any good news once a patient is accepted by those facilitators."

"I guess it's part of the reason she and Valentina were always so close. They have the same soft heart for suffering. Just not mine."

Luca rolled back his head and groaned toward the ceiling. "Enough already. I just gave you some encouraging news."

"What's so positive? Has she tried to contact me? Did that tender-hearted woman send me *one* school picture of my son? A crumb of news to feed my soul," Sal continued, pinching three fingers together as though holding something infinitesimal.

"You're hurt. I get that, but I don't believe your heart is stone cold. I saw the curiosity in your eyes when I informed you that Mom was still alone," Luca added a glint of light in his own eyes. "We're Italian for crying out loud. It's hard for us to contain all of our emotions, especially around each other."

Sal shrugged, but when he spoke, his voice was husky. "I was surprised, that's all."

"Have it your way," Luca told him. "I just want to say one more thing. If you want to talk about her, or anything else for that matter, I'm here. Also, you should understand anything you say to me stays confidential, unless you signal otherwise." He polished off the second drink faster than the first, and rubbed his hands together. "Now—what can I do to help you?"

"Rocco was going to come in early tomorrow to restock the bar. If you want to get started on that, I'll give him a call and let him know he can take his time. He'll be grateful, considering this week is going to be just as demanding. On top of the heavy tourist traffic, we have an engagement party, and something called a baby reveal celebration in the banquet room."

Luca nodded. "Yeah, having a party to share the baby's gender is a big deal these days. Let me wash up these dishes, and if you'll unlock the stockroom, I'll get to work."

"About that," Sal replied. "I'll just get you a whole set of keys to everything."

Luca paused midway to the bar's sink. "That wasn't a hint."

"I know. But think about it. Instead of stopping me every time you or someone else needs something, you can do it yourself. It'll start taking a load off."

"Well, I want you to know I appreciate the vote of confidence," Luca said, quietly. "That's a big deal."

Sal smiled. *"Avendoti a casa `e un grosso affare per me."*

"I get 'home...big affair for me,'" Luca said, trying to translate.

"Having you home is a big deal for me," Sal replied. He patted Luca's back. "We'll have you fluent in no time."

WITH LUCA TAKING care of things behind the bar, Sal was freed up to work in the office. He put together the Saturday deposit, then paid several invoices, which otherwise wouldn't get done until much later today if not tomorrow. It was a pleasure not to feel rushed. By the time he returned to the front, he found Luca was finished and studying the smaller wine inventory at the bar.

"Do you see room for improvement?" Sal asked.

"I don't know your clientele well enough to say. Those are good house brands, though, and on a hunch the moderately-priced wine list seems logical for the kind of traffic you get."

"Good." Sal brought out a smaller wine list and handed it to Luca. "These are the expensive vintages. We don't show it to everyone, since a pricey wine list could scare off more people than it attracts. Aside from Valentina and myself, Tony is the only other person to know when to offer that. But enough work for now. I'm hungry, how about you?"

Luca pressed a hand to his abdomen. "I thought it was my growling stomach that brought you out of your office."

"On Sundays, I like to check out different menus. There's a new food truck on Seawall Boulevard. I hear the fish tacos are a big hit. You game?"

"I could be. I had a nasty experience which just about cured me of ever trying them again, but if we're talking local fish fillets, I'm definitely interested."

After they did a small side-trip to drop the bag in the bank's night deposit drawer, and the bills at the post office, Sal drove to the seawall. Skateboarders and bike riders were in abundance, zipping between pedestrians and four-wheeled traffic.

Luca studied the hotels, restaurants, and souvenir shops with interest. "None of this is familiar to me."

"Well, you were so young when you left, and Galveston has changed quite a bit. I still miss The Balinese Room."

"That doesn't ring a bell, either."

"Probably because after surviving Hurricanes Carla and Alicia, Ike took it out in 2008," Sal explained. "But back in the '40s and '50s it was the Texas Atlantic City. The pier went out six hundred feet and all the big names came to perform—Sinatra, George Burns, the Marx Brothers. Your grandfather got to go once because the owners were Sicilian, and they had a dish request for a special party that supposedly he made better than anyone." Seeing Luca grin at him as though not certain whether to believe him or not, Sal said, "No lie."

"What was the dish?"

"*Pajata.*"

"No, that one escapes me."

"It's the intestines of a calf not yet weaned. You leave the chyme. During cooking, the heat coagulates everything helping to make a rich, creamy sauce. You cook it with stewed tomatoes and serve with rigatoni pasta."

"I think I could skip that one without any regret." Suddenly Luca snapped his fingers. "Wait a minute. The Balinese Room...that's where the margarita was said to be invented. The bartender was a big fan of Peggy Lee, who was headlining there."

"No one could ever prove the story. You should have seen it. It was this long Tiki house—with a shadow life. Hell, Houston oil barons came down, and not just for the shows. The place also ran an illegal gambling operation. I swear if nature didn't churn up a big enough storm to take down the place, some lawyer or politician would still be lying through their teeth to keep the enterprise going."

"Navigating the jungle," Luca replied. "Let's not ruin the day going down that path. Hey!" He pointed toward the ocean as a pelican dove straight into the sea. "That's it! That's what I remember."

"They don't have pelicans in Chesapeake Bay?"

"Not the redneck variety."

Sal was still grinning when they parked. A few spaces away was the yellow food truck adorned with comical pictures of aquatic life wearing sombreros. A line at least six deep stood waiting to order.

As they joined the group, Luca leaned toward his father and said quietly, "If you had shut the door in my face, I would have considered a venture like this."

Noticeably startled, Sal replied, "I don't know what throws me more—you thinking I would be so callous, or learning this type of business would draw you. It's pretty much a gypsy life."

"It's independence," Luca said with a shrug. "A modest overhead compared to leasing or purchasing—and definitely building a place. It also means you're free to move. You know location, location, location is the blessing and curse in business."

"Enough." Sal held up both hands like a traffic cop. "I was raised that a father hopes to have something to pass on to his children. You're my only heir. The restaurant will be yours if you want it."

This time Luca was the one looking astonished. "Dad, hold on. I didn't come here with my hand out. I came looking for a relationship with you. Getting to reconnect with Aunt Val and spending more time with Uncle Leo would be a bonus."

Once Luca was born, Sal had contemplated his life and evolved his perceptions and fantasies: he would teach his son everything he knew about the restaurant business from humbly washing dishes and sweeping floors, to how to maximize profit, but not at the expense of quality and service; how during summers he wouldn't just teach him about food, he would instill in him the pedagogy that separates a chef from a cook. As time passed and those designs turned into the bitter taste of dust in his mouth, Sal had struggled to keep caring. Simple pride was his sole companion, the satisfaction of a job well done had to be enough. Adding insult to injury, was Fate laughing at him as it presented a son who not only matched what he'd accomplished, but clearly could surpass anything beyond what Sal ever imagined?

"Well," Sal said, suddenly unsure of himself, "that's the way I feel, so it's there if you want it."

"Wow," Luca murmured softly.

Pleased and even daring to feel a seed of hope, Sal nudged him with his shoulder. There settled between them several minutes of peaceful introspection. By the time they had their food and were looking for a place to sit, they were joking about what Sal constituted as a traffic jam compared to what Luca told him about congestion in Washington, D.C.

With no tables around and all the benches already occupied, they settled on partaking their fare in the van. At least they had relief from the sun and the air conditioner to cool them off. Beyond the sidewalk railing was a drop to the beach, where bikini-clad beauties lay worshipping the sun, while men and boys played volleyball and Frisbee. The lifeguards had assumed their posts on their wooden towers, spending as much time eying any good-looking female that passed, as they watched the bathers romping in the water. Below them children were trying their hand at building sand castles. People with toddlers were running to and from the surf. From beyond the last seawall an ocean liner cruised out to sea.

"Now there's one thing I've never had the urge to do," Sal said.

"What? Be a sailor?"

"Okay, also. There must be no genetic links to Christopher Columbus in our DNA. But what I mean is the universal fascination with cruising as a vacation option. Though, I would like to see the country of my ancestors."

Swallowing a mouthful of taco, Luca asked, "Do we still have family there?"

"Cousins at the very least," Sal mused. "Maybe an aunt or uncle could still be hanging on. Ask Valentina. I sure haven't had time to dwell on the family tree."

"Aren't our people from the Tuscany area?"

"My part is from a little village near Greve."

"I'm not familiar with the name."

"It's in the heart of the province. Greve is south of Firenze, and north of Siena. It's where the Chianti Classico brand is produced. Did you notice the black rooster plate in the bar? It's their logo."

"Cool. So, it carries an even deeper meaning."

"There's a little more provenance to the rooster. These two knights were given rights over the land, and they were told to divide the area between them. It was agreed that when a rooster crowed at dawn, they should each start walking toward the other and when they met, that would be their land's boundary. So, the one smartass puts a rooster in a box and doesn't feed him the whole day. Come dark, the knight starts toward Siena with the box. When he gets within hearing distance of the city walls, he lets the rooster out of the box and it starts crowing. *Fini.* There's nothing to divide."

Luca laughed as he opened his bottled beer. "Mom never talked about our ancestry. She once said if it was such a great place, then why did the family leave?"

"The war," Sal said bluntly.

Luca murmured his agreement. "That may be why she would say, 'You're an American,' like nothing else mattered."

"I can't explain that," Sal replied. "Your grandparents would have told you anything you wanted to know. Both sets were well-versed in each other's lineage."

"Grandpa Jacques got sick when I was ten," Luca explained, "and I never saw him again after he was taken to the hospital. Grandmother Marie got really quiet after that, and wore black the rest of her life like Aunt Val does. I guess she missed Grandpa more than I could understand at the time. She died before I got to junior high. My uncles, Paulo and Antonio were always too busy to spend any time with me, so I didn't get much out of them, either, unless it had to do with their particular interests."

Sal scowled. "They should have seen to your education and future. A boy needs a man in his life."

With a sound of pleasure, Luca nodded at his food. "This is perfect. I'm glad you recommended we come here. The chipotle and adobo goes great with the seabass. And the extra crunch that comes with using Napa cabbage instead of lettuce is great."

"Quit changing the subject," Sal grumbled. However, he, too, bit eagerly into his taco. He'd chosen fried oysters with citrus salsa and avocado.

"Okay, to be fair, I wasn't the kind of nephew my uncles were expecting," Luca said. "Uncle Paulo always had his head under the hood of a car at his auto repair shop, and as a master carpenter, Uncle Tony was constantly booked up. To this day, Aunt Ginny complains she's married to the invisible man."

"I bet she doesn't complain that the money isn't invisible."

Shaking his head at his father's dogged negativity, Luca reminded him, "Don't forget, they had their own kids, too."

"I've heard enough. You don't need to make excuses for them. But while we're on the subject of your mother's family, how's her baby sister, Carmella?"

Luca's expression grew amused. "Aunt Carmella is raising her own village. They have six sons."

"Ha! If they were younger, we could have invited them down to meet Vinny's daughters. Who'd she marry? He'd better be a bank president or something that pays well."

"John is a pediatrician and loves kids as much as she does."

Mollified, Sal offered a crooked smile. "Then God bless them. So, what happened to your grandparents' place? The two times your mother and I managed to get up that way after they moved to be closer to the rest of the family, we saw that Jacques' grapevines were starting to look promising."

"The house burned down right after Grandma died. Mom and the rest of the family had no proof, but they suspected vagrants or drug dealers taking over the neighborhood. They sold the property after Gran's estate was probated."

"What a shame. Your grandparents brought a little of the old world with them, and now it's all gone."

As he watched his father finish his beer, stuffing the empty bottle and food wrappers back into the bag, Luca said, "I didn't mean to depress you."

"You can't stop the sand pouring through the hour glass."

"Speaking of... what are your plans for the rest of the afternoon? I'm free if you need help with anything."

Sal hooked a thumb over his shoulder. "I promised your uncle I'd stop by. He's been abrupt when I call. Leo demands physical proof that someone cares, so I have to make an appearance."

"Poor guy must be lonely."

"Which is why Fredo Busto gets a steady paycheck. If the board of health allowed dogs in the place, it would be a helluva lot cheaper to get Leo a four-legged buddy. God knows, even a Saint Bernard would eat less."

"I take it Leo's not missed much work?" Luca asked. "I mean except for the time after the accident."

"Second only to me."

"Then if you don't mind, I'd like to tag along."

"I'd be grateful. Maybe that way Leo won't gnaw me raw." He watched as his son bagged his remains, as well. "Afterwards, I'm heading over to *Romo Italia*. You might enjoy that."

Luca hesitated. "More food? Why didn't you tell me sooner? I wouldn't have ordered the grande size taco."

"Relax. We'll eat, but not until evening. By then you'll be hungry, believe me. We have a standing game of bocce there," Sal explained. "I'm guessing you don't play?"

"Nothing beyond knowing how to spell it."

"So, today you'll learn. Go toss these bags in the trash bin. If we're stopped, we don't need to get into trouble for the open container law."

IT PROVED TO be a full and lively day. There were three permanent bocce courts built behind the restaurant, surrounded by umbrella-covered tables and park benches, all of it fenced to keep out both two and four-legged trespassers. Luca also learned the game wasn't exclusive to men. Women and children had a court, too, although it was also used during mixed couples' matches. While not a physical game, adults often acted decades younger than their age as they strategized and cheered during a competition.

"I wish Uncle Leo could have come with us," Luca said, less than an hour into playing. Having finished his turn on the first court, he collapsed into a chair and accepted the bottle of cold water his father pushed toward him.

Sal shrugged. "He may sound like his cantankerous old self, but the doctors want him to stay off his feet and see what things look like once the swelling goes down. What could we do?"

"Tiny seemed game for a change of scenery."

"He has the same expression when he's hungry."

For the moment, there was only the two of them at the table and Luca leaned forward to ask quietly, "I've been meaning to ask. Has there ever been anyone for Uncle Leo?"

"Lisabetta Tuscano. Lovely girl, good family, but then there was the accident and . . . Leo refused to see her. It was the worst part of his self-destructive period."

"What happened?"

"Her parents took her on a trip to cheer her up. She met and married a California winemaker."

"And that was it? Ever?"

"You saw him. Who wants to keep company with such a sour-puss?" Sal's team called to him to return to the field. Pushing himself to his feet, his mood lightened and he grinned at his son. "Prepare to pay up. Your team is about to lose."

AS THE AFTERNOON waned and evening approached, a considerable group of family and friends arrived to cheer on the players. Lights strung around the yard were turned on. At first merely cosmetic, adding to the festive atmosphere; by dusk, they were necessary to complete the game. As the last balls were played, the final points would have been impossible to determine without the added illumination. Sal came out on top with the highest score, and his team won the tournament. Beer and wine glasses were lifted and the toasts were poetic, awarding Luca a gratifying glimpse of his father's position in the community.

"To our brother Salvatore," Dominic Tomei said, speaking last. "You've also been such an uncle and godfather to all of the youngsters, and we salute you as your own son returns. Now I invited everyone to come over to *Dominic's Real Sicilian Pizza*. Let's party!"

Luca had enjoyed watching his father with the kids. He was a natural teacher, tender and playful with the youngest, while patiently instructional with the older ones. As everyone began to disperse, Luca couldn't resist teasing his dad. "So, Godfather, is there going to be a backroom processional at Dom's where we'll all be expected to kiss your hand as a sign of allegiance?"

"You're laughing now," Sal drawled. "What you don't know is they're schmoozing me because every mother and father with a daughter of marriageable age has been sizing you up all day. You'll be lucky to get two bites of pizza down your gullet before the matchmaking hints start dropping like baseball-size hail."

Holding back, Luca glanced yearningly toward the van. "Any chance I can plead heatstroke and get you to drive me back to Aunt Val's?"

"Not one. I can't tell you how many weddings I've sat through, envying the fathers of the brides and grooms. Now here you are like the golden calf, and that's before anyone even knows you turned down Alexander Silver and marriage to his daughter."

"Dad, so help me," Luca began, a queasy feeling growing inside. "I told you that in confidence."

"My lips are sealed."

DESPITE KNOWING THAT tomorrow was a workday, no one seemed in a hurry to end the day. Each of the Italian eateries in the area took their turn hosting a dinner after a tournament, and with it being Dominic's turn, the group only had to walk a few doors down the street to where Dom's staff was well into preparations.

As they navigated their way around the crowded room, Luca noticed a big gallon-size jar on the counter by the cash register with a slot to slip in money. The men paused to make their donation, and Luca realized it was to help cover the cost of food, beverages, and to pay for the staff working extra hours.

"Smart idea," he said to his father. He followed his lead and drew out a crisp twenty. "I wondered how you all handled this."

"No one knows what entertaining costs better than we do," Sal replied. "Besides, we're family and this is one of our traditions we don't want to lose. Usually a couple of the priests from Saint Mary's join us, but I heard they were tied up with a few baptisms and a funeral today."

After that there was little chance to get a private word due to people wanting to meet Luca. Overall, he didn't mind; during the tournament, everyone had been relaxed and friendly, but now he felt like a prize piece on a chessboard with moves running out. It was a relief when his father drew him to where they were to sit.

The square tables were slid into one long line across the room. A shorter row was placed by the window for the children. As the day's champion, Sal was expected to sit at the head of the table with host Dominic and family. Naturally, Luca was directed to take the seat beside him.

More wine and beer were served, and soon an assortment of large pizzas was brought out in a procession from the back of the kitchen. Placed down the middle of the makeshift banquet table, they reached from one end to the other.

Dorotea Ecco, wife of Claudio, had been introduced to Luca hours ago when the two men played on the same team. Seated across from one another, it was difficult for him to miss her surreptitious glances, or the secretive smile curving her mouth. It didn't escape her husband's notice, either. About to finish his second slice from the mushroom and pepperoni pie, he dropped it onto his plate.

"What is it with this flirting, *mia*. We may be married twenty-six years, but I still have a few jealous bones in my body."

The attractive woman in the print sundress that flattered her tan and gently rounded figure, leaned into him to chide softly. "Silly man. You know I was thinking of our Jessica."

"Just checking." Claudio winked conspiratorially at Sal.

"Forgive me if I embarrassed you," Dorotea told Luca. "Jessica is our eldest, a teacher. Of all times to be on a field trip to Austin with some of her students. I would love to introduce you to her some-time—unless you're already involved?"

"Believe me, I'm flattered."

It was easy for Luca to speak with complete sincerity considering that a schoolteacher was an improvement over the introduction he'd endured earlier. Seated only a few people down, the mortician and his wife were hanging on his every word hoping for another chance to mention their daughter. "She's licensed herself, and will take over the business," they'd shared proudly. "What a perfect match, eh? We could handle the funerals, followed by receptions at *Vita e Spezie*. Keep it all in the family."

With that unpalatable offer still haunting him, Luca continued, "But as it happens, there is someone."

Sal's head whipped around. "There is?"

"Somewhat."

"What kind of relationship is 'somewhat?'" Claudio demanded with mock scorn.

Reaching for his wine, Sal said, "Exactly what I was thinking."

"Meaning new and—fragile," Luca said, with another apologetic smile toward Dorotea.

"Sweet," she crooned, before squeezing her husband's arm. "Now that's respect. He's already considerate and protective of the girl's feelings." To Luca she added, "Well, if anything changes, please let me know."

BY THE TIME Sal and Luca were in the van heading back to the restaurant, Sal wasted no time in returning their conversation to the subject Claudio's wife had broached. "So, what was that all about?"

Aware of his father's intense scrutiny, Luca bought himself some time by pretending to misunderstand. "Taking your keys? You had more to drink than I did, even if it is only a few blocks." He turned onto the street, and at the next traffic light pulled up beside a patrol car. "See?"

Sal waved to the grinning officers, and replied, "Are you kidding? I keep those two in meatball sandwiches. Believe me, my mind is working fine. I'm talking about the way you answered Dorotea when she tried to hook you up with Jessie—who, by the way, is a cute little number. Smart, too. I would be proud to have her as a daughter-in-law."

Luca shook his head. "I only got here, remember? The timing is all wrong to try to juggle a new job *and* a new relationship."

"That's right. But that's not what you said."

"I had to say something to stop what was going on." The light turned green and Luca was relieved when the patrol car moved on, and he could ease into their lane preparing to turn at the next block.

"As long as that's all," Sal said. "Because the only person you've had time to meet so far is N'awlins, and you know I don't want you starting anything there."

"There are the waitresses," Luca added, prompted by an emotion he couldn't begin to explain.

"Get real," Sal muttered. "You're no more a cradle snatcher than I am."

"You're starting to slur your words."

"I am a bit tired. All that sun. It was a long day, but one of the best ever." Sal reached over and gripped his shoulder. "You had a lot to do with that."

"I'm glad you think so." Luca pulled into the restaurant's parking lot and shut down the van. Releasing his seatbelt, he considered his father. "I also think, instead of you risking the drive home, it would be a good idea if we crashed in your office. You can sleep on the couch, and I'll take the chair."

A goofy smile spread over Sal's face. "You're worried about your old man." In playful, slow motion, Sal pressed his fist into his son's arm. "I like that. It'll be like a campout we never had."

"Oh, brother," Luca sighed.

DAYLIGHT WAS BARELY brightening the high, barred window when Sal and Luca were awakened by a commotion outside, followed by angry pounding on the door. Father and son exchanged bleary-eyed glances before scrambling to their feet and hurrying down the hall.

Despite the security mechanisms, Sal still kept a steel bar across the back door when they were working late or if he was spending the night. Punching the code on the wall pad, he opened the door to find an aggravated Leo, a guilty-looking Tiny, and an abashed Olivia standing there.

"What the hell, now you're barricading the place to keep *me* out?" Leo demanded.

"Yeah, everything is always about you." Checking his watch, Sal added, "You know I don't trust electronics. And since we spent the night here—wait a minute." He quickly rubbed a hand over his face, willing away the last of his lethargy. "You're supposed to be in the hospital." He looked past them to Olivia. "And you're forty-five minutes early."

"I sold out of quite a bit, remember?" Olivia was apologetic as her gaze darted between father and son. "If I waited until the usual time, I wouldn't get done before the lunch crowd. When I saw both of your cars here, I assumed it was okay. Then...they pulled in beside me."

"We thought we could beat her here."

It was a moot point whether it was Tiny's admission, or his almost girlish giggle that earned him an elbow in his side from Leo. He immediately deflated and ducked into himself.

"I repeat," Sal said to his brother, "what are you doing out of the hospital?"

"Saving the insurance company, and us, money. I'm tired of being a pin cushion and donating blood. For what? So, I got dressed, used Tiny as a decoy, and slipped out."

"Well, whatever you had planned for here isn't going to happen," Sal declared. "Olivia, come in. You two go home."

Since Olivia was blocked by the two men in front of her, she stayed put. Leo and Tiny didn't budge, either.

"I have every bit as much right to be here as you do, Salvatore." Swelled up like a blowfish, Leo faced down his brother.

"Oh, this is so wrong." Olivia started to back away. "I don't need to work in such negative energy."

"Don't take another step," Sal ordered before addressing his younger brother. "Yes, you have rights—but not when you're a danger to have around, and can't work at the speed and capacity needed."

"I'll manage. I always do."

"I'm serious, Leo. This is for your own good. You want a cup of coffee, you're welcome, but on the rest, I'm firm."

"Bah! You'll be lucky if I ever cross this threshold again," Leo groused. "Come on, Tiny. Let's get out of here."

Olivia pressed against the building to make room for them to pass. When she finally entered the restaurant, she met Luca's sympathetic gaze. "I feel so badly about this."

"Don't. Dad will handle everything."

Sal shut the door. "He's right, N'awlins. This is long overdue. Don't give it another thought. You go get started while we clean up. It was a late night and we had to crash in the office. The security system is off, so don't unlock the door again unless you recognize who's on the other side."

"I'm only heading upstairs, so I'll be back pretty quick," Luca assured her, as his father went to grab his keys and wallet. "If you'd start a pot of coffee, I would appreciate it."

"You look like you could use a whole one by yourself."

"And here I was going to compliment you by saying you look as fresh as a morning glory."

As promised, Sal returned quickly from his office and they both departed with Luca whistling a familiar, romantic tune that had Olivia blushing before she could lock up behind them.

She slumped against the solid door. Heat tempted her to unbutton her chef's jacket for quicker relief, although she only wore a thin white tank top beneath it. Perspiration dampened her forehead, back, and chest. As for her heart, it pounded as though she'd run from Tempest's house. She hadn't, of course; once again using her car—and not only due to the latest supplies she'd picked up yesterday.

"And this job was supposed to be the smart choice to keep my mind off my problems?" she whispered.

The Angeloni family was proving more high maintenance than first anticipated, and Luca was getting under her defenses too easily. It wouldn't do. She was scheduled for an appointment next week to see if she would be approved to join a medical study group. Somehow, she had to stay balanced, even if things spiraled out of control around her. Along with that pep talk, she began the deep breathing exercises meant to stabilize her condition. Once the symptoms subsided, she carried her bags to the nearest prep table, and wet a paper towel to cool her face and throat.

Outside, a street sweeper passed, and in back a garbage truck came to empty the restaurant's metal industrial-size container. The sound effects didn't remotely resemble the melodic sounds of sea and surf; yet they represented normalcy, welcome in its own way. With a last, deep breath, she tossed the wet sheet into the trash and started a pot of coffee as Luca had requested.

Once she heard the machine gurgling as it spewed fresh brew into the glass pot, she picked up her bags and carried them to her part of the kitchen. She unpacked the fresh berries and put them into the refrigerator, spices particular to her recipes into their racks. That task completed, she collected the pans and ingredients she needed for the new supply of Doberge.

Working with a satisfying focus, she was pouring batter into four pans when she heard the click of the deadbolt at the back door. Hoping it was Sal, she slid the pans into the convection oven before turning to greet her boss.

Her welcoming smile waned. She'd been foolish to hope wherever Sal lived, it was close enough to beat a man half his age down one flight of stairs. With his wet hair and T-shirt clinging to his body, she wondered if Luca had taken the time to towel off before racing back?

"Worried about what I was getting into all by my lonesome?" she asked.

"Nope." Luca went straight for the coffee machine. "Aunt Val is at church, so I didn't have to wait for the bathroom."

He carried his mug to her workstation. "Want one of these?"

"Thanks, but I had some green tea earlier."

"It looks as though you've been keeping a killer pace since I ran upstairs. Your cheeks are pinker than ever."

And he knew exactly why, so Olivia disregarded his bogus observation. But there was no ignoring the subtle waft of deodorant soap emanating from him, or that he looked more fit than ninety percent of chefs she'd ever met.

"Please go away, Luca."

"I don't want to. This is borrowed time. In a few minutes, it'll become a beehive again. And my father will shoot visual daggers at me if he sees me anywhere near you."

"He's a smart man. And our boss."

"I respect that. Except where you're concerned."

Her mind going blank, Olivia had to check the list she'd drawn up last night as to what she should do and in what order. Determined to change the direction of their conversation, she asked, "So, you and your dad had a big time yesterday? I'm just going by the bloodshot eyes and the *eau de* brew wafting around you two when you opened the door."

"I was in my first bocce tournament."

She raised both eyebrows. Who would possibly lie about such a thing? "You play?"

"Dad won."

Olivia couldn't completely repress a smile. "Is it difficult?"

"Rather like marbles, but with bigger balls." As soon as he spoke, Luca uttered an oath. "Excuse me. Caffeine deficiency. Not that I jump through hoops on behalf of the PC police. I only—oh, crap."

Olivia had been collecting the ingredients for the cheesecakes, and couldn't help feeling sympathetic for his verbal contortions. "I bet he was beside himself getting to show you off."

Luca held up his mug. "There were toasts. Many toasts. Which is why we crashed here for the night."

"Someone was still thinking clearly." Olivia felt her wall of resistance suffer another few cracks. "I'm sure you felt badly for denying your aunt your company—"

He gave her a guilty look. "The truth? It was a relief to escape spending another night on her couch."

Giving in to an obvious need, he massaged his sore back, which had Olivia suggesting, "No doubt your father will invite you to his place, if he hasn't already. Does he live far away?"

"I have no idea."

Olivia tapped her wrist where a watch would have been. "You've been here three days and you still don't know where your father lives? Here I was convinced you Italians were as bad as Cajuns about being in each other's business."

"Dad likes me keeping an eye on Aunt Val, so the subject hasn't come up yet. Even if it does, I don't think it would be wise for us to spend too much time together. Everyone needs their space."

"Can't fault you there."

About to finish off his first dose of caffeine, Luca paused with the mug inches from his lips. "Didn't you say you'd moved to some quaint boarding house? Are there any other rooms available?"

7

THE MOUND OF SWEET POTATOES PILED BEFORE OLIVIA
vanished before her eyes. All she saw was Luca Angeloni emerging
from the single bathroom at the end of the hall at Tempest's boarding
house wearing nothing but a towel around his waist. A distraction she
didn't need, and couldn't allow.

Mentioning the place had been an accident. Since then, she'd convinced herself of how he was too sophisticated with an appetite for
the good life to be satisfied with anything so—did he quote her as
saying "quaint?" She would never use the word "quaint" in relation to
anything about Sister Tempest Fleuraugust.

"I—uh," she began.

"Forgot where you live?"

She slid him a warning glance. "Wouldn't you prefer something...more?"

"More will have to wait."

Another thing about the man was how he refused to say anything
to her without it having a double meaning. "I don't know if Tempest
would be interested in a short-term boarder."

"Heartening news," Luca replied smoothly. "I mean about you assuring her of intending to stay in Galveston."

He was tying her in knots. Thankfully, a reprieve came in the form
of Valentina rushing in from the back, breathless and concerned. "Olivia, thank goodness you're here." Dressed in yet another black ensem-

ble, she wound her way around the work stations until she could grasp the younger woman's shoulder. "Would you believe I was through an Our Father and started a Hail Mary when it struck me? You don't know about Wednesday or Friday."

Putting a steadying arm around his aunt, Luca said to Olivia, "I'll bet this has to do with either the engagement party or the baby reveal. I've seen the schedule."

Both women stared at him in disbelief, and said in unison, "You know about baby reveals?"

"Life in the Beltway isn't entirely insular."

Olivia refocused on Valentina. "Which one is on Wednesday?"

"The baby reveal. I made the reservation and my notes are in my book in Sal's office. I'll get it for you."

Drawing her to a stool, Luca urged her to sit down. "Tell me what it looks like? I'll get it. Aside from needing to catch your breath, you're as white as Olivia's chef's jacket, and your hands are clammy."

Valentina didn't argue. "It's the red leather binder sitting on top of the in-box."

Nodding, Luca said, "I recall seeing it. Be right back."

As he left, Olivia put down her paring knife. Luca was right; Valentina didn't look well at all. "Can I get you something? You shouldn't have rushed. I'm afraid you got overheated."

"I'll be fine."

"Well, please don't worry about the events. There's plenty of time to handle whatever is needed for both parties."

"What can I say? I'm used to Leo keeping up with his side of things. However, with him in the hospital, it slipped my mind."

"Oh, dear. You don't know," Olivia said. Seeing Valentina's confusion, she added, "He's out."

"They let him go?"

"Not even close."

Valentina closed her eyes. She looked like she was about to slip off the stool, prompting Olivia to put a bracing arm around her shoulders. "Luca! We need you!"

"Don't make a fuss, really," Valentina entreated. "I was only startled by Leo's actions. Whatever possessed him?"

"He doesn't like hospitals."

"Who does?"

Gratified by her gentle sarcasm, Olivia said, "Please let me get you something cool to drink—water?"

"I'm afraid it would be too raw on my stomach. There's some pomegranate juice in the same cooler," Valentina said. "Maybe a little glass will revive me."

"Excellent idea. Hang on." Before she finished pouring, Luca returned.

"What's happening?"

"I told her about Leo. I thought she was going to faint." Olivia held the glass, until she was assured Valentina could hold it. As soon as her hand was free, Olivia touched her forehead. "I think you have a fever. Let me check for..." She gently pinched the skin on the back of Valentina's hands and to her dismay, it stayed puckered. "It's as I feared, you're dehydrated."

"Leo is the one who needs to be checked on," Valentina insisted.

"Tiny is with him at Uncle Leo's place," Luca assured her. "Drink, Aunt Val. Dad will be back any minute, and if he sees you in this condition, he'll send *you* to the hospital."

The warning was enough to make Valentina comply. In the meantime, Olivia got a fresh paper towel, wet it with cold water, and held it to the breathless woman's forehead.

"Did you get any rest?" Luca asked.

"Of course. But I don't need as much sleep as some."

Luca and Olivia exchanged glances. He gave her the subtlest shake of his head before handing over the book.

Taking the hint, Olivia let Valentina cool herself with the towelette and paged through the planner until she found the applicable entry, "About this baby reveal, how many guests are we to plan for? Here it is—approximately thirty."

"Denise couldn't be sure. She said some of the invited may be out of town for one reason or another. As for the specifics, you'll see her doctor told me the Thompsons are having twins, one of each. The couple signed a release so the obstetrician could share the information with me."

Olivia smiled. "How perfect!"

"In the future," Valentina told her, "feel free to check that on your own, in case my memory fails me again. Or maybe you should start handling these kinds of calls."

"If it would help you," Olivia said, a bit surprised at her willingness to delegate something so important. After all, there were more arrangements involved than a cake. "Perhaps Luca should be the one to take this on, since it's the entire restaurant's reputation at stake."

"I see what you mean," he replied. "I'll check with Dad, but I'm sure he'll agree you and I need to make this a team effort."

"Goodness, your handwriting is gorgeous, Valentina," Olivia declared too brightly. "And what detail. Luca have you seen this? 'Customer for twenty years. Customer for ten years. Cousin to Councilman John Porter. Bride's colors are lilac and ivory. Work this anniversary party around their song, *I've Got You Under My Skin.*' You've made things as easy and clear as possible for Chefs Leo and Vinny."

Luca shifted closer until they were touching shoulder to elbow. "The social secretary at the White House couldn't have done a better job. You're invaluable, Aunt Val."

"Everybody is replaceable," she replied, with a sad smile. She set her half-empty glass and the paper towel on the table. "I'm going to leave you young people to your work and return to my apartment to rest a bit before I'm needed back here."

"Hold on," Luca said. "Maybe you should sit out today's lunch service, as well. We've got this."

"One little glass of juice can't have resolved your hydration problem," Olivia pointed out.

"I wouldn't mind the extra time, and Mondays can be less busy, as far as the dining room is concerned." Speaking as though trying to talk herself into the idea, Valentina pushed herself to her feet and kissed Luca's cheek. "Could I inconvenience you a moment longer to help your pathetic aunt upstairs?"

"If you didn't ask, I'd insist," he told her. "Provided you stop insulting yourself. Back in a flash, Livie."

As good as his word, he returned in five minutes; however, his expression was devoid of the humor and lightness he'd exhibited when talking to his aunt. Olivia paused as she rinsed the peeled sweet potatoes, momentarily shutting off the water so she could hear what he had to say.

"Tell me you don't buy what she's selling?" he asked.

"No," she admitted slowly. "It really doesn't seem to be merely a case of heat exhaustion. There are degrees of fatigue, though, and your family and the rest of the staff have been keeping a demanding schedule. Then again, she's the only one near collapse."

"Except for Uncle Leo," Luca reminded her.

"He's accident prone."

"Or something."

Olivia stepped back as he lifted the heavy pot of potatoes and carried it to the stove, where he proceeded to turn on one of the back, gas burners. Something was nagging at him, and it overrode her impulse—unwise as it would be health-wise—to insist she could manage the task by herself. Against her better judgment, she asked, "What are you trying to say?"

"I learned something yesterday. It seems to explain everything going on here."

"Well, please don't tell me. I learned something, too, and I wish I didn't."

Luca stared. "Why not?"

"Because it's none of my business, and . . . it's too sad."

Frowning, Luca's tone held challenge. "Are you the same person who showed so much compassion for that troubled family on Saturday night? Is it easier to care about strangers because once they're out the door you can forget about them?"

He made her sound awful. "That's a horrible thing to say! You might want to consider how everyone carries baggage, Luca, even if we don't appear to be in the shape of your aunt and uncle."

This time he was the one to look stricken. "I'm sorry. I can't believe I said that. Given the pace of business and added responsibilities Aunt Val's absence will put on you, you must be worried about suffering a relapse."

It would have been so easy to let him think he'd guessed correctly—although, in a way, he wasn't far off—but Olivia was dealing with enough deception. "Oh, Luca, that's not it. Yesterday, I discovered Valentina isn't just a widow. She lost her only child."

He sighed heavily. "It gets even worse. Uncle Leo was driving the truck."

She pressed a hand to her mouth to keep in a sound of anguish. How on earth had the poor woman survived such a thing, let alone continue to function as well as she did? And suddenly, Leo's behavior, unpleasant as it was, made more sense. "Dear God. This isn't a restaurant, it's an Italian opera."

Luca murmured his agreement. "And you only know half the story. My mother left my father thinking he was having an affair. To punish him, she kept me from him. Later, I stayed away thinking he didn't want me."

"How awful for you." Olivia bit at her lower lip against impulses, but made herself ask, "Was it true? About the affair?"

"I hope I'm enough of a judge of character to say, I don't think so."

She drew in and expunged a deep breath. "At least that's something."

"Except for fighting residual anger toward my mother for not being honest with me. And some bitterness toward Aunt Val, since she would come visit us in Houston and kept my mother's secret."

Trying to stay in motion, which saved her eye contact, Olivia salted the water in the pot. "Especially if she'd already lost her husband and son." Even though Valentina knew Luca was safe and thriving, where was the empathy for her brother's suffering?

"Bullseye. We left only weeks after the accident. Mario Junior and I were both five."

Regardless of his tough pose, with his bare arms crossed over his chest, Olivia didn't think twice about offering comfort; in this case, resting her hand on his forearm. "I'm so sorry. I've read whether they mean to or not, parents damage their children. I guess close relatives do, too."

"It helps having you to talk to."

Alarms went off inside Olivia. His voice reflected vulnerability, his gaze desire. Contrasted against his strong arm, dusted with slightly rough hair, and mixed with sinewy muscle, Olivia's resolve shifted into crisis mode. She had to be the strong one, the one to disengage and keep things professional.

Returning to sweep potato peelings into the trash, she said, "Dare I hope you made sure your aunt has more juice or something by her bed?"

"I did, and saw that she drank a little more before I left. Excuse me."

He went to the back, but not before Olivia caught the wry twist of his lips and disappointment dulling his eyes. She knew he wanted to linger in the cocoon of intimacy that had settled between them. However, someone was going to arrive at any moment, and one of them had to keep things from going too far.

When he returned, Luca was slipping into a chef's coat. As he buttoned it, he stopped beside her to check the notes again. "What do you think of this extra work?" he asked, sounding as though the last few minutes hadn't occurred.

"It will be my first reveal for twins. I'd really like to go with a pink and blue glaze. Then it'll create all the more excitement for the expectant parents to cut into the cake only to see more pink and blue. I also have some gingerbread man cookie cutters. I could place the cookies onto the sides of the cake in alternate colors with question marks drawn in white or yellow frosting. Another cute idea would be cupcakes surrounding the main cake, alternating with pink or blue frosting."

"You lit up when Aunt Val said there would be twins. You really like kids."

"I'd better. I have a whole passel of nieces and nephews back in Louisiana."

"Has it triggered an itch to have a couple of your own?" Luca asked.

Grateful his tone was lighter again, she drawled with mock warning, "My itches are none of your business, Angeloni. You're lucky I'm not the kind of female with a knee-jerk tendency toward sexual harassment lawsuits."

"I wouldn't have said anything if I didn't sense a kindred spirit. Me, I like the idea of a 'passel.' As an only child, I was envious of my friends who came from big families."

The way he slipped so easily from amused to wistful made her heart ache. "I feel sorry for the lonely, little boy you were."

"Not the lonely big boy?"

"Him, too. But now you have your father," she said with a gentle smile, "and I think you're going to be just fine."

The back door opened again. This time an agitated Sal strode in blustering into his Smartphone. "All right, all right, I get it. Do what you can." Disconnecting from the call, he slammed the door shut with his right foot. "Can you believe it? The sun is barely over the horizon and already crap is hitting the fan."

"What's happened?" Luca asked, as his father drew nearer.

"Andi just called. She's come down with a stomach virus."

Unfamiliar with the name, Olivia asked, "Who's that?"

"You haven't met her yet," Sal replied. "She and Janine do tag-team hostessing during the week. The rest of the time Andi is a nursing student and interning in the pediatric wing at John Sealy Hospital. Damn it, I knew that giant incubator for germs was going to cause us headaches. Don't tell Vinny I said that. From day one, he told me, 'Don't hire her!'"

As soon as the words were out, he grimaced and sent Olivia a sheepish look. "I know that sounds cold, but she and Janine are friends outside of work, too, and all we need is for Janine to show signs she's coming down with this, and I guarantee there'll be a domino effect running through this place. We'll be lucky if we don't have to shut down for a day or two."

Luca and Olivia exchanged worried glances. Could it be they had an answer to the mystery of Valentina's condition?

"Dad," Luca began, "Maybe that's already happening. Aunt Val was here a while ago and I took her upstairs."

"She's sick, too?"

"We can't be sure, but she hurried from church, upset to have forgotten two events scheduled for this week. Olivia was certain she was running a fever."

"And dehydrated," Olivia said. "If Luca hadn't been here to convince her to go upstairs, I'm sure she would have fainted."

Sal rubbed at his freshly-shaved jaw. "I'll call her in a minute. Jeez, we've never had the whole hostess team wiped out before."

"You have me, Dad," Luca reminded him. "If you want me to handle seating, we can run over the dining room chart before lunch."

Before Sal could reply, Vinny arrived with Benny right behind him. Sal held up his hand, stopping them in their tracks.

"Either one of you feeling under the weather?"

"It's Monday," a sleepy-eyed Vinny said with a shrug. "A cup of coffee will help." It was characteristic of the head chef to thoughtfully tiptoe out of the house with shoes in hand, without taking time for a dose of caffeine in order for his wife and girls to sleep.

"I had my coke and peanuts on the way over here, boss," Ben replied. "I'm pumped."

Sal grimaced. "How many times do I have to tell you not to drink soft drinks? You're killing your taste buds and ruining your stomach ingesting that garbage."

"I'm weaning myself," the young sou chef assured him. "I'm down to indulging only on Saturdays and Mondays when I need the energy the most."

"Who's sick?" Vinny asked Sal.

"Andi."

"I told you not to hire a nurse."

Sal merely turned to Luca and Olivia with a "See what I mean," look.

Oblivious to the exchange, Vinny went into his spiel. "They got more sanitized soap, rubbing alcohol, and bleach in those hospitals, but every time I talk to someone who's just been released from one, they have an infection and need antibiotics. Right, Sal? They cure the disease, but the remedy might kill you!"

Sal signaled him to drop the matter. "What do you want me to do, put a sign in the window? We get a lot of business from our medical centers. Zip it. Just check your crew and the rest of the staff, as they arrive. Anyone looking green around the gills, send them home. I gotta go before you complain today's fish looks more like bait and chum."

In total, only one waiter called in sick, and the lunch service ran smoothly, as did dinner, despite Sal giving Valentina firm instructions not to consider coming down again before tomorrow. Luca handled the host position, backed up by Sal and Tony, when two larger groups arrived without reservations. Considering all of the bad news lately, no one could have asked for more.

TUESDAY WAS ALMOST a repeat, except the waiter was back on the job giving Sal the idea his absence was more about a hangover, than any bug going around. However, both of their younger hostesses remained ill. Valentina insisted she was feeling strong enough to do the dinner service; nevertheless, Sal remained adamant. He told her she needed to be at her best for the baby reveal event the following day.

"You're not punishing me because I kept in touch with Rosa and Luca, are you?" she asked, when he came up to the patio for the day's herbs for the kitchen.

Through the years, her green thumb had saved them a small fortune. The raised beds along the wood railings were lush with basil, parsley, rosemary, chives, oregano, lemon grass, and mint. In happier times, the two of them would sit up there after the restaurant closed to enjoy a nightcap, and breathe in the intoxicating scents mixing so enticingly with the sea air. However, those days might be over.

While he couldn't bring himself to make eye contact, Sal replied somberly, "No. But I'm not ready to discuss the matter."

"I understand, brother," she said. "Let me simply tell you that what I did, I did for completely selfish reasons and in doing that, I didn't choose sides. I love you and Rosa too much and always will."

HARMONY RETURNED ON Wednesday. While Valentina missed the lunch service to assist Tiny in getting Leo to the hospital for the tests his doctor wanted, she was there for the evening. Like the fresh flower arrangement in the entryway, *Vita e Spezie* was aglow with ambiance, the staff in full cooperation, and the diners reacting to the positive vibrations. The hum of steady conversation, seasoned with laughter left Sal and Valentina beaming as they made their rounds through the room. Their pace remained as relaxed as the Perry Como arrangement playing in the bar and lounge.

As Sal came up to a long-time customer's table, the man lifted his wine glass to him. "Salvatore, I have to say I've been bringing my family here since the first week after you moved in. I don't think we've had a better time. What's different?"

Sal shook hands with the big-deal concrete contractor from Houston. "You honor me, Carmine. It's just a little finessing here and there brought on by my son joining us, as well as pastry chef Olivia Dumont."

"What did you do with Leo? I can't see him taking the competition well."

"He didn't have much choice," Sal replied with brotherly sympathy. "He suffered a mishap that looks like it's going to force him to finally have the hip surgery he's been avoiding for years."

"That's a shame. I wish him the best. But I have to say his replacement improves the view in the kitchen a thousand percent."

"We've hit the motherlode with N'awlins. She bakes as well as she looks. Make sure you leave room for dessert."

Valentina eased behind Sal and stopped where another familiar couple was obviously celebrating something special with their oldest son and his date. Their half-eaten meals triggered her concern. "Do we need several to-go boxes here? Charlie, are you attending something special and have to leave early?"

"Yes, please, for the boxes, but no, we're not in a rush. We're celebrating and wanted to be sure we left room for champagne and dessert." He gestured behind them. "I couldn't help but overhear about Leo. He could always be relied upon to put a little something extra with our desserts for a birthday or an anniversary."

"I can assure you, Olivia won't disappoint you."

Charlie Barnett looked meaningfully at his son and the pretty brunette beside him. "Charlie Junior and Melissa got engaged this evening."

As the bride-to-be extended her hand to exhibit a sparkling diamond solitaire, Valentina murmured her admiration. "It's lovely, and I'm so happy for you both. You two have looked perfect for each other since the first time you came in together."

She turned back to the electrical contractor, who had done all the work in *Vita e Spezie*. "Would you like to look at the dessert menu, or have us surprise you?"

Alecia Barnett leaned toward her husband. "Let's let them choose for us."

"The boss has spoken," Charlie said. "We'll leave it to you, Valentina."

Once in the kitchen, Valentina directed Kat to deliver to-go boxes to the Barnett table. "But don't prepare a bill yet. They're having dessert and champagne. Give them the wine menu to choose from." Continuing on to the other side of the kitchen, she came upon Luca and Olivia in an animated conversation.

"I get the visuals of the swans on creamy gelato," Luca said, "but that puffed pastry will get soggy in no time."

With a confident look, Olivia replied, "These are for the kids at table nine. They'll be gone seconds after Tony sets the plates on the table."

"That looks charming," Valentina said. "Now I have another challenge for you. The Barnetts at table seven have just announced an engagement. They want something memorable to match the occasion."

"*Lagniappe!*

"And that is?" Luca asked.

"It's a Cajun expression meaning a little something extra, as in a surprise."

"I don't know what you had in mind," Valentina said. "Leo would add a rosebud or two to the plate. Once, he dusted sugar on grapes that came out very pretty."

"The Crème Brule," Olivia countered. "I'm going to slice it, so it lays thin on a saucer and crystalize it with my torch. Tell the couple the cracks that form represent how life's journey takes us every which way. The two swans will be angling toward each other, until almost touching beaks, like a brushed kiss across a cheek. I'll unite them with a red ribbon tied in a loose bow around their necks, the ends connected to two chocolate-covered strawberries to signify that everything is surmountable through love." A new thought jerked Olivia out of her vision. "You do think sharing one plate will be all right?"

"Absolutely," Valentina replied. "How delightful. Let me get their wine preference and I'll be back in a minute."

As soon as she was out of earshot, Luca drawled, "Well, look at you. Miss I'm All Business has a romantic side."

"I thought that was evident last Saturday when I said I'd like to make swans."

"They require a technical touch as much as anything else. What you're doing is creating a visual story to address the happy couple's future. Are you familiar with Antoine de Saint-Exupery?"

"I'm afraid not."

"'Love is not just looking at each other, but in looking together in the same direction.'"

As Olivia watched him retreat to check in with Chef Vinny, her heart lifted, only to beat in her throat like the flutter of dragonfly wings. She'd long understood how intellectual seduction was far more intense than sexual attraction, but the two combined were irresistible.

"Heaven help me," she whispered.

Sighing with relief, Olivia created the confections she had described. Catching Valentina's eye, she brought the desserts to the partition. "I hope they please."

"How could they not?"

Olivia's smile of pleasure lasted until she returned to her station, where Luca waited. He had placed a small plate bearing a sample of eggplant parmigiana on the table. As she arrived, he cut a ladylike piece, dipped it into the sauce, and held it up to her lips. "Eat."

"What are you doing?"

"I haven't seen you do more than sip water all day."

"And I'm not about to do more with a few hundred people behind me."

"But they don't know what I know. Someone has to take care of you."

"You're putting me in an awkward position with your father, as well," she reminded him.

"Not if he knew you were compromising the investment he's made in you."

"You are the human version of a gnat—irritating and deserving of a whack with a fly swatter."

"I can't hear you and I'm not going away until you eat."

"I hate you. Can you hear that?"

"Yes, but I don't believe it."

Afraid he would say what he did think, she slid the food off the fork with her teeth. But she had to chew an inordinately long period of time to swallow due to her stressed state.

Almost laughing, Luca warned, "Don't you dare try to tell me it's tough, or I won't be responsible for my actions."

Snatching the fork, he held out to her, she seethed, "I swear if you don't go away, I'll put a *cunja* on you."

He did, but in his own style. He was only three bars into humming, *That Old Black Magic* when she let the eggplant slide off the plate and into the trash.

With the baby reveal group arriving, even if Luca wanted to say anything about what she'd done, there was no time. Suddenly, all havoc broke loose. It began when Valentina called Olivia to the back.

"What's wrong?" Olivia asked, as she was drawn toward the hallway, out of sight of the dining room.

"I need you to get the cake to the banquet room."

She looked terrible and was barely coherent, compelling Olivia to ask, "Do you want me to get Sal?"

"No! I simply failed to acknowledge my limitations sooner."

The remark proved an understatement when, seconds later, she crumbled to the floor. Olivia barely managed to catch her head before it hit the hard tile.

"Miss Val!" Stu cried out, as he saw her falling. He came running, with Benny only a step behind him. "What's happened?"

"Get Sal," Benny said.

"No. Get Luca." Gaining their attention, she explained. "Sal is out front. Let's not start a commotion. Luca is in the reserve wine closet in back."

Olivia didn't watch him take off; she could see that not only was Valentina conscious, but she was determined to get back to her feet. "Give yourself a minute. Can you tell me what's going on?"

"The excitement just got to me."

"We both know that's not true," Luca replied, dropping to his knees beside them. By now there were a few waiters and waitresses also hovering close, as well. "Someone go get Sal back here...*discretely.*"

Valentina made a faint sound of protest. "Luca, I almost forgot—two cappuccinos for table five."

Luca glanced up and focused on Benny. "Get it for their waiter. Everyone else, aside from Olivia, back to your stations and customers."

When that directive was obeyed, Luca swept his aunt into his arms and carried her to the office, where he eased her onto the recliner. "Now tell me straight before Dad arrives, what's the last thing you remember?"

"Work... that's not getting done."

There was no time to try again. Sal appeared in the doorway, his expression closed. Seeing his sister pale, but alert, he spoke with gruff tenderness.

"What's going on?"

"She was just asking me to handle the baby reveal when she collapsed," Olivia told him. "Maybe the virus finally caught up with her."

Sal kept staring at his sister. "What do you say?"

"Perhaps a little low blood sugar."

"That much I believe," Sal replied. "Luca, call 911."

The ploy didn't work any better than it had with Leo. Valentina grabbed for his hand. "Salvatore, no. I admit I'm tired and if you can lend me Luca for a minute, I'll call it a night and retire to my apartment."

"You're done for the day, all right," he told her. "But you're staying put where we can keep an eye on you."

As the three of them walked down the hall a minute later, Luca reached out to stay his father and Olivia near the rear exit. "You can see she's not telling us everything?"

"What else is new?" Sal muttered. "Women." When he saw Olivia bow her head, he added a hasty, "Present company excluded."

"This is a private conversation for family," she said. "Let me go handle the Thompson event."

"In a second." Luca gave her a look of entreaty. "I'd like your input. Frankly, I'd feel better if Valentina let us call an ambulance. Maybe I should reach out to Mom to get her take on this?"

Sal bristled. "Like hell you will." He pointed in the direction of the office. "Those two have been in communication all along. Whatever is going on, your mother knows about it. So why isn't she here?"

8

"YOU MIGHT HAVE AN ANSWER IF YOU LET ME CALL," LUCA replied.

Nevertheless, Sal remained resolute in his perspective. "You can still say that after all the revelations you've learned since arriving here?"

Once again, Olivia sought her own escape. "Someone has to face a few facts. You're going to have some extremely unhappy guests in a minute, so I'm going to handle the reveal. Good luck, gentlemen."

Luca wished he was going with her. "She's right about unhappy guests, Dad. Let's tell the guys to watch the back door in case Aunt Val tries to sneak out—if she's even capable of walking in her condition. Then we need to finish the evening schmoozing."

Sal chose their first stop at an intimate booth for four. "Judge D'Amato, Mrs. D'Amato, I'd like you to meet my son, Luca. You two have something in common, Judge. Both of you worked for the government."

The tanned, silver-haired man in the well-tailored suit leaned forward to extend his hand to Luca. "Uh-oh, should I start worrying about job security?"

"You know Dad's sense of humor," Luca said, with a firm handshake in return. "I just finished a six-year run as a White House chef."

The well-coifed woman beside him gasped. "How exciting! Sal, we didn't even know you had a son. You must be so proud."

The judge motioned to Luca. "My wife, Vivian…and this is my brother, Ricardo, and his wife, Joy."

"I can't imagine how many dignitaries you've met," Vivian gushed.

"Most of whose names I can't begin to pronounce."

Leaning forward, Joy asked in a loud whisper, "What about the Hollywood crowd?"

"We all had to sign confidentiality agreements, but if you know anything about the A-list, I'm sure you can think of a few of them," Luca said diplomatically.

"Joy, look at you," the judge said gently taunting her. "Your husband is a golf coach who has worked with the likes of Jack Nicklaus, and still, Hollywood turns your head."

With a good-natured laugh, she shrugged. "I can't help myself, Frank. When I'm shopping, ask me if I'm looking at polo shirts or diamonds."

Ricardo linked his fingers with hers. "Need I remind you it also takes a polo shirt guy to keep the diamond market in good shape?"

"What does it take not to get embarrassed on the greens around here?" Luca asked him.

Ricardo's expression lit with interest. "What's your handicap?"

He told him, and shrugged at the man's surprise. "That's not to be taken too seriously. I don't get to play much."

Ricardo D'Amato gave his brother a wide-eyed look then reached into his pocket for a business card, and quickly scrawled his cell phone number on the back. As he handed it to Luca, he said, "I'm here for a month. If your father can possibly spare you for a few hours, I'd like to see your game."

"Me, too," Sal said under his breath as they continued around the room. "I'm beginning to think you blew the bocce tournament to spare your old man total humiliation, and now you're dazzling my best customers with your golf. Keep it up and I'll be ready to be put out to pasture by Christmas."

He led him to a booth occupied by two priests. "Father Flynn, my favorite confessor," he said to the eldest.

"Salvatore, my favorite sinner."

Sal put his arm around his son. "Father Patrick Flynn, in all seriousness, I want you to meet my only saving grace, Luca."

"You can say that again," the burly, silver-haired priest said, extending his hand to Luca. "Good to meet you, my son. I knew I smelled rebirth in the air. This is Father Domingo Torres, our recent transfer from Jalisco, Mexico."

Luca shook hands with the slender-faced man, who could have been the subject of an El Greco painting. *"Buenas noches, Padre. Espero que la transicion has sido facil para ti."*

A beatific smile warmed the sad-eyed priest's countenance. "Very much. Everyone has been most welcoming."

Sal couldn't contain a burst of laughter. "Pardon me, but . . . I'm just realizing I sired a one-man United Nations."

"You have much to be proud of." Father Flynn nodded with satisfaction. "So, Luca, you finally left the White House."

Taken aback, Luca was slow to offer an awkward, "Uh—yes, sir."

Beside him, he could feel his father all but reeling at the observation. Then, without a word, Sal walked away, and exited the dining room through the second set of swinging doors.

Wishing he could vanish, as well, Luca uttered an almost apologetic, if cryptic message. "Aunt Val must have had a lot to say in the confession booth."

With dawning realization, Father Flynn dropped his head into his hands. "Merciful Mother. I really screwed up."

"Well, you'd have to get in line to see if you won the top prize."

The priest shook his head in disbelief. "Sal really didn't know anything about you?"

"He's catching up fast. Appearances aside, it's a rewarding if not perfect homecoming." Luca leaned closer to offer a quiet word. "You should probably know, Aunt Val collapsed earlier. I can't help but think it's related to all this family subterfuge." Seeing the seasoned priest nod, he added, "Between her grief and this deception, it's as though she's being devoured from the inside. Would you pray for her?"

"Of course. Is she in the hospital?"

"Like my uncle, she resists. If stubbornness was a virtue, my family would be walking around with blinding auras." He added soberly, "I can't see how this can continue."

Father Flynn clasped Luca's hand with both of his. "We will pray for your entire family. And remember our doors are always open, my son."

Thanking him, Luca went in search of his father. In the kitchen, he was stopped by Benny.

"If you're looking for the boss, he went storming out the back door."

With a quick nod of appreciation, Luca followed. Just outside they nearly ran into each other.

"Dad..."

Holding up both hands to silence him, Sal demanded, "Tell me one thing. Who the hell doesn't know, besides me?"

"You'll have to ask someone else. I'm the other guy who was left out of the loop."

"Don't remind me." With a growl of frustration, Sal resumed his pacing. "If I wanted to permanently cripple myself, I'd put my fist through this wall."

Luca struggled to think of something to say that didn't sound like empty rhetoric. The warm, humid air taunted him. It muddled his thinking like dense dough clogging a pasta press. However, he'd come too far to lose these tender beginnings.

"Dad, we will get through this."

"Every morning of my life, my first thoughts have been about wondering where you were—if you had enough to eat, getting a good education," Sal said as though he hadn't spoken. "The only way to endure those days was to make choices, protect the family I had left. Your uncle, your aunt... I had to atone for not doing right by you—only to learn *she* helped keep you away from me. What's there to get through? My life has been a joke."

"Dad, I'm here."

Sal struggled under the weight of his emotions. "I missed your graduation from high school. Don't even know what your first date was like. Even when you were wobbling around on training wheels, I was looking forward to teaching you how to drive. You were never going to make the mistakes I did." With a groan, he bent over, bracing his hands on his knees, as though the poisonous thoughts consuming him for decades, sought exodus all at once. "Could we possibly have tried any harder to screw up?"

"Now you're starting to sound like Father Flynn."

"Flynn." The priest's name was a growl rising from Sal's throat. "That greeting you heard? It's a standing joke between us because I haven't been to confession since—"

"The last time you went to church?" Luca offered with a crooked smile. "I get it."

Sal pointed to the restaurant. "Well, I'm done feeling guilty for that. And he'll go to his day of judgment for being complicit in my humiliation."

"You expected a priest to repeat a confession?"

"The Irish *sedere* drank my wine and best cognac."

Luca laughed. The fact he'd had enough restraint not to say *culo* instead, spoke fathoms. He'd already learned how any priest entering *Vita e Spezie* was not to be presented with a bill at the end of dinner, and he doubted anything would change. Regardless of his rants and threats, his father's heart was as generous as his faith was secure.

He approached his father, arms spread wide.

Sal grabbed him as though locking onto the last handhold before being swallowed by quicksand. "I don't deserve this," he rasped.

"Don't say that. You've made me happier than I can ever remember being in my life."

Sal patted his back several times before releasing him and rubbing his wet eyes with the backs of his hands. "And it's going to get better. I promise you."

"Now, Dad, take it easy. Don't forget, there's Uncle Leo and Aunt Val who are going to need us, on top of all the demands of the restaurant. Believe me I'm just grateful I got here when I did. Let's take it one day at a time. No one needs excessive pressure put on them, particularly you."

With an uncomfortable laugh, Sal turned away, raking both hands through his hair. "You have no idea what a foreign concept that is to me. It's been all on me since I took over things from your grandparents. Don't think I'm not crediting your aunt and uncle's efforts. But look at them. If Leo waits too long to have surgery he's going to end up confined to a wheelchair, and Valentina is on the verge of God knows what."

"Perhaps greater forces are at work to help you out. I'm certainly intrigued how I was nudged to come back here at this particular time."

"If that's the truth, I'll have Valentina light candles at St. Mary's to show my gratitude."

"Or you could do it yourself."

"I wouldn't give Flynn the satisfaction."

Returning inside, they found Vinnie struggling to maintain control of the kitchen, while Tony anxiously searched for help with the front. With Olivia handling things in the banquet room serving the baby reveal cake, Benny was filling dessert orders. From the looks of things, everyone's sweet tooth was acting up tonight.

Sal said to Luca, "You get things in order here. I'll get the front back in shape."

Luca came up beside Vinnie as he wiped away a tiny splatter on the edge of a plate. "I'll get this. Go ahead and start on the next orders. Where's Stu?" Joey was scrambling to get a tray full of salads ready.

"Stu needed a bathroom break. I told him to check on Valentina while he was back there. Here he comes."

"How is she?" Luca asked, handing him two plates to pass to the waiter on the other side of the partition.

"She claims she's feeling better, but she doesn't look it. She's been crying, too."

"All right, I'll see what I can do as soon as we get caught up."

He returned to Vinny and joined him on the next dozen entrees. By the time they'd recovered lost ground, they were both in need of a bottle of cold water.

Vinny touched his plastic bottle to Luca's. "Thanks. If this momentum continues, we're both going to have more work than we can handle."

"Better growing pains than having to move product, and lure customers by having specials," Luca replied.

THE GROUP IN the banquet room lingered longer than expected, and they were among the last to leave the restaurant, except for the people in the lounge and bar. As they departed, they were enthusiastic in their thanks. While Olivia wheeled the cart with the minimal remains of the cake, and bins of dirty dishes on the lower shelves, Sal escorted the expectant couple out.

"Thanks again and congratulations! Be sure to send us pictures of the *bambino* and *bambina* when they arrive."

Once she reached the kitchen, Luca took over and rolled the cart the rest of the way to the dishwashing area. Then he followed her to her station.

Easing onto the first stool she came to, Olivia massaged the corners of her mouth. "I would not make it as a Miss Whatever, never mind a restaurant hostess. This face is not used to smiling and talking so much at the same time."

"Appearances to the contrary. Everyone left looking happy."

"How's your aunt?"

Luca took her change of subject in stride. "Pretending she's sleeping. Her tears give her away."

"Maybe I should go see her?"

As she started to rise, Luca gently urged her back. "Maybe you should think about yourself for a moment."

"She fainted, Luca."

"Yeah. And my gut says to call my mother, but I'd hate to do anything behind Dad's back. He's been hurt enough by those tactics." At Olivia's confused look, he continued. "Mom's a RN and hospice nurse—and most importantly, she's kept in touch with Aunt Val all these years. She should have answers."

"More interesting family dynamics."

"You can say that again. For example, even after all this time, and the cold war going on between them, my parents aren't divorced."

She practically gaped. "Who does that these days besides aristocrats, politicians, and corporate moguls?"

"Apparently, old school Italians."

"You have to stop," Olivia told him. "I'm about to enjoy myself and I don't think my cheeks can take it."

Luca sat down facing her. "Not to worry. Things get tedious from here on with my list of Must Dos. For example—if we can't convince Aunt Val to go to a hospital, I have to make other arrangements. She needs observing tonight—I'll handle it—but, thereafter, things are going to change. Would you mind if I contacted your landlady? I'd like to see her tomorrow morning if Aunt Val is stable."

"You still want to do that?"

"I can't have my aunt tending to me like a nanny. And she doesn't sleep, so I'm not getting any rest, either."

"I—I'll let Tempest know she can expect a call from you."

As she retrieved her cell phone and showed him the number so he could enter it into his device, there was no missing how his request triggered negative responses in her. Yet he couldn't let that stop him. She was his north star in a crazy sky.

"Livie, I don't mean to make things awkward for you. I just have a lot to get done and no time to do it. So much for the idea of a leisurely reunion. Next, I'll buy some wheels, in order to return my rental. Both mean a return trip to Houston. Only, look at how things went this evening—Dad can't spare me."

She continued to look like the person in the room with the short straw. "I told you, the boarding house is within walking distance."

"A huge relief after spending fifteen to seventeen hours on our feet."

"Okay. I can move my supplies from the passenger seat to the back."

"I knew there was a marshmallow heart behind that crusty sea salt and fibrous caramel exterior."

"Disgusting. Who would ever double up on sweetness like caramel and marshmallow? For that I'm going to point out what you obviously or intentionally overlooked—your aunt rarely uses her car."

Snapping his fingers, Luca declared, "You're right! It needs rescuing from turning into a piece of salt sculpture. Now resolve my dilemma as to how to be here and still get the rental returned, and I'll hire you as my personal assistant."

"Thanks, but I think I'll keep my day job—unless Tempest decides she doesn't want you as a boarder and it gets me fired."

He gave her a mild look of reproach. "You have to know how little chance there is of that happening."

"Luca, are you the last person on the planet to realize there are car rental offices everywhere these days, including on the island? You can drop it off here."

He honestly had no idea. "There's proof of how infrequently I've rented in the last several years."

Despite compressing her lips, one corner of Olivia's mouth betrayed her amusement. "It's refreshing to find you're human. There are rumors among the wait staff of you being a well-programmed robot. 'He has the handicap of a pro.' 'He's multi-lingual.'"

"I told you, I fill the emptiness of my life with things that interest me."

"Okay, Renaissance Man, make a long overdue call to your mother. She should be a fountain of enlightenment."

Pulling his cell phone from his pocket, Luca checked the time, then hooked his thumb toward the back exit. "I'd better do this outside. Don't tell Dad."

"Not my business."

Outside, Luca hit the button for his mother's number.

"Your ESP must be working," she began, "I was thinking of you as I drove home. I'm pulling into the driveway."

"Another late night. I hate you driving alone at this hour."

"My patient's time ended tonight. I should have a little break."

Although she cared deeply about her patients and her responsibility to them, Luca knew she avoided using words like death and terminal to protect herself, as much as relatives to her patient. "Ah, Mom. I'm sorry."

"Thank you, darling, but it's okay. What's on your mind?"

"Aunt Val collapsed this evening."

"Is she in the hospital? Has the doctor talked to you yet?"

Feeling as though she was two steps ahead of him, he said, "You're not in the least surprised."

"Where is she, Luca?"

"Lying down in Dad's office. We're about to close for the night."

"Okay. In that case give her a kiss from me."

"Say what? Mom, she refused to let us call for an ambulance or take her to the hospital ourselves."

"Don't yell, Luca. I can hear you."

"Then tell me what the hell is happening."

"It's not my right to betray her trust. She has to share whatever she wants in her own time."

Pacing up and down the parking lot, Luca stared at the black asphalt which was as opaque as his mother's words. "Mom, do you realize how bizarre you sound? This isn't the time for hedging or prevaricating. Are we talking cancer? Her heart? A brain tumor? What the hell?"

"Luca, I've said all I can say. Just know I love you. Goodnight."

Luca stared at the blank screen.

"Hey!"

Luca whipped around. He hadn't heard the back door open or his father's determined strides across the parking lot. His father's surprise approach told him what his mother's reaction had done to him.

"Dad, you're not going to like this."

"You don't look like you do, either."

"No. I called Mom and before you get bent out of shape, let me explain. I hoped if she would share what she knows with anyone it would be me."

"So?"

"She refused to break a confidence."

Sal erupted into a burst of Italian, Luca only half understood. It was enough to determine it wasn't anything to be uttered in a church or around polite company.

"Dad...I don't blame you for being upset, but we already have two members of the family who should be in the hospital. We can't afford a third."

Pointing toward the restaurant, Sal said, "Well, I know one thing, we're going inside and she's going to tell us what the hell is going on."

Valentina was emerging from their private bathroom, dabbing at her face with a dampened paper towel. Their grim expressions made her instantly wary. "I know, it's closing time. I was just freshening up a bit before I came to help."

"The only thing you're going to do is come clean—and don't give us the same song and dance Rosa did," Sal declared.

Gasping softly, Valentina pressed the towel to her throat. "You spoke to Rosa?"

"I phoned her," Luca said. "Call me slow, or call me too trusting, but it didn't hit me until a little while ago that Mom would be the only person you would confide in. So, what's going on, Aunt Val?"

"If your mother talked to you then there's nothing else for me to say."

"Did you anticipate this moment?" Luca asked, "Because that's exactly what she said to me."

"A promise is a promise, Luca, especially when two people are as close as sisters."

Sal put up a staying hand. "Knock it off. She made promises to me, too. She took *vows*. And you are *my* blood. What's that worth to you?"

Tears brimmed in Valentina's eyes. "Salvatore, don't you understand, my only intention was to spare you unnecessary concern. I had some tests done, and I have some issues, but there's no need for worry right now."

"Sure. Everything is under such great control. You collapsed in front of all of us."

"I was foolish and skipped lunch. If it will make you feel better, I'll leave the closing to you and retire to my apartment."

"Just so you know, neither one of us is buying that," Sal replied. "But, I, for one, don't have the stomach to fight you. Luca, get her upstairs. I have things to do."

OLIVIA DIDN'T EXPECT to see Luca again once he left with Valentina. Nevertheless, she'd just finished a lengthy shopping list for the morning when he returned. She watched him head straight for the bowl of leftover tortellini soup and spooned two ladles into a to-go container. She couldn't resist his expression. He looked so troubled.

"Is she feeling any better?" She spoke softly, not to be overheard by the others who were cleaning their own areas.

"No, I don't believe so, but she did agree to eat a little soup."

He had yet to meet her gaze and, as he snapped on the lid, she could feel the anger emanating from him. "If you need a few minutes for yourself, I can take that upstairs for you."

Luca placed both hands flat on the counter, as though struggling for self-control, and stared at the stainless backsplash. "She won't tell us what's going on."

"Your mother?"

"No. Yes. Her, too, but I'm talking about Aunt Val now."

"She must have her reasons."

"Then what's the point of having a family? What's the point of trying to keep it together?"

"Sometimes a family's concern is too much, until there's no more oxygen to breathe."

"How can there be too much love?"

It was an admirable concept, and one she wanted to believe in herself, but sometimes people exchanged love with control and pretended they were the same thing. "Oh, I don't know," she mused. "Maybe when two powerful, impassioned Angeloni men are ganging up on you?"

Finally looking at her, his expression reflected his incredulousness. "You see this as bullying?"

"Mm... borderline."

Luca turned around and slumped against the counter, deflated.

Pocketing her shopping list, Olivia went back to her station and picked up her bag. Upon returning to Luca, she reached for the soup.

"Love should be its most generous in the face of pain," she told him. "I'll see you tomorrow."

OLIVIA LET HERSELF into Tempest's house and locked up only to discover her landlady in the kitchen, chopping dried herbs for tea. The fine scent of lemon grass, orange blossoms, and blackberries was a lovely homecoming. "I don't even need the tea to make me feel relaxed enough to sleep," she said, stopping by the other side of the counter.

"But you look like you better have a cup. Sit down, child. It will only take a minute. I have hot water ready."

Although Olivia would rather have retreated to the privacy of her room to better ponder over the matter of Luca and his family, she accepted the invitation out of gratitude and consideration. She did appreciate being so welcomed here, and thought perhaps the older woman got lonely at times in this big house.

She watched Tempest prepare her drink in a rather dainty mug decorated with lilies of the valley. She'd taken the piece of china from a shelf full of mugs, no two alike. It made Olivia wonder if she'd chosen the cup randomly, or if it had some significance? She concluded that Tempest rarely did anything randomly.

A large bowl of finished product sat in the middle of the island, surrounded by smaller bowls almost empty save for dust, bits of leaves, and stems. "Are you making this for a client or for your shop?"

"Marnie's Tea House downtown. I supply her with several blends." Tempest carried the steaming mug to the table. "Come take a load off. You carried a world of worry in with you. Did things not go well today?"

So much for thinking she was adept at hiding her emotions, Olivia thought; however, she accepted how Tempest had gifts she hadn't begun to understand yet. "It started as a perfectly fine day. We had a special event for expectant parents—a baby reveal, are you familiar with those?"

"Any excuse for a party."

"Now that's often a man's perspective, but they both seemed pretty excited about the whole thing. I was pleased with the way the cake turned out. But then Valentina fainted. It overshadowed everything, since we soon realized she's keeping some matter about her health a secret. It's extremely upsetting to her older brother and nephew."

"To you, too."

Olivia glanced at the majestic woman, still an impressive figure despite having removed her jewelry and head scarf for the day. Was she insinuating she better than anyone understood how conflicted Valentina was, and why? "Well, I can hardly pretend to be as close to her, as they are. But, yes, I find her special and so very soulful. In a way, you have that in common. She has this motherly quality about her making you believe with her hugs, everything will remain all right. Sadly, I don't think it will be. For her. And her family is at their wits' end."

"What will be, will be," Tempest replied in her lilting way. "For the sake of your own health you need to focus on something that won't tie you in knots. Maybe that building you're so interested in."

Olivia was glad she hadn't yet picked up the mug, certain the seemingly innocent phrasing wasn't so innocent, and she would have spilled some of the steaming contents. "Yes, *Vita e Spezie,* which had been the post office. It is a fascinating place, and I'd love to delve deeper into its history, but I haven't had the time. What's more, it would be inconsiderate to trouble Valentina with questions when she's not feeling well."

"The city's central library, The Rosenberg Library on Sealy is only blocks from here. There's much information about The Great Flood, and might offer you some useful insight. People speak of the Moody Mansion on Broadway providing background, as well."

Olivia had passed both a number of times as she'd acquainted herself with the city, but had yet to go into the island's central library, or the Romanesque, thirty-one-room house. "Thanks. I'll keep them in mind if things settle down." Not wanting to linger on the subject, she took a tentative sip of her tea and almost choked as she remembered Luca's request. "I almost forgot."

"You need honey for the tea?" Tempest asked, about to rise. "Is it too strong?"

"No, it's perfect. I mean I almost forgot to pass on a message from Luca."

"A message from Golden Boy? You have my full attention."

"It looks as though he's going to stay, meaning join his father at the restaurant. But sleeping on his aunt's couch in the upstairs apartment is a strain for both of them. I made the mistake of telling him about you and this place—"

"A mistake?"

Olivia could feel her cheeks warm, and took a sip of tea hoping it would look as though the heat rising from within was the cause. "An unintended admission before I thought better of it."

"That, I believe. He's easy to talk to, eh? So he wants a room. Shall I turn him down?"

Olivia squirmed under her opaque scrutiny. "Not because of me!"

"Then you want me to let him have a room?"

"It's not any of my business."

"No? You'll both be upstairs, the next thing to roommates, and it would seem your schedules are the same. Familiarity will not breed contempt?"

It would breed something; that's what worried her. "You have to do what's right for you."

"Which is sustaining harmony in this house. Let me pose my question this way—are you telling me you like him more than you did?"

With a shallow sigh of resignation, she allowed, "Please don't read too much into this. I'm not open to anything more than a compatible work environment."

Tempest smiled. "Every journey to tomorrow starts at its own entryway."

At the risk of burning her tongue, Olivia gulped down her tea. "I'm not even going to attempt to analyze that. I've fulfilled my obligation. Now I'm going to take my weary self for a shower, and plan to be asleep before my head hits the pillow."

"Sweet dreams, *mon petit.*"

"IT'S GOOD OF you to see me on such short notice," Luca said to Tempest Fleuraugust early Thursday morning. "Love the *Gele.*"

"How do you know of such things?" Tempest's demand held a touch of censure, as though he was stealing some of her energy, the way remote peoples avoided cameras when first exposed to them.

"We hosted an African Summit at the White House, and several of the dignitaries' wives wore headscarves popular in their nations. How do you get such perfect color placement?"

"I whisper to silkworms I keep in the shed out back," she replied.

"That sounds exceptionally time-consuming," he replied, managing to keep a straight face. "At best, I would have deduced great skill at tie dying, matched only in wrapping expertise."

He thought her an exotic woman in her purple-and-yellow print caftan and matching head scarf. A human wind chime, her every movement sent music in the air, thanks to the multitude of bangle bracelets adorning her strong arms. Her hoop earrings were the size of bangles, as well.

"It's not a bad guess—for a man." Tempest led the way to the stairs. "I know from Olivia how your line of work leaves you with precious little time for anything else. Would you like to see the room?"

Luca began to open the leather folder he'd brought with him for the list of references and financial information he'd drawn up for her. "I brought this for you."

Tempest waved it away. "Save it for someone with more file space. From what you told me on the phone and what Olivia said about you, it's not necessary. Life works best if you keep things simple." At the base of the stairs, she gestured toward the second floor. "You may choose one of the two bedrooms on the right. Olivia is in the far left bedroom. You'll excuse me if I don't join you, but at my age steps are no friend."

"Am I right in thinking we're your only tenants?"

"Yes. I base the number on who my renters are, and don't think it's fair for more than two to share a bathroom, particularly if your hours are similar. Just lost a long-time boarder before Olivia arrived. He was an intern at the hospital and has relocated to Boston. He had worse hours than you two do."

"You may be the most considerate landlady I've ever heard of."

"No doubt about it. Why else do you think I'm such an entrepreneur dabbling in everything? My CPA berates me constantly about how my life would be easier if I'd simply rented out the rooms."

"You would like my father. Only yesterday, he told me his accountant said he could raise his prices by twenty-five percent and not lose traffic. All he had to do was exchange the clientele he currently serves for a more affluent public that is particular about whom they dine with."

"I would change accountants. The man sounds like someone in need of gallbladder surgery." Tempest kept her bejeweled hands clasped like an opera singer, parallel to her diaphragm. "You'll have a key to your room and the front door. All I ask is for you to maintain your own space, and share the care of the bathroom. As with Olivia, you are welcome to the kitchen, provided I'm not in a rush to get one of my orders out. The laundry room is beyond the kitchen."

Thanking her, Luca jogged upstairs. He could already gauge this arrangement would suit him well. He'd been charmed by the tree-lined street with its tropical-colored houses, so similar to Charleston, New Orleans, and many seaside communities. The house, though old, bore a welcoming ambiance, completely dissimilar to his condo on the East coast, where he only slept and stored his belongings, and never finished decorating.

Passing the first bedroom, Luca went straight to the one opposite Livie's. The quartz-blue room was serenely lit with filtered light from old-style, knee-to-ceiling windows facing north. His view of the house next door was diminished by a magnolia tree at least twice his age, and trumpet vines gone wild over the privacy fence and everything else they could cling to. The tubular orange blossoms were bobbing from visits by hummingbirds and bumble bees.

Below, there was a walkway that appeared to circle the house. Flowers, herbs, bird baths, and garden art continued the pattern from what he'd passed through to get to the front door.

The room's antique oak furnishings were Quaker spare with a queen-sized bed, a solid oak chest of drawers, a high-backed chair upholstered in a shade of evergreens, and small drop-leaf table that could serve as a place to dine or work on a laptop. Considering how little time he anticipated spending here, it was more than pleasant.

As he exited to the hallway, Luca couldn't help but consider Olivia's closed door. The temptation was strong to see what view she woke to daily. However, he was getting used to a number of temptations where Olivia Dumont was concerned, and settled for checking the black-and-white subway-tiled bathroom. He took in the claw-footed tub and separate shower stall, and smiled in satisfaction. It looked as though it hadn't been used, which told him Livie was as neat here as she was in the kitchen.

Back downstairs, he found Tempest shaking some dry cat food into a bowl which she placed just beyond the door on the back porch. "There you go, Mister. I know you're powerful hungry seeing as you were keeping us up half the night serenading your lady friends." She stroked the hefty, ring-tailed gray tabby, nearly the size of a potbellied pig, before shutting the door.

"That's an impressive-size cat you have," Luca said as she re-entered the kitchen.

"Mister is not mine. He belongs to no one. I call him my outside boarder."

"He pays rent?"

"In his way. Best mouser I've ever seen. And a true gentleman. Shares with his neighbor ladies, even at the cost of depriving himself, which is why I supplement him. He's worth it."

Luca scratched the side of his nose thinking that animal knew nothing of deprivation. "I think he's found your soft spot, Sister Fleuraugust."

"I'm sure you're correct, Mr. Angeloni. But this way he's just plump enough not to jump fast or high enough after the birdies. So, what do you think of the room? I hope you tested the bed and found it acceptable?"

"I didn't ma'am. After sleeping on a couch designed to keep a chiropractor in business, I'm sure your bed is as pleasant as everything else. If you'll allow me to write you a check, I'll bring my belongings upstairs, before I get back to work."

SLIGHTLY OVER AN hour later, Luca entered the restaurant, relieved to note there was no sign of Valentina. While it was still early, he hoped she'd listened to him about staying put and letting fully-recovered Andi handle the lunch crowd. To his left, he spotted his father talking to Rocco at the bar, so he sidestepped the others to have a quick word with Olivia.

"Hi, neighbor."

Finished with beating enough eggs for three cakes, she turned off the mixer. "You need a bullhorn. I don't think all of the wait staff heard you."

"Do you want to keep us a secret?" Luca asked, low enough so only she could hear.

"There is no *us*, but I do hope you don't snore. I have a hunch insulation was invented after the house was built."

Luca knew she remained ambivalent about having him living under the same roof with her, but her mild sarcasm was an improvement over her initial responses to the idea. "I don't believe I do, but if it turns out anything I do bothers you, feel free to knock on my door. Anytime."

"Not with those creaking floorboards."

"Afraid you're going to give our landlady the wrong idea?"

"Her and you."

"No matter. I have enough optimism for both of us. In the meantime, I have my fantasies."

Shooting him a quelling glance, she asked, "Now all you have to do is look up the location of the rental office."

"Nope, that's done, too. As soon as I brought my things to my room, I drove over there and turned in the little money pit. One of the clerks was about to go on break and I gave her a crisp twenty to drive me back."

"She would have probably have done it for free," Olivia said drolly.

"But far be it for me to give her the wrong impression."

"Oh, damn," she muttered.

"I'm just playing with you, Livie."

"No—behind you," she said.

He turned around right when the rest of the kitchen went silent. Leo and Tiny were in the building.

"Don't get your shorts in a twist," Leo grumbled to the room at large. "I only came by to see Valentina. Sal called and told me what happened."

Luca went to give his uncle a hug, and gave Tiny a friendly pat on the back. "Have you already been upstairs?"

"I figured I'd check here first."

"We're hoping she takes it a little easier today. At least for the first shift."

"Bravo. Another good reason to have you home. If she'll listen to anyone, it's you." Leo's expression reflected his worry. "What do you think is going on with her?"

"Nothing good. Did Dad tell you Mom was evasive, too?"

Shaking his hand as though burned, Leo said, "Whew! Was your father hot when he learned your mother has information and wouldn't share it."

"Can you blame him?"

"Not at all. We're Valentina's blood. We're the ones who have been here for her all along."

They'd walked over to Vinny at the stove. In a simple gesture of comradery, Leo placed a hand on the other man's shoulder, and the two exchanged knowing nods.

"Females," Vinny said. "It's a conspiracy with them. I know. I can walk into a room at my house, and all six of those girls and their mother will go silent. They'll stare at me like 'Who are you? Get out!'"

Leo snorted. "Don't give me that. I've seen how those little beauties are around you." He told Luca, "It's all, 'Oh, Poppy,' this, and 'Poppy,' that. The rest of the time they climb all over him like kittens."

Grinning, Vinny shrugged and returned to stirring his marinara sauce, while Luca drew his uncle a few steps farther into the kitchen.

"Speaking of communicating," he began, "weren't you supposed to have another test today?"

"Yeah, yeah. It's done." He dismissed the experience with a flick of his hand. "'We'll call you,' they tell me. I'm still waiting for news about the last test. If I'd stayed in the hospital, they would probably have operated on me and I wouldn't know what for!"

He limped over to the baking area where Olivia was measuring dry ingredients for the Doberge. "So, how's it going? You look settled in."

Hoping he wasn't going to say something to offend Olivia, Luca was about to speak. But she beat him to it.

"Getting there, Chef. Unfortunately, I had to disappoint a customer yesterday. Apparently, he was craving one of your special brownies, and naturally, we didn't have any."

Leo's face lit with delight. "Pauly Macaroni! How could I forget? Once a month, I make him a big pan of them. He would buy them every week, but his wife gets after him to watch his weight."

Olivia gestured to the next table. "If you're up to it, would you like to make him a batch? He was very upset to learn you're not feeling well and sends you his regards."

Tiny had been shadowing Leo like a faithful hound; however, Olivia's invitation had him springing to life. "He can't. The doctor told him again he couldn't work and to stay off his feet."

"Put a lid on it, will you?" Leo snapped. "They gotta tell you something to charge you an arm and a leg. Go on to the gift shop and see if Nancy still remembers your name." To Olivia he added, "He's sweet on the sales girl next door. She likes to call him by his Christian name—Alfredo. She thinks it sounds sophisticated."

Blushing, Tiny said, "She's from Arkansas. How many Italians do you think she's met in her life?"

"A half of one." Laughing at his own joke, Leo cupped the back of his head and added affectionately, "It's okay. Take a few minutes for yourself."

Once Tiny left through the dining room, Leo turned back to Olivia looking less confident. "You're sure you don't mind?"

"By all means. I'm intrigued."

He made a face, his manner almost sheepish. "It's not much of a secret. You simply add raspberry jam on top of the brownies before frosting them. It adds an extra moistness."

"So that's what all those jars of jam are for in the pantry," Olivia mused.

Leo was slipping on a chef's jacket when Sal entered the kitchen. Seeing his annoyance, Luca caught his arm before he could rebuke Leo.

"It's okay, Dad. Olivia told him about Pauly missing his brownies. He's sharing the recipe, and I called Pauly to tell him to come down in about an hour."

"Yeah, Sal," Leo said, with a smug smile. "Not everyone thinks I'm always the bad guy."

HAVING LEO BACK at the restaurant turned out to be a pleasant enough interlude, helped by its moderate duration, and skillfully managed by Olivia's diplomatic and generous demeanor. The results were a big success and Pauly was effusive with his thanks. By the time the restaurant opened for lunch, Leo and Tiny left beaming and in the best humor anyone could remember in a long time.

"That was extremely generous of you," Luca told Olivia as soon as the back door closed.

"Thanks, but I've already received my reward," she replied with an impish grin.

"How so?"

She slid the tray of extra few dozen brownies, she'd encouraged Leo to make for the restaurant into the display case. "These are really quite good, but now that I know how he does it, I can cut the excessive sweetness by making the berry compote from scratch. It will avoid the extra sugar commercial manufacturers use for an added shelf life."

"My mouth is already watering. But Leo will be crushed."

"No, he won't. I'm going to share the recipe."

VALENTINA CAME DOWN for the dinner service. While she thanked the staff as each made a point to greet her and voice their concern about what happened, she and Sal discreetly avoided each other, something that visibly seemed to pain Valentina.

Olivia observed the whole situation from her vantage point in the kitchen and remained concerned about Valentina's condition. While there was no real physical change in the Angeloni sibling, the strain from the familial undercurrents was draining her fast. Worried she would suffer a repeat from the other night, Olivia coaxed her into taking a break before the restaurant filled completely.

Valentina sat at Olivia's station with a cup of tea and picked at one of Leo's brownies when an envelope floated to the floor. "Look," she whispered, pointing.

With a sound of excitement, Olivia snatched it up. Once again there were only one word on the front. *God.* She offered it to Valentina.

"You open it and read it to me."

Not needing to be asked twice, Olivia glanced over her shoulder toward the dining room to see if anyone was watching, and discreetly removed the single sheet of note paper. The handwriting was in script with a straight up and down flow and generous loops.

Dear God,

Thank you for making me the happiest woman on earth.
As you know, Keith proposed, but I haven't been able to
summon the courage to break the news to my parents.
They see his music profession as a pipe dream at best,
and at worst a future of poverty, and loneliness for me
as he travels. Maybe even heartbreak when I have to deal
with an endless assortment of awe-struck groupies at
every event. But I love him and I believe you gifted him
with this talent for a reason.

Rather than become even more stressed than I
already am, we've decided to elope and plan to be
married by a justice of the peace here before we go back
to Omaha on Monday.

I read about your special mailbox in a brochure so
I'm adding this note to go with my prayers that you bless us
and our marriage.

Yours,
Lacy

From up front at the hostess table came Tony's call. "Order for Lacy?"

Olivia and Valentina exchanged glances, hurried to the front counter, and craned their necks and peered around the corner to see a young, petite brunette with waist-length hair accented by a pink braid. Her white tee shirt advertised *The Keith Burke Band*.

"She's adorable," Olivia whispered.

"But so young," Valentina replied.

"That's all the more reason for you to light a candle for her tomorrow at church."

"Maybe three. Two for the happy couple and a third for her undoubtedly terrified parents."

As Lacy accepted the change from her bill, Olivia noted, "Well, look at it this way, that's an awfully nice engagement ring, and they can still afford a good dinner, so they can't be on poverty row yet."

"You're right. One has to remain positive."

Olivia would have been elated by Valentina's acquiescence if only she didn't hear the sadness in her tone, or see it reflected in her eyes. She barely repressed a shiver as she accepted a dessert order from one of the waitresses.

9

EARLY FRIDAY MORNING, OLIVIA STOOD IN TEMPEST'S KITCHEN
taking a first eager swallow of a fresh-fruit smoothie. She'd always struggled with pills and the size of her current medication only worsened
matters.

Popping the last tablet into her mouth, she attempted to wash it
down with a big gulp, hoping momentum would do the trick. Wholly
focused on getting through the morning ritual, she was unprepared
for the storm door to open and to hear a masculine hoot.

"Caught you! I knew you were hiding something."

The combination of surprise and dread had Olivia trying to gasp—
under the circumstances a physiological impossibility. As her body rejected the impulse, she lurched to the sink, her hand clapped to her
mouth, and grappled with the faucet in a race against time.

In that fraction of a second where she registered the thought of
how things couldn't get worse, they did. Part of the smoothie went
down the wrong pipe.

Violent coughing ensued—and its equally forceful opposite reaction—breathing. The combination triggered such knifelike pains in
her throat and chest, she thought she was going to die. And, in the
midst of everything, she had to endure the added humiliation of Luca
looming over her, patting her on the back with increased vigor.

"Damn, I'm sorry. I was only teasing."

It took several more wrenching coughs before her airway cleared enough for the spasms to ease and she could loosen her death-grip on the lip of the sink. Still blinking away blinding tears, she desperately rinsed her face and hands then splashed the rest of the pink down the drain.

"Lucky me," she wheezed.

Her voice sounded like a mortally wounded victim in a slasher movie. Disgusted with the whole situation, and wondering if that last pill ended up down the drain, Olivia ripped off a length of paper towels. She proceeded to pat her face dry, as well as the water and drink soaking her white T-shirt. Seeing her bra clearly visible through the wet cotton, she was belatedly grateful she hadn't followed her first impulse, which had been to come downstairs in her thigh-length sleepshirt.

"Are you all right?"

Ignoring the concerned expression that made him more handsome than a jogger deserved to be at the end of a run, she gave Luca a baleful glare. "Do I look all right?"

After a too thorough and intimate inspection, he said, "A little unsteady on your feet, not quite saturated enough to be in a wet T-shirt contest, but otherwise, as lovely as ever."

"Don't be ridiculous." Reaching for her glass—which miraculously still contained half of her drink—she brushed by him and headed for the stairs. "You'd better be prepared to apologize to Tempest for waking her."

"I will." Luca followed her. "Want me to carry that for you? Your hand sure is shaking."

"Of course, it is." The more agitated she became, the worse she croaked. "You scared me to death. I thought you were still upstairs."

It was barely six o'clock and she'd tip-toed around the creaking floorboards she'd memorized so far in order not to wake him. Instead, he had already done some running if his damp tank top and jogging shorts were anything to go by.

"In our business, and with my genealogy, it's smart to stay proactive to burn off calories. Otherwise, I'd already be looking like Tiny."

"Please don't tell me you're marathoner." Given her current limitations, it was too easy to envy people with his kind of energy.

"Hardly. Just a mile or two a few times a week to keep my metabolism going. What about you? How do you stay in such great shape?"

Since the truth would only raise eyebrows, she asked, "How do sea snakes stay slim?"

"By never stopping?"

"There you are. I'm leaving in ten minutes, if you don't want to walk."

Even though he had his aunt's permission to use her vehicle, he'd caught a ride with Olivia. He'd left the sedan at the restaurant in case Valentina reconsidered and wisely sought medical help during the night.

"What's the rush?"

"I want to catch your father before he heads off to the wharves. I need off on Monday."

The news had Luca pausing in mid step. "I can imagine how Dad's going to react. This is the Fourth of July weekend. Besides, you only started days ago."

"The restaurant is closed Sunday. And this was something already scheduled." She could tell by his silence that he hoped she would elaborate. She didn't.

"Give me five minutes to shower," he said, his long strides allowing him to catch up with her. "I'll meet you out front."

THEY LEFT THE house before Tempest emerged from her room, so Luca jotted her a note and left it on the island in the kitchen. Once in the car, he hoped Olivia would pick up the conversation where they left off; however, she remained silent.

"Want me to apologize again?"

"Why? Didn't you mean it the first time?"

Luca decided cranky was cute on her and, while he knew her throat had to still hurt, it emphasized the sexy quality of her voice. "Okay, I'll leave you alone. Obviously, you're deep in thought."

With a sigh, she said, "I'm having doubts about the Jansen retirement party. Did you hear his kids' idea of funny? They asked for a cake in the shape of a casket—with wheels."

"It is a family-owned mortuary."

"I tend to think a head shot of him inside, and a sash across the casket imprinted with 'I'll be seeing you,' is tasteless and disrespectful."

"Ostensibly, maybe. Yet the funeral directors I've met seem to have a good sense of humor. Who do you think thought up the 'Dying to get in' joke?"

Olivia remained unamused. "If Mrs. Jenson had barroom humor in mind, she would have chosen a different venue than *Vita e Spezie*."

"I'll admit, you have a point there," Luca said. "Do you have something else to offer them?"

"No," she admitted. "Because it's not as though I've had a great deal of notice."

They pulled into the parking lot right behind Sal. Luca noticed his father had a funny expression on his face when he spotted them, and could guess why. Although Luca had told him he wouldn't be staying with his aunt any longer, and shared where he'd gotten a room, apparently the sight of the two of them arriving together reseeded certain thoughts.

"Everything okay?" Luca asked him.

Sal's gaze shifted between them. "You tell me."

"We're neighbors," Olivia said, brusquely, "and I don't know about Luca, but Mister was carousing outside my window half the night. If my eyes are bloodshot, that's why."

Intrigued, but grateful she hadn't shared the real reason, or blamed him, Luca explained, "She's referring to the free-range Tom our landlady feeds." Mouthing, "Thank you" to Olivia, he added, "Looks like I got the best room."

"Be patient. He's an equal opportunity annoyer—like someone else I know."

"What's wrong with your voice?" Sal demanded. "You're not coming down with something just when we have a full crew again?"

"Morning allergies. My landlady has quite the green thumb."

"Dad, Olivia needs to run something by you. Do you want me to give you some privacy for that?" he asked her with an innocent smile.

"That won't be necessary. Your opinion doesn't matter."

At the back door, Sal stopped and frowned at both of them. "What the hell is going on? I don't even know who to look at."

"Me." Olivia squared her shoulders. "Sal, sir, I need part of Monday off."

"It's the July Fourth weekend. Galveston is swamped."

"And I'm here. But Monday is the fifth. Everything will be back to normal."

Sal narrowed his eyes in suspicion. "Don't tell me you're quitting already?"

"No, but I should have told you when you hired me about this complication. I'm certain to be back in time for the dinner service."

"Is everything all right?"

"Just a prior commitment I can't get out of."

"Then do what you have to do. It's not like this is going to be a weekly thing. *Right?*"

"Thank you, sir. If you'd like I can come in Sunday to catch up on product if it looks as though we'll run short." Seeing his frown deepening, she quickly amended, "But not if I'm going to inconvenience anyone."

"Inconvenience someone on the Fourth of July by asking them to work?" Sal unlocked the door. "If there's anything else, could it please wait until I've had some caffeine? It's too early for all this."

As he went on ahead, Olivia pinched Luca's side. When he jumped, she whispered, "You tried to undermine my conversation with your father."

"You called me annoying."

"Insinuated. There's a difference."

"Do you split hairs with the truth, as well?" Seeing her eyes widen, Luca found himself blurting out something he hadn't even considered until that moment. "One thing you don't want to do is test my loyalties, Livie. I'm a guy who hates secrets."

A PARTICULARLY STRONG thunderstorm compromised the lunch traffic. Once again, Sal had called upstairs to tell Valentina to stay home, this time the entire day, since the threat of repeat of storms would continue. He used the excuse that he didn't want her slipping on the slick stairs.

For a while, things were so slow, Luca and Sal retreated to the office for what Sal called an impromptu business pow-wow. As soon as he shut the door he reached into his pants pocket and handed Luca a set of keys.

"What's this?" Luca asked. He'd already been given those related to the building.

"Keys to the house. They belonged to your mother. She left them behind."

As a particularly close clap of thunder shook the building, Luca tried to determine why he was getting this set. "Dad, it's not necessary. I appreciate the gesture, but I'm not going to move in with you."

"Good. I don't want you to."

"So why?"

Sal rubbed the back of his neck and paced beside his desk. "Because, God forbid, you may need to check on me if something happens and I don't show up at the restaurant one morning, or you need to store some of your stuff, I don't know." When he noticed Luca's unconvinced stare, he snapped, "Because I don't know how this is done, okay?"

"You seem to be doing all right."

"Well, I'm not. All that garbage I mentioned is valid, I guess, but what I really want to say is that I want to ask questions. I want you to ask me questions." He pointed beyond the closed door. "Out there I think it's going good for us. Better than good. I think we're getting close to brilliant. But we're alone only minutes a day and I feel clumsy around you."

He was right. Luca experienced moments like that himself. "It's going to take time."

"It seems to be going pretty fast with you and N'awlins."

Luca bowed his head, unable to repress a hopeful smile. "Ah. Yes, well, that may be nothing. You don't know what it took to get a room at her boarding house."

"She's who you were referring to on Sunday when the mothers were trying to hook you up with their daughters?"

"Yes."

"I wouldn't have hired her if I thought she could turn your head so easily."

Luca accepted the admission with quiet resolve. "You have no idea how much armor I've put around myself to avoid repeating my mistakes. Don't blame Livie. She's rebuking and rejecting me at every turn."

"But she tried to get your help to take Monday off."

"No. I forced her to broach the subject sooner hoping she would accidentally or intentionally tell you why she needed to be gone."

"You're sure this isn't about another job offer?"

"No, because she said it was something arranged before she took this position."

"Then it's about a guy." When Luca frowned, Sal shrugged. "Think about it. Her family is too far away for it to be about them. What's left? Protect yourself. She's as smart as she is beautiful. I don't want to see you get played again."

Exasperated, Luca said, "I should never have told you about the Silvers."

"I would feel the way I feel, regardless. I'm a father. I finally get to worry about my son."

With a slow grin, Luca replied, "I'll bet you've been practicing that line since I got back to town."

THE STORM MOVED on, and tourists returned to the streets. While the bar had stayed busy, the restaurant began filling, as well; partly with people who were enjoying their conversations so much, they opted for an early dinner. Others passing in the street heard the happy sounds emanating from inside *Vita e Spezie* and wanted to join what appeared to be a happening place. Before long, the skeleton crew they had to handle the interim hours between lunch and dinner were bustling around at top speed, and Sal phoned a few of their staff to come in as soon as they were able. The holiday momentum had begun.

The results had a positive effect on the kitchen staff. Still fresh after a light lunch service, everyone was energetic and upbeat. They moved with a spring in their step, and conversations were as lively as the music flowing from the bar and restaurant. Everyone, save Luca.

Oddly enough, the more cheerful Olivia became, the more it put him out of sorts. At the moment, she was laughing and pausing in her work to clap to Vinny's impromptu tarantella. Even some of the diners closest to the kitchen were clapping and cheering with enthusiasm.

"Vinny, I had no idea you had such moves," she declared, as he skipped around her. But when he tried to get her to join him in the Italian folk dance passed on from his family's district, she waved him away and retreated to her station.

"Olivia," Joey said, pointing to their head chef. "I don't know this man. You're bringing out a side of this work horse we've never seen before."

As a winded Vinny returned to his orders, he scoffed with good humor. "That's because all you guys do is talk about sports, more sports, and your broken-down jalopies and motorcycle. Not a one of you has any culture."

Still wiping tears from the corners of her eyes, Olivia was startled when Luca slammed down a dessert order slip he'd plucked from the counter where it sat unnoticed. "If you don't watch yourself you're going to have all the guys in here battling each other for your favors."

He was being ridiculous, since half of the staff was younger than her, and Vinny was a happily married man. "Is everyone supposed to enjoy themselves around here, but me?"

"Yeah, damn it."

Painfully aware of what a fool he'd made of himself, Luca couldn't get out of the kitchen fast enough and found himself aiming straight for the bar. He needed a drink. Jealousy was a new emotion for him and to be fair, Olivia had done nothing to provoke it. It was good to have harmony in the kitchen, but he wanted her attention on him. He wanted to be the one who made her laugh so hard she wept. Maybe he had more of his mother in him than he'd realized—and not all of it good.

Rocco was tied up with customers at his end of the bar, so Luca took the last seat at the other end. Chanel finished serving a customer a margarita and came down to greet him

"You look like you need something. Relief that comes in a shot glass?"

"You're right. Give me a hit of Absolut."

Although he felt no small chagrin at exposing his feelings so easily, he appreciated the tall redhead's casual acceptance. They hadn't had many opportunities to get to know each other, but he liked the green-eyed personal trainer. When necessary, she was all business, yet knew how to make customers linger for good conversation over a second drink. After placing the shot glass before him, she deftly filled two other orders and returned to find it remained untouched.

"Now I know this isn't about you and your father, so it has to be Olivia." At his stunned look, she rolled her eyes. "I've been on this side of a bar for over ten years and married to a cop for nine. Reading people has become second nature."

"This is impossible," he muttered, rubbing at his forehead, as though trying to wipe the thoughts churning in his head out of his mind. "I only met her a week ago."

Chanel smiled. "My husband says I had him the moment I walked into his party—and I was with a fellow cop, slash, buddy of his. A definite sin inside the brotherhood. Fortunately, it was only our second date, so there weren't too-hard feelings. Are you having to deal with competition?"

"You'd think she'd share at least that much information, but I don't know."

About to reply, Chanel was called away again by new arrivals. When she returned, she nodded at the still-untouched drink. "You keep this up and I'm going to make you pay for wasting good vodka."

"I guess I don't like feeling out of control."

Glancing over his shoulder, she observed the activity in the kitchen. "She doesn't strike me as a collector."

"You lost me."

Chanel raised her left hand wiggling her fingers, making the diamonds in her engagement ring and wedding band sparkle. "You know, a trophy hunter. Mercy, you're naïve for someone who's been swimming with the big fishes."

"I've learned enough to know I don't like shark meat."

"Then you didn't waste the education."

With a small nod, Luca finally downed the drink. "Thanks for the balm to my ego." He cast her a sidelong look. "So what do you really think about her?"

"She's an interesting little thing. First impressions—a breath of fresh air. Bottom notes—strong, stable, but she keeps her cards close to her chest."

"She has brothers. I suspect she learned more from them than how to play poker."

"That would explain part of it, but not everything. Be patient. It's a compliment to want to know everything about someone, but not everyone is comfortable with the open-book tendencies that social media is making the norm."

Despite finding reassurance in Chanel's words of wisdom, Luca grew increasingly restless and eager to have time alone with Olivia. It left him feeling worse than dealing with the flu. When ill, he'd known he had a two-week stretch of misery ahead of him, yet he'd been fed up with the bug after two days. As the evening wore on, it appeared even their customers were willing to antagonize him.

In the middle of the Jansen retirement party, some debonair guy who looked like he owned an avocado or cocoa bean plantation in South America demanded the chef of the *"magnifico!"* dessert take a bow. To her credit, Olivia had outdone herself, resolving her personal aversion for the humorous cake. She'd ended up making a second, classy, and obviously tasty alternative—given how little of it was left—as a gift from her. While the Jansens were more than kind in their praise, Luca found himself gritting his teeth as the Latin lothario kissed her hand, and thereafter refused to let go.

Luca watched from the doorway of the banquet room to stay out of the way of the servers, miserably noting how every compliment turned Olivia's cheeks pinker and her smile brighter. Yet, when the man slipped a business card into the pocket of her chef's jacket, he could barely resist hauling her back to the kitchen.

When she finally returned to her work station, Luca was close on her heels. Before he could stop himself, he muttered to her, "I hope you have your passport in order. *Señor* Suave doesn't strike me as a man to wait on American red tape."

"What on earth are you talking about?"

"I saw him slip his business card into your pocket. Did he try to convince you he really wanted a personal chef, or does he even care that you have a culinary arts degree?"

Her eyes flashed like blue lasers. "Be glad for this open view to the dining room, or you'd be sitting on your backside, wondering what hit you."

FOR THE REST of the evening, Olivia ignored Luca. Considering her initial impulses, she thought she was doing him a favor. Even when he brought her a few tickets for dessert orders, she filled them without comment, avoiding eye contact as much as possible.

After closing, when it was the norm for the staff to share a glass of wine, she excused herself and left. She wanted nothing more than the security of her quiet room, where she could deal with the anger and regret warring within her.

What was wrong with him? she'd fumed on the short drive home. She'd tried to keep things professional between them, all but implored him to help her. But Luca was about to ruin everything.

She'd made it to the second floor when she heard the front door open and bang shut. About to reach sanctuary, she heard the thump of footsteps on the stairs. Her hands began to shake as she tried to slip the key in the door's lock.

Glancing anxiously over her shoulder, she saw him striding down the hall toward her, a dark silhouette in the dim light coming from below. Although she felt anything but, she tried for assertiveness.

"What are you doing here? Your father needs you. You're just going to make things worse."

"It's your fault." Although breathing heavily from the run, he swept her into his arms and closed his mouth over hers.

While his actions weren't a complete surprise, Olivia's pulse pounded in her ears from the assault on her psyche and senses. He was everything she dreamed a lover would be: that breathtaking mixture of passion and yearning. Only he was the wrong man at the worst time.

The arms used to crush her close, perfectly aligning their bodies, confirmed he was as fit as her eyes had gauged. Each inch of hard muscle and taught ligament and tendon spoke of desire unrestrained, and it battered at her defenses, triggering a heat that fueled her longing. To realize this moment was hers if she wanted it, that all she had to do was turn the doorknob and they could yield to each other's cravings, all but broke her heart.

Instead, she wrenched her lips from his, and whispered raggedly, "Luca, I can't."

"Don't tell me you don't want this, too."

"No, I won't lie to you, but it's still not something I can give in to."

"You don't think Tempest can see what's between us? Nor does she strike me as a prude. Livie, I know it's crazy fast, but I mean it when I say it's never been like this for me."

She caressed his cheek, regret a new and different ache in her chest. "I'll cherish that. But I'm not going to sleep with you."

He still held her close, but now the pain of rejection showed in his eyes. "There's someone else."

She cancelled that conclusion with a single shake of her head, "Not in a long time." And never like this. However, she couldn't give such power away when he already had so much control over her.

"Then why? We're not kids, and we've shared enough to know neither one of us is impulsive."

"Says the man who just ran from the restaurant where I'm on probation."

He relaxed a little and almost smiled. "Dad will understand, and he knows what a gift you are to us. I'm sure he'd be happy to assure you that your job is permanent."

Olivia struggled with more rationale, since she couldn't tell him the truth. "Your father has enough on his plate, and you need to be there for him—what with this latest development with your aunt, your uncle needing serious surgery, and your parents' relationship seeming to hold everyone's future in their hands."

"None of which has anything to do with us." Luca's tone held finality and he sought and found another kiss.

The intimate contact had its effect on Luca and, feeling the strength of his arousal, Olivia knew if she allowed it to go on another moment, anything else would be on her conscience alone. That is *if* she survived it.

Pushing against his chest, she used his surprise to open the door, ready to slip inside. "Go back, please. We can talk tomorrow."

He let his arms fall to his sides, studying her for several seconds. "You're not going to try and sneak off in the middle of the night, are you? Don't make me have to leave my door wide open to keep an eye on you, because I don't sleep in pajamas."

Unable to resist, he reached out to stroke her hair, only to sense her tensing. He let his hand drift down, grazing her shoulder, run along her arm, until he hooked one of his fingers with hers. Their gazes held, seconds stretched until the silence was filled with only the sound of their shallow breaths.

Olivia looked down at their entwined flesh and ever so slowly, drew away. "Goodnight, Luca," she whispered, and retreated into her room.

≈≪≫≈

KNOWING LIVIE WAS right, Luca returned to the restaurant; however, his body protested the decision, and his mind was awash with the sensations of what their first kisses had done to him. She'd tasted like one of her confections, her sleek body seemed designed to fit his, and her fleeting touch had left him aching to be naked with her in a place where they had all the time in the world to explore each other.

Everyone had already collected in the kitchen, and his father was giving the celebratory toast. Although Luca hung toward the back, it didn't go unnoticed and was met with curious looks, as well as a few knowing grins. He did his best to ignore them, steeling himself for his father's reaction. It came minutes later when, done with his side of things, Sal signaled for him to join him in the office.

The moment he shut the door, Sal demanded, "For crying out loud, what was that all about?"

Choosing not to prevaricate, Luca was blunt. "I stepped out of line and said something, a few somethings, I shouldn't have to Livie."

"You ran her off. Practically everyone saw it."

"And I apologized."

His father looked him over with a mixture of concern and relief. "Well, at least you're not bleeding. What did you say?"

"I'd rather not talk about it."

"Of course. The national anthem of the Angelonis."

Taking a stabilizing breath, Luca said, "That's funny. But not tonight."

They both took a moment—Luca to unbutton and hang his chef's coat on the empty hanger on the back of the door, and Sal to take a seat behind his desk. The weight of the day, of many days, was catching up with them and once Luca lowered himself into the recliner, they considered each other solemnly.

"Is she okay?" Sal asked.

"I might be able to better guess at that if she's still here in the morning."

"And if she isn't? Will you be all right?"

"No worse than you."

"Then you'll live."

His father's grim retort triggered a spasm deep inside Luca that had him slumping in the chair. "Exactly how long do you want to exist like that, Dad?"

"Damned if I know," Sal replied with unexpected candor. "When it's all there is, you get used to it."

"That's nuts...and unacceptable."

His father see-sawed his hand between them. "You're at the start of your life. It's different from this side of things."

"Yeah, since you're such a dinosaur." Luca tilted his head toward the direction of the restaurant. "I see the ladies—single and attached—hanging on your every word."

"Well, that will end fast enough with you here.—fresh blood and all."

He wondered if his father had a true conception of what he'd been inviting? Maybe a little flirtation had been his vitamin pill to get through the loneliness of his life.

"The point is I don't want the superficial," Luca replied. "I want the real thing. I thought you did, too." Rising, he added wearily, "I'm going to go see if Rocco needs help with restocking."

Their bartender welcomed the assistance. Between the two of them, they cut a good half hour off the task and it was only minutes past midnight when the last of them exited the building.

After Sal locked up, he faced his son and gestured to his car. "You want a lift?"

"Thanks. I think I'll walk and burn off some adrenaline."

Sal hesitated. "You know I'd be happier if you got involved with someone other an employee, but I want you to know I'm here for you."

With a simple nod, Luca shoved his hands deep into his pockets. "Night, Dad," he said, and headed back to the house.

The first buzz from those kisses shared with Livie had been fading since he left her; fading as sadly as the initial pleasure from tasting a rare wine. What remained was the knowledge of loss and it left Luca with a void where melancholia settled like the heaviest fog.

Cars whizzed by pulsating with music that spoke of anger and sex. He crossed streets and passed brightly lit houses where—having reached another weekend—people were in full, mindless revelry. It was the hour for slow, grinding dancing and long, tongue-tangling kisses, and Luca was relieved when he finally reached the oasis that was Tempest's house. Oddly enough the white hollyhocks and gladiolas glowing in the light of the full moon reached up like fingers, as though cupping the house in a mystical, protective grasp. Luca passed through the white picket gate with relief. Here he could think without his thoughts being tainted by the impulsive and the reckless.

Preoccupied with his own notions, he didn't see the creator of all this imagery, until he reached the stairs at the base of the porch. She looked like a sphinx sitting there in a high-backed white rocker, stately and calm.

"Back to stay this time?"

Accepting the wave of chagrin that swept through him, he nodded. "I was loud when I ran in earlier. I apologize."

"Again."

"Yes, ma'am. I sincerely apologize. I swear this is conduct wildly out of character for me. But I won't blame you if you're regretting your decision to let me stay here."

She chuckled and dismissed his concern with a wave of her hand. "I was awake. Moons like this aren't for sleeping."

No, he thought looking up at the hazy sky that still allowed the celestial orb to provoke them. There had been no other storms, which was a relief. The atmosphere carried enough energy without adding dangerous lightning and bone-rattling thunder.

Wondering how much she'd heard, Luca leaned against the porch railing. Olivia's car was parked out front, sparing him from having to ask if she was still here. But had she come downstairs seeking Tempest's advice?

Tempest resumed her rocking. "Has it crossed your mind that our girl has a lot on her mind without you complicating things?"

The unmitigated censure had Luca torn between bristling and relief for her honestly. "Do you know what's going on with her?"

"No, and if I did, I wouldn't tell you. That's her business."

"I only want to help."

"You *want*," she crooned. "At least you got one word right."

Having a virtual stranger stare at you as though reading your most personal thoughts was embarrassing, and yet in a matter of a few sentences, Luca felt as though she was forcing him to have a conversation with himself.

"I don't expect you to believe me, but it's more than what you're insinuating. I don't know how to explain it. I just know."

"Regardless, delicate things can never be forced."

The crickets ceased their chirping. The tree frogs fell silent. Everything seemed to be listening and Luca knew he needed to, as well.

"That's the second time I've heard words to that effect tonight." He was still for a moment, struggling with what else he wanted to say. "It's hard. I'm afraid she'll run away before she realizes she can trust me."

"A cornered animal is supposed to trust?"

Luca groaned. "I know, I *know*."

"Patience is the hardest virtue to champion."

"I wish there was a secret to it."

"No secret, but some kind of recipe. You're in the recipe business, you should already know it."

'What's that?"

"Stay busy and keep the faith."

10

"WILL MY BEING HERE MAKE YOU UNCOMFORTABLE?"

It was Sunday morning, the Fourth of July, and while most of the city appeared to be sleeping-in to recover from a night of partying, and to reenergize for yet another, activity-packed day, Olivia and Luca kept to the agreement made Friday to return to *Vita e Spezie* at their usual early hour. The plan was to complete the baking as soon as possible, so they would have the rest of the day to enjoy the holiday, too.

They'd made it through Saturday simply because the restaurant had stayed busy from opening to closing. However, Luca's question brought back the reminder—one hardly needed—that they were alone this time with nothing and no one to distract them from each other and the electricity humming between them.

"It would help if you didn't keep staring at me the way you have been since we left the house." Olivia knew if she'd let him drive, the problem would have been resolved, but then she would have been left to fidget, even those few blocks.

"Well, Livie, the fact is I like to look at you," he replied with matching candor. "And today is the one day I can do it without an audience."

While she respected his frankness, and was secretly thrilled by the sentiments, she couldn't encourage him. "Yes, it's just you, me, and the security cameras."

Grimacing, Luca started to retrace his steps. "I'm shutting them off."

"Don't! We have to assume your father is going to check them. What conclusions will he come to if he sees they were down while we were here?"

Luca stopped, his back still to her. Moaning toward the ceiling, he uttered, "You're right."

Slipping on her chef's jacket over a turquoise, scoop-necked T-shirt and white Capri pants—her indulgence for working through personal time—she suggested a way that would give them both some relief. "Maybe you should check upstairs and see how Valentina is feeling. You could take her to church."

He glanced down at his black T-shirt and cargo-style Bermuda shorts. "I could at least drive her, yeah."

"Exactly. If she's feeling well enough to go, you know she'll think it's too close to drive. But it can't be safe for her to walk."

Luca checked his Smartphone for the time. "Although I fully intended to help you with the work, you're right. I'll lock up after myself. Call if you need me."

As soon as the door closed behind him, Olivia breathed with relief. With luck, he would be gone at least an hour. Hopefully, Valentina would want to attend first Mass, and it would be longer.

She was doing this for both of their sakes. For her part, it was difficult to be around him and not relive what it felt like to be in his arms. Friday night had been a sleepless one for her, and last night not much better. They'd returned to Tempest's and found the house dark, indicating their landlady had retired. It had been an oddly intimate experience to climb the stairs and walk down the hallway together like a real couple heading for the same bedroom. But then Olivia had turned left at her door, and Luca had stopped across the hall at his.

"Goodnight," she'd said, trying to sound normal.

"Livie."

The wistful entreaty in his voice had her missing the lock and scratching the paint next to the knob. Fortunately, her phone jingled, a clear signal as to who was calling.

"It's my mother," she said, holding up her Smartphone as proof. "I have to take this. I haven't done more than text her a few words since her last two calls and owe her a serious *vay ya*. Goodnight."

While relieved for the escape, Olivia didn't get off easily. Her live-wire, chatty mother had gone immediately into her version of the third degree.

"Why aren't you out on a hot date?"

Olivia had pictured the vibrant sixty-one-year-old dusting the living room or reorganizing the pantry with one hand, oblivious of the hour. Dropping her purse on the blue Queen Ann's chair, Olivia had toed off her non-skid, black work shoes and sighed with true exhaustion. "Because I've been on my feet for eighteen hours, and all I want is to get horizontal and sleep."

"My poor *boo*. It's those *cro-cros!*"

"Better ugly shoes than a dangerous fall. I told you one of the chefs here injured himself and that's why I have my job."

Her mother made a sound of reluctant acceptance. "Well, what about tomorrow then? Big plans for the holiday? You said the place is closed Sundays. How old school, but good for you. Everyone is open seven days a week these days. Your brothers make the *babbin* all the time."

"Yes, we're closed." Unbuttoning her black slacks and tugging her white T-shirt over her head, Olivia had been careful not to share she would be working anyway—and definitely stayed away from the reason why. "How are those pout faces otherwise?"

"Don't change the subject. Good grief, *Bebelle*, haven't you met anyone yet?"

She'd closed her eyes upon hearing the loathed nickname. *Boo/ Honey* was bad enough, but doll was so demeaning. Her brothers were called Bertrand, Maurice and Remy. Always. But she was forever *Bebelle* or *Boo Bebelle*.

Bebelle with a culinary arts degree, damn it.

"No one wants to date a woman with bags under her eyes. Give Dad a hug for me. I'll call you tomorrow and we'll catch up then. Love you."

She felt guilty for cutting off her mother; however, not guilty enough to tell her the truth. There would be time enough for that later. Maybe. Depending on what she found out tomorrow.

The sound of a key in the deadbolt brought her back to the present and Olivia's breath caught. Surely Luca couldn't have missed Valentina.

"She didn't answer the door," he began. "I almost came down to tell you I'd run to the church to make sure she'd made it okay when I remembered I still have a key to her apartment. Well, it's the one on the restaurant ring Dad gave me."

Olivia felt her heart grow heavy. "Luca, what are you telling me?"

"She was still in bed."

By itself, the news was anticlimactic. Olivia would be languishing back at the boarding house, too, if not for tomorrow's appointment. But conscientious and faithful Valentina Angeloni off her long-time schedule was a serious matter. "Oh, no. Is she—?"

"Sorry. She woke once I tapped on her bedroom door. She insists she's okay, but admitted to being too drained to go to church this morning."

That was not like her at all. "Do you think you should call your father?"

"I suggested that. She said it was nonsense and insisted I don't bother him on his one day off."

It stacked up to be a lose-lose situation. Did Luca call Sal anyway, and offend Valentina, or honor her request and invariably face Sal's displeasure should things grow more critical? "How does she look?" Olivia asked.

"Like a woman without makeup."

He was being entirely serious, which had Olivia rolling her eyes. "The more things change, the more they stay the same."

"Meaning?"

"In the era of the geisha, I doubt a man would recognize any of those ladies if they'd passed him on the street in less than full regalia."

He dropped his chin to his chest, accepting his guilt. "Can I get a raincheck on being pummeled with feminist stones? I'm trying to figure out what to do."

"I'm thinking. Did you notice any pill bottles on her bed stand? Used tissues? A water glass?"

"Come to think of it—only a half-empty cup of tea, and her alarm clock. How am I doing, Sherlock?"

Olivia shook her head, not liking what she was hearing. "A woman with a broken heart, who's clearly not well would have photos close by, tissues for the endless nights of tears, medicine bottles. Rosaries! Cajuns are Catholics, too. If there isn't a Crucifix on the wall by her bed, she has to have a little rosary box within reach to help ease her torment and suffering."

"The first night I was there, I heard her moving around in her room as though she was putting up things," Luca said. "Maybe she stuck everything in the bed stand drawers because she didn't want me to see."

"Now you're on the right track," Olivia replied, only to give him a look of dread. "I'm afraid she's been ill for some time, Luca."

Luca remained stoic as he digested the grim news. "I told her I'd be back to check on her."

"Of course, you must."

"We should still have some soup left from last night."

"If she can't or won't eat, it will be another sign to gauge her condition."

"I'd make her something fresh, but I don't know that she could handle anything substantial." He ran his hands through his hair, his expression uncertain. "God, I'm babbling. Give me something to do, Livie, before I drive us both nuts"

She indicated the ten pounds of sweet potatoes on the next table. "Peel. I'm midway through preparing the Doberge batter, and I'll put those pans in the convection oven. With Vinny not here, we can bake the cheesecakes in the other stove. We'll finish all the sooner and that will free you up to do whatever you may have to do."

Although he continued to look troubled, Luca nodded his agreement. Washing his hands, he reached for a paring knife.

After the silence grew too palpable, Olivia asked, "Where is your father today?" She didn't like talking for the sake of avoiding silence; however, she also didn't want him brooding too much. "Is there another bocce game?"

"Yeah. Dad said he was going to pick up Uncle Leo and Tiny."

"Can your uncle play in his condition?"

"I doubt it, but it will be good for him to socialize a little. And I'm sure he'll be good with the kids."

Realizing he would be missed, Olivia added, "I'm sorry for keeping you from being there, too. Your father has to be peeved."

He shrugged. "He hasn't said anything to me. Besides, he knows this was important and there'll be other opportunities. There was no contest, as far as I'm concerned."

"Luca."

"I know. You don't want me to say things like that."

On the contrary, she wanted to hear every sweet nothing he was thinking, only it wasn't fair to encourage him. But she could make some kind of gesture.

"There's something you should know," she began. "About the gentleman at the Jansen party."

"Could we drop that? I know I acted the fool."

"No, listen, please. Mr. Estevez and Mr. Jansen were old Navy buddies. Pilot and navigator landing their fighter on an aircraft carrier, and there was an accident. They crashed into the sea. Mr. Estevez was injured and would have drowned, if not for Mr. Jansen saving his life. They've remained friends all these years. He's with the American consulate in Panama and came all this way to celebrate with the family. He retires in two years. The business card he put in my pocket was the name of his granddaughter, along with her email address. She wants to become a chef and he asked if I would consider giving her some tips, since her parents don't want her to go into the profession because it's still so male dominated."

Luca stopped peeling and stood there in a state of something worse than dumbfounded. "And there endeth the lesson."

"I don't understand. I was just trying—"

"What an ass I've been, and I humbly apologize. Livie, I swear to you, I'll never pull anything like that again. My reactions that night have haunted me. I don't want to follow my mother's choices—reacting and judging without a dialogue. If I ever get to take vows, I want them to mean something. At the very least not prejudicial perspective without communication."

Although he sounded like he was talking to himself, Olivia said, "I believe you."

He grew silent after that, and she left him alone to deal with whatever internal coup or configuring he needed to do. This time the quiet felt almost companionable.

"Did you email her yet?" Luca finally asked. "The granddaughter."

"Yes. Last night. I only had to remember the continental and elitist snobbery I faced to make myself forget how tired I was and take the first step," she replied. "Then I saw her Facebook photos and realized how petite she was—shorter than me—and I was doubly in her court."

His expression grim, Luca said, "I'm sorry it was a rough haul for you, Livie. If we'd been in school together, I would have stepped up and been your champion."

"Only to compromise your own future?" Olivia shook her head, adamant. "The only way to change that type is to crush them with success." She chuckled. "In my case, it's to wear them down to a half-hearted surrender, but I'm hoping to build our small army one tiny voice at a time...soon to include Isabella Estevez."

"You have a lifetime ally in me."

IT WAS TWO o'clock when Olivia washed the last of the pans and wiped off her station. Luca did the same with his area. They'd worked well together which, as hoped, had taken hours off her initial estimation for the day.

"I don't know about you, but I'm starved," Luca said.

She had a one-word answer. "Valentina."

"I'll bring her the last of the soup," he assured her. "If she seems stable, there's no reason to hang around and have her upset about taking up our time."

He'd gone up to check on his aunt twice already, and both times he'd reported marked improvement in her status. He'd also taken over the chore of watering the herbs she babied for the restaurant to save her more worries.

When he returned this time, he gave Olivia a thumbs-up, and drew her from her stool where she'd been waiting. "She's sitting up in bed and watching TV with a cup of tea. She even put on some makeup and seems to be feeling better."

"Good! I'm so relieved," Olivia said. "Attitude means a great deal." As they walked to her car, she gave him a last out. "But are you sure you shouldn't appease your father and make an appearance at the game?"

"Only if you come with me."

"Whoa," she said, literally backing away from the idea. "I don't think I have the courage to face your father at the moment."

Grinning, he said, "Then where to?"

"Oh, you." Recognizing that he was toying with her, she continued,

"Someplace with fresh air, where we can people watch. Last Sunday, Tempest and I had a walk on the beach and I've only dealt with recycled oxygen ever since."

"Fisherman's Wharf," Luca said with a nod in the correct direction. "It's a couple of blocks that way and if you get tired of people watching, you can take in the cruise ships and shrimpers. Don't worry about ignoring me. I'm used to having my feelings hurt."

In reply, Olivia tossed him her keys.

The restaurant was as crowded as one would expect for a holiday weekend in a resort city. However, after a short wait, they were shown to an outer table with a great view of the bay.

Olivia sat back in her chair, took in her surroundings, then breathed in the humid mix of aromas that soothed the senses the way the breeze caressed her skin. "I never get tired of this ambiance."

"That's shades of what my dad said."

"I'll take heart in knowing we agree on something."

"Besides a soft spot for his son."

Olivia let him get away with that one. "So, what are your other favorite geographic aromas?"

Continuing to peruse the menu, he replied, "Aside from the surprisingly seductive waft of lemon balm and basil on your hand as you caressed my cheek Friday night, I occasionally enjoy the cleansing jolt of alpine air."

"Ah," she murmured, unable to deny how the unexpected compliment undermined her resistance to him. "I've developed a sneaky habit of pinching a bit of both herbs from Tempest's plants along the walkway when I get home. I find it soothing to breathe in their scent while I'm trying to fall asleep."

"One mystery resolved, dozens to go. By the way, on you those fragrances become heady stuff."

"How often do you get your jolt of alpine air?" She was running out of barriers to keep him from heading too far down Charisma Lane.

"Infrequently enough to forget I really don't care too much for freezing my butt off, and that I'll never be more than an adequate skier."

Their waiter arrived with silverware and napkins. "May I interest you in a something to drink?" he asked. "We have some nice selections from Texas wineries and breweries."

"Do you have Pellegrino Mineral Water?" Olivia asked.

"Yes, ma'am."

"Then that will work for me, and...the red snapper with fresh vegetables."

"What's one of your most popular artisan beers?" Luca asked.

"Our head bartender dabbles a bit on the side and has created a wild version of a popular pineapple-and-jalapeno light ale."

"Welcome back to Texas," Luca said with a chuckle. "You know you're home if everything has jalapeño in it. Let's give it a try, and I'll have the snapper, your house salad, instead of the other sides, and to start we'll share an order of Shrimp Kisses."

When the waiter was out of earshot, Olivia leaned closer to Luca. "I hope you're as hungry as you said, since you'll be eating those appetizers on your own."

"You have to try at least one."

"I think you only ordered it because of its name."

"Could be," he mused, with an irreverent grin.

In the end, she did try one of the starters, only to drink most of her mineral water before any feeling returned to her mouth. She also, relented, and took the tiniest sip of his ale to put an end to his coaxing. His enthusiasm to share everything with her was irresistible.

"I get it," she said, savoring the flavors, "but the jalapeño is reigniting the heat in my mouth, and I think I'd prefer my pineapple in salsa or chutney with a cod or halibut."

"A white fish for sure. Sea bass. Although it's not on the menu. Dad's turned down the last few suppliers, who've offered him some."

"I'll bet he's fun to watch when he's doing his thing."

"A few other adjectives crossed my mind," he mused.

"I can imagine a whole room full of Angelonis playing off each other. I'd find a comfy chair in a safe corner and take in the free entertainment."

"And I would be right beside you—ready to cover your ears, which odds are would be frequently necessary."

Their light-hearted banter continued through the meal, and when Olivia declined dessert, Luca signaled the waiter that they were ready for the check. Olivia reached for her purse.

"Don't you dare," he murmured.

"You can't buy me dinner. This isn't a date."

"Live in denial if you must."

When they exited, a line had begun to form outside. "We timed that just right," Luca said, only to have a pair of passing bicyclers win his attention. "Want to rent a couple and work off some of those calories? Correction, my calories. You ate like a one-winged bird."

"My strength hasn't completely returned yet for something that arduous," she told him, "but I'll take a walk on the beach if you're willing?"

"Anything to prolong the day."

THEY DROVE A fair way southwest to get to a stretch of beach that wasn't packed with tourists. Even so, privacy was a haphazard thing.

"Considerably warmer than the beaches around Chesapeake Bay," Luca noted of the tepid water, once they finally reached the surf.

"Were you brave enough to swim up there?"

"Nah, I was never tempted. What about you back in Louisiana?"

"It's bayou country," she reminded him. "If you can't see your feet, you don't know what's in the water with you. I did everything else, though. Climbed trees, played baseball. Having all brothers, I had this ridiculous idea that I could keep up."

"Oh, yeah? What position?"

"I was the youngest and smallest. They stuck me in the outfield. The only way I could stop a ball was if it hit me while I dozed under the old turkey oak tree at the end of my grandparents' property."

"So, I take it you didn't try to shoot hoops?"

Olivia held her arms out inviting his scrutiny. "Look at me. And all my brothers stand head and shoulders above me. I'm competitive, not suicidal."

"What do you think they'd make of me?"

"I'm sure they'd say, 'You're a great guy. Run as fast as you can.'"

"I would never have taken you for being an exaggerator."

"Oh, pathological."

"Uh-huh. Do Cajuns have as much blarney in them as the Irish?"

"More if my family is anything to go by." Studying the bits of shells the waves washed over her feet, she asked, "Are you going to try for a reunion between your parents?"

"I won't deny the temptation is there, but they've been apart for so long that might not be possible. If it's not, I would at least like to see them happy again." As though suddenly self-conscious, Luca asked, "How often do you talk to your parents?"

"As you probably gathered from last night, I'm weening them. You may not get this, but despite my accreditations and accomplishments, they have a knee-jerk instinct to do what your mother could have done to you. I've developed a deep-seeded rebellion to excessive coddling."

Luca pivoted around to walk backwards so he could study her. "It seems only natural they would be that way. Three strapping sons in a row, and then this little bit of fairy dust enters their lives? It was irresistible."

"Arrete toi!"

"And what does that mean?"

"Stop you! I'll give you a perfect example of what I'm talking about. My brothers were always addressed by their Christian names. They were seen as future businessmen by my parents before they stopped sucking their thumbs. But I didn't know what my given name was, until I started school. From day one, I've been called *Boo, Boo Bebelle* or *Bebelle*."

"Which is . . . ?"

"Honey, or Sweetheart, Honey Doll, or Doll."

"Outrageous," he said. "How did you bear living with such hideous people?"

Olivia kicked into the surf sending a spray of water at him. Laughing he darted out of reach.

"From now on, that's what I'm going to call you when we're alone. *Boo Bebelle.*"

"Then you *better* lock your door at night and live in fear of me coming to strangle you."

She sprang at him, intent on pushing him into the shallow waves, but he was faster and dodged out of the way again, only to grab her from behind. His lips caressed her ear.

"I wish you would come to my room."

Holding her tighter, he spun her around and around. Olivia gasped and screamed, the momentum lifting her legs high. She had a fleeting image of people grinning as they strolled by, and birds zooming low over the water. Then her vision started to fade.

"Luca—please!"

The panic in her voice had him immediately setting her down in the frothy surf, but when he felt her legs buckle, he quickly caught her, although this time they were facing each other.

"Livie—are you all right?"

She gripped his biceps to steady herself. "It's okay. I just got dizzy for a second."

"You're sure? I'm sorry." He kissed her forehead, then drew her against him for a gentler hug. "I got carried away and spun the breath out of you."

Olivia soaked in the wonderful feeling of being in his arms. She felt so safe and strong there. Even though it was unwise, she rose on tiptoe and pressed a sweetly erotic kiss to the side of his neck. "It just tells me how exhausted I am. Would you mind taking me home?"

"I'm not ready for this to end."

"But you really should spend a little time with your father and uncle. You're welcome to use my car."

THE BOCCE TOURNAMENT was well underway when Luca arrived. He was greeted with raucous cheers at the table where his father and uncle were sitting. From the number of glasses cluttering the surface—a mixture of beer mugs, wine goblets, and things that looked like the remains of a Tom Collins, Singapore Sling, and maybe the lethal Long Island Iced Tea—Luca knew in advance not to take anything that would be said too seriously.

"What do you think, Luca? You were part of the White House." Dominick Tomei's long cigar sent a curling blue plume toward the top of the red umbrella protecting the group from the baking sun. It seemed to be helping to chase away flies.

Not having a clue as to what the subject was, Luca said, "Guys, I would tell you, but they imbed a device in us that has audio and video abilities, as well as GPS features." He pointed upwards. "The satellites are watching. I'm sworn to secrecy for five years, and was told if any of us are caught breaking our oath, we're collected like stray cattle. When they're finished with us, we end up in a drum headed to North Korea for use as fertilizer."

Nodding solemnly Leo laid a paternal hand on Luca's shoulder. "*Silenzio.* That's the Angeloni way."

As Claudio drew him a chair from another table, Sal eyed Luca with as much amusement as pride. "You would have pulled that off if you hadn't added the video part."

"The price of thinking on your feet."

"I'm glad you made it. How'd everything go?"

"Fine," Luca assured him.

"Sal said the man's been working. Get him something to drink," Claudio yelled to no one in particular. "What's your pleasure?" He held up his beer and the half empty plastic cup of water nearest to him.

"Any cold beer in a bottle would be greatly appreciated, thanks."

Looking around the group and then out toward the yard, Luca asked, "Where's Tiny?"

"He left an hour ago," Leo replied. "He's at a picnic."

Luca recalled the name from the other day. "Nancy? Nice."

Leo sniffed with disdain. "She's about to have a reality check, but for once he has a good seat for the fireworks. Her father is the city manager or something and is producing the show this year."

Wishing the younger man better fortune than what his uncle foretold, Luca accepted the dripping bottle Claudio handed to him. "Thanks."

There came a call from across the yard. "Claudio! Dominic! You're up!"

After they left, Luca took a long swallow of beer, silently wishing he was still on the beach with Livie. If he closed his eyes, it would take no effort at all to imagine the feel her lips.

The memory was interrupted by his father's inquiry, "So, how's N'awlins?"

Blinking, Luca said, "She gave it her all to get things in shape for tomorrow. Lent me her car in case I needed to get back to Valentina."

Sal grew instantly alert. "What's up there?"

It hadn't been his intent to go down that track yet, but he decided it was just as well. "She didn't go to church today."

"That's never happened!" Leo declared.

"She probably caught the same bug that Andi and Janine caught, Uncle Leo," he said, not breaking eye contact with his father. "But I fed her some of Vinny's soup and she was feeling better this afternoon."

Sal nodded and patted his arm. "You tell me if you think I need to go over there."

"I checked on her three times, Dad. She almost looked herself on my last trip upstairs."

That seemed to relieve Sal. "And N'awlins? Did she tell you what's up for tomorrow?"

"No." *Damn it*, he thought to himself.

Leo perked up and looked from one to the other. "What about tomorrow?"

Looking like he'd swallowed a bad olive, Sal said, "She needs a few hours off."

"What, already? She's only worked for us a couple of weeks."

"That's why she worked today," Sal intoned. "To make sure we'd have enough product."

"No worries. I'll take her place."

11

"ARE YOU SURE?"

Perched on the front steps of Tempest's front porch, Olivia gazed at the darkening sky. She hadn't heard any fireworks except for the little firecrackers and cherry bombs kids were shooting off in the neighborhood. Behind her, Tempest rocked in her chair humming some unknown melody between breaks in their conversation.

"Been this way for ages. Don't know why it would change because you've come to town."

Grinning, Olivia said over her shoulder, "Not questioning, just excited. It's been a few years since I've had the opportunity to witness a show. I don't know when I'll have a chance again."

"Listen to you," Tempest said. "Talking like things don't change."

"I know they do, but a chef is usually busiest during the hours when these productions take place."

"Uh-huh. Your excitement ain't got nothing to do with you hoping Golden Boy might come back earlier than you're expecting?"

"Hush. He's with his family and that's exactly where he needs to be." Olivia regretted telling Tempest why she was home alone, and without her car. "Did you have a good day? I saw your closed sign up."

"I went to church and had lunch with friends. Then had me a nice nap with a soothing avocado mask on."

Olivia cooed softly. "You go, girl. Is that the secret of your lovely complexion?"

"No, but I get free samples in the mail from time to time, and I like to compare their concoctions to my own."

"I'm not sure you should subject skin like yours to such an experiment, but I applaud you for ascribing to truth in advertising."

"Especially when I can deduct it from my taxes."

As Tempest laughed at her own joke, the first rocket exploded in the air. Olivia gasped and clapped.

"It's starting!"

Every explosion offered its own formation and color. The noise decibel was louder than she'd expected, but then they were only a few miles away from the barges launching them.

Several of Tempest's neighbors were outside watching, too. Some of the children were dancing with sparklers, while others were laying on the grass just looking up. It was as she watched one child try to mimic one sky-wide burst by throwing her sparkler in the air, that Olivia saw a vehicle come down the road, and park directly in front. It was her car.

"That's my sign to turn in," Tempest said, easing to her feet. "All is right in this house."

"What?" Olivia spun around. "Don't go."

"I've had me a good day, darlin'. You finish it up."

The front door shut just as Luca made it to the steps. As another explosion sounded, he looked over his shoulder. "Did I miss much?"

"Only a half dozen or so." He sat down beside her, and Olivia momentarily forgot about the show. "What are you doing here already? Is the game over? Isn't there some kind of party still going on?"

"Yeah. But I wanted to be with you."

Since they were touching shoulder to hip, when he turned to meet her gaze, they were close enough to kiss. He wanted to. Olivia could tell by the way he focused on her lips.

"There you go disappointing your father again," she said, her throat suddenly going dry.

He grinned. "My, you worry about him a lot. I spent almost four hours with Dad, and tomorrow we'll be together all day. He's fine, believe me." He added in a more seductive tone, "Are you glad to see me?"

"Yes. But I feel badly that Tempest went inside."

"I saw that." Luca leaned against her slightly. "Think she's got some matchmaking in mind?"

Olivia had no doubt whatsoever, but made herself say, "She admitted she'd had a full day." She could tell by Luca's expression he knew she was all but squirming under his admiring scrutiny. Thankfully, another series of explosions began.

"Oh, those are my favorites!" she said, as the sky filled with white spheres, followed by long sparkling tendrils flowing down.

"Willows," Luca said. Then as smaller eruptions occurred on either side, he added, "Those are horsetails...and that's the fish."

Olivia shook her head. "You even know the names?"

"Washington, D.C., puts on some major shows, and I had a front row seat. There's plenty of opportunity to pick up little details."

A blend of pink and red rockets spread across the sky. "That must have a flower name," she said.

"Peony."

"Oh, I can see that." Yellow followed in a similar pattern, but with shorter petals or tails. "Mums?"

"Chrysanthemums, good."

The next made her laugh. "It looks like a Tina Turner wig."

"It's actually named after a famous Japanese hairdresser—Kamuto."

Had she called him a Renaissance man? He was a walking encyclopedia. "What don't you know?"

"Whether or not you'll go shy on me and run, if I kiss you?"

That was her cue to wise up and head inside, too. But Olivia couldn't. Tomorrow was looming and with it greater fears. She didn't want to leave him thinking she didn't care. She cared too much.

Cupping his cheek, she leaned closer and touched her lips to his. Her thumb stroked his jawline and the slightly rough texture of his five o'clock shadow. Grateful he let her lead, she tasted his lower lip and then traced his upper lip with the tip of her tongue. There she discovered he'd helped himself to the mints she kept in the car, and his breathing was as shallow as hers.

Resting her forehead against his, she whispered. "I'm glad you came back early."

"Did you get some rest?"

"Enough to stay awake for the fireworks."

"What fireworks?"

Olivia started to smile, but Luca was seeking another, deeper kiss.

With a soft moan, she yielded to it. Life had been demanding such a hectic pace lately, it was the most luxurious feeling to linger in the moment and fully experience each sensation as it flowed around and into her. She could tell Luca was feeling much the same from the way he stroked her hair, caressed her hand, and only then slipped his arms around her, so that their hearts were nearly beating as one.

She sensed his hunger, and yet he was unbelievably careful with her. Tender. It made her eyes sting with the threat of tears.

Only the pace and loudness of the explosions broke the spell, and Olivia started from it. Luca chuckled and coaxed her to lay her head against his shoulder.

"That's the best prelude to a finale I've ever experienced," he said.

They watched the rest of the show like that. Olivia had never felt safer or more at peace. They weren't even bothered by mosquitoes for all of the citronella plants and lavender Tempest had growing around them.

When the last blinding balls of fire lit the sky and shattered the night with staccato bursts, they sat content until the smoke left behind blended with the darkness.

"Are you going to fall asleep on me?" Luca asked. "Because you know we have better options."

Sighing, she lightly kissed the corner of his mouth and sat up. "You know I can't."

"I should have kept my mouth shut, let you fall asleep, and carried you upstairs."

"Romantic, but I'm a light sleeper."

Luca rose and extended his hand to help her up. But then he kept it and lifted it to his lips. "Won't you tell me what happens tomorrow?"

"Tomorrow. When I get back."

"I'll be watching the clock and the door all day."

OLIVIA'S DRIVE NORTH to Houston proved one of dread and agitation. When she wasn't worrying about what she would hear from the doctors, she was annoyed with not taking into consideration Monday traffic and how much it might slow her down. She ran into accidents every few miles, until she started to wonder if she'd make her appointment time at all, despite having left ninety minutes earlier than the trip should have taken.

As much as she enjoyed music, her subpar car radio crackled with static more than music. Since fiddling with the thing was a danger of its own, she had to ride in silence, and that was an enemy to her psyche.

She finally made it to the heart clinic with only minutes to spare, and all but collapsed in the reception area.

"Ma'am, you need to sign in."

Olivia lifted her hand, signaling the clerk by the window that she'd heard her. "As soon as I catch my breath."

The woman began to rise from her seat. "Do you need me to call for a wheelchair?"

Afraid she looked worse than she felt, she forced herself to her feet. "Thank you, but that won't be necessary. Olivia Dumont. I have an appointment with Dr. Acharya."

The receptionist nodded, finding her name on the screen and said, "I'll let them know you're here. In the meantime, we have paperwork for you to fill out, and I'll need copies of your driver's license and insurance data."

That was nothing new. Olivia had lost count of how many forms she had completed at various medical facilities. It took her several minutes by the time she completed all the documentation, but once the receptionist scanned everything, she said, "It shouldn't be long before they call you back."

Olivia returned to her chair and studied the people around her. The young child of no more than six looked in the worst shape and found little interest in a box of Legos. His coloring was the awful yellow-gray that speaks to insufficient oxygen and the threat of organ failure. As if that wasn't bad enough, the parents looked like extras from a horror movie; their condition appeared little better than their child's.

Sitting closest to the door leading to the examination rooms was a frail couple, the man in a wheelchair bearing an oxygen tank.

See, she thought to herself, *it could be worse*. While the room wasn't full, she looked healthier than everyone there.

Knowing it could be a while before she could check her phone again, she drew it out and began to answer long delayed text messages and emails.

The elderly couple was called first and left before the child and his parents were brought in. From their expressions, she could tell the news they'd been given wasn't good. That had Olivia wondering if she, too, would be sent away without hope.

The door opened and she was taken back. Expecting a long wait, she only sat on the exam table for a couple of minutes before the doctor came in. He a was small, wiry man with riveting brown eyes that looked as if they could glow in the dark from all the passion exuding from them.

"Miss Dumont, how was the drive up from the coast?"

"Nothing I'd like to do every day."

He set his laptop on the table, opened it to bring up her history, and proceeded to adjust the earpieces of his stethoscope.

"Take a deep breath," he instructed, as he held the diaphragm to her chest. "Let it out slowly. And again."

He did that several times shifting his location to various parts of her chest and back. Finally, removing the ear pieces, he set the stethoscope on the table beside his computer and clasped his hands, clearly about to make a pronouncement.

"I have news, not all of which will reassure you at first, but I believe your trial will soon be over."

"Oh my God," Olivia gasped. "Are you telling me I'm dying?"

"Well, we don't like to put it in those terms, although it's always a possibility," he admitted, his manner congenial. "You would not be here otherwise. But in your case, help is near. However, it also means you are no longer a candidate for the aortic stenosis trial. Your condition has passed our requirements."

She felt as though she was being thrown down an open elevator shaft. "Wait! I was told without this I can't survive."

"Which was how long ago?" he asked, with an understanding smile. "This is how quickly and brilliantly technology advancement comes to us. Though your condition has advanced, I'm convinced new techniques available will serve you well. In fact, a colleague I trained is now at John Sealy where you are located and would save you the deplorable commute. How marvelous is the universe?"

Dazed, Olivia shook her head, trying to take in what these revelations meant. "I don't understand. My medical problem is so bad, you won't work with me, but I'm a candidate for surgery?"

"Of course, we could do it here, but you've confirmed that you now work and live down in Galveston, where an equally adept surgeon would save you stressful travel time, and ease your recovery and rehabilitation requirements. With your permission, I'm going to send her your records. In the meantime, we'll get you fitted with an ambulatory electrocardiogram."

"A what?" Olivia all but squeaked.

The doctor patted her arm. "A heart monitor, but rather than the larger machine you've been hooked up to before, you carry it on your person throughout the day. Calm yourself, Ms. Dumont. It is entirely pain free and easy to operate."

Visions of the contraptions they attached to convicts' ankles played out in Olivia's mind. "How conspicuous is it going to be? I have a new job and anything that stands out will raise eyebrows. I haven't told anyone about this. Likely, no one would have hired me if I did."

"No problem. It looks exactly like a Fitbit."

"Great. Now I just need to explain why, after all the years of not wearing a watch, I'm wearing one of those?"

"These days, with everyone being more health conscious, people will think you're keeping track of your daily activity." Placing a reassuring hand on her shoulder, he said, "I'll be back in a minute. Let me see if Dr. Pham has confirmed my request. In the meantime, I'll have the nurse get you fitted and show you how the device works."

Olivia sat there numb. What had just happened?

"Congratulations, you're rejected."

What kind of good news was that? Everyone knew Houston had the best heart specialists. How could a facility in a vacation resort town compare?

In the next few minutes, as the nurse arrived and put her through a quick lesson, Olivia could only give her part of her attention. The other part of her mind was racing through ways to convince the doctor to allow her to be part of the trial. With every argument, she heard Dr. Acharya's verdict again.

"Your condition has deteriorated."

"But I don't feel any different."

The nurse gave her a concerned look. "Pardon?"

"Nothing. I'm just—what did you say about a diary?"

"You'll need to keep a record of what you were doing when you feel an episode coming on and what time it happens."

Olivia's anxiety was already pushing up her heart rate. "I'm a chef under scrutiny all the time. I can't be stopping to jot notes every other minute."

"When did you last feel an episode of lightheadedness or dizziness?"

She wasn't about to tell her it was last night when she and Luca were kissing, so she only admitted to the previous experience. "I was at the beach. Playing in the surf." She could feel her cheeks heat from her lack of forthrightness.

"Then that's when you'd want to write down the time and detail the occurrence and activity."

Olivia could just imagine Luca's reaction to that. "This is turning into a nightmare."

The nurse left, and Dr. Acharya returned and handed her a card. "It's all set. You see Dr. Pham tomorrow at 10 a.m."

"NO," SAL TOLD an obstinate Leo. "How many times do I have to say it? We don't need you. Olivia said she'll be back for the evening service."

"Saying and doing are two different things." Leo jutted forth his chin in challenge. "She said she was ready to work when you hired her, and after two weeks, she's already asking for time off? What kind of reliable employee does that?"

"But she worked yesterday to make up for this morning, Uncle Leo," Luca reminded him. He kept his tone easy in the hope of avoiding animosity between the brothers.

Sal gestured to his son. "Exactly what I was about to say. Everything is taken care of and under control."

"What if someone comes in with a special request?" Leo asked.

"It's Monday," Sal replied, exasperated. "Who's going to come in with something like that today?"

In one of life's ironic moments, Kat entered the kitchen waving an order receipt. "Where's Olivia?"

"Not here," Leo announced like a judicial verdict.

The waitress handed him the slip of paper. "Someone is out front in a hurry. They're asking if they can buy a whole Doberge, but they want a going away message written on it. Do you have time to do that?"

Leo sent his brother a smug smile, and reached for his chef's jacket. "Sure. I'm on it. Tell them to give me ten minutes."

As he collected a stainless bowl and the ingredients for a frosting, Luca patted his uncle on the back. "Glad to see your trip wasn't wasted, after all."

Sal threw up his hands. "I'm getting out of here before we have an accident with all this extra traffic in here."

As he strode away in the direction of his office, Leo winked at Luca. "He hates to admit when he's wrong."

Everyone returned to their individual tasks. Periodically, someone mentioned something they'd done yesterday. Someone else complained about their internet reception being out all day.

"Hey, Leo," Vinny called over his shoulder. "Yesterday, my youngest hit a home run. Man, that kid has arm strength."

"Good thing she looks like her mother," Joey chimed in.

Leo was scooping his frosting into an icing bag. "See? And you gripe about not having a son. Now everyone be quiet while I do this writing. I can't mess up."

He bent over the cake and started slowly drawing the letters. After a minute, Tiny stepped closer to peer over his shoulder.

"Where do you think she's going?"

"Am I a mind reader? They want what's written on the paper—'Annie, we'll miss you! Good luck!'"

"You going to put a candle or something on there?"

"It's not her birthday. Go get me a box."

As Tiny scurried off to the storage area by the display case, Kat leaned over the partition between the dining room and kitchen. "Leo, how much longer?"

"A minute. Tiny! The box!"

"I can't find any the right size."

"Bah! Luca, tell Sal his genius pastry chef left the place without restocking her station. Never mind, Tiny. I'll get one."

Leo circled the table and headed toward the far side of the kitchen where the main supply was kept. At the same time, Benny lifted the large stainless pot of steaming marina sauce. The two collided sending a wave of red sauce into the air and over Leo. Screams followed, then the sound of the crashing pot as sauce landed on Benny's hands, making it impossible to keep his grip.

Leo went down, while Luca, Vinny, and Joey came to his aid. Everyone stared at horror. In the harsh, fluorescent light, the sauce looked like blood.

"Sweet Jesus," Luca breathed. "Somebody call 9-1-1."

"He didn't say, 'Behind you,'" Benny said. "He should have said, 'Behind you.'"

"Holy Mother!" Vinny said, crossing himself. Seconds later, he collected his wits and hollered, "Towels! Clean up this mess before someone else falls."

"Call 9-1-1, damn it!" Luca yelled again, as he dropped to his knees beside his uncle.

"They're on their way," Kat assured him from her position on the other side of the counter. Her cell phone was pressed to her ear.

Luca went to work ripping apart the chef's jacket to try to remove Leo's clothing. He knew the boiling-hot sauce would only continue to burn skin. Time was of the essence, and Leo was already starting to shake from shock. But kindly, he hadn't yet regained consciousness. "Vinnie, give me your sharpest knife. We have to get everything off him. The marinara is melting his flesh."

Sal appeared at his side. "What do you need next?"

"Clear out the place of as many people as you can. When Leo regains consciousness, it's going to sound like hell in here, and we'll have to fight to hold him down."

Sal squeezed his shoulder and was gone. He was replaced with Vinny.

"His clothes are saturated, Luca. They won't cut easily. "I'll lift him, you pull off his things."

"Get me clean tablecloths," Luca yelled. "*Now!* Kat, tell the ambulance to come to the back. Stu, go out front and direct them back there if they happen to come up front. Tiny, go out back and wait for them."

By the time Luca had everything off Leo but his underwear, which was only lightly stained, he had him covered with the sanitary linens. It was then his uncle began to groan. Agony seeping through his unconsciousness, Luca leaned close to his uncle's ear. "Hang on, Uncle Leo. Try not to move. Help is on the way."

"Don't worry about me. Get little Mario out."

It was an emotional sucker punch, and for a second Luca thought he would be sick. Just as quickly he fought the wave of nausea and leaned close to his uncle's ear. "It's okay. Everything will be all right. You just hang on."

Sal led the EMS responders into the kitchen. Everyone backed away and avoided eye contact, afraid of what they would see in the other person's face. Radio calls were made to the hospital and none of it sounded good. Someone choked back tears when the paramedics did the count to lift him onto the gurney. It was all motion again as a keening Leo was rushed to the ambulance.

Just outside the door, Luca heard a cry. He turned in time to grab Valentina, stopping her from chasing the paramedics and Leo.

"*Mia adora*. What happened?" she demanded of Luca. "Why didn't you call me? I must go with him."

He held her firmly. "Aunt Val. Let them do what they need to do. We'll follow the ambulance to the hospital."

THE ABRUPT SWITCH from air conditioning to Houston heat via sliding glass doors came as a physical shock to anyone exiting a building. Add the glare of the morning sun, and a perfect scenario evolved for the two preoccupied and rushing people leaving and entering the hospital.

As they collided, Olivia uttered a breathless cry. Her shoulder bag went flying and she started reeling backwards. Although the other woman's groan was louder, she recovered faster, and grabbed Olivia's upper arms to steady her.

"Oh, God...thank you," Olivia gasped. "I was sure I was about to crack my head open on the concrete. I'm sorry for not looking where I was going. I was trying to turn on my cell phone."

"My fault," the woman in dark-pink nurse's scrubs replied, just as quickly. "The sun reflecting on the glass blinded me. Well, I'm not quite myself, either. I just lost a patient, and was running back inside to pick up some papers I'd forgotten." As soon as she spoke, she covered her eyes with her hand. "Apologies. I should never have said that."

"Bless you. I more than understand," Olivia replied, dismissing the inappropriate sharing of information. "This place does strike me as a portal to life and death. My doctor told me I'm as good as dead."

"Sweetheart, you need to sit down for a minute." The woman led her to one of the wood-and-wrought-iron benches tucked under a cluster of pines some yards away. "Take a few moments to catch your breath and calm your mind."

"My purse!"

"I've got it."

Olivia watched the woman with the coal black hair collect her bag and shove the things that scattered out of it back inside. She gauged her to be close to her mother's age, quite attractive given her harried state and the bad news she'd shared. "Thank you," she said as the woman handed her the bag and cell phone. She turned it on right away.

"Good," the woman said, sitting down beside her. "It's not broken. And, you, how are you feeling? Do you think you should go back inside and let someone take a look at you?"

Before Olivia could answer, her cell phone lit up, alerting her to an incoming call. As she looked at the name on the screen, she bit her lower lip, torn over wanting to answer, but knowing she couldn't speak yet.

"*Luca Angeloni?*"

The woman's exclamation had her glancing up in confusion. "Yes. Do you know him?"

"He's my son."

12

AS OLIVIA'S PHONE WENT SILENT, SHE PLEADED TO THE woman, "Don't tell him you met me."

Right when Rosa began to respond, *Chopsticks* began playing inside her purse. She drew out her phone, and showed Olivia the screen. "Luca."

"Please, let it go to voicemail, Mrs. Angeloni."

Rosa did, but as soon as things went silent again, she asked, "Why would he try calling both of us?"

"I don't know, ma'am."

Giving her a wry look, Rosa replied, "I have a feeling you'd better call me, Rosa. Let's see what message he left."

> *"Mom, I'm on my way to the hospital with Aunt Val and Dad. There was an accident, and Uncle Leo is badly burned. I wanted to let you know in case something got on the news up there. I'll call with an update as soon as I know something. Love you."*

Gasping, Rosa blurted out, "Did you hear? Leo has been burned. It must have happened at the restaurant."

"He's not supposed to be there."

"Well, obviously he was. Did Luca leave you a message?"

Olivia shook her head already knowing the answer. "I wouldn't tell him why I needed off, or where I was. Now I haven't answered my phone. He's going to be extremely upset with me." She rose. "I have to get back."

"I'm coming with you."

"Really? Okay." Olivia's confusion was born out of her awkwardness. What would it look like when the two of them appeared in Galveston together? "Are you sure that's a good idea?"

Rosa lifted her eyebrows. "I see you know about me, yet I know nothing about you."

"Only a little, and mostly out of necessity." She thrust out her hand. "I'm Olivia Dumont, filling in while Leo was supposed to be recovering from another fall, and then have hip surgery."

Rosa's handshake was firm and warm. "So, you're the one I've been hearing about. I'll bet you were a blow to Leo's ego."

Guessing it had been Valentina who had mentioned her, Olivia offered, "I can't imagine anyone would like to be replaced, even if only temporarily. But, yes, the Angeloni men are a proud lot."

"I wouldn't still be here by myself if they weren't."

Taking a calming breath, Olivia tried to discretely massage her chest. These revelations on top of her news from the doctor were taking a toll on her heart. She didn't want to check her monitor for fear of what it would tell her. "That brings me back to my original question about us riding together. How will you get back?"

Rosa shrugged. "Luca will have to help me. The point is, we've both been dealt big blows, and Leo's accident makes it worse. Neither one of us should be driving, or be alone right now. I can drive, if you need me to, but I'd like to make some phone calls to my office first."

"I'm okay," Olivia told her, thinking to herself, *Provided there weren't any other shocks coming.*

"Fine. Then if you'll wait for me to run inside for the paperwork I forgot, you can drive me to my car, and I'll pick up my bag. In my line of work, I've learned to always carry some essentials just in case."

It was several minutes before they were on their way. Olivia used the time to jot down the monitor data and the time in the little notebook she kept in her purse. The data was undoubtedly off a bit, since she was starting to calm down; however, it would have to do, since she wasn't yet sold on the idea of keeping a journal in the first place.

Once they were out of the parking lot, Rosa offered her services again. "I can delay my calls for a little while if you need me to drive?"

"I don't think so. Am I doing something that makes you think you should?"

Rosa reached over and patted her shoulder. "No, dear. It was my way to get you to talk to me. What did you mean, your doctor said you were as good as dead? That's not usually the approach they use."

"It might as well have been. I came here anticipating joining this drug trial, only to be told my condition has deteriorated so much, I'm no longer a candidate. A minute later he tells me not to worry. If I don't drop dead in the next day or week, there's a new procedure for aortic stenosis."

"Why, that's reassuring news."

Olivia frowned, still unconvinced. "Or else he was giving me false hope to get me out of his office. Not every guinea pig gets to be a lab rat."

"Who's your specialist?"

"Dr. Acharya."

"I've heard of him. He has an excellent reputation. Who's he sending you to?"

"Dr. Pham at John Sealy in Galveston."

Rosa smiled. "Maybe I can reassure you a bit. I had a patient that was given no hope and your Dr. Pham saved him."

"Excuse me—I happen to know what kind of nurse you are."

"Then listen to me. Miracles happen."

Olivia took in the information. It was humbling how badly she wanted to believe what she was hearing. "You're not just trying to make me feel better, are you?"

"One of my strengths—and weaknesses—is that you get the truth, ready or not."

"Okay, then. Thanks," Olivia said. "I guess I'll at least go see what she has to say."

They drove in silence for a few minutes. Once they were southbound on Interstate 45, Rosa asked, "How long have you known Luca?"

Convinced she already knew if Valentina had been talking about her, Olivia said, "We met the day after he returned to Galveston."

"Not long at all. Yet you've made a strong impression on him."

What was she supposed to do, agree? Deny? Apologize? This was a private matter, even though Rosa was his mother.

"All right," Rosa continued. "Then let me ask, what do you think of my son?"

"That's not exactly a fair question, given what I've tried not to tell *him*."

"What else are you going to do for the next forty minutes to an hour? Fret over Leo when there's not a thing you can do about it, or listen to country songs about heartache?" Rosa chided. "That will improve your condition."

"It has crossed my mind to pull over to let you take the car, and I'll call for an Uber ride or UFO."

Rosa pointed at her. It was then that Olivia noticed she wore no jewelry, except for a watch, and her nails were unpainted, and as short as her own.

"I'm the mother of a professional chef. You are a professional chef. That tells me, while you may look like puff pastry, you have the fortitude to overcome challenges important to you."

Luca's mother was giving her too much credit; however, she wanted to get through this ride in an amicable way. "Not because he's your son," she admitted slowly, "but he's special."

"You're falling in love with him."

"I know my situation. He doesn't need to deal with what that means, or could mean."

"It wouldn't stop him," Rosa said, with a knowing look.

Olivia was sure she was right; however, it wasn't what she wanted for him. "All I can think of right now is the nuclear explosion that's going to erupt when we arrive together."

GETTING TO THE hospital was an exercise in visual and audible agony, thanks to traffic and the emotional state of his passengers, but once they reached the emergency area, Luca dropped off everyone and went in search of a place to park his father's car. There had been no question about him getting behind the wheel.

When he finally caught up with the group in the waiting room, the others traveling separately had arrived, as well. Valentina was weeping into a handful tissues. Beside her, Vinny kept saying, "I can't believe it. It all happened so fast," while his father was pacing like a caged animal.

Noticing Benny and the prep team huddled across the room, distressed and deep in conversation, Luca spoke with them first. That's when he realized Benny was trying to overcome his own pain from his burned hands. Placing his arm around the trembling, young man, Luca led him to the receptionist's window.

"This is Ben...Benjamin Bosco," Luca began.

"B-Benedict," Benny mumbled.

"Sorry. Benedict Bosco," Luca said. "He was hurt at the same time, as my uncle, Leo Angeloni, who's inside. Can you have someone see to him, as well, please?"

When the woman saw Benny's fiercely red, swollen hands, and his stressed state, she called for assistance. Moments later, the door opened to receive him.

Feeling his hesitation, Luca leaned closer to whisper, "I know you're worried about the expense. We'll take care of you." Then, squeezing his shoulder, he gave the young man a slight push.

He turned to see Sal had spotted him and had come over. "Dad, you need to pull yourself together."

"This is nuts. Why can't we get any information?"

"They only now got him here, and he's not the only patient." He nodded toward his right to indicate the rest of the room with several other people watching them.

"Excuse me," the admittance clerk said. "There's paperwork to fill out on both parties. Who's going to do that?"

"I will," Luca replied, only to smile. "Pardon—I'll need Benny's wallet to complete his." He motioned beyond the doors. "It's in his pocket."

Having witnessed his paternal care with Benny, she leaned forward and whispered to him, "I'll buzz you in. But please don't linger."

"Thank you."

Upon his return, Luca went to the far corner of the room where his family was huddled. "Bear with me as I get this done."

The minutes dragged on, and Sal returned to pacing. "Are they leaving him back there to suffer until they get an insurance number?"

Finishing his uncle's paperwork, Luca handed Sal the wallet and the clipboard with the paperwork. "Hand over the clipboard, pocket the wallet. Try not to mix up the process."

"Smartass."

"Yes, sir," Luca said, bowing his head over Benny's forms.

Sal handed Leo's wallet to Valentina to hold. She stroked it as she would Leo's hand. Upon opening it, she made a choking sound and pressed the wallet to her breast.

"Oh, my sweet brother. Look, Luca," she showed him the picture of his Uncle Mario giving Mario Junior a piggy back ride. "Leo has carried it with him all this time. Dear God, what if he dies, too? Who will remember?"

Sal stopped before her. "Don't be ridiculous."

"He can't go before me."

"Nobody's going anywhere, Valentina. Stop it."

After several more minutes, Luca finished filling out Benny's forms and took his license and what ID cards he could find to the front desk. Behind him he heard Tiny whine, "I should never have agreed to take him to the restaurant."

Startled, Luca glanced over his shoulder. He hadn't seen Tiny since the accident. He must have driven here by himself.

"It's not your fault," Valentina assured him.

"No, I was supposed to take care of him. I am stupid, just like Leo said."

With no energy to deal with the dynamics of that relationship, Luca turned his back on the whole scene, only to have something else capture his attention.

The glass doors slide open—and Olivia and his mother walked in.

AS WITH EVERYONE else, Sal heard the emergency room doors open. He did a double-take realizing one of the two people entering was Olivia. His overwhelmed mind accepted that, at some point, Luca must have found an opportunity to call her. What made a farce of such reasoning was the woman beside her.

He felt something cold and awful wrench inside him, followed quickly by a fury that propelled him across the room. "Are you kidding me?"

Sal stopped in time to block Rosa and Olivia's path, only to seethe at his wife, "What the hell are you doing here?"

"The same thing you are. Luca called me with the news."

Valentina rushed forward and gripped her brother's arm. "Salvatore, *per favore.* You're causing a scene. Come, all of you. Let's sit down."

Valentina linked arms with Rosa and led her to the back of the room. Glaring holes into his estranged wife's back, Sal followed. As Olivia brought up the rear, she saw Luca out of the corner of her eye. Giving him a look of commiseration she continued after the others, who were taking their seats.

Rosa asked Valentina, "Has there been any news yet?"

"No, and as you can see, we're all stressed to our limits."

"What happened?"

"They tell me it was an accident," Valentina explained. "Leo was excited to have a special order."

"But he wasn't supposed to be working," Olivia said.

"Well, somehow he was," Valentina replied. "And he turned without thinking and ran straight into Benny carrying a boiling pot of sauce."

Rosa crossed herself and glanced Olivia's way. "Hip surgery will be out of the question for now. The risk of infection from the burns would be too great." Returning her focus to Valentina, she asked, "Did the sauce reach his face?"

"No, thank God."

Sal glared at Olivia. "And how do you two know each other?" he asked, wagging his finger between her and Rosa. "Is this where you tell me you two are pals, and you've been stabbing me in the back the same way my sister has?"

"No!" Olivia cried. "We only just met. A simple run-in, as I came out from of my appointment. Then Luca called and she saw his name appear on my phone, and we started putting two and two together."

At that point, Luca joined them. "And moments later I called you, Mom, and you didn't answer, either. You didn't have your phone with you?"

"Please don't rush to judgement, Luca," Olivia said. "She already had too much going on, having just lost a patient right before we bumped into each other."

Valentina wrapped her arms around Rosa. "My poor sister. What a horrible day you're having."

"Hold on," Sal interjected. He hooked his thumb over his shoulder to indicate the emergency area. "The person who's having a bad day is Leo. I'm done listening to 'poor this, poor that' nonsense. You're not going to make me overlook the fact that you two have been conniving behind my back for years."

Rosa shot him a pitying look. "Right, Sal. Be sure to always make everything about you. You cared so much that not once in all this time did you come for me. The only one who cared was Valentina."

"Why should I chase after you when you're the one who left?"

"Because you're the one who needed forgiveness. You were the one who was having the affair!"

THERE HAD ALREADY been too much pain in this day. Olivia couldn't bear another moment of it. The ugly words meant to punish threatened to suck all oxygen out of the room. Desperate for relief, she ran for the door. Her heart was pounding in her ears and—when the midday heat assaulted her—she thought she would become ill.

As she reached out for the white brick wall to steady herself a hand closed around her wrist. A breathless moment later, she was pulled against Luca.

"Where do you think you're going?"

"Luca, please, I'm going to be sick."

Her expression must have confirmed that. With greater care, he helped her lean back against the building. "I'm sorry. I didn't mean to overreact. It was just seeing you and Mother walk in together. It made me think ... I don't know what."

"That's pretty much how I reacted, as well. Once I learned who she was."

"Your appointment," he murmured. "Is that where you got this?"

Despite some judgement and suspicion remaining in his tone, Luca frowned as he stroked the band on her wrist with his thumb. Belying his tone, his touch became a caress.

With a resigned sigh, she nodded.

"So, you're not simply recovering from a bad bug. It's far more serious."

Olivia closed her eyes waiting for her world to turn right side out.

"You have your family to worry about, and they need you. Now's not the time for this."

"It is for me. At least I know the truth of why you wouldn't let me in your room the other night."

"Couldn't."

He swallowed, and his fingers briefly squeezed her wrist. "Are you on a donor's list?"

"No, it's something different."

"Operable?"

When his voice broke on that single word, Olivia's gaze lifted to his. What she saw in his eyes made hers well with longing and fear. "Luca...I—I...can barely breathe let alone think."

When the last word became a sob, he drew her into his arms. As his body absorbed her small frame's trembling, he kissed the top of her head. "What I don't want to think about is how long you've been carrying this by yourself. Who else knows?"

"Your mother. On the ride up. You know how she is."

"I'm getting a fast-track education. What's the prognosis?"

"I'm not entirely sure. My doctor told me I no longer qualify for his study, and he's referred me to someone here who is a specialist in aortic valve disease. I have an appointment with her tomorrow."

"I'm going with you."

Easing away from him, she wiped away tears. "Luca, you know that's not possible. There's your uncle, your mother's going to need a ride home when she decides she's going back, and your father probably hasn't begun to think of how invaluable you'll be in dealing with the restaurant."

He framed her face with his palms. "Do you not realize you're every bit as important to me as they are?"

"Let's not talk about this right now," she entreated.

"Livie," he whispered, his voice raw. "A part of me worried you wouldn't come back."

Her eyes filled anew. "I was coming back."

This time he kissed her on the lips. It wasn't the kiss they both knew he wanted, but the damned sliding doors kept opening and closing.

"All right," he said. "One thing at a time. But you are going to tell me all of it, aren't you?"

"I promise."

WHILE EMPTIER THAN before, the stress level in the waiting room remained pretty much the same. Vinny and Joey were on their phones calling employees to relay news, while Sal's pacing had advanced to an even grimmer stage. He moved around the large reception area like the last surviving gladiator in a coliseum, ready for whatever came next. In their corner, Valentina and Rosa sat almost forehead to forehead, deep in discussion.

"Family of Leo Angeloni?"

Sal signaled everyone to stay put and followed a weary-looking man wearing scrubs into the ER hallway. Once the door shut behind them, Rosa reached over and touched Luca's knee.

"You should go, too."

"No, he clearly wants to handle this alone for the moment. Let's respect that."

"And are you all right, Olivia?" Valentina asked. "The way you ran out, I thought..."

"She was trying to give the family space in an awkward moment," Luca said, sparing Olivia the need for any explanation.

Looking pleased, Rosa leaned closer to Valentina. "She told him. That's good."

Shaking her head, her expression uncertain, Valentina replied, "I think all we do these days is speak in mysterious and even secretive phrases."

With a self-deprecating sound, Rosa said, "I guess that's my fault. I started it all."

"We both did."

There was no protest and their words hung in their air like incense after Mass. It was a relief to see the doors open and Sal emerge. Although from the haunted expression on his face, and the slump of his shoulders, questions were unnecessary. He had nothing good to share. Even so, both groups merged into one, eager to hear what he had to say.

"On top of everything else, his bad hip is broken," he said bluntly.

A low-key series of groans and cries spread through the group. Hugs were shared, hands were clasped. Usually the most vocal, the youngest of the kitchen staff simply hung their heads.

"Will they let us see him?" Valentina asked.

"He's heavily sedated."

Rosa and Sal spoke simultaneously, which earned her a scathing look from her estranged husband. Neither of them followed up on the statement. Rosa merely looked to the left and Sal averted his gaze to the right, an unspoken agreement not to make things worse than they already were.

"The next twenty-four hours are critical." Sal glanced at Rosa, daring her to speak again. "Everything depends on his resuscitation from the shock."

"Then it will be about comorbidities," Rosa added. "That's dealing with two or multiple conditions or diseases that thwart recovery. In Leo's case it's the burns, broken hip, as well as depression, and anything else that's cropping up given his age."

Seeing his father's near-seething expression, Luca stood. "Dad, I think we all should get out of here. I know you'll want to stay with Uncle Leo. Vinny and the boys can help me clean up at the restaurant. Hopefully, Mom can get Aunt Val to rest and Olivia, you should, too. Keep Tiny here to drive Benny home when they release him."

"Yeah, good idea," Sal replied. "See that you put a note on the door that we're closed for the day."

"It's already done."

"Oh. Right. Well, have Janine call and cancel tonight's reservations with our apologies."

"Not to worry, Dad. I've got this. Call me when you know more."

No sooner were they outside than Valentina began to protest. "I really should stay."

"We don't need two of you in the hospital, and you know you're not up for this," Luca replied. "Mom, talk to her."

"He's right," Rosa told her.

Extending his hand to Olivia, Luca asked, "Let me drive?"

She dug out her keys and passed them over. "But don't even think of dropping me off at Tempest's. I want to help with the cleanup."

His gaze dropped meaningfully to her wrist. "What I said to my aunt goes for you, too."

"I won't overdo, but you have to understand, I won't rest with tomorrow preying on my mind."

He waved to the others heading for Joey's car, then opened all four doors to Olivia's white Prius to let out the intense heat. Leaning inside, he started the engine and turned the air conditioner on full blast.

Olivia didn't wait, and collapsed onto the passenger seat, laying against the head rest and closing her eyes. Valentina was nowhere near as quick, but equally determined to ease into the back seat behind her.

In a loud whisper, Rosa pointed over the roof in Olivia's direction and said to her son, "I like her."

"God help us," he replied.

"Is that a way to talk to your mother? And you didn't even offer a hug when I arrived."

He kissed her cheek. "Get in."

As he fastened his seatbelt, Olivia said, "I heard all that."

"Then you know never to criticize your family again. Mine has yours beat."

After he paid their parking fee at the booth, Valentina said to Rosa, "We should go to church. We need to light candles for Leo." With a soft gasp, she added, "And the patient you lost. How rude of me to overlook that."

"Well, technically, it's two this week, but thank you. Only, don't do that to yourself. You're always thinking of other people," Rosa said, patting Valentina's hands, tightly clasped in her lap.

"I'll drop you off there as soon as I unlock the restaurant for the guys," Luca told them.

"It's only a short walk," Valentina protested.

Luca pointed to the screen on the dashboard. "See that temperature? It means the heat index is 105 degrees."

"He's right, dearest," Rosa said. "Olivia, would you mind if we borrow your car for another hour?"

"It's fine."

Hearing Olivia's listless reply, Luca glanced into the mirror, his gaze challenging his mother's. "Aunt Val's car is in the parking lot right below her apartment."

"This one is already cooled down."

He was getting a crash course in how willful his mother had become—or had she been that way all along? Of course, she had; love and respect had just blinded him to reality. "Things are definitely due for a change."

IN THE NEXT hour, all the overload of stress and energy was redirected into cleaning up the disastrous effects of the morning. It was when Joey Farina and Stu Ciccarone asked about trashing perfectly good sauces on the stove that Vinny looked questioningly at Luca.

Grasping his unspoken message, Luca glanced around the kitchen. "What do you say we try for the evening service?"

"We only have one type of pasta made," Vinny reminded him.

"There's time to get the others done if we're not opening for lunch," Luca assured him.

"We already called the staff to tell them we're closed," Stu added.

"I'm in," Joey declared. "I can't afford to miss a paycheck. It's only the fifth of the month and my bank account is already overdrawn."

The last comment had Luca turning to Olivia. "Take down the sign out front and put one up that says we're reopening for dinner service at five. Everyone else, get to work."

A resounding, "Yes, Chef!" filled the room.

"Cut prep quantities in half," Luca added. "I'll handle the pasta. Vinny, get the soup on before you start the meatballs. I'll call our waiters and waitresses and see who's still available. Our bartenders, too."

Luca went to the office to use the Rolodex and make the staff calls. Olivia appeared with the reservations book.

"There are only six, and they're all between seven and eight o'clock. I can call and let them know we're able to accommodate them after all."

"Folks tend to be annoyed when their plans are compromised," Luca warned her. "Are you sure you're up to handling that?"

"How angry are they going to be if they understand there was a tragic accident, and that *Vita e Spezie's* dedicated staff insisted on opening, eager to oblige them?"

Luca came around the desk and framed her face with his hands. She looked so young and pretty in her frothy, flower print blouse and white Capri pants. "I had visions of taking you home and carrying you upstairs to your room to watch you sleep in my arms. Instead, you're another female in my face telling me how it's going to be."

"Poor you."

After a brief chuckle, Luca grew serious. "Seriously, Livie. How are you feeling?"

"If I hadn't told you anything, you wouldn't ask that."

"But you did, and if something happens to you, what do you think I'm going to do? Kiss you goodbye and say, 'Great knowing you? You were a trouper?'"

"No. Much more." Olivia reached up to kiss his strong chin. "Luca, I'm a water girl. I was certain Houston held a medical solution for me. But I knew I needed the coast and sea air to keep going, so I came down here planning to commute. That's as far as my plans and expectations went. I never counted on meeting you."

"But now that you have?"

"I want to live and dream."

13

SAL'S HEAD AND HEART WERE FILLED WITH LAUGHTER. ON some level, he knew he was caught up in a dream, partly based on truth and happier times. He and his brother had gone deep sea fishing in the past, but then fantasy took over, and the fish on the end of his line wasn't just a feisty red snapper, but a record swordfish. It was trying to yank his limbs from his torso. What also didn't fit was Leo abandoning his fishing rod to help his older brother finish hauling in the catch of the day. *Not in this lifetime,* Sal thought, even in his dream.

"That's the one!" Leo cried. "Don't lose him, Sal. You've got him."

"I've got him!"

"Who? Who have you got? Salvatore, are you all right?"

Jarred fully awake, Sal straightened in his chair and saw his sister and Rosa frowning down at him. In the unpleasant juxtaposition of realities, irritation had Sal swatting at them as though they were gnats buzzing his face, and hastily wiped away the rest of his sleepiness.

"What? Yeah. It's nothing. What are you two doing back here?"

"We wanted to know if there had been any change," Valentina whispered, although the emergency room reception area was currently empty.

Not yet fully acclimated, Sal rose. "Hang on a second. I need to splash some water on my face."

Once in the restroom, Sal did exactly that, and rinsed his mouth before staring into the mirror to gather his wits. Although a glance at his watch told him it was mid-afternoon, he wasn't ready for his sister to be back; to have to deal with Rosa again was too much. For a moment, he considered phoning Luca to ask why he'd let the two women out of his sight, but that would be unfair.

The issue was Rosa. Condemnation was easy in absentia, but now that she stood before him as a living, breathing human being, his whole psyche fell into turmoil.

"You're the one who had the affair."

There had been no affair. Since she left there had been women, sex, of course. He was a man, but that had nothing to do with her, let alone, *them*. Was she going to pretend that she'd had no needs in twenty-five years?

A new wave of irritation pulled him deeper into his rancid anger, polluting his thoughts. No, she was not going to put the past all on *him*. Besides, as head of the family, there was Leo to deal with, and the mystery of Valentina's condition. Who else would handle that? Not Rosa. Now that she knew Leo would live and she'd had the opportunity to spew her accusations, she would return to her *career*.

With adrenaline once more pumping in his veins, he returned to the waiting room, strode straight to the desk and asked for a report on his brother.

"He's resting comfortably, Mr. Angeloni."

"Can our sister see him for a minute?"

Earlier, Sal had been allowed a few minutes with Leo. He thought despite the bandages and tubes hooked up to his brother, Valentina would feel better hearing the steady beats and hums of the machinery. It didn't fester on his conscience at all that what he really wanted was a few minutes alone with Rosa.

"Send her over. I'll have someone take her to him," the attendant said kindly.

When he returned to the women, he focused on Valentina. "They'll buzz you in. Go have a minute with Leo."

Murmuring her gratitude, she started that way. Something about her slow, cautious steps made Sal not want to watch; but left alone with Rosa, he didn't want to look at her, either.

"Thank you for that," Rosa said.

"Shut up."

Ignoring her arched look, he continued, "Let's get one thing clear. I don't need your input or approval of my behavior. It means nothing to me. I have treated my sister with the respect and courtesy she has always deserved. Correction, what I believed she deserved, until I learned how much contact she's had with you. Even then, I restrained myself."

"Yes, you're a saint among men."

"I'm the head of this family and don't run away from my responsibilities."

"Good for you. Except, you still know nothing about women. Listening to you talk, I don't think you like us."

Sal slid her a sharp glance. "I liked my sister. Until she met you."

Rosa shook her head. "You just said it yourself. You saw it as your job, especially once your parents died. Your poor widowed sister is your responsibility. That doesn't mean you feel any real joy and abiding love in your relationship with her."

"What the hell am I supposed to do, get up every day and throw rose petals at her feet? There's a restaurant to run with almost two dozen employees who rely on me for their income, including her and Leo."

"Yet you don't see she's vanishing before your eyes?"

The quiet condemnation was a cold pail of water in his face. "*I see.* But I'm just her brother. Not someone to confide in. You're the one she chose for that. It's your shoulder she wanted to lean on. Cry on," he sneered. "How careless and obtuse am I, Rosa? Because by God, I figured out that much."

"I told her you would be hurt," Rosa said, her tone resigned. "But she thought it would be easier on you this way, considering her illness would be a long journey."

Knowing what was coming, Sal motioned her to stop. "At this point, I don't want to know."

"She has ovarian cancer. The one they call the silent killer."

His strength left him in a vacuum, and Sal dropped into the next chair. As the years passed, and they said goodbye to their elders, life had its way of preparing them for impermanence, everyone's finite number of days. Nevertheless—and maybe it was due to the closeness of their ages—there was no escaping the stark difference between pragmatism and reality.

"Sitting here today, I started to figure out it was something like that." He stared at the pale, mottled tiles between his feet. "How does she do it? She faithfully goes to church every day, sometimes more, embracing the God that took her husband and baby. And now, the very part of her which could have brought new life is killing her, too?" With a choked sound, Sal buried his face in his hands.

Shifting over to the chair beside him, Rosa started to reach for him, only to check herself. Instead, she laid a calming hand on his knee. "God isn't punishing her."

"Don't treat me like one of the family members of your patients," he snapped. "I see things as they are. Not how I'd prefer them to be."

"I don't think so, Sal. Val's accepted what is, but she could see you would have difficulty with this, and she didn't want your pity."

"I could at least have listened."

"Since when?" As he stiffened, Rosa said wearily, "Don't get all bent out of shape. We're actually communicating for the first time in decades."

After a few seconds, he exhaled and said in resignation, "Go on."

She took her time. "I know Luca told you I'm a hospice nurse and aside from providing compassion, and physical comfort, what makes us invaluable is our commitment to listening to the ill and the dying. Just know this, if I hadn't been available, she still would have reached out to someone else in my field, rather than you."

"That's cold."

"You have to get over thinking this is personal."

"It is, damn it! She's my sister."

"So, it's never crossed your radar that people tell more to strangers than they do to family?"

The truth had him looking around the room for an escape. How long had Valentina been gone? Long enough as far as he was concerned.

"If you think I'm going to thank you for the enlightenment, or being the one she turned to, you're wrong."

Rosa laughed softly. "I'll bet God always looks forward to your one-sided conversations with Him."

Turning his head away, so as not to smile at Rosa's accuracy, he was stunned to see Tiny in the farthest corner of the waiting room by the drinking fountain and snack machines. "Just a second," he muttered.

When he reached the younger man, he said, "Tiny, you're still here. I didn't see you."

"No one ever sees me."

A wave of shame pushed Sal down into the chair beside the heavy-set man. He was right in that everyone took him for granted. He was Leo's shadow, Leo's responsibility, and Leo's truest friend. Where else should Tiny be, but waiting for his next directive from the most important person in his life? His parents were gone, and Sal's father had promised to see to the care of Pietro and Renata's slow son. However, "slow" did not mean ignorant, and yet Sal was as guilty of treating him that way as anyone.

"I'm sorry. Did you hear any of the reports by the nurse? Leo's going to be all right. Only they can't do any surgery on his hip until threat of infection has passed."

When Tiny failed to respond, Sal prompted, "So, what are you going to do?"

Innocent and unguarded brown eyes stared into his. "Wait."

Realizing he was serious, Sal placed a comforting hand on his back. "You can't do that. Even I'm going to leave in a little while."

"Somebody in the family has to be here for him."

A ghost of a memory came out of the shadows of Sal's mind and he remembered how Tiny had spent so much time at the nursing home in the last days of his mother's life. Eventually, many thought he was a resident there, too.

"You're a good cousin, but you're going to make yourself sick with worry if you do this. Go home. Get some rest and build up your strength because you know when it's time to do therapy, Leo's not going to want to do it. We'll count on you to make sure he does. Call that girl of yours Leo mentioned. Ask her to dinner, or at least let her know you're thinking about her. Make plans to see a movie or go for an ice cream. You're going to have some free time on your hands. Do something for yourself."

Tiny's double chin tripled as he bent his head to ruminate over the advice. "Okay, Sal. That seems like the right thing to do. But . . . would it be okay if I come back tomorrow?"

The hopefulness in his voice tugged at Sal's heart. "He's not going anywhere. You come when you want."

As Tiny lumbered out the door, Sal returned to Rosa. He had seen her watching them and could just imagine what she was thinking.

"Is that Fredo? Alfredo Busto?"

Sal had forgotten she was the only one to call him by the diminutive of his name just like Tiny's mother had done. "The one and only."

"God bless him, there's a poster child against having children late in life."

"It wasn't exactly planned," Sal reminded her. "Even you should remember the story of how his mother's doctor suggested aborting the pregnancy. Oblivious to the fact that she was Catholic."

"It's a doctor's job to share all issues and options with a patient," Rosa said, only to add sadly, "It appears he's had a lonely life."

"You don't have to be mentally challenged to be lonely."

Holding her hands up in surrender, Rosa said, "You're right, Sal. All decisions have repercussions. If we knew how ours would affect us, we might have done things differently. Good for you that you have it all figured out."

Because she said it without rancor, he could rein in some of his acrimony. "All right. I'm sorry. Maybe love is wasted on the young."

"That's education."

"You're going to contradict every stinking word out of my mouth?"

Immediately contrite, she replied, "Absolutely not. Except I do agree with the theory that it's not over 'till it's over."

He studied her as she stared at her clasped hands. Although it stung that she didn't wear her wedding ring, her white knuckles gave him the courage to ask the question that shot through his mind like white lightning.

"Are you telling me something?"

"I don't know," she sighed. Then she offered a one-shoulder shrug. "I do know it's good to see you again, and…I didn't expect all this inner turmoil."

Sal thought the news should have caused a seismic shift on the Richter scale, considering the jolt it gave him. It gave him the courage to speak as frankly as she had. "Rosa, I swear on all that's holy, I didn't cheat on you. What you think you saw was somebody else's idea, and I put a quick end to it."

"Okay."

"Look at me."

She kept her head bowed. "I can't because everything I did was based on a belief that I thought was right, and right to protect our child. Now you're telling me not only was I wrong, but I was a fool?"

"We were both fools. I didn't fight for you."

"Did you want to?" she asked in a small voice.

"If your father was still alive, he could attest to it."

Rosa frowned. "He didn't tell me."

"Well, he said plenty to me. He told me to get lost and let you live your life."

With a delicate snort, she said, "That's the first time you listened to my father."

"It was the first time he spoke to me as an equal and not someone who was stealing his daughter away. Later, I hated him again because as a father himself, he was okay with you taking my son from me."

"He was concerned we would tear Luca apart."

"In the meantime, Luca thought I didn't care about him. Was that okay with you two?"

Slow to answer, Rosa looked up, only to gaze out the tinted hospital windows. "It was convenient to think Luca wasn't as aware as he probably was."

"I finally get an admission."

She rose and paced for a few steps like someone fighting her own restraints. "You want me to leave, Sal? Because if this is too much for you, I can go. Only you need to understand, I'm not here about Leo. Valentina doesn't have much time left."

Feeling the room closing in on him, Sal turned away. It was all too much.

"Sal, please, for once, listen to me."

"I'm listening. I may not have always known something was going on with her besides her grief," he said. "But I'll be damned if I need you to lecture me." Rising, he looked everywhere except at his wife. "I've got to get out of here. I need a shower, or I'll never be able to stand the smell of marinara sauce again. Can I count on you to get Valentina home?"

"We're supposed to be talking, and you're running away?"

"I'm not the runner. You are. I'm the guy who doesn't like people who pull strings. The ones you're toying with are connected to my heart, and they haven't been yours to play with for a long time."

"TIME?"

"Ninety minutes to opening, Chef!"

"Are people coming to a dinner service or a funeral visitation?" Joey asked, setting two stainless bowls on the prep table beside several bundles of Romaine lettuce and another mound of spinach. "Where's the music?"

About to taste the Alfredo sauce, Luca paused. "Damn. You're right, Joey." He crossed to the partition between the kitchen and dining room. "Chanel? Can you get the stereo on?" he called.

"What's your pleasure?"

"Harry Connick, Jr., Michael Bublé? A little mix of the classics with some new flavors for a change?"

Seeing her give him a thumb up sign, he returned to the stove. Once again Vinny spooned a sample of the Alfredo sauce for him to try, as he did for Sal every night.

"Chef?"

"Perfect," Luca replied. Are you satisfied with the marinara?" With Benny gone, Vinny had made a new batch. *Vita e Spezie* was known for their marinara given that they took the time and expense to use San Marzano, the beautiful plum tomatoes with denser flesh and fewer seeds.

The older chef's expression mirrored his ambivalent mood. "Given another hour, it will be fine. Only Sal knows I don't like to serve a sauce that's not four or five hours matured."

Luca got a fresh spoon and tasted it. It was good but, as Vinny fretted, so young yet, like wine. "The hour will help. If you crank up the flame a hair, you'll get closer to your usual quality, though you'll have to watch it more. It's your call."

"I can do it."

As Harry Connick Jr.'s mellow baritone voice added an indescribable sheen to the atmosphere, Luca's attention was drawn to the dining room. He saw Olivia with a tray of small vases she'd refreshed and was returning to the tables, since the wait staff was still dribbling in one-by-one. All the while, she was softly singing along to Harry's vintage, *Blue Light, Red Light.* He thought it adorable that she made little tilts with her head coinciding with his inflections, as though she was in the room with Harry as he recorded.

His heart swelled, even as he worried for her. Given the news she'd finally shared, she should be home getting some rest. Instead she was taking a big risk, insisting on helping get through tonight's dinner service. It was an act of pure selflessness. How could a heart contain that much goodness? Whatever fears he'd harbored in the last few days were being quickly replaced with feelings soaring too high for a small word like love.

As though she felt his eyes on her, she glanced over. He pointed to her, willing her to realize he'd requested the music especially for her, and she broke into a dazzling grin.

It was going to be a good night.

AFTER ADDING A bit of water to the front arrangement, Olivia went around the corner to thank Chanel for the music. Joey had been right; it had gotten entirely too gloomy.

"Have you heard anything new about Leo?" The redhead was busy filling the last snack mix bowl before screwing the cap on one of the big plastic jars they bought in bulk. Like the rest of the wait staff, she was in a white tailored shirt and black pants, but today her slacks were leather, and emphasized her killer figure, and her hair was in a sexy ponytail over one shoulder.

"Sal called a bit ago and said Valentina was able to get in for a short visit. Obviously, Leo is stable enough to see immediate family. Rosa was supposed to bring her back to the apartment for the rest of the day."

"Shut up. *The* Rosa?"

Olivia felt a tinge of guilt at the curiosity Chanel's surprising response triggered, but had to ask, "You know her?"

"No, I didn't start here until years later, but even then that name was only mentioned in a whisper. I can't believe she's here. Luca must have called her."

"She drove down with me," Olivia confessed. "We happened to run into each other."

"Down from where? You two are acquainted?"

"Houston. No, we literally collided. Moments later, Luca called me, and she saw his name on my phone. It's a long story, and I have to get back." It wasn't fair to keep Chanel hanging like that, but Olivia wanted to delay as many details as possible about her condition, until she knew when the procedure would happen.

"Well, I'm dying to know, so when you get a break, come chat for a few minutes. Hopefully, it won't get like New Year's Eve in here tonight, since I'm soloing it. Do not tell Luca I'm wishing him less business," the redhead added with a chuckle.

"Understood. But why are you subbing for Rocco tonight? Could Luca not get hold of him?"

"No, we switched schedules a few days ago." Her green eyes twinkled with amusement. "Have you noticed Janine isn't here, either?"

The relevance escaped Olivia. "What am I missing?"

Chanel winked with conspiratorial humor. "I don't think it's a coincidence."

Olivia couldn't have been more surprised. "Isn't he in his mid-thirties?"

"If it works, what's a little gap in age?" Chanel replied with a shrug. "But do me a favor and keep it to yourself because I don't know how her family would take it, let alone Sal."

"You don't have to worry about me. There's enough drama going on as it is." Olivia left to avoid any further conversation and wished she'd never heard what Chanel had told her. Secrets were a sore point with the Angelonis and having just come through a critical situation with Luca she wasn't ready to keep yet another one from him.

Movement up front caught her attention, and she felt a wave of relief as Andi Baker walked in. "Great to see you! I didn't think we'd have a hostess tonight."

"I was ending an extended late shift at the hospital and late getting the message we were opening after all. Sorry for cutting things close."

Olivia accepted the explanation from the tawny blonde with the calming personality. "The important thing is you're here. Tony was going to have his hands full otherwise. I'd love to help out, but—" she spread her arms out to draw more attention to her unprofessional attire "—I'm not exactly dressed for my job, let alone yours."

"I'm ready. Thanks, Olivia. How's Mr. Leo?"

"Holding his own. They have to watch for infection, though."

"Of course. Poor man."

The front door opened and a group of six walked in and Andi handed her purse to Olivia. "Could you give this to Chanel? She and Rocco kindly watch our things for us behind the bar."

"Will do." *And that,* Olivia thought, as she took the bag to Chanel *was probably how Janine started conversing with Rocco.*

Returning to the kitchen, Olivia announced, "Get ready! Party of six about to get seated."

WHEN SAL DROVE to the restaurant after seven o'clock that night, he felt physically better for having had a shower and changing into a light gray summer suit. His mood would have been improved, too, if he'd allowed himself a scotch on the rocks; however, since he hadn't yet had a bite to eat all day, he resisted.

It had only been when he came down the street and saw the full parking lot, and all the lights on that his spirits soared. Despite accepting that they'd needed to close *Vita e Spezie* for the day, Luca and the staff had managed to open after all. He could only imagine the enormous effort it had taken to prepare in time.

Inside, he found business was bustling, yet the staff moved steadily and with confidence. It was also evident how everyone seemed to be cooperating with each other. The two lanky paisans, Joey and Stu, were handling their duties and whatever else Luca directed, as he acted as sou chef to Vinny. Olivia was transferring an impressive tray of cannoli and cheese cakes to the partition where Rosemary carried it off to one of her tables.

Out front a quick visual tally told him the dining room was seventy percent full, and Tony was doing an admirable job keeping the two other male waiters, and Rosemary moving. To Sal's relief, he didn't notice one impatient or otherwise disgruntled face.

"There he is now."

Hearing that Stu had spotted him, he went over to pat both young men on the back. "Good going, guys. Beautiful job."

When he joined Luca and Vinny at the stove, he asked with mock concern, "Trying to show me up?"

"Trying to take a load off," Luca replied. "And keep up with Vinny."

"I couldn't continue this pace every day," the older man told him, but I also haven't had so much fun in a while."

"What's the latest on Uncle Leo?" Luca asked.

"Status quo. They're going to keep him sedated through the night, but they say his vitals are holding up well."

"What about Aunt Val and Mom?"

"They should be upstairs. Valentina's car is outside."

"They used Olivia's."

"It's outside, too. By the way, what's going on with her?"

Ignoring his father's sliding glance toward Livie, Luca said, "I'll fill you in later. Mom hasn't asked for some food? Aunt Val doesn't keep much of anything in her refrigerator."

"I guess I'd better get upstairs and check on things, not that I expect I'll be a welcome sight."

Luca slid him a look of dread. "Did you fight again?"

"What again? All you saw was a little depressurization. What do you expect after all this time?"

Clearing his throat, Luca nodded to the pots and platters of food. "I'm going to make a small variety of things for you to take upstairs."

"Would you have N'awlins box a couple of slices of cake, too?"

While his son did that, Sal made the rounds up front. It was easy to praise the young people who were tending tables; Tony was showing exemplary initiative and deserved consideration for increased responsibility if he wanted it. Several regulars had heard about the accident, and Sal had never worked harder at making small talk. The price of having his mind pulled in too many directions.

It was a relief to return to the kitchen where Luca walked him to the back door with the bag of take-out containers. "I'll be back as soon as I can," Sal told him.

"Take as long as you need—as long as you're *talking*. Say, 'Hi,' for all of us. *Please* bring back Olivia's keys."

As Sal climbed the steps to Valentina's apartment, he felt like a man heading for the gallows. What was he supposed to say to his sister when right now he thought he might start bawling like a baby at the sight of her? He'd been thinking about Rosa's pronouncement for hours. His sister was dying and all he had been doing was lashing out at her for keeping secrets about Rosa and so much more. He felt ashamed and sick to his stomach, all at the same time.

Upon reaching the top of the stairs, he mumbled to himself. "I can't do this."

The door opened, and Rosa peered out at him. "What took you so long?"

Thinking the worst, Sal crossed the deck. "Is something wrong? Is she feeling worse?"

"No, her doctor provides her with medication for when the pain gets to be too much." Rosa waited for him to do something. When he didn't, she asked, "Are you coming in?"

He held forth the bag. "I brought soup and stuff."

"That's good. She might be able to keep down a little later. Anything heavier would be out of the question." Rosa took the bag and led the way inside.

Shutting the door, Sal said softly. "I should have noticed she wasn't eating. I knew she was losing weight."

"Regardless of what I said, don't beat yourself up over this. The only control she had was over who knows what and when. She didn't intentionally want to hide things." Setting the bag on the counter, she took out the containers. "This smells heavenly. I can't remember the last time I had a soup that didn't come out of a can."

"You must be starved. Luca told me there's no food up here. You should have called downstairs. They would have been happy to bring you something."

"I didn't realize you would be open, until I heard faint music."

"The staff stepped up to the plate for Leo. Luca sends his love. Everyone is being supportive."

"From what I saw at the hospital, it seems like you have a good group still." She glanced at the closed bedroom door. "Tell them Valentina had a small bowl of fruit. She's sleeping now."

"What about you? You're not sick, too, are you? You're too skinny."

"Italian men," Rosa mused. "You'd have all of us looking like overstuffed sausage."

"A man wants something to hold on to."

"Did I not just say that?" However, studying him standing in the middle of the room, an understanding smile curved her lips. "This is a lot of soup, even in one container. Have you eaten?"

"Nah, I didn't think I could keep anything down yet."

"Sit. We can share."

Sal lowered himself at the table with only two chairs, while Rosa plucked bowls from the cabinet, and split the beef-noodle concoction between them. Once she also had the spoons, she unwrapped the foil package of warm, buttered garlic bread and set it on the table, as well. She had changed from her nurse's scrubs to a short, white cotton robe. With her bare feet, and her hair brushed loose in careless waves around her shoulders, he couldn't help wondering what she wore beneath it.

"Eat. I know Valentina has some wine stashed someplace," Rosa said searching from cabinet to cupboard. "We've all put you through the wringer today. Heaven forgive me, but I wouldn't say no to something with a kick."

If she was weaving him into a black widow's web, Sal wasn't sure he cared. "Knowing Valentina, if there is any, it's turned to vinegar by now."

Fortunately, they didn't have to experiment. Rosa found an ornate brandy bottle that had never been opened. She brought it to the table along with two aperitif glasses. "This must have been a gift from someone who thought she might need a little help getting to sleep."

"More likely she kept it in case one of the priests stopped by."

Pouring a shot into each glass, she held hers up to him. "Thank you for not chasing me away. I didn't know what to expect."

"And yet you came."

"My concern for Valentina and how she would react to Leo's injury outweighed any fear I had about facing you again."

Growing introspective, Sal laid his hands on the bare table, palms upward. "Did I ever leave you with the impression I would harm you?"

"That's not what I was afraid of."

He thought some more, only to shake his head, unable to follow. "You're going to have to spell it out for me. You're right. Anything I thought I knew about women has proven to be less than nothing."

"I was afraid coming back here, I wouldn't be able to resist you."

That was never one of the responses Sal considered when he

lay awake at night and played this moment in his imagination. If he couldn't understand that she'd left in the first place, and never accepted the possibility of her returning, why would he draw the pompous conclusion she would remain attracted to him?

"Because I thought you would take revenge."

"Well...you might have been right at one time." Finally picking up his glass. "But you know what molten lava does, Rosa?"

"Devours everything in its path."

"Afterward. It cools off. It hardens. It becomes just another face for a foot to step on."

Rosa covered her mouth to muffle her laugh. "Oh, Sal. There is no one like you, and that's God's truth."

He shrugged and touched his glass to hers. The delicate clink of crystal was muted by the clumsy clunk of ice cubes falling into the bucket inside the freezer. To Sal it was a perfect analogy of life; there were these precious moments, but if you didn't pay attention, life's routines and cycles could obliterate them.

After sipping, Rosa studied his profile. "You really didn't have an affair, did you?"

"You can ask a hundred times, and the answer's still going to be the same."

Upon seeing her stricken expression, Sal pushed back his chair and drew her onto his lap. As tears filled her eyes, Rosa wrapped her arms around his neck. Sal crushed her even closer and buried his face in her hair.

"It killed me to see her mouth on yours," she moaned against his neck. "That was my place."

"I never thought I would know this scent again. I love the smell of your hair and your skin. The feel of you."

With a whimper of yearning, she kissed him as though wanting to hold the very air that had carried those words to her heart. He whispered her name before deepening the kiss too long withheld.

Distant thunder rumbled, sounding like applause. The first rush of wind blew across the deck, slapping the taller herbs against the windows, urging them to hurry. What seemed far away was often closer than expected. That was the thing about time, it could be two-faced.

With a groan, Sal pressed his forehead to Rosa's. The dimly lit room brightened with lightning giving each a clearer glimpse of the reawakening in each other's eyes.

"I have to get downstairs before the storm is on top of us," he said.

"Hurry. Don't take any chances. It's bound to wake Valentina, too, if it hasn't already."

Sal caressed her shoulder to hip, refamiliarizing himself with every curve and hollow. "But I don't want to go."

"I feel the same way," she said, stroking his freshly-shaven cheek, and lower lip that was moist and darker from her kisses.

Just as Sal caught her fingers to press a kiss into her palm, a stronger clap of thunder sounded. "Try to get Valentina to eat something."

"Will you come back after you close?"

"Are you sure you want me to?"

"Valentina will be sorry she didn't get to see you. She'll want to hear about Leo, and there are things you two still need to say to each other."

"And you?"

"We haven't begun to talk yet. Others' needs are more important."

Sal nodded. It had always been their way, getting things out of order because they were too eager to be together. Not always wise, as history proved; nonetheless, it was happening again.

Rosa fixed her robe that had begun to part yielding a glimpse of a lacy camisole. "Go. The wind is carrying in the cell fast."

At the door, he paused to look back at her. His smile held hope. Hers offered promise. Coming on the heels of today's disastrous moments, and with the darkest angel again looming in the future, Sal recognized he was a man at another precipice. There had been too many of these moments. However, for the first time in decades, he didn't feel alone. Someone was waiting for his safe return.

14

THE NIGHT WASN'T FINISHED PRESENTING SMALL GIFTS AND token blessings. After locking up *Vita e Spezie*, not only did Olivia hand over the keys to her car without Luca having to ask for them, he saw his father returning upstairs to Aunt Valentina's apartment. He'd known something had changed when his dad had come back to the restaurant after his initial visit. A storm was blowing in, but amid all the fierce lightning and claps of thunder, there had been a gleam in his father's eyes that had stopped Luca in his tracks. In that instant, Luca had known things were considerably improved between his father and mother.

"Will you look at that," he murmured.

Olivia followed his gaze. "If you're worried they might fight again, you should go up there, too. I'll wait in the car. Valentina doesn't need to be exposed to any more upheaval."

"I don't think that's an issue," he drawled, putting his arm around her. "My thoughts are running along the lines of wondering how long it will be before Mom asks me to help her move down here. At which point, I may tell Dad to take a couple days of vacation and hire a crew."

Olivia did a doubletake. "Are you for real? Okay, maybe he can see how Valentina could use Rosa's help, but anything else would be premature—wouldn't it?"

The storm had dissipated, but a humid breeze continued to dance around them. With a bemused smile, Luca unlocked the car, and held the door open for her. He only answered when he was behind the wheel. "You didn't see how different he was after he first came down from there?"

Over the sound of the engine starting, she said, "We were short three waiters, and the storm had everyone lingering over coffee and dessert. Thank goodness Sal let me work yesterday because, despite not having a lunch service, all the cannoli are gone, as well as the swans. Believe me, I didn't notice your father until he started ushering everyone out and locking up."

Seeing the day's events had caught up with her, as she collapsed against the seat, too tired to care about fastening her seatbelt, Luca did it for her. "Damn, Livie, I'm sorry. Even without all the commotion today and your drive to and from Houston, you would be beat. And I didn't do a thing to make things easier for you."

"Exactly when were you supposed to have the time? You were covering for Sal, helping Tony, Andi, and even Chanel when that rowdy trio needed escorting out of the bar, all the while keeping tabs on the kitchen, since we were without our sou chef. If you had managed anything else, I'd be checking where you hide your Lithium battery and calling you a bionic man."

"Yeah, well, a robot would do a better job noticing you're looking as spent as I've ever seen you."

"Everyone looks pale under ugly street lights." Holding up her left arm indicating the monitor on her wrist, she added, "My sidekick here says I'm doing okay. Let's just go home, so we can crash."

"I hear that." Luca smoothly exited the parking lot. The street remained fairly busy despite the midnight hour. "Remind me again about the time of your appointment?"

"Nice try, but you are hereby released from all good intentions. Your dad needs you more than ever, what with him having to divide his time at the hospital with Leo, and doing what he can for Valentina."

Sal had shared the heartbreaking news he'd learned from Rosa with Luca, who had told Olivia; however, they hadn't had a chance to discuss it yet. Nor had anyone informed the rest of the employees. Sal's directive had been to give Valentina the privacy she wanted for as long as possible.

"If Dad has ever been in a position to understand extenuating circumstances, it should be now. And Aunt Val couldn't be in better hands with Mom monitoring her. Good intentions aside, having Dad underfoot would probably make my aunt uncomfortable."

Murmuring a sound of agreement, Olivia sighed. "If what you're saying is true about your parents coming to some understanding, I wonder what it's been like between them today? Twenty-five years...I can't imagine. Is there the same heart-fluttering magic there was before? Now that I think about it, it's easy to imagine. They're both still striking people."

"What about your heart?"

"Oh, don't worry about that. Your dad's not my type."

"You'll pay for that."

When they parked in front of the boarding house, there was a single light on, the lamp in the front parlor. Olivia said, "Tempest's gone to bed. No funny stuff going upstairs."

"Which brings me to the question, why on earth did you rent a room that requires you to climb to a second floor?"

"I loved the house, the location, and the rent. Besides, it's not like I'm going back and forth much, let alone sprinting."

"Will you placate me and let me carry you this time?"

"I said she went to bed. I didn't say she'd be asleep. I'm sure she'll notice if she only hears one set of footsteps."

"Yeah, because they'd be really heavy ones."

"Wretch."

Luca released her seat belt and used their proximity to steal a kiss. "I'll bet if she did realize I was carrying you, she'd smile."

"Well, we'll never know."

Before Olivia made it through the gateway, Luca was beside her. Once again, he slid his arm around her waist in support.

"Livie..."

"No piggyback ride, either."

"I'm trying to be serious."

"Hasn't today been serious enough?"

"I want to stay with you tonight."

"Says the man who sleeps naked, and me with a heart condition."

"I promise to be appropriately attired," Luca said.

"But I still have my imagination."

At the top of the stairs, he turned her to face him. "Thank you, darlin'."

Olivia closed her eyes. "Don't look at me that way, and don't use that voice."

"It's the only one I've got."

"I might agree to keep my door open, and you can keep yours open. Satisfied?"

"It would make me feel a lot better to be close in case you need something. Hell," he sighed. "I just need to hold you."

Finally opening her eyes, Olivia searched his face. "The truth is . . . I'd like that, Angeloni."

Upstairs, she stopped outside her door. "I'd let you shower first," she told him, "but if you did, I'm afraid it might take a crowbar to get me out of bed for my turn."

"No problem. I'm going to text Rocco and make sure he comes in tomorrow. He needs to understand the situation at the restaurant, in case he has any ideas about taking another day off."

"Oh dear."

Her troubled expression had Luca crossing over to her. "What's wrong?"

"Maybe give him the benefit of the doubt, and wait for the morning to see if he does call in?"

Narrowing his eyes, he drawled, "What do you know that I don't?"

"Technically nothing. Nothing I can confirm."

"Out with it, Boo."

She gave the front of his shirt a warning tug. "I told you not to start that."

"Then 'fess up before I go outside and yell, 'I'm nuts about Boo Bebelle Dumont!'"

He'd already raised his voice to a normal speaking decibel and Olivia shushed him. "Luca, I gave my word to Chanel that I wouldn't say anything."

"You two are getting mighty chummy. Sharing secrets already."

"It's not a secret, it's a matter of discretion, and I don't even know if Rocco knows anyone has guessed."

"Guessed what?" he groaned. "If you can't trust me with this, you'll have proof you can't trust me with anything."

Nevertheless, Olivia visibly writhed until she blurted out, "Janine intentionally changed dates with Andi a few days ago." At Luca's blank stare, she squeaked, "They're *together.*"

"You can't be serious. She's a kid, and he's—Rocco."

"Janine is legally an adult."

"Don't get me started on that," he muttered. "*I* was legally an adult at eighteen, and worked every bit as much as my mother did to pay her back for what my education cost her. Even then I flirted with things not good for me and screwed up plenty. Janine at twenty-one is an incubated princess. This is her first job, and Mr. Tucci will have Mancini's male parts and more if he finds out that Italian Samson has been sniffing around his baby girl. Dad said the only way he let her work at the restaurant is because she was under Aunt Val's wing."

"That tells me you were only paying me lip service when I told you I didn't date through high school."

Luca wagged his finger negating her suspicion. "You and Janine are two different things."

"Janine is a studious artist. She needs someone with more experience and broader horizons."

"She hit the motherload with him."

With an arched look, Olivia replied, "Talk about getting chummy, in this short time, you two have already been comparing war stories and conquests?"

"Enough to recognize my life is that of a monastic monk by comparison."

With a delicate snort, she brushed him aside and entered her room. "Let it alone, Luca. You never heard anything. Are you going to listen to your father when he continues to warn you off me?"

"He's stopped doing that." At her skeptical glance, he added, "At least he hasn't called you Mom's chauffeur again."

WHEN LUCA WAS through with his turn in the shower, he walked in on the sight of Olivia with a pillow over her face. Acting on sheer reflex, he lurched across the room and tore the thing from her fisted hands.

"Je vas te passe une calotte!"

"What?"

"I'm going to slap you."

"Well, what are you doing? I thought you were suffocating your-self."

She yanked back the pillow. "I'm frustrated. My mind refuses to shut down."

With a sigh of relief, he picked up the two pillows he'd brought from his room and added them to the one on the left side of the bed. Laying down on top of the single sheet covering her, he drew her against him.

"I can help."

"Then you should have worn a T-shirt over those jogging shorts, and left off the aftershave."

"Why, thank you, Boo," he crooned. "Although, technically, it's only my soap and my natural yum-ness." He plucked at her oversized, LSU jersey. "Speaking of . . . this is adorable. Only whose number are you wearing? A particularly skinny linebacker's?"

"It's my dad's number. He was a quarterback. A star in his time, only not good enough for the NFL."

"Just checking. But I bet that number sells the hell out of BBQ."

Olivia smiled and fingered his chest hair. "You would so get along with my brothers."

"Correction, I will." When she didn't offer a comeback, Luca al-lowed a question that had been nagging him. "Why aren't you telling your family about what's going on?"

"I told you how they are. It would trigger a waterfall of Dumonts, and they would try to whisk me back to New Orleans and turn me into a true invalid, suffocating me with their idea of TLC."

"That seems a natural impulse for anyone who loves deeply."

"It shouldn't be at the cost of what you know is right for you."

He kissed the top of her head. "You are ardent in your indepen-dence. I'm awed by that."

"Yeah, right. Then why am I here using you as a pillow?"

"Because I asked Tempest to put a spell on you?"

"Oh, I think she's more like Valentina. Prays rather than casting spells."

"You have something in common with my aunt, too. You keep way too much to yourself."

"It's one thing to know what you know and withhold information until circumstances necessitate sharing. It's another to be an open book, only to have to live day in, day out seeing a constant question in loved ones' eyes. 'Is this the day you drop dead?'"

Luca hadn't considered her perspective before and it made him rethink his frustration with Valentina for keeping her secrets. "There are no easy answers, are there?"

Olivia drew away, only to turn off the lamp on the bed stand table. When she resumed her position, Luca stroked her hair.

"Tired of my talking?"

"No, I need to say something and it's easier in the dark," Olivia admitted. "If something happens to me, don't let my family blame you for my keeping this to myself."

"Don't talk like that. You're going to be fine."

"It needs to be said."

"How long is the convalescence time for something like this?"

"I won't know until after tomorrow's appointment."

"Olivia, please let me go with you?"

She didn't reply. Thinking she intended to ignore the question, he told himself he'd have to live with that, and wait to give the matter his hard sell in the morning. The last thing he wanted was to stress her out and keep her from getting any rest.

"Yes."

He twisted his head trying to see her face in the darkness. "Really?"

"Yeah. You may have to lend me some of your courage if the procedure starts sounding like more trouble than I think it's worth."

With the gentlest of hugs, he said, "Consider it done."

WHEN OLIVIA OPENED her eyes the next morning, it was to the unhappy realization that Luca was watching her. "For pity's sake, Angeloni. Tell me you haven't been doing that all night?" His bloodshot eyes already gave him away.

"I slept enough. The important thing is you did." He sniffed the air. "I smell coffee."

"Lucky you. My needs have to wait until the blood suckers can take another few vials at the hospital. When are you going to tell your dad about coming with me?"

"Did it while you were sleeping. It's all under control."

She hadn't heard or felt a thing, which spoke volumes as to how comfortable she'd been with having him near. "You're not just saying that?"

"It's a new day, Livie," he said, stroking her cheek. "Can't you feel the change in the air?"

Anything would be better than yesterday, she thought, shifting to sit on the edge of the bed. The memory of Leo's accident, and the truth emerging about Valentina all but blotted out the hopefulness of Sal and Rosa's reunion. Her own pending situation finished her descent into myopia and pessimism.

"It rained," she said. "That's all." Reaching back, she patted his thigh to ease the censure in her voice and headed for the bathroom.

When they made it down to the kitchen, Tempest directed them with her spatula to sit at the table. "Get your mugs. I'll start breakfast right away. What's your pleasure?"

Olivia and Luca exchanged glances. He squeezed her hand before he veered off to get some coffee.

"Nothing for me, thanks," she told their landlady, taking the seat nearest the window.

"I can wait, too," Luca said.

Already at the refrigerator, Tempest closed the egg box, and then the door. She studied Olivia with concern. "You don't even want any juice?"

"I appreciate the thought, but not right now. What are you doing up so early?"

"The air changed." When Olivia covered her face with her hands, Tempest asked, "Did I say something wrong?"

"I said the same thing," Luca replied, taking his seat. "She doesn't want to hear it."

Tempest reached for her coffee mug and sat facing them. "Are you going to let me in on what's happening, or do I have to guess?"

"Routine blood work," Olivia said with a shrug. "You know how it goes."

"No. But I do know you're not planning to get a marriage license, since a blood test isn't required anymore," Tempest said. "Guess I'll just mind my own business and wish you the best."

As she started to get up, Olivia reached across the table to clasp her hand. "Forgive me. I have an appointment with a heart specialist this morning."

Outside in the garden, Mister slept on a white wrought iron chair, exhausted from a night of socializing, while hummingbirds chased each other from a nectar bottle. Tempest faced the scene, but her vision seemed focused on another place. "I knew there was something about you."

"Don't mention pale," Luca said in a conspiratorial tone, clearly trying to lighten the mood. "She hates me noticing, too."

"It's not that," the older woman replied. "She's been keeping too much company with the other side."

Startled, Olivia jerked back. "I am not."

Tempest took hold of her hand again and focused on her palm. "Not in the way you think. Do you not see her in your dreams?"

"I don't dream," Olivia said, genuinely perplexed. "At least not that I can remember."

"You're too tired. But she's there."

"Who?"

"Maybe she means my Aunt Valentina," Luca said. He told Tempest, "She's more ill than we thought. She's terminal."

Olivia cast him a look of reproach. "We agreed to let Valentina handle this her way. Privately."

"You trust Tempest."

Olivia was embarrassed to answer. "Of course, but I'm feeling overwhelmed. Because I'm supposed to be focusing on *my* health, but instead I'm caught up in the worries and heartache of people I didn't even know this time last month. And now, Tempest is scaring me with this talk of dreams and a woman I don't know."

Their landlady offered neither apology nor explanation. She simply watched the dynamics between the young couple before her.

"Anyone would feel overwhelmed, Livie. And I'm sure Tempest is only trying to reassure you." He paused to give the older woman a chance to speak for herself. She didn't. "Today you do have to focus on yourself," he continued. "Life goes on and, despite everything, you still have your life to live."

"I'm starting to hate that cliché. Life does not go on. Not for everyone," Olivia replied. "Hospitals and cemeteries are full of people who never expected to end there as soon as they did. Look at the Marios for goodness sake. So, why should I expect a different result?"

"I can't speak to that," Luca said slowly. "And I get your fear. The truth is I am, too. All I know is you keep fighting. You fight for us."

Olivia wanted to scream, lash out, or explode. Maybe all of it. If she'd wanted positive reinforcement, she would have stayed in New Orleans. All she wanted was silence—and to be done with living in limbo. However, even as those thoughts pummeled her, she felt ashamed for her own impatience and lack of gratitude. She glanced up and caught Tempest's knowing look.

"You'll feel better now that you got that out of your system. Just don't chase this one off, darlin'. The good ones be few and far between."

∞∞∞

UPON WAKING, SAL reached for his cell phone and went straight to his contact list, even before his normal trip to the bathroom. He wanted to make sure the number that Rosa had put into his directory was still there, or more accurately, not a figment of his imagination. He had his reasons. After all, he'd slept alone, as usual. In their house. In a bed he'd replaced some five years after she'd left him, for the pitiful reason that while he'd washed her scent from the sheets, the depression of her body in the aging mattress continued to linger. To prove something had really changed, he now had her number.

Whatever the day held, he also had the memories of last night, after Valentina had returned to bed. Sitting on the deck with Rosa, after the refreshing rain, they'd talked. There had been no accusations, kindness instead of sarcasm and, finally, a goodnight kiss to remember the rest of his life. Every moment shimmered in his mind like shards of diamonds in a world gone chaotic, rife with new and pending grief. All he wanted was to hear her voice, and he would be able to get through the rest of the day, no matter what loomed ahead.

But when he initiated the call, the phone only rang. He hadn't been counting—was that four or five rings? She didn't have it set up for taking messages? Six rings. Had he said too much last night? Women say they want honesty, but were the skeptics right in saying, "Only when framed in compliments?" Seven rings. What if she was on her way home using Valentina's car. Because...?

"Don't hang up!"

Sal purged a held breath. "I was about to. What's wrong?"

"Nothing. I have the phone on vibrate not to disturb Valentina, and was just getting out of the shower."

"That's going to be my favorite image for the rest of the day."

With a throaty laugh, Rosa said, "It's too early for that. How did you sleep?"

"For the first time in ages, I had to rely on the alarm. You're a tonic for what ails me," Sal said, his tone insinuating. "How about you?"

Rosa sighed heavily. "These aren't days for good rest, *mia.*"

Despite the news, her endearment had Sal's insides melting like the seductive richness of one of N'awlins' desserts. "Are you seeing more decline in her condition?"

"No, but she's needing more and more pain medication."

"I would be there, but Luca is taking Olivia to a specialist's appointment this morning, so I'm doing the morning shopping on my own."

"God bless her. And him," Rosa added. "I've been waiting to become a grandmother, but not with the cold-blooded glamour pusses he's been with so far. Now he finds an intelligent, talented woman, and there's this."

"It was moving too fast anyway," Sal said, trying to be pragmatic.

"Sal! Don't you dare let Luca hear you say that."

"Of course not. I'm having a conversation with my wife. Anyway," he continued, "I called the hospital. If Leo remains as good as he is right now, they'll probably move him to a room later today."

"Then put this side of things out of your mind. As much as possible," Rosa amended. "I'm here with Valentina and we'll only go to see Leo if I feel she's up to the physical and emotional drain."

Sal was grateful. "Thank you. I can't afford to leave until mid-afternoon. Let me know what you want for yourself and Valentina's lunch. I will make the time to bring it up myself."

"And call anytime," Rosa reminded him.

The caress in her voice warmed him to his core. "You, too."

AT THE HOSPITAL, Olivia signed in and was quickly escorted to the phlebotomist for the latest drawing of blood. Right after, she was directed to the doctor's office. Luca accompanied her and appeared equally astonished that she got in so quickly.

A diminutive Vietnamese woman, perhaps an inch or two shorter than Olivia, rose from behind her desk and extended her hand as they entered her office. "I'm Meredith Pham." After Olivia and Luca introduced themselves, she said, "Have a seat. I'm grateful Dr. Acharya sent you to me. I've studied your files and, of course, I need to examine you and run tests for myself, but if everything holds to what I've seen, I think I can help you."

When Olivia said nothing, Luca reached over and gave her clasped hands a gentle squeeze. "That's great news, right, Livie?"

"We'll see."

Dr. Pham nodded, as though understanding her reticence. "I can see you've had your hopes raised and dashed enough to make you wary. While your case isn't rare, I respect that each patient brings his or her own uniqueness to a situation. Generally speaking, aortic stenosis is detected in childhood. Can you tell me if you ever experienced any episodes of weakness, or something to cause you to faint, or otherwise feel ill?"

Olivia shook her head. "No, and I was a tomboy, keeping up with three brothers. Well, they were bigger than me, but I was fine."

Luca frowned. "Didn't you tell me that when you played baseball with them, you fell asleep under the tree in the outfield?"

"Because they ignored me and I got bored."

Even so, the doctor made a few notes on Olivia's chart. "It does sometimes happen that the patient experiences nothing until adulthood. When did you sense your first episode?"

"The summer I graduated from culinary school. I was immediately accepted at a two-star Michelin restaurant. If anything, the hours were more brutal than school, but you're working on adrenaline and passion, so nothing else matters."

"You thought you had the flu," Dr. Pham said with another understanding nod.

"Of course. Friends recommended vitamins, herbal tea, steak tartar to build up my blood."

"Did anything make you feel better?"

Olivia couldn't keep back a wry smile. "Nothing like the high of a perfect dinner service or receiving accolades from other chefs in my field."

"It's common for young people to think they can't be suffering from a serious illness at their age."

"Well, I'm glad you're not going to scold me for not going to a doctor."

"I'm not in the business of reprimanding. I'm in the business of healing. But what finally made you seek medical input?"

"I fainted." Ignoring Luca's sharp intake of breath, she explained, "It had been a rough day at work, and I don't mean busy. I was in Paris at the time when a club on the same block as our restaurant was hit in a lone-wolf terror attack. We were forced to shut down and quickly leave. I was so stressed and breathless when I got to my apartment, I barely got the door closed when I collapsed. The next thing I knew it was hours later. Night. The next day I gave my notice and booked a flight back to the States."

"Livie, why didn't you tell me any of this?" Luca asked.

"When has there been time?" she asked wryly.

Dr. Pham asked, "And when did you see a doctor here?"

"About six weeks later."

"Any incidents during that period?"

"Some weakness now and again, but I was extra cautious, so, no. There wasn't another fainting spell."

The doctor asked several other questions, constantly writing. When Olivia left out her spell after her job interview at *Vite e Spezie*, Luca stroked her arm, and reminded her.

Aware of the heat rising in her face, she looked away. "That wasn't the work, that was you," she told him.

A slow smile spread across his face. "Now comes the truth." Luca said to the doctor. "I thought she didn't like me."

"He's my boss' son. I didn't expect him to be there, and the way he kept looking at me—"

"She hid it well," Luca interjected. "But it was pretty much love at first cannoli for me."

Olivia closed her eyes and shook her head. "Stop. Dr. Pham is going to think we're ridiculous."

"I love a good romance as much as anyone, but can I see your monitor for a minute?" When Olivia took it off and handed it over, the doctor checked some buttons. "Are you keeping a diary?"

"Not yet. Things have been very stressful for all of us." She briefly recited Leo's status and Valentina's plight. "I didn't see how all of that could reflect an accurate reading."

"One thing it does reflect is that you're extremely susceptible to Mr. Angeloni," Dr. Pham mused. She looked at Luca. "I'm afraid I'm going to have to ask you to return to the waiting room until we finish. Otherwise, we'll be here all morning trying to get any reliable reading."

"THIS IS SUCH a nice car." Rosa drove Valentina's silver Buick Lacrosse out of the restaurant parking lot and, once on the street, she drove toward the hospital. "Compared to my little Kia, I feel like I'm driving a limousine."

Valentina waved away the compliment. "It's all Sal's doing. As little as I drive, I wanted something economical and easy to park, but you know Italian men. 'You're an Angeloni, a part of the business. You have an image to uphold,' he said. 'Besides, I don't want you driving some sardine can that ends up looking like an accordion with the smallest fender bender.'"

Rosa chuckled at her pitiful imitation of a man talking. "He's a good brother, bossy and concerned at the same time."

Valentina gave her a sidelong look, filled with affection. "Yes, and you have the same stars in your eyes that you had when you two first met."

After a slight hesitation, Rosa allowed herself a youthful sigh. "I didn't know what to expect coming back the way I did, but Valentina, after he got over his initial shock and anger, he's been the man I fell in love with."

"You think so?" Valentina's expression turned skeptical. "I believe he's changed a great deal. Oh, he's as passionate and temperamental as ever, but he's learned from his mistakes. He's missed you terribly. He just had to get out of his own way. Angeloni pride is doubly hard on the men in this family."

"In which case, as guilty as I am for my own mistakes," Rosa told her, "I'm not sorry I spared Luca too much exposure to it."

"There are no perfect answers or solutions."

At a stop light, Rosa studied her sister-in-law's graceful profile. She hadn't wanted them to leave the apartment, which was why she'd agreed to go sooner than later in the afternoon. Seeing how quickly Valentina was losing strength, Rosa feared she would take a tumble down the stairs. Plus, she knew the poor soul was swallowing ibuprofen like candy, which also could trigger dizziness and drowsiness, among other things.

Hearing the vagueness in her voice, Rosa said, "Now we're finally talking about you. I was starting to feel awkward about hogging the conversation to get responses out of you. If I was being reviewed, believe me, they'd reprimand me."

"I wondered why you were so enthralled with my car."

Rosa offered an impish grin. "If Sal told me to trade in my KIA, I'd tell him where he could go with his ideas. I love that thing."

Making a soft laugh-mewing sound, Valentina finally turned her full attention on Rosa. "I need you to help me. How long can you stay?"

"As long as you need me, even if it gets me fired. But sweet sister, do not ask me for something I cannot do for you." Rosa would never say the words to her, but in her line of work, talk of suicide was the unspoken whisper in every hallway she'd ever walked.

"You know me better than that," Valentina replied. "I would never put such a burden on a loved one. Only...Sal is still upset with me for keeping this illness from him. He doesn't want to see it was the one way I could do something for him. To pay him back. To spare him worry. Everything, the restaurant, our family, has all been on his shoulders. Too often he would sleep in the office and not bother going home. Leo would get upset, because Sal wouldn't discuss much with him. Honestly, can you blame him? The only numbers that work for Leo are measurements in baking. The rest he loses interest in fast. And to Sal's credit, things always seemed to work out. Only maybe it would have been easier if he would have shared a little with us. This way, Leo wouldn't have grumbled so much and grown more obstinate, and I wouldn't have become the pitiful church mouse I am."

"You are not and never were a church mouse. You're too elegant.

But it may take time, dearest. People are uncomfortable with the subject of death."

"Time is the one thing I no longer have."

"Then remember you are his baby sister. Did he not agree when I
told him to hold lunch and we would go see Leo now?"

Rosa had also phoned Dr. Ingrid Tobin, Valentina's doctor this
morning and introduced herself, explaining the current situation. Dr.
Tobin shared her frustration about her patient, but agreed it seemed
like Valentina's time was running out. "According to our paperwork,
you are the designated person to receive information on Valentina,
and I have no problem with you giving her the morphine she'll need
once the ibuprofen ceases to help," she'd said. "But I expect you to
keep me informed."

Rosa hoped to take a few minutes and seek out the good doctor
if it was safe to leave Valentina and Leo alone. Certainly, credentials
needed to be shared and authorization signed.

"Leo will be even more difficult." Valentina's brooding broke into
Rosa's thoughts. "Heaven knows, I can't tell him while he's in his present condition."

"Then you better dig into your purse and put on a little blush and
lipstick," Rosa said, trying to keep her tone light. "Because seeing you,
he'll think he's already passed over to the other side." She knew Valentina had been as much mother to him as sister. Leo would as soon
stop breathing as stop loving her.

At the next stoplight, as she neatly opened one zipper and took
out a tube of lipstick, Valentina asked, "If you had to do it all over
again, would you?"

"You've just given me goosebumps," Rosa said, rubbing at her
arms. It felt strange not to wear scrubs. Hospitals were so cold, you
needed to wear layers, but today she wore a black tunic borrowed
from Valentina's closet, and black slacks she'd packed in her week-
ender suitcase. She looked like Valentina's shadow. The way things
were going, she would need to run to a discount store and grab a few
things because she planned never to wear black again, unless it was a
cocktail dress.

"After I got my nursing degree," she continued, "I chose my specialty. I chose the worse cases no one else wanted as penance in the

hope God wouldn't punish me for taking Luca away from his father. At the end of my workday I could step away from that grimness, all of those sad people. I trained how to do it, just as I trained to be a nurse. But the rest? My private life?" Rosa shook her head. "That was my cross to bear because I created it." She gazed wonderingly at Valentina. "Yet, you seem at peace with your decision."

"We grew up in the same kind of family. After church and lunch, what did the men do while the women were in the kitchen first cooking, then washing dishes? They played cards—at least in the colder months. And what do gamblers say? You play the hand that is dealt you."

Rosa took that in and nodded for a good while. "I may have felt I had no choice but to leave Sal, but within a few years, I stopped believing I was dealt a bad hand. I chose to stay away. What if I'd just scratched that little tramp's eyes out? Would he have loved me more?"

Valentina smiled, but shook her head in disbelief. "What if, what if? It happened. It's now that matters."

"Now, then, when . . . I thought about coming back after Luca went on to chase his career," Rosa said. "The more you told me there was no one in Sal's life, the more I daydreamed. But I didn't have the courage to take a chance. That can't be why *you* chose to stay alone?"

Valentina shook her head. "I just didn't know what to do with the pain. No man deserves having to deal with another man's ghost, or the ghost of a child."

Rosa pulled up to the hospital's drop off/pick-up zone. She intended to obtain a wheelchair for Valentina from the attendants on standby. She figured they could leave the chair outside of Leo's room. Valentina had balked at first, but she made no fuss now.

"Time to change the subject," Valentina said during the seating shift. "I've been thinking of turning over the letters we receive at the restaurant to Olivia. She's very interested, and it could help convince her to stay here. I know Luca is half in love with her already. They have enough in common to make a strong partnership. They remind me of Mario and me."

Rosa didn't reply. She let an attendant take Valentina into the building's foyer while she found a parking place. She needed time to choose her words.

"I like the way you think," she said rejoining Valentina. "There's just one problem. Olivia is ill herself."

"She *was*," Valentina replied, lifting a hand to enunciate her words, "but she's better now. She told us."

"Sweetheart, in the simplest terms, she needs a heart valve operation," Rosa told her. "As a matter of fact, she's somewhere in this maze speaking to a specialist."

"That poor child," Valentina said. "Do you think she'll be all right?"

"Her case is out of my area of expertise, but I have heard they've been making great progress in that type of thing."

Pondering the reply, Valentina said decisively, "She will need time to recuperate. The letters will give her something to do when Luca can't be with her."

Rosa kissed her cheek. "Brilliant. You be the matchmaker. At least that will keep me out of trouble a little longer with my son."

AFTER OLIVIA CONCLUDED her appointment with Dr. Pham, she and Luca started down the elevator to the lobby. Alone for the moment, Luca couldn't wait for answers.

"Well? What's next?"

"I wait," she said stifling a yawn. The whole thing had been exhausting. "Dr. Pham has to look at the new bloodwork and other tests to see how they compare with what Dr. Acharya's records show."

"Damn. I wanted them to set a date for you. So how long will that take?"

"Soon, Luca. Can we please change the subject?" As the door opened, Olivia had an idea. "Let's detour and see about your uncle before we return to the restaurant. You know the staff will ask if we saw him."

They stopped at the reception desk to find out where Leo was currently placed. He had been transferred to a room, but in another wing. Fortunately, a close one.

Minutes later, they started to enter Leo's room, only to be met with an outcry. "Don't come in! Keep her out!"

Startled, Olivia backed away. "It's not a problem. I'll wait in the hall."

Luca returned inside and took in the dimly-lit room. "Why'd you do that, Uncle?"

"I can hardly bear to look at myself. "I don't need a reason. This is my room. But if you must know, there's no reason for anyone else to have to look at this."

Luca inspected his uncle's condition. "The swelling is down. I heard there's less and less sign of infection."

Hardly mollified, Leo mumbled, "What are you doing here, anyway? You should be back at the restaurant."

"Olivia had an appointment and I wanted to see you."

"Okay, okay, but where's Tiny? I haven't seen him since they put me in here."

"Last I heard, Dad told him to go home and get some rest while you go through the worst of this."

"He agreed fast, huh? Doesn't want to come. I wouldn't blame him."

Luca shook his head. "I'll find out where he is. Maybe he got lost. This is a big place. How are you feeling?"

"Like a skinned catfish."

"Have the doctors been in to see you today?"

Leo snorted. "Yeah, a puppy and a guppy. I have socks older than those two. At least they're telling me I won't need any skin grafts."

"Better news yet," Luca replied.

"I'll still look like a monster...or a piece of modern art."

"Uncle Leo, I'm going to find Tiny. I'll bet he'll do more for you than a new IV bottle."

"That's what I've been saying to the night crew from the crematorium," Leo replied, nodding toward the door.

Outside of the room, Luca drew Olivia with him. He stopped at the nurse's desk.

"Excuse me, my uncle is in 303 and I'm sure you don't need me to say his name to know who he is?"

The four nurses looked at him with a mixture of emotions from disappointment to disdain. The least impressed had the beginning of a tattoo peeking from the neckline of her scrubs that appeared to be ears or horns, and what looked to be an animal tail at the end of a short sleeve. Luca suspected she was the one with whom his uncle had the most conflict.

"Have you seen a man not much taller than Olivia here, about two-hundred thirty pounds and appearing a little lost?"

"We shot him downstairs," Tattoo Girl said.

"With or without the elevator?" Luca asked mildly.

Giving the young woman a warning glance, the eldest said, "He left."

"He needs an attendant of his own," Tattoo Girl added. "What is he supposed to be a watchdog or playmate? I don't need anyone hovering over my shoulder watching every move I make. It creeps me out."

"He does ask a lot of questions," the older woman admitted.

"It's natural curiosity, and he is protective of my uncle." Luca drew out one of the restaurant's business cards and started writing on the back. "His name is Alfredo Busto. You may call him, Mr. Busto." He looked pointedly at Tattoo Girl. "My uncle will refer to him as Tiny. He's a cousin. I'll speak to Fredo about slowing you down as you do your job, but you'll find my uncle will be more cooperative if you allow Fredo to stay with him. This is my number." He handed the card to the eldest nurse. "If there are any future problems, I'll see to them immediately."

Once downstairs, they found Tiny wandering around the lobby. He looked hopeful when he spotted them.

"Did they throw you out, too?" he asked.

"It was a misunderstanding," Luca told him. "You can return to Leo's room. He's very unsettled without having you around."

"I tried to tell them," Tiny replied with a shrug.

"Just step back or into the hall when the nurses work, okay? Sometimes they're a little busy and don't have time for questions."

"Okay. I'm on this." Tiny bump-fisted Luca.

As they watched him happily return to the elevators, Olivia entwined her fingers with Luca's. "Can I say it?"

"Not too loudly," he said, lifting her hand to his lips. "You know I blush easily."

"My hero."

15

AT ELEVEN O'CLOCK ON TUESDAY, MOMENTS BEFORE THE lunch service began, Sal met Luca and Olivia coming in at the back of the restaurant. He'd been walking up the hall from the office, ready to unlock the front door.

"Talk about cutting it close." He looked as relieved as his tone indicated. "How did it go?"

Since his gaze fell on Olivia, she offered a cautious, "Promising. I should have some definite news in the next day or so. Luca checked in on Leo."

Without missing a beat, Luca said, "And would you believe Tiny was MIA? We found him drifting around in the lobby. It appears he had the misfortune to cross the path of the one nurse who chose the wrong profession. I left the restaurant's card with my number on the back in case there's any other problem. I figured you wouldn't mind."

"God love him," Sal said, shaking his head. "Yeah, you did good. It's mind-boggling he can put up with your uncle's cranky nature, but any conflict with anyone else intimidates the poor guy. I should have remembered that."

"Have you heard anything from upstairs?" Luca asked, nodding his head toward the ceiling. "I noticed Aunt Val's car is gone."

"She insisted she was strong enough to go see Leo, too. I brought coffee and biscotti to them when I first arrived." With a sheepish smile, he added. "Your mother used to have a soft spot for the chocolate dipped variety."

"I'm proud of you, Dad," Luca said.

Sal shrugged. "We're lucky she's here. Valentina can't be alone any longer, and she has the skills and experience to do what needs to be done."

"That, too," Olivia said. "But a woman likes to know she's being thought of."

Sal touched his index finger to his temple. "Before I forget, Rosa says Valentina wants to talk to you. Maybe once the lunch traffic slows down, you could take a few minutes and go upstairs?"

"I'll be happy to," Olivia assured him.

As Sal moved on to unlock the restaurant, Olivia turned to Luca. "I could make biscotti if I knew someone wanted it."

"Like you aren't doing enough already? Dad told me he picks up a box for Aunt Val now and then in the gourmet section of the market. Mom is the only other person I know who likes the stuff. Although, she said when I was a baby, those things were my teething ring."

"Sweet. I want to see your baby pictures."

"You may regret saying that. Mom has a closet full. I think she recorded everything from my first experience with solid food to me in my first chef's jacket."

"Your father will be elated."

Luca glanced over her shoulder. "Benny's here. Let's welcome him back."

Benny's hands remained red and sensitive; however, it was a testament to his dedication that he'd come in to work anyway. He reacted shyly, but pleased with Luca and Olivia's warm greeting.

From there on, it was business as usual, although Luca stayed in the kitchen to assist Benny on things he didn't need to be dealing with yet. Olivia reviewed inventory in her department and started the puff pastry recipe. It was just another day—and yet so very not.

LUNCH WAS A clean, error-free service, which helped settle everyone down.

Shortly after two o'clock, when the kitchen was back in order, Olivia told Luca, "I think I'm going upstairs and see if Valentina is up for company. I'm curious to know what she wants to talk about."

"I'm going with you," he told her.

"Don't you have something else you should be doing?"

"Nothing that can't wait. Besides, I can entertain Mom while you and Aunt Val chat."

"I'll send her downstairs to see you. Has she seen the restaurant yet? I'll bet she'd like to compare it to what she remembers it looked like back when."

"Dad can give her the grand tour another time. Do you need it spelled out?" he asked softly. "I'm not about to let you out of my sight."

"I didn't leave New Orleans, only to take on another flesh-and-blood guardian angel."

Luca held her gaze for several dizzying seconds. "Boo, who have you kissed, the way you've kissed me? End of conversation."

"So underhanded."

"Yes, ma'am, unabashed, unadulterated, and unapologetic."

Olivia discovered Luca's mother was as adept at maneuvering things the way she wanted as her son. After receiving a hug from Rosa, she soon found herself nudged toward Valentina's room, while Luca was directed to the kitchen table.

With the door quietly shutting behind her, she approached the bed where Valentina lay as still as a corpse. Decorating-wise the small room gave new meaning to minimalism and was as clean as the rest of the apartment. It made Olivia think of an adobe-washed bedroom in a convent. As had been the case with her grandparents' bedroom, she saw a modest wood Crucifix hanging over the bed. A strand of onyx rosaries lay coiled neatly over a worn Bible on the bed stand. On the chest of drawers, stood a foot-tall statue of the Virgin Mary, a rack of votive candles positioned before it. A hint of incense hung in the air, suggesting it hadn't been long since the last candle burned out. Every-thing confirmed an existence spent in prayer.

"I'm not asleep."

As Valentina patted the ample space beside her, Olivia sat down on the edge of the bed. The shadows under the good woman's eyes were increasingly pronounced against her translucent skin. It looked as though she had taken that first step between this world and the next.

"Are you able to sleep at all?"

"There'll be time for that soon enough."

"Don't say such things," Olivia entreated. "Everyone downstairs is beside themselves with worry."

Valentina gave her a tender look. "There's no need. In time, you'll know how to explain things to them. Rosa will help you."

Had they spoken about the future? Rosa staying? Wanting to be reassuring in return, Olivia said, "Sal lights up just saying her name. He's a new man."

"*Ave Dio.*"

"Yes," Olivia said softly. "It almost makes you catch your breath when you see them together."

"So much history, so much lost time. But soon, everything will be better. It's the one thing I'll regret missing out on. Well, maybe two," she added, with a brief, sly look her way.

"Valentina. Don't. You're going to make me cry and I'm not a pretty crier."

"You're thinking from the perspective of youth, dear. Don't ask me to apologize for being ready."

Olivia managed to nod. "That wasn't my intention. Only, please tell me if there isn't something I can do for you?"

"It's why I had Rosa ask you to come up." She pointed to the closet. "In there. They're yours now."

"What is?" Confused, Olivia glanced over her shoulder.

"All of the letters. The stories and secrets people have bestowed on the building. They're yours to carry on with as you see fit."

In other circumstances, Olivia would have been thrilled, enthusiastically ready to get to work and share her ideas of researching at the library and elsewhere for more information about Nathan Burroughs, his family, and the mysteries that kept luring people to this building. However, such a gift was coming at a heartbreaking price. It had her pulse pounding in her ears like the ominous sound of a bell tolling.

Humbled, Olivia had to protest. "I'm temporary. I'm not family. I have no business accepting such a gift." Her unspoken thought was her fear of not being able to fulfill such a responsibility.

"You and Luca are the future of *Vita e Specie*. I see that as clearly as I see my own."

"The restaurant belongs to the Angelonis—Sal, Leo, and you."

"Today. Tomorrow brings changes, as it should."

Even so, Olivia felt the need to present stumbling blocks. She wasn't about to impose her health problems on the dear woman; however, there were plenty other justifiable arguments to be made. She would have made them if not for a shadow crossing Valentina's countenance that suggested the return of pain.

"Do you need me to call for Rosa? Is it time for your medication?"

"In a moment," Valentina finally whispered. "First go to the closet."

Olivia opened the door and saw almost three decades of human frailty, hopes, and heartache contained in two oversized plastic, lidded tubs. Even if she was completely healthy, she would have struggled to get them downstairs.

"Call in Luca," Valentina said. "I hear him talking to his mother."

"Why don't we leave them here and we can work on them together."

"Because there's no time."

When Olivia saw the opaqueness in Valentina's eyes, and the darkness that speaks to deep seas lacking any oxygen and no future, she slumped against the closet door, grateful it momentarily kept her knees from buckling.

"I'm sorry for my abruptness and the shortness of this visit," Valentina said, covering her eyes with her hands. "But you need to get Rosa now."

Nothing else would have stopped Olivia from trying to figure out a way to avoid all of this. She didn't even say goodbye. She couldn't. She simply exited the room and quietly closed the door behind her. It was as though she'd stepped from the Valley of Death.

The apartment was too small not to be noticed immediately. Luca and Rosa had been sitting at the dinette table with mugs of coffee and whatever her expression exposed, it brought Luca to his feet.

"What's happened?"

She waved away the question and said to Rosa, "She needs you. The pain is surging."

Without a word, Rosa went to the bedroom and disappeared inside. Olivia made it only halfway across the room before Luca had her in his arms. "You need to sit down."

Olivia simply laid her head against his chest. "This is surreal."

"You're both exhausted and not well."

It was obvious he didn't quite grasp what she meant, and she wasn't sure she could put it into words. Her conversation with Valentina had almost been like talking to Tempest.

"We're losing her, yes. Yet she wants me to take all the letters people have been putting through that mail slot through the years."

"You don't have to feel obligated to take them."

"Are you kidding? I've wanted to get my hands on those things ever since the first day I witnessed the arrival of one. But this is your family's heritage, just like *Vita e Spezie* is. It's as though she's realigning, or rather *aligning* our destinies."

Placing his fingers under her chin, he coaxed her to meet his gaze. "Is that such a bad thing?"

"You don't understand, Luca. She knew what I wanted even before I did."

Whispering her name, Luca kissed her as though they were the only two people in the apartment.

BY CLOSING THAT night, a unique and strange aura permeated everything and everyone in the restaurant. The dinner service had been as successful as lunch; nevertheless, there was no ignoring Valentina's absence, which cast a shadow over everyone's mood. No official word was given, nor needed. With rumors spreading that Rosa Angeloni, a hospice RN, was now staying with the living saint of *Vita e Spezie*, the worst was feared.

Most of the staff murmured endearing and emotional sentiments as they left. It took its toll on Sal. When Vinny lingered to assure him, "If you need me to come in earlier, or to stay later while you all go through this, just say the word. Anytime."

Sal could only nod and squeeze the chef's shoulder. He had to keep his lips compressed to keep them from trembling.

Once Vinny left, he settled on a kitchen stool, exhaling heavily and focused on a concerned Luca and Olivia. "I didn't feel this tired after our grand opening."

"Well, you're not thirty anymore and this is an ordeal, not a dream come true," Luca reminded him. "Do you need anything before I take Olivia home?"

"Nah. You go on." Then his expression softened. "I couldn't have done it without you, kid."

Luca nodded. "Give Mom and Aunt Val a kiss for me. But we'll wait until you're locked up."

After Sal waved them off, he relied on the help of the banister as he climbed the stairs to Valentina's apartment. A flash over the building caught his attention. The ship channel and points north toward Houston were being affected by an unusually strong low-pressure system. It was triggering aerial art. Hidden by clouds, the lightning created a Monet canvas in the pinks, lavenders and corals of a painter's palette. Since the wind was still blowing in from the Gulf, he couldn't hear any rumbling of thunder, but for a moment Sal felt a whimsical urge to collect Rosa and head up the highway in his car to relive what it was like to sit in a downpour and help nature steam up the windows.

With a wistful sigh, Sal noted there was only a slight glow coming from behind the mini blinds. While it was normal for Valentina to keep a light on in the apartment throughout the night, he had a hunch Rosa would still be awake. He knocked softly.

She opened the door, her hair slightly mussed and immediately stepped aside to let him in. "You should have gone home to get some rest," she whispered.

"Yeah, that's going to happen." He glanced beyond her toward the direction of Valentina's room. "How's she doing?"

"I had to call Dr. Tobin and get permission to increase her morphine dosage."

Sal could feel the blood drain from his face, and crossed himself, something he hadn't done in years. "I knew it was bad, but *morphine?* Shouldn't she be in a hospital?"

"They can't do anything there that I'm not doing here, and she's not interrupted by intercom announcements, helicopters coming and going, not to mention someone constantly coming in to take her blood pressure." Rosa had informed him earlier that she'd visited with the doctor and had signed the necessary paperwork to handle Valentina's home care.

Sal stared at her as if he was looking at a stranger. "You even sound like a nurse."

"I should hope so. I worked hard enough to earn the credential letters behind my name."

She was no longer the girl he had married. The jolt once again left Sal at a momentary loss for words.

Seeing his stymied state, Rosa took hold of his hand and led him to the dinette table. "If you're not too exhausted, why don't you join me for a little nightcap?"

"Me? How about you? I can see I interrupted your rest," he said. But he didn't mind seeing her in that sexy, short robe again.

"Broken nights are part of my job description." Rosa got the bottle of brandy from the cupboard, as well as the two short-stemmed glasses. As Sal took his seat at the table, she poured.

"I should have brought you some more food."

"We still have leftovers from the last time."

"A little dessert would have been nice with the brandy."

"You've become such a considerate man. For that alone, I cannot regret the lost years."

"Nobody pays a compliment like you do, Rosa," he replied dryly. "I feel like I'm stuck in an elevator between Heaven and Hell."

"Sometimes it's best not to overthink things. We both needed time to mature. The more I think about it, the less I feel there's anything to be ashamed of." Settling onto the other chair, she raised her glass to his. "Don't brood. I expected to come back here one day to find you with three more kids and a restaurant still turning out good food, but crumbling around your ears. No one has ever been more proud and relieved to be wrong."

"Thank you." Sal touched his glass to hers. "But I'm the one who's impressed. How did you do it—get a degree and everything?"

"The usual way, a day job and online courses at night, until I had to do my clinicals. As you must have guessed, my parents were a big help with Luca when he was little."

Mulling over her choices, Sal asked, "How do you enjoy work like yours? The last days of a life—they're the worst time. There's the pain, the emotional family."

"We see it as a calling. Technically, it's ensuring another pair of hands and eyes to make sure the patient is made as comfortable as possible through that difficult passage. In some ways, I'm a conduit between the patient and the family. I make the time to answer questions relatives don't or won't ask staff in a facility, either because of shift changes where there's always a new face and the patient is just another case. Whereas, I'm the patient's advocate around the clock until the end. I lend a sense of normalcy to patient and family, even peace."

"And I thought Valentina was a glutton for punishment running to church all the time."

"Well, as far as Valentina is concerned, she doesn't always go to church, sometimes her destination is her beloveds' graves."

"I know. Early on, I followed her, until I felt confident she wasn't going to harm herself. Luca learned as much himself. He followed her the morning after he arrived."

"I hate he had a reunion with his cousin and uncle in such a way. If I could change the past, it's one of the things I would have done differently."

"It needed to happen at some point," Sal told her. "You don't think Little Mario's death didn't mark him as much as we did? Luca is thirty and still single. We were barely out of school when we were married."

"Yes, we were definitely a living advertisement for marrying young."

Sal lowered his gaze, and fingered the fine leaf engraving around the liqueur glass. "I don't want to fight."

About to take a sip of brandy, Rosa eyed him over its rim. "We're having a discussion, Sal. Not an argument."

"I guess I need more practice. If I'm not butting heads with Leo or someone else in the kitchen, or threatening to walk from a supplier I catch trying to pull something over on me, I'm the showman, putting on a performance for the customers. I'm not always sure who the real me is."

"They all are. As the saying goes, you wear many hats. From what I've heard from Valentina, the entrepreneur you've become couldn't have achieved the success you have without a certain amount of sensitivity to adapt to whatever the business needed."

"Now who's schmoozing whom?"

Sipping her drink, Rosa said, "You've become someone easy to be around."

"There's something every guy lives to hear. Next you'll use the comfortable old shoe analogy."

"It's a good comparison. Reassuring. Soothing. Believe me, edgy or exciting can wear out a person on the receiving side fast."

Sal looked anything but pleased by that observation. "And what experience is this based on?"

"You." She saw his skeptical look and scoffed softly. "You think I could survive another young Salvatore Angeloni?"

Sal didn't know whether to feel disgruntled at her questionable praise or relieved she wasn't comparing, referring to someone from another relationship. But his brooding was soon replaced by a memory that put a sparkle in his eyes and a heat in his belly. "Do you ever think of the afternoon you came to the old restaurant to tell that young Angeloni you were pregnant? We made love on the desk in office."

"You're the only one to ever tempt me to ignore my head and go with my heart."

"If Valentina wasn't only yards away, I'd take you to the couch. But there's a perfectly good desk going to waste downstairs."

"And that is what makes you even sexier now, Sal. I know you're flirting has a line of respectability and responsibility you won't cross, because you won't ask me to leave your sister."

Sal gestured helplessly. "How the devil can I be sexy when you can see through me easier than clear wrap?"

She started to shift toward him. "Because I'm trusting you'll give me a raincheck. Now drink up, kiss me, and go home."

BY THE TIME Luca carried the second box upstairs at the boarding house, he found Olivia with the lid off the first one, paging through letters. A roll of thunder mirrored his mood. "Oh no, you don't. You're not staying up all night turning yourself inside out over all that human turmoil."

"But, Luca, listen to this. There was this woman. She was a nurse and she fell in love with a man whose life she saved when he was injured in the line of duty. He was a U.S. Marshall, but she'd been raised to hate guns and couldn't bear the thought of him having to be gone so much, let alone being killed. So, he accepted a transfer and she moved on. A few years later she relocated with her husband and child only to find him in the same town and still single. The love between them still very real. She's miserable because she'd settled for security at the cost of love."

Wind started to gust outside and, despite the glow from a single lamp, the room brightened with increased flashes of lightning. "Let me tell you about miserable," he said, turning off the air conditioner unit. Pulling up the blinds, he tugged open the other window.

As the wind blew in, Olivia gasped and quickly pulled the lid over the container. "Don't do that," she cried. "Everything will fly all over the place."

"I have a solution for that, too." He hoisted the box off the bed and set it on top of the other in the corner. Turning off the light, he then stretched out on the bed, drawing her to him. "You don't need to be focusing on other people's unfulfilled longing tonight. Think about mine...ours."

Without her chef's jacket, she was achingly tempting in her little white tank top that lovingly molded itself to her breasts, while the cool wind caressed her before he could, pronouncing taut nipples through her thin bra. It was a grueling exercise in discipline to be around her all day and not get trumped up by his fantasies. He would be damned if he had to share the night with her commiserating over someone else's unrequited love.

In the next long flash of lightning, Olivia saw his intense, strained face and it all but froze her breath inside her lungs. Her fingers were unsteady as she traced his lips. "Oh, Luca, I'm sorry. I wish I could be what you need right now."

He drew her closer, until their bodies conveyed what words couldn't adequately describe. "You don't think I know that? What makes it bearable is that you're what I need forever. I would never risk your safety no matter how badly I want you."

In-between his whispered utterances, he caressed her with his lips, her cheeks, chin, the space between her eyebrows, and throat. Only when she sought more, did he close his mouth over hers and give in to the deep kiss he'd been craving.

It was a risky indulgence and it did push them to the brink—until a particularly harsh, and close, crack of thunder sent Luca off the bed. He gripped either side of the window pane, defiantly facing the storm. He ached so badly, the lashing of cold, stinging rain was a relief. Only when he felt in control again, did he shut the window.

Soaked, he stripped off his shirt and slacks before rejoining Olivia.

She was still trembling with the residual effects of her own unfulfilled needs. He folded her tenderly in his arms. "How are we going to explain your monitor readings to Dr. Pham?" he asked, hoping he sounded more amused than he felt.

Olivia kissed his collarbone. "She chased you out of her office. I'm sure she'll figure it out."

16

ONCE AGAIN, THE NIGHT'S STORM CLEANSED THE AIR, AND
seabirds of all types were soaring through the sky searching for a
morning meal. Sal knocked on Valentina's apartment door, still bleary-
eyed and carrying a tray of coffee, cappuccino and treats for his ladies.
To his surprise, it was his sister who opened up. Although she was in
the wheelchair Rosa had obtained for her, she was actually smiling.

"Good morning, Salvatore, dear. Rosa is still getting ready. Come
in. I'm not very good yet with maneuvering this chair."

'Yet?' The connotation of the word inferred a future mastery. Was
she telling him something?

Sal recovered in time not to drop the tray, and closed the door behind him. "Ah…should you be out of bed? I mean you look beautiful.
Great compared to yesterday, but—"

"I feel well enough to go to church. I wish you could join us."

He hated having to disappoint her. "If I could, I would. For you.
But you know I have to get to the docks for fresh fish. But I tell you
what, if you're feeling this well on Sunday, I promise to join you then."
Seeing his sister's sad acceptance, he bent to kiss her cheek and added
quickly, "Are you up for a cappuccino? A biscotti?"

"I've already had tea, thank you, but I will sit with my two favorite
people."

Rosa emerged from the bathroom, wearing a navy-blue knit top,
and lighter blue slacks. With her hair held off her neck by a tortoise

clip, she looked fresh, and lovely, yet oddly somber given Valentina's improved condition.

"Good morning." He gave her a light kiss on her lips, his gaze reflecting an unasked question. "Isn't it wonderful to see Valentina doing so well?"

"Excuse me, I forgot my bag in the bathroom," she replied.

"I'll get it," Valentina said, immediately starting to wheel toward her room. "I need mine, as well."

As soon as she disappeared through the doorway, Rosa drew Sal as far into the corner of the dinette area as possible and whispered in his ear. "Don't be fooled by this. She's not better."

"But—"

"It's an illusion. Some call it Fate's last cruel joke. I see it all the time. Just before the last spiral to the end, there's a day or two of what seems like a patient's remarkable recovery. There's euphoria, an appetite, it's startling to family witnessing it. However, it's always followed by the final decline."

Crestfallen, Sal dealt with the ache in his throat and burning in his eyes. What did Valentina make of this? Did she know?

Rosa quickly kissed his cheek, whispering, "I'm sorry to be so blunt. She's coming back. Do not let her see you understand."

And how was he supposed to do that, when he hadn't adjusted to the idea of her pending death? Now he was being told it was imminent? Certain he wouldn't be able to speak without his voice shaking, he bought himself precious seconds by reaching for the cup he'd brought for his sister. As though to mock his strategy, his phone rang.

Swearing under his breath, he drew it out of his pocket and checked the screen. *"Good going, God,"* he thought. *"More gratifying news?"*

"It's the hospital," he announced.

For the next minute, he listened to a nurse tell him about Leo's latest escapade. It was no surprise that once he disconnected, both Rosa and Valentina were staring at him with concern. Of course, they'd heard enough of his side of the conversation to know the situation was bad.

"What's happened to Leo?" Valentina demanded. "Why did you tell them to do what they had to do?"

"Your brother," Sal muttered. "Always convinced he's the smartest eggplant at the market. He decided he'd had enough of the bandage changing and cleansing. Not only did he rip out his IV, he tried to get out of bed."

"But his broken hip!" Valentina cried.

"Fortunately—or unfortunately—they managed to keep the idiot from falling flat on his face."

"Salvatore!"

"Valentina, you know you own a big chunk of my heart, but I'm done with making excuses for him."

Because he was still seething with anger, Rosa quickly tried to re-direct his focus. "What happened to Tiny? You said he was staying with Leo."

"The nurse didn't say." Sal shrugged. "Who knows, the bathroom, the cafeteria. I know if it was me, I'd be on the roof preparing to jump."

As Valentina crossed herself, Rosa asked firmly, "Sal, seriously, when you said what you said, did they tell you they were going to sedate him, or wanted your approval to secure him to the rails along either side of the bed?"

As impressed as he was with her knowledge of procedure, Sal gestured toward his sister. "Does she need this?"

"Salvatore," Valentina declared with quiet dignity, "I'm not a delicate flower who needs to be protected from the smallest draft. Tell us."

"They want me over there to sign a consent form for the restraints."

"They're tying Leo to the bed?"

Rosa put a calming hand on her sister-in-law's thin shoulder. "This is a touchy subject for hospitals, for every caregiver. They have strict written policies to protect patients' rights and to avoid the need for litigation. But they also have to protect their staff from assault and injury. We're talking carefully placed Velcro bands at his wrists to be removed as soon as Leo calms down and stops being a threat to his own safety. Surely within the hour, but no more than twenty-four if Sal is going to give them written authorization."

"I'm going, too," Valentina said. "He'll listen to me, so none of this is necessary."

"Dearest, you need to understand how Leo has already compromised himself. Given the spill from the bag, the new bleeding, not to mention staff grabbing him before they could put on gloves, they're going to have to watch Leo even more closely for the threat of infection. That will only delay his surgery. You know you don't want that."

"No," Valentina agreed. "But it's all the more reason for us to go to church first, and then the hospital."

"Time, Valentina," Sal groaned. "Can God not hear you if you pray in the car?" At Rosa's reproachful look, he hung his head in surrender. "I'm not going to fight both of you, but—" he checked his watch and did some quick mental calculations "—I have to make a call first."

LUCA AND OLIVIA had just pulled away from the boarding house when he glanced her way. "'Chocolate melts in a child's pocket.'"

She slid him a perplexed look. "You know that old saying?"

"No, it's one of the several interesting things you recited in your sleep."

Blushing, she said, "I heard a British chef say it as a reminder not to overheat the chocolate in a Florentine cookie recipe. Otherwise it will cloud when cooled."

"And why do I want the cheaper chocolate?"

"Cheaper?"

"If it's under seventy percent cocoa bean, isn't it cheaper?"

"Not necessarily. The lower the number, the easier it is to work with, especially for tiramisu. You're making fun of me."

Luca placed his right hand over his heart. "I told you, dessert wasn't a strength. But I can honestly say I've never met anyone who recites lessons and tricks in her sleep."

"It's not so different than counting sheep to relax so you can nod off."

"More likely it was a thing you developed to keep from worrying about your health."

With a sigh, Olivia admitted, "No, Dr. Freud. I was in denial about that. However, I was scared to death I couldn't prove my abilities to more experienced bakers. During tests, presentation can mean thirty to fifty percent of your score in your areas of culinary arts. In mine it's everything before they even taste what you've created."

"I'll give you that. And I would rather deal with a State dinner and all of the white-glove inspections than have to survive a hands-on fussy bride changing her cake request every other day."

"Did you have a favorite one of those?"

"The one for the Rumanian prime minister who came into the kitchen, not only to thank us for the meal, but to give us tips on how to make blood sausage. His father had been a butcher."

"Disgusting stuff," Olivia muttered. "I'll eat oysters three times a day for a week—even during a month without an R in it—before I'll touch that gruesome concoction."

That was another common-sense lesson Luca expected to hear her recite in her sleep one day. Oysters were less likely to contain harmful bacteria in cooler months, all of which were spelled with an R.

"Hopefully, with tequila or vodka chasers as antibiotics," Luca drawled.

She laughed and gave him an incredulous look. "You're scary."

"Excuse me?"

"You think as fast as anyone I've ever met, you're practically a walking computer of knowledge, and not simply witty but a raconteur, you've almost succeeded making pasta only one or two people on the planet can make...where are you hiding your feet of clay? You're too good to be true."

Luca went silent. There was no denying a minute disappointment, especially after their closeness last night. It would never cross his mind to expect perfection from her; her humanness was part of what made her fascinating. Endearing. Irresistible. However, she'd just told him she suspected he was hiding his shortcomings.

"'Feet of clay...' I'm sure they exist, given my genetic cocktail, but all I've strived to do is to make the best of life with what I have."

With a moan, Olivia reached out to touch his arm. "Lord, Luca, I offended you. I am such an ass."

He recovered quickly; she was, after all, his Livie. "I'd hardly go that far, darlin'. But from here on we're going to have to play the `Who loves whom more' game. I win this round."

"And I'm going to start calling you Saint Luca for your goodness."

"Don't you dare. I've no interest in becoming a beatified fossil before we consummate this relationship."

Luca's Smartphone started ringing as he turned into the restaurant's parking lot. In one of those perfect one-two moments, he saw it was his father on the line and, also, standing by his black Mercedes parked next to the steps to Valentina's apartment. At the top of the stairs stood his mother, with his aunt in a wheelchair.

"Something is going on," he said to Olivia, giving the horn a tap. It worked. The phone went silent; they had been spotted.

Parking beside the Mercedes, he got out just as his father reached him. One look at his face told Luca whatever was going on, it wasn't good.

"We're on our way to the hospital," Sal said, and gave him a quick update. "Can you help me get your aunt down to the car, then handle the fish pick up this morning?"

Luca waved at the female members of his family. "Of course. Aunt Val looks almost perky."

"Well, she's not." Sal repeated what Rosa had told him.

Olivia had just joined him and clutched Luca's arm. "Don't worry about anything here," she assured Sal. "We have it covered."

"I know you will."

Luca easily carried Valentina on his own. In her condition, his aunt weighed nothing now, and it broke his heart to understand what that meant, even without his father's news. As he set her into the back seat of the elegant car, he kissed her tenderly. "I'm glad you're able to go. Dad will check his temper better with you there."

Loading the wheelchair into the trunk, he also kissed his mother, then waved them off. Moving Livie's car to its usual spot, he rejoined her at the back door. His mind was racing like a bullet train.

"I hate to leave you alone," he began.

"I'll be fine. Are you going to take Vinny up on his offer to come in as soon as possible?"

"I hate to, but I see no way around it. If I'm getting the fish, there's no one to make the pasta. He can get it started, until I get back. That means we need Benny in, as well, to do the sauces and soup."

"That may be a bit stressful for him," Olivia said.

"Overcoming experiences like he's had is part of rising in the business. But there's nothing wrong in creating a better atmosphere for him—all of you—to work in. I'll turn on the stereo. Vinny will know to monitor things. Don't you hesitate to draw out Benny with small talk, until Joey and Stu arrive."

Once the calls were made, and the music was playing softly—the same Harry Connick Jr. album from the other day—Olivia walked him to the back door. "Is there anything I can pick up for you?" Luca asked.

"I'm good, thanks. I'll just dash upstairs to get Vinny what he'll need from Valentina's garden."

"There'll be no dashing. Let me get the containers and scissors and I'll bring everything down to you." When she gave him an impatient look, he waved away any further protests. "Humor me, Livie. I don't think I could keep it all together if you ended up in the ER, too."

IF SAL HAD his way, they would have driven straight to the hospital. But it had been several days since his sister had been to church—and if Rosa was correct, Valentina's next visit would likely be her last. A journey where others would be lighting candles for *her*.

He stayed in the back near the exit, although they had the place almost to themselves. One of the priests was checking the alter, and watering the plants, while on the far side, an elderly man sat looking as though he'd prayed himself into a nap.

Just when Sal thought he might perspire through his clothes, Valentina signaled Rosa that she was ready to leave. But then they paused to light candles.

Finally exiting the church, Sal blinked against the glare of sun and haze. He was wheeling Valentina to the Mercedes when he heard a baritone rumbling of his name.

"So, my eyes didn't deceive me." Father Patrick Flynn strode up the street, his silver, leonine mane trimmed and shaped into restraint. Clearly, he'd just come from having a haircut. He stood a head taller than Sal, and in his black suit and Roman collar, his robust girth competed with the church's stone pillars.

Beaming, he extended both hands to Valentina and held them to his heart. "How is our most faithful lamb? We've been so concerned about you."

"I just needed a little rest, Father." Valentina sent Rosa a look of entreaty. "Rosa, dear, you remember Father Patrick Flynn? Father, our Rosa is home again."

The priest's blue eyes darted between Rosa and Sal before he turned to extend his hand to Rosa. "What joyous news, and how won-derful for you to escort your ladies to church this morning, Salvatore."

With a wry smile Sal nodded. "Go ahead and rub it in. You're en-titled."

"What brings you out this early?"

Grimacing, Sal said, "We put in a request with your boss, before we head over to the hospital."

"Salvatore, show some respect," Valentina chided. "It's Leo, Father. You've heard about his latest misfortune?"

"Misfortune my—" Sal intercepted his wife and sister's glares and managed to repress his blunt opinion on the accident.

"He walked into poor Benedict Bosco, our sou chef, as Benny was moving the marinara sauce," Valentina explained. "I'm sorry I didn't call, Father. I've been under the weather myself."

Watching Sal pinch his nose and turn away, he took great care as he patted Valentina's hands. "Dear Valentina, the fault is mine. But you have been in my prayers. Leo will be, as well. What's his prognosis? Can he receive guests?"

"Probably not at this time, Father," Rosa said. "He also broke his bad hip in the fall. They can't operate, until the worst wounds close and the threat of infection recedes. Unfortunately, he pulled out his IV this morning. Considering the additional surgery coming up, his veins didn't need that kind of abuse."

The priest's expression reflected his concern. "Oh, dear, that's se-rious. I'll be on standby and await your call at any hour. I know he doesn't come to services any more than you do, Sal, but I also under-stand why. It might give him comfort to realize that like The Father, The Church remembers him regardless."

"Thank you so much, Father," Valentina said.

The older man gave her a soulful look. "You know I'm here for your entire family. Father Torres will be pained by the news, as well. He very much enjoyed meeting Luca. He gets homesick, and finding someone who speaks the language was a gift. Do you mind if he stops by to see Luca? I suspect the youngest Angeloni is holding down the fort at the restaurant?"

Valentina told Rosa. "Father Torres is the newest member of the parish and is Luca's age."

Rosa nodded with satisfaction. "Excellent idea, Father. The one thing I worried about while my son was in Washington, D.C., was his spiritual health."

Patrick Flynn smiled with amusement. "But they have glorious cathedrals in our capitol."

"Yes, but like his father, he's been totally focused on work," Rosa said gently, leaning into Sal.

"He had a position of responsibility," Sal reminded her, only to look at the priest. "Doesn't the Bible say, 'to whom much is given, much is expected'?"

Father Flynn's blue eyes lit with merriment which also brought heightened color to his rosy Irish cheeks. "That's an interesting perspective. I think our Lord was more referencing our devotion to spreading His word. However, our Heavenly Father also approves of His industrious shepherds. I'll go now and speak to Domingo. God bless you all."

WHEN THE THREE Angelonis arrived on Leo's floor, every nurse at the station exhibited relief. They also tried to speak all at once.

"We were about to draw straws to see who was the unlucky one to go check on him next."

"Not that he doesn't already have a sitter in there," the shortest nurse added, pinching the first speaker's arm lightly. "A man. Mr. Angeloni doesn't seem to like women."

"He's still being well taken care of, despite everything," the oldest nurse added. "We understand he's in a lot of pain, that even with medication is substantial, and changing bandages on a burn victim isn't for the faint of heart."

"Can you tell us what he's on?" Rosa asked.

When the woman stared at her, Sal said, "This is my wife, Rosa Angeloni. She's a hospice nurse. This isn't a haphazard question."

Rosa touched his arm. "Why don't you go inside with Valentina, Sal. It will be all right."

As Sal sucked in a breath so deep it tested the buttons on his white dress shirt, Valentina placed a steadying hand on his forearm. If it wasn't for her own precarious condition, he wasn't sure he could resist shaking her off.

"We're so sorry ladies," Valentina began. "This isn't like my brother Leo at all."

"The hell it isn't," Sal muttered.

"*Mia,* getting upset isn't going to help anything," Rosa said.

"*'Getting?'* I've got news for you. I've been dealing with that for most of his life," Sal said pointing toward the door of Leo's room. "He always makes people suffer even when they're trying to help him. I don't care how injured he is, there's no excuse for his actions."

"This is our job, sir, and we were wrong to burden you with our problems," the senior nurse said.

"That's good of you to try to cover for him, but I meant what I said. I know my brother."

Before anyone could say anything else, there was a crash from behind the closed door directly across from the nurses' station. As one of the nurses covered her eyes with her hand, Sal gave the senior nurse a speaking glance.

"Prepare whatever you need me to sign so that stops," he told her, and strode across the hall to enter the room.

Tiny was on all fours scrambling to wipe up the water and a milky substance spilled around him. Leo, with both wrists fastened to the bars on either side of the bed, continued to kick like someone gone berserk, or a child throwing a fit. The male attendant, wiping the same concoction from his face and clothes, took one look at Sal's expression, and started for the exit. "I'll get someone to clean this up."

As he left, Sal told Tiny, "Take what you have there and let the nurses show you where to toss it. Then take a break."

Tiny stumbled for the door, delayed by Valentina entering. Once she was inside, he shut the door behind himself.

"And you—" Sal finally faced Leo "—I don't care how bad the pain is, stop making everyone's life hell."

"You have no idea," Leo snarled.

Sal pointed at their sister. "No, *you* have no idea!"

Valentina gasped, "Salvatore, don't."

Sal was oblivious to anything but his own fury. "You may be hurting, but *she's* dying."

He knew he was breaking his promise to allow her to tell Leo in her own way. However, soon there would be no Valentina to handhold their brother through the rest of his life. As far as Sal was concerned, all deals were off.

Stricken, Leo rasped, "You're lying."

"No, what I am is the only person in this family dealing with reality. She is dying, and you are laying there like what happened to you is everyone's fault but your own. It hurts like hell, Leo, we get it. But you did that to yourself. Always in a hurry, always doing what you want, when you want, however you want. Then when everything hits the fan, you swing back and forth from having a pity party to throwing a fit like a spoiled baby to avoid apologizing.

"There's a young man at the restaurant half your age," Sal continued pointing out the door, "that you could have blinded or maimed for the rest of his life. So now I'm telling you for the last time, get your act together, or I'll clean out our bank account to pay you off. After that, I'll never want to see you inside *Vita e Spezie* again!"

Sal stormed out of the room with no idea of where he was going. Years of pent up anger and frustration had taken his toll. He would carry guilt for exposing Valentina to this, but he couldn't tiptoe around her feelings any longer. What Leo did at the restaurant was awful and wrong; however, disrupting the operation of a hospital was unconscionable.

When he stopped at the end of the hall he realized he was out of options. To his left, were just more rooms and to the right were double doors with a sign that stated *No Admittance.* He slumped against the nearest wall, exhausted. He had no idea Rosa had followed, until she stood before him.

"Well, that's one way to clear the air," she drawled.

WITH JUST THE two of them in the room, Valentina wheeled her chair as close as she could to the bed, and stretched her hand toward Leo. "Forgive him. He's had too much on his shoulders for too long."

"I don't care." Leo muttered.

"My poor brother." The tangled blankets let her see too much, a man covered in gauze from neck to thigh, and medication over the burns where skin had not peeled off. "Lay back. Calm yourself, please. I'll get someone to fix your bed."

"Stop. Just tell me—is it true?"

Valentina slowly nodded.

"Did he know and not tell me?"

"No one knew except Rosa. Not even Luca."

"Are you sure there's no hope?"

"It's certain."

"How long?"

She touched his fingers. They were all she could reach. "I'll come to see you every day, as long as I can."

Tears bled from the corners of Leo's eyes and he uttered a long wail. *"No!"* Then he burst into sobs that allowed no further conversation.

Valentina wept as well, but not out of self-pity. She hated having to bring him this grief. "Listen to me dearest. Rosa will be here to help you."

"But she's not you."

"Leo, I'm tired of hurting and I want to see my husband and child again."

"You would still have them if not for me."

Anguished by the realization he'd been carrying guilt all this time, Valentina ached to hug him, but had to settle for stroking those few, trembling fingers. "No. Hear me. You must stop this once and for all," she said gently. "It wasn't your fault that someone ran a red light."

"I was talking too much and teasing Little Mario. If I'd paid attention maybe I could have stopped, swerved, done something."

"Enough. Promise me from here on you will look toward the future. We've all spent long enough living in the past."

PREP WORK WAS moving along well, even if Joey and Stu were trying too hard to be cheerful. It was welcome compared to the long faces there would be if everyone knew how bad things really were.

Olivia checked the time, aware Luca should be returning at any moment. The wait staff would start arriving soon, too. There would be little chance to ask if he'd talked to his family, but as long as he was here, that would be reassuring.

A Dean Martin song came on. Joey grabbed a spoon and held it like a microphone as he danced over to Olivia to croon, *"That's amore!"*

Smiling, she shook her head at the handsome, young Italian. "If I don't get these entremets piped and into the oven they won't cool in time for lunch."

"And you won't be finished, either," Vinny warned the younger man. He pointed with his spatula. "Vamoose."

Olivia had just gotten her layered, mousse-based creations in the oven when her phone rang. Thinking it was Luca, she quickly dug it out of her chef's coat pocket. Her smile waned when she saw it was her cardiologist.

Dropping down on the nearby stool, she said, "Olivia Dumont," covering her free ear with her hand due to the noise.

"Good morning, Olivia. This is Dr. Pham calling with your test results."

"Okay, doctor. I should warn you my heart just dropped into my stomach, but I'm ready to hear whatever you have to say."

"Well, that's totally understandable and justified. Your situation is more serious than we thought. I'm sure I asked you before, but do you recall any relative that had some sort of issue like this because frankly, I'm amazed you've functioned so well for this long."

"You did ask, but I don't have anything different to tell you. There's no one."

"Interesting. With your kind of case, there usually is a history, but all right, we move ahead," Dr. Pham said. "The tests revealed your heart valve has become stenotic, which means stiff. As a result, the heart must work harder to pump the blood through the valve. The situation is nearing critical and I'd like to get you into surgery as soon as possible."

Olivia was glad to be sitting down. "When?" was the only word she could force through her lips.

"Next Tuesday morning at seven o' clock. You'll need to come to the hospital Friday morning at nine for pre-op and registration. Clear your schedule for a couple of hours. In the meantime, you need to get as much rest as possible. You'll also have to arrange to take a leave of absence from work. Recovery time is four to eight weeks."

Olivia yelped in shock. "Our other pastry chef is in the hospital's burn unit with hip surgery pending. I can't be off that long."

"You don't have a choice."

When Olivia disconnected, she realized she was shaking. She wasn't even aware Luca had returned until she saw him crouching beside her. He took her phone and checked her calls.

"What did she say?" He asked softly.

"Surgery is next Tuesday."

"Whoa. That soon. Then what you're not telling me is it's more serious than she first thought?"

"Yes. Delaying isn't an option." She was finally able to meet his studious gaze. "Luca, if it's successful, recovery time is one to two months."

"What do you mean `if?'"

Ignoring the question, she focused on what was right for the restaurant and the family. "Your father needs to fire me and bring in someone else." She let her head drop back and gazed at the ceiling. "Oh, I've made such a mess of things."

Luca rose and glanced over his shoulder. "Joey, Stu, the van needs unloading."

As they took off, he crouched again and covered her clasped hands with his. "Listen to me, Livie, there'll be no talk of quitting. I can cover for you."

"You're the one who admitted pastry isn't your forte."

"But I can do it, and I've been watching you enough to learn a few things. And if I run into trouble at some point, I can call, and you can walk me through the rough spots."

"You and your father are going to be pulled in enough directions as it is with Valentina and Leo."

"Mom is here. It's all under control. We'll make it work."

Taking a steadying breath, she managed a weak smile. "You know we're now at two to zip, don't you?"

As his dark eyes brightened with understanding, he measured an inch with his index finger and thumb. "And that much more."

17

ON THE FOLLOWING TUESDAY, LUCA ACCOMPANIED OLIVIA to John Sealy Hospital's cardiac unit, where she signed in at the registration office. As soon as the attendant brought up her file with all the data from Friday's appointment, she printed her ID information and snapped the plastic bracelet onto her wrist. A moment later, another individual led them down the hall to an assigned room where Olivia changed into a hospital gown.

Before she climbed into the bed, Olivia handed Luca her tote to keep for her. "All of my worldly possessions," she quipped.

"Not funny."

"Nerves. And I'm freezing. If they're trying to slow down my overworked heart, they're succeeding. It's going into a coma."

A nurse entered and heard her distress. "I know, dear. I'll get you a couple more blankets as soon as I hook you up to the IV. Once the medicine goes in you'll start to feel relaxed. Don't fight it. Have a little nap if you can."

As soon as she left, Olivia glanced at Luca and said, "They're about to stop my heart and she's talking about taking a nap?"

Luca caressed her other hand. "Try to focus on the idea that in a couple of hours you'll be a new woman."

"With a big, nasty scar," she added.

"It will make you all the more precious to me and I plan on kissing it to make it better every chance I get."

"Oh, sure. Get me all hot and bothered again when there's still not a blessed thing I can do about it." She frowned, realizing something. "Dr. Pham didn't even tell me how long I would have to wait before having sex."

Luca's chest shook with his repressed laugh. "Whatever they gave you is having some effect, although probably not what they intended. You would never have been this frank with me otherwise."

She clamped her hand over her mouth and said, "What did I say? I hope I stop before my parents get here."

Olivia had been tip-toeing around her parents for so long, she doubted they could handle the person she'd become at this stage. As it was, her mother had cried and voiced her hurt when told about the surgery, while her father had gone straight into take-control mode, wanting to drive up that night. Precisely the conduct Olivia had been avoiding all this time. They weren't ready for the independent, self-reliant woman she'd become in the last few years.

As luck, or fate, would have it, a tropical storm had edged a little closer to New Orleans than first expected, delaying their arrival; however, they were now on their way, and would probably be at the hospital by the time she made it to recovery. Olivia had no doubt Luca would have them eating out of his hand every bit as quickly as he'd won her over.

The warm feeling triggered by that last thought was short-lived as the nurse and two orderlies arrived, ready to take her to the operating room. Olivia gave Luca an apprehensive look. She began to reach for his hand, only to hesitate.

"What?" he asked, leaning closer. "Tell me."

Despite the lack of privacy, she clenched his fingers tightly and said, "You should know...I love you."

A short time later, as he headed for the waiting room, he thought of her expression when he had replied, "I'm glad I didn't have to ask you to say that." But it was nothing compared to what she looked like when he said loud and clear, "Hurry back to me."

Not so pleasant was the scene in the waiting room. It made Luca doubly grateful Olivia's parents hadn't arrived yet. It was good of his family to be here for moral support, since today was an important day for Leo, as well. Even more touching was his father insisting *Vita e Spezie* close for the day, while assuring all their staff full salary. However, his father was acting as though the room was his office and he was on the phone directing things in the next hospital wing where Leo was supposed to be undergoing hip replacement surgery at this very minute. From the sound of things, Tiny was panicking as usual.

"Get a grip, Fredo. All that is normal. They know what they're doing. I'll get there as soon as I can. He'll be fine. Get yourself something to eat." Spotting Luca approaching, he added, "I gotta go," and disconnected.

"They just wheeled her in," Luca told his three family members. Setting Olivia's tote in an empty chair, he shoved his hands in his pockets, shuffled for several seconds, then looked at them with over bright eyes. "She finally said she loves me." He had to look away and swallow a few times before he could speak again. "We've both played around with the subject. It was so new, and she was skittish, only I didn't know why."

As his father resumed his seat beside Valentina, Rosa leapt up and embraced him. "I knew she was special from the moment I met her."

Laughing softly, Luca replied, "She said the moment you met her, you called her a blond dingbat, who needed a seeing eye dog to get her wherever she was going."

Rosa gasped. "I swear, I did not, *mia*. Did she really say that?"

"No, Mom. I'm only kidding you."

"Good, because a *nonna* wants to be adored by her daughter-in-law, so she can babysit as much as she wants." Rosa framed his face with her hands. "Her doctor was telling her the truth? Babies are possible?"

"Yes, Mom, but one thing at a time, okay?" He hugged her again. "I didn't believe this was going to happen for me."

SAL SAT ENVIOUS of mother and son. He wanted that for himself. He wanted Luca to reach for him, so he could assure the beautiful man he'd become, *"Of course! Who wouldn't love you?"* But he was getting control of those knee-jerk emotions—thanks to Rosa. She was giving him back as many pieces of lost time as she could. Sharing anecdotes, giving him copies of photos and videos she kept on her phone.

Hands tightening on his forearm drew his attention back to the present. He looked over to see Valentina with the sweetest expression he'd ever beheld in his life. About to apologize for daydreaming, she dismissed it with a lilting laugh.

"Isn't that perfect, Salvatore? It's all going to be all right."

There was no time for him to gently tease her again about being a romantic. She simply laid her head on his shoulder and was gone. Reality didn't sink in for several seconds; he thought she was just resting against him, but then a strange knowing came upon him. Shifting to take her into his arms, she collapsed onto his lap. He uttered a cry, a sound unlike anything that had never passed his lips.

Rosa extricated herself from Luca's hug, took one look and called for assistance. Luca stared at his aunt, then his father with the questioning eyes of a lost boy.

Everything Sal knew he was guilty of, and deserved retribution for, hit him like God's own fist. It was over. There were no more chances to assure Valentina he would work things out with Leo. He had run out of opportunities to tell her how much he appreciated her for sustaining his heart in the times when *he* wanted to give up. All he could do was bow over his privacy-loving sister one last time to protect her from curious eyes, as people trickled into the room to see what was going on. "Valentina, I'm sorry," he rasped. "I'm so, so sorry."

THE NEXT HOUR was a blur, lost in the chaos of technicians, doctors, and procedure; everything that happens when you're in an institution functioning on strict policy. Sal didn't judge. He was in a holding pattern above the earth waiting for God or somebody to please tell him there'd been a monstrous mistake, and everything would go back to normal in a minute. He did know what to say when Rosa asked him to confirm which funeral home they should call. However, she already knew. He understood without asking, it was another thing she and Valentina had discussed.

The two sons now running Parisi Funeral Home came to take Valentina. They, along with their parents, were long-time customers at the restaurant, and so hugs were shared, and words of condolences. While everyone was circumspect Sal couldn't contain an utterly base groan as his sister's covered body was rolled by him on a gurney.

"Fino a quando ci incontreremo di nuovo, più dolce anima."

Rosa crossed herself, and whispered into Luca's ear, "Until we meet again, sweetest soul."

Having been too young to remember his father's reaction when the Marios died, an emotional Luca put his arm around his father's shoulders. "What can I do?"

When Sal failed to do anything, but watch the cart get loaded and shake his head, Rosa said, "Luca, call the family florist. Have them put a tasteful wreath on the restaurant's door with a black ribbon. White roses. She loved white flowers."

TIME IS IRREVERENT. It has no patience or interest in human emotions. Its job is simply to continue. By sunset, Leo had a new hip; Olivia had a new heart valve; and Valentina lay alone at Parisi Funeral Home.

Olivia's parents arrived about three hours later and were overjoyed to learn their daughter would see many more sunsets. Suzette Dumont was exactly like her daughter had described—a petite, energetic, strawberry blonde, with the attention span of a terrier puppy. Husband Claude looked like what Luca expected when he thought of a Cajun—just under average height, sinewy in build, with shrewd eyes, and an animated mouth that wanted to smile.

Introducing himself, Luca offered his hand. "And I hope you grow to like me," he added, "because I intend to marry your daughter."

When Olivia's mother sent her husband a worried look, Claude shrugged with a, "we'll see" attitude. "At least he's polite, *cher*," he told his wife.

Luca quickly assured them. "I wouldn't be so presumptive if she hadn't assured me her feelings are mutual. Don't worry, though, we'll give you plenty of time to get used to the idea."

Before he could say more, a nurse came out and said quietly, "The doctors will allow a visitor now."

Luca wanted desperately to push past everyone and go in first, but he forced himself to tell the woman, "These are her parents just in from New Orleans. I know she's eager to see them."

Once alone, now that his parents had gone over to the other wing where Leo was, he rested his elbows on his knees, and covered his face with his hands. He was dizzy from the day's turmoil. To keep his mind off what was going on in ICU he thought about his aunt and what his parents were going through. Had they told Leo yet? He dreaded that for everyone involved. Tonight, it felt as though the Angelonis owned most of the tears in heaven.

OLIVIA SLIPPED IN and out of consciousness. At one point, she thought she'd seen her mother, and wanted to ask when she'd let her hair grow so long, but the words wouldn't come out of her mouth. Something was in there. *Ventilator.* The feeling was awful, and she welcomed the darkness pulling her back into nothingness.

The next memory she had was of seeing Valentina. While she was delighted, it seemed odd that no one else in the family had joined her.

Things went dark again, and the next time she opened her eyes, she saw her parents. She couldn't understand what they said, but she felt their kisses, and the gentle stroking of her hand. That little bit of awareness exhausted her and she fell asleep before she could ask for Luca.

"I'm here."

She heard him before she sensed him hovering over her. Her olfactory senses were doing a better job at waking up and had her reaching toward the scent of him. She found his cheek, but only for a second. Her hand weighed a ton.

"What took you so long?" Her lips were so dry and stiff that she doubted she made any sense, but then she felt a soothing kiss on her forehead and nothing else mattered.

"I had to wait my turn."

Struggling against the medication, Olivia blinked and tried to reach for him again. The room filled with beeping sounds, and soon a female voice directed her to lay still and rest.

"You're going to scare the nurses if you move around too much," he told her.

"You're here. I thought I saw my mother, but then it was my other mother. My parents. I don't know."

"It's okay. It's the anesthesia."

"No. They let Valentina come by herself."

The strangest guttural sound slipped through Luca's lips that drew her back to full consciousness faster than anything could. Only when she saw the pain in his romantic, dark eyes, she wished she hadn't awakened yet.

Olivia found his hand and curled her fingers around his. "What's happened?"

She saw his mouth open and then he tried to turn away. Tightening her hold, she refused to let him go.

He pressed a kiss to her fingers. "She insisted on being here for you. We were all in the waiting room and I'd just told them that you loved me. She was so happy. She laid her head on Dad's shoulder and... she was gone. Aunt Val is gone, sweetheart."

Valentina. Olivia struggled to make sense of it all through the blur of drugs and with her other hand stroked his hair.

A stern nurse entered the room. "Sir, you need to let her rest."

"His aunt just died," Olivia said. "Here."

Realization lit the nurse's face. "That's your family? We heard. I'm very sorry, but we need to let her sleep now. She's had entirely too much excitement for this early after surgery."

Nodding, Luca kissed Olivia again. "I'll be here waiting for them to let me in again."

"No, Luca," she told him. "Go help your family. They need your strength."

He shook his head. "But I need you."

"I'll be here."

AFTER TALKING TO Olivia's parents and making sure they had a place to stay, Luca sat in his car in the parking lot not sure what he should do next. *Tempest.* Olivia had asked him not to forget to call her. Their landlady answered before the end of the first ring.

"I'm so sorry to be late in calling you."

"I've been turning cards all day," she replied. "I thought I saw that everything would be all right, but then the Queen of Hearts kept showing up, followed by the Ace of Spades, the Death card. I couldn't help but worry."

"Olivia's surgery went great. Her parents are with her. It's my Aunt Valentina, who..." He had to swallow against the blockage that returned to his throat before he could continue. "She passed away while Olivia was in surgery."

"The woman in black. Now she walks in light, and not alone."

"That would be a good way to think of her."

"If the Dumonts need a place to stay, don't hesitate to call. They would be welcome here."

With a husky, "I'll tell them," he thanked her and disconnected.

The call had cleared his head somewhat and his first impulse to drive to his father's house changed to an instinct to go to *Vita e Spezie*. It turned out to be the right choice once he recognized several cars parked in back: his father's, Rocco's, Vinny's, and several others. Word had obviously spread and there was undoubtedly an Italian version of a wake going on.

He walked in and found some of the bocce players cooking in the kitchen while everyone else was grouped in the bar. The glow of candles was everywhere. He recognized Vivaldi playing softly on the stereo, one of Aunt Val's favorite composers. The lilting notes matched the gentle tones of conversation and supportive hugs he witnessed as he drew closer. His mother spotted him first and, drawing Sal behind her, hurried to him. "How is she?" she asked, kissing both of his cheeks.

"Okay. Mom, she took one look at my face and knew."

Rosa hugged him and crooned, "Of course, she did."

When he turned to his father for a hug, he asked, "How's Uncle Leo?"

"He's taking it as hard as we expected."

"I should have gone over there before I headed this way."

"You had enough going on. Tomorrow is another day."

Luca tilted his head toward the kitchen. "What's happening in there?"

Sal's smile of appreciation cloaked some of his sadness. "It's the Italian way. You need a drink. What's your pleasure? Chanel, take care of Luca."

As he stepped up to the bar, Luca caught sight of Rocco with a protective arm around Janine, Valentina's niece from her husband's side. Even with her long hair up in an elegant bun, she looked like a goldfish gazing dreamily at a great white shark.

"So that's really happening?" he asked Chanel.

Shaking her head, she replied, "I should have known Livie couldn't keep from telling you. One thing you've got to say about life, it keeps going on." She reached for a bottle of cognac. "I think you need a spot of this as long as you promise to eat something, too."

"Yeah, sure."

"How's our girl?"

"Amazing."

Chanel patted his hand.

By the time the rest of the people who had heard about Valentina had gotten there, the dining room held close to fifty people, including Father Patrick and Father Domingo. Tables were rearranged into a long line and huge bowls of food were set up and down, filling the room with Mediterranean scents.

Father Patrick rose, touching the Crucifix that lay on a gold chain over his chest. "Tomorrow," he began, "we will return to mourning our cherished sister and friend. But tonight let us remember her as she would want us to. In the words of our beloved Pope John Paul II, 'To maintain a joyful family requires much from both the parents and the children. Each member of the family has to become, in a special way, the servants of the other.'"

Sal nodded solemnly. "That was Valentina. And she succeeded." He looked at Rosa and reached for her hand before gazing across the table where Luca sat next to Father Domingo. "She reunited the family." Lifting his glass of wine, he said, "To Valentina and *la famiglia*."

"*La famiglia!*"

EPILOGUE

VALENTINA ELEONORE ANGELONI PASTORE WAS LAID TO REST on an overcast day. Someone was heard to remark how it would take a gentle soul like Valentina to convince God to give them relief from the scorching temperatures.

Saint Mary's had been filled to capacity, and not a prayer candle remained unlit in the back of the nave or the transept areas of the cathedral. Though not surprised, all of the Angelonis were touched by the show of respect and love by so many. Among those who had not been able to attend, were Olivia's parents who had to return to Louisiana. However, both Olivia and Leo had been able to witness the moving service, albeit in wheelchairs and in Leo's case, with a medical attendant.

In the week between Valentina's death and her funeral, Luca drove his mother home where he helped her arrange for moving her possessions to Galveston, back into the house his father had not changed much since she left twenty-five years ago. Rosa had taken one look at the place and told Sal, "I'm honored, but this is beyond ugly. Why did you ever marry someone with such hideous taste?" Sal had grinned like a bridegroom.

Luca saw it as another of Aunt Val's intercessions how things were to evolve between his parents. Not perfect, but real. Rich. No dull moments. His mother had never looked so vibrant. As for his father, he was evolving into a different person, an eternal smile lighting him from the inside, and he was apt to break into song without notice whenever the mood struck him.

It was another month before Olivia finished her rehab, while Leo continued his rehabilitation sessions several times a week, and would for another month. Tiny provided his dutiful assistance and did so without apprehension, due to the changes in Leo himself. The loss of Valentina had shaken him to his core and brought out a humility and consideration in him, all of which was welcomed by everyone.

On the first day of autumn, as tourism eased, giving everyone in the restaurant business a little more time, Sal and Rosa announced their desire to renew their vows. The pending event was what Luca and Olivia were talking about one night in bed as she lay in his arms. Although she had been medically restricted and had suggested they return to keeping their separate rooms until she completely healed, Luca would have none of that, insisting they not be apart again.

"Your father must be acting like the first groom ever," she said, fingering the nest of hairs on his chest.

"If I wasn't so happy for them, I would find the whole experience embarrassing."

"Well, I have news, too," she said, rising on her elbow. "My doctor gave me a full medical release today. You know what that means."

Luca frowned. "Already? I remember them saying up to two months. Are you sure?"

"Do you need to see some signed paperwork?"

She thought when she inched closer and started brushing her lips over his chest he would put any concerns behind him. It had been a long, hot summer for them in more ways than one, but to her amazement he eased her back against the pillows and said quietly, "Not like this, Liv."

She watched in disbelief as he left her room. She could hear him entering his, and wondered what she had done wrong. Had he changed his mind? Had he forgotten his phone and thought he might need it should she suffer a medical emergency? *What?*

He returned, shutting the door behind him. When he stretched out beside her, nerves had her quipping, "Was it something I said?"

"Yes. We're free now to pick up where we left off." He shifted so she could see the little black box. "Livie, will you marry me? I've been waiting to give you this since your surgery."

Her lips parted in a perfect silent, "Oh!"

She opened the box to see a glistening solitaire diamond set in platinum. She held up her hand and said, "Yes, please."

THEY WERE MARRIED a month later at Saint Mary's. Olivia hadn't wanted to make a fuss about her dress, but both Suzette and Rosa had insisted she indulge, and she had to admit she did feel like a princess in the lace and silk creation. The look on Luca's face alone as she walked down the aisle of the church on her father's arm was worth the silliness of fittings, choosing flowers, music, and everything else.

Olivia and her mother were upstairs in Valentina's apartment while everyone else was down in the restaurant, already starting the reception. She still tired easily and had voiced her concern about changing into more comfortable shoes.

"Have you checked the storm path in the last hour?" Olivia asked, as she removed her veil. "Do they think it's changed?" A late season tropical storm was forming again in the Gulf.

Suzette Dumont flicked her fingers to dismiss her concerns. "Your father says it's going to get swept into Mexico, thanks to the front pushing down from the plains."

Olivia sighed with relief. "I don't mean to wish trouble on anyone, but that's a relief. Given where we are, I can't help but think of the great hurricane of 1900 and Mr. Burroughs writing his letter in this very building."

Her mother brightened. "Hmm? You tried to tell me about that right after your surgery and I thought you were still under the influence of anesthesia."

Olivia wasn't surprised her mother had forgotten. She rarely kept two thoughts in her head for longer than a minute because she was fascinated with the next thing that grabbed her attention. "No, it was real. It's why the restaurant is so famous. He wrote this lovely letter to his wife, Mia, thinking he was going to die here." She corrected herself in the next breath. "Actually, he wrote it to God with his wife and children in mind."

With a soft, "Ah, I have always liked that name," her mother said. "Of course, it's a diminutive of Amelia. I had a great aunt who was called Mia."

"You never told me about a great aunt." Fluffing her hair, Olivia exited the bathroom.

"That's because no one ever talked about *my* side of the family. Conversations have always been about your father's people because they're around us all the time," she said rolling her eyes in mock despair. "What did you say the man's name was?"

"Burroughs. Nathan Burroughs."

Her mother's eyes grew wide and her mouth fell open. "Nathan and Amelia Burroughs."

Olivia felt the floor shift and sank beside her on the couch. "Yes." "That's them."

"Are you sure?"

"Well, I guess I would know my own flesh and blood. Mia Bertrand Burroughs, just as I'm Suzette Bertrand Dumont. I'm told I favor her somewhat, although I don't know how she managed all that hair," she said, patting her own chin-length bob. "Are you telling me her husband survived the storm in *this* building?"

"*Yes.*" For a moment Olivia thought she might be having a heart episode as she strived to take in the information. "Did you ever meet her?"

"Sadly, no, dear. Although someone in the family may have a photo somewhere. We'll have to start asking. She died relatively young after giving birth to her third child. It was her heart." As soon as she spoke the words, she gasped. "Oh, my."

"And I asked you whether we had any history of heart trouble in the family!" Olivia cried.

"I'm sorry! I didn't think that far back. And my mother never had any trouble. I don't, but..."

Tears filled Olivia's eyes. "Yes," she agreed. "But. I think she came to me after my surgery, the way Valentina did. Maybe more often," she murmured, remembering Tempest's comments about her dreams.

"Are you sure, dear?"

Olivia nodded. "Tempest told me I was keeping company with a woman from the other side. What if she was guiding me?"

Her poor great-great aunt had not had the medical technology to help her have a full life. Yet by some miracle, Olivia would not suffer the same end, and had found her way here, to the very spot Mia's beloved husband cheated death. She gripped her mother's hands. "Do you see it, Mom? There are no accidents."

She and her mother all but flew down the stairs to join the others. Only steps inside, Luca was there, impatient to embrace his bride.

"Are you okay," he asked, concerned, as he held her close. "You're so flushed."

She wrapped her arms around his neck and kissed him with joy. "Mother and I have made the most amazing discovery. Luca, I was meant to come here all along."

"I know, darlin'."

Laughing, she took hold of his hand and lead him further into the restaurant. "No, no, you don't. Not half of it. But you're about to. Let's find Rosa and Sal...oh, and *Tempest*. Have I got a story to tell you!"

ABOUT THE AUTHORS

Helen R. Myers & M. Gail Reed
co-authored

A Flock of Sparrows

writing as part of the team Helen Foster Reed.

They live in Northeast Texas
and more about them can be found at
www.myersandreed.com, www.helenrmyers.com,
and on Facebook

They are currently working on their next collaboration.

Made in the USA
Middletown, DE
15 July 2019